DO YOU THINK
I CRIED TOO LONG?

ELAINE KELLIHER

ISBN: 979-8-218-15724-1 (Paperback)
ISBN: 979-8-218-15725-8 (Hardcover)

There will be haters,
There will be doubters,
There will be non-believers,
And then there will be YOU,
proving them wrong once again.

~Jennifer Van Allen

Acknowledgments

To the little girl in me who knew she had to survive—if for nothing else than to tell her story.

I also want to thank my mother, Ellen, who lived long enough to give me enough love to last my lifetime, and my siblings, Lorna and Orville Jr., for reminding me about unconditional love.

My teachers, especially my elementary school teacher, Mrs. Kerr, and my high school English teacher, Mr. Wilson, for sharing their joy of learning and reading: inspiring me to pursue my dreams along the way.

My family: my son Ronald, who in his own quirky way kept bugging me to finish my book; my daughter Renee', who taught me that even when you're down, you're not finished; and my youngest, Niambi, who pushed me, kicking and screaming, into a book publisher's arms.

To the bohemian poet, Clive Matson, whose weekly writing workshops kept me grounded in the writer's world.

A special shout-out to my long-time friends, Billie, Ruby, and Kennetta, who have been encouraging me from day one.

To my husband Giles, I could not have asked for a more supportive partner. Thank you for believing in my book's potential and for arranging my forgotten mother's gravestone. It meant the world to me and my siblings.

Prologue

"For life and death are one, even as the river and
the sea are one." –Kahlil Gibran

A shotgun blast pierced Lily's ears, causing her temples to pulse and her slight body to propel itself upwards from the front porch steps. Her brother, Deenie, stood up, eyes wide with fright, and stared at his big sister. His two-year-old eyes glanced from Lily to the screened-in front door and back to Lily again. Lily could see him trembling. Neither Lily nor her brother had ever heard a shotgun going off, and the reverberating sound scared them. Deenie clutched his sister's gangly legs and whimpered.

The Jenkins' house was a half-mile from the nearest road. A car hadn't passed by for over an hour, and Lily could hear the fieldworkers outside plowing the nearby beet fields.

The frightening blast left Lily's heart pounding so hard that she thought it might jump from her chest. She could hear her mother moan from inside the house, and she thought she heard a car at the end of the driveway, but they were alone; her stepdad, Orville, had already left. Maybe it was the tractors in the beet field. Lily freed herself from her little brother and ran inside.

She saw the blood before she could reach her mother's bedroom. She stopped, unwilling to take another step. Her mother moaned again, and Lily resumed walking, this time taking small, cautious steps toward the mother she could not yet see.

Lily peered into the bedroom. Her mother was lying face down in a pool of blood. It poured from her stomach to form a red river, about to touch Lily's bare feet. She stepped back, this time noticing her baby sister in her crib near the window. Lorna wasn't crying, just staring, glaze-eyed at their mother.

Tears rushed down Lily's face. What to do, what to do, what to do? She had no idea. Lily watched as baby Lorna responded to the scene unfolding in front of her with a loud, piercing scream.

Her little brother was calling for her. "Sissy, come get me. Me want Momma."

"Stay there, Deenie. Just stay on the porch."

She had to calm herself down. She was eight; she was the oldest. She had to do something. She ran to the kitchen sink, grabbed a glass, and filled it with water. She came back and sprinkled it on her mother's face, careful to avoid the widening pool of blood. They did that on the Three Stooges. They always came back to life when water hit their faces. Yet, her mother didn't budge. Oh, she rose on one elbow, but only for a second before slumping back down.

She had to get help, but where? Then she remembered the field-workers. They could help, but how was she going to get out there? How could she cross the recently plowed field, with clumps of wet dirt piled higher than her knees?

Leaving her screaming sister in the crib, she grabbed her brother. They walked out to the farm workers, trying not to sink in the deep rows of dirt gutted by the tractor plows. Her brother's shoes kept getting stuck in the mud, and he started crying. She stopped and firmly grabbed his tiny fists. "You stay here. I'm gonna get help. Don't move, Deenie. You hear me?" He nodded.

When she reached the worker, he was sweating in the blistering October sun. His black eyes peered out from under the wide-brimmed cowboy hat that covered most of his sun-burned face.

As she approached, she noticed dotted beads of sweat above his full, blood-red lips. She shouted over the noisy tractor engine, "You've got to come help me; my mother is dying!" Her heart felt like it skipped a beat. Did she just say dying?

The field hand spoke no English and gestured to his white foreman, who was driving the tractor. The foreman cut the tractor's engine and strutted over to Lily. She noticed he had on tall rubber boots that made it easy for him to walk in the mud. He looked annoyed. Lily repeated herself and saw him: blue eyed, with hair the color of wheat, stare at her in suspicion. The other workers watched curiously as her brother, several rows away, bawled loudly with snot running down his face.

Lily pointed toward the house. "She's in there. You've got to help us!"

Convinced something was wrong, the foreman signaled to the two other workers to come with him. They all followed her into the house.

CHAPTER 1

Rude Awakening

More than a painful year after her mother's death, Lily sat outside on a log next to a cottonwood tree in her grandmother's backyard.

"Lily, bring me some water. Shit, it's hot out here!"

This was about the third time grandmother had sent Lily on errands to fetch this and that.

"Golly, grandmother, you call me too much!"

Lily watched as her grandmother stopped, pivoted abruptly in her direction, and slapped her hard across the face. The stinging pain was immediate, and she cried out, with tears gushing down her cheeks.

"Now, go get me some ice water, and don't give me no back talk. You hear me?"

"Yes." She caressed her cheek, feeling the warmth of her grandmother's slap. "Yes? What, I done told you, girl, ever since you moved in with me? It's 'yes, ma'am' and 'no ma'am.' You hear me?"

"Yes, ma'am, grandmother."

"And I told you before, you might as well call me Momma 'cause you ain't got none now, so just call me Momma."

"Yes, ma'am." Lily knew better than to argue, pout, or frown like she used to do at home when she got in trouble with her real family. This mean woman tolerated no back talk, even if you didn't open your mouth!

Lily's grandmother had directed her to call her 'Momma' before, but, from Lily's perspective, this was not a war that her grandmother would win. She would not talk back to her grandmother, but she would never call her 'Momma'–ever! When she had spoken to her dead mother, she promised her she would not forget her and that no one would take her place. Lily would wait until she had eye contact with her grandmother before speaking or directing any comments or questions to her. Today was no exception. It was never mentioned again. She was grateful not to have to fight about what to call her grandmother and was able to keep her promise to her mother.

As Lily walked inside to get the ice water, she felt the cool breeze blowing and heard the rustling sound made by the mulberry and cottonwood trees that stood next to each other on grandmother's tiny two-acre farm. On her way back with the water, she stuck out her tongue to taste the air and contemplate what her life would be like living with this mean, old woman.

She could hear her mother say, 'I'm here, Lily,' and she felt comforted.

For sure, living without her mother had been hard. Lily had over-heard her grandmother telling someone on the phone that her sister Lorna and brother Deenie were living with their Uncle Cecil, Orville's brother. And Orville was somewhere driving trucks, but never stopped to see about his kids. She missed them all, but especially her mother.

The lack of her mother's daily presence for almost one school year now, left a deep, hollow spot in her heart, and she had cried herself to sleep so many nights that she had lost count. But when she awakened each morning, the sun rose in the east, and no miracle brought her mother, baby sister, brother, or stepfather back. Sometimes, grandmother was nice, but mostly she was mean and constantly complained about how much she sacrificed to "keep" Lily.

CHAPTER 2

Dreams, Oh Dreams, Leave Me Be

Pet, as she liked to be called, wiped the sweat already dotting her forehead and dripping down her armpits. She was about to go inside to pack, but she stopped and cast her gaze upon Lily. How in the world had she ended up taking her in? The morning's scorching sun and the responsibility of caring for Lily weighed heavily upon her. Not only did she look like her mother, they both also had the same temperament: easily hurt, timid, and easily frightened.

Pet dragged a rusty lawn chair to the nearby cottonwood tree and plopped down. The image of her dead daughter, Ellen, immediately appeared. Pet cleared her throat and spat on the grass in front of her. She waved her hand in front of her face, trying to shoo the image aside, but Ellen's haunting face remained. Try as she might, Pet could not stop the painful images of her dead daughter from appearing. The memory of Ellen locked her into the lawn chair like a prisoner strapped to an electric chair. Rather than fight it, Pet sat back and allowed the painful movie to play.

News of Ellen's death had spread rapidly around the colored communities of Merced and Sacramento. The rumors ranged from murder by her husband, staged to look like a suicide; to murder by a nearby Mexican field hand; to accidentally shooting herself, to just plain suicide.

Pet favored the murder-by-her-husband theory, but she wasn't any-where near Clarksburg when it happened. Orville had left his wife, Ellen, and her children secluded in an old farmhouse twenty-two miles from Sacramento. No one but the children were around when it happened. Orville was tight-lipped and wouldn't talk about her death except to say he wasn't there and he didn't do it.

The thought of Ellen blowing a three-inch hole in her abdomen and bleeding to death, surrounded by her three young children, alone in the middle of no-got-damn-where, made little sense to Pet.

Strapped to her chair in an unwanted, unplanned memory ride was too much for her. She was getting too old for this, especially with the extra burden of caring for Lily. There had to be a way out of her predicament.

A cool breeze suddenly wafted across her face, and she awakened from what seemed like a memory trance, wrested herself from the chair, and resumed packing.

CHAPTER 3

Black Beauty

Lily watched as her grandmother loaded more junk into the car. As she waited, she felt both afraid and excited. Remembering past trips, this was her third trip this school year, she thought of the fun she had traveling with her grandmother. The closeness began when they were on the road, so Lily sat, digging her too-small Buster Brown oxfords into the dry, patchy grass. Thankfully she would not have to wear them into the next school year,

Gazing up at a nearby branch of the cottonwood tree, Lily watched with disgust, as a fat, lime-green caterpillar munched greedily on one of the cottonwood's leaves. She wanted to kill it but knew from experience that its slimy green blood would end up all over her shoes.

Boredom was settling in, and Lily wanted to go play with one of her friends. She waited for eye contact, "Can I go play with Bee Nahas? They just live around the corner, and I could ride my bike."

The words were barely out of Lily's mouth when her grandmother's face turned into a cold, hard, mean stare. Her grandmother dropped the box of tools she was lugging to the car, pulled a handkerchief out of her muumuu dress pocket, and wiped her brow. "Lily, I just don't understand you. You see me trying to pack up this car so we can get up outta here, and you want to go PLAY!"

Lily dropped her gaze and stared down at the ground. She wasn't used to living with someone so mean. She couldn't help it; the tears flowed down her face. She didn't wipe them because she didn't want her grandmother to know that she had made her cry. All Lily could think about now was her lost family.

Why did her mother have to die and leave her with this mean, old woman? And why couldn't she at least visit her brother, sister, and stepfather? Before coming to live with her grandmother, when she wasn't at school, she played all the time with her mother, baby brother, and sister. And Orville too, when he wasn't away driving trucks for a living. Life was just not fair!

Lily walked back to the log under the cottonwood tree, this time keeping her eyes on her grandmother as she continued her steady pace of packing the car. The thought of riding in Black Beauty with grandmother caused her brows to furrow and a tenseness to envelope her small frame.

From previous experience, Lily knew that other drivers along the highway would speed by with children in their back seats gawking at her grandmother's car with the springs and shocks that sagged and swayed, nearly causing her grandmother to fishtail into other cars. For her, it was embarrassing. She would slump and hide until they were well out of town, away from anyone who could recognize her. Once they were on Highway 99, Lily could relax and enjoy the precious intimacy that could only be shared in an automobile.

The car had been a fine automobile earlier in her life. The 1949 Ford, originally named Black Beauty, seemed to compel each owner to maintain her name. Her grandmother told her that.

Many years of life had produced a musty, worn smell. The many owners' odors lingered so that one intimately knew of each of her inhabitants. People and time and dust surrounded her, and you knew she had been everywhere and done everything a good old American car could do. Her grandmother packed her well.

"Girl, whatchu doing staring at me? Can't you think of anything to do to help?"

It appeared to Lily that the more stuff grandmother added to Black Beauty, the meaner she got. Lily had no idea how to answer. When she had tried to offer help before, her grandmother had screamed at her for not placing the stuff in the right place.

"I, uh, could bring my clothes."

"Don't you know that the clothes go in last, just before the mattress?" Her grandmother's face, swollen from the heat and sheer exhaustion, dripped with sweat.

The tears started again, but this time she remembered the last reprimand and mumbled, "No, ma'am." Lily pretended to look around at anything but her grandmother, but periodically peeking out the corner of her eyes, she watched as grandmother placed the heavy items on the floor of the back seat.

Dishes, pots and pans, and jars of staples stood stoically on the floor. Utensils, food, and bath items were packed next. When Black Beauty was fully laden with household goods, clothing was laid on top. Grandmother packed tools and other items too bulky for the back seat in the trunk. She stored food and drink to eat along the way on the floor of the front seat.

Stepping into the hot mid-morning sun and shading her brown eyes as her grandmother finished the packing, Lily marveled that they were moving so soon. Only three months in this town and now on to another.

At least school was out this time. No gawky stares from kids who had always gone to the same school. Who looked upon her as if they'd never heard of anyone changing schools during the school year. No long stares at her leggy brown frame. There would be lots of new kids on the first day of school.

No living with strangers while her grandmother looked for work, either. She'd get to stay home and play with her rock collection. She had already secretly stored her rock collection underneath the front passenger seat. It lay in a worn jewelry box adorned with plush, black velvet that showed off each piece exquisitely. Sometimes she'd pick up each piece, one by one, and hold it in her hand while marveling at the precious stone. Her two favorites were the shiny, black onyx and the green copper ore.

It was time for the mattress, and Lily scurried to help load her bed on top. This was the fun part of packing. With the mattress on top of everything else, she had a perfect bed. She loved making up her bed from the lying down position. She'd flatten out the crisp white sheet and tuck in the corners deftly among the junk as if she'd been making up her car bed all of her life.

Maybe she'd meet some real friends at the new school. They wouldn't have to know that she'd probably move soon after they had confided their best-kept secrets. She'd pretend this was her first move. Maybe her teacher would like her. Maybe some kid would feel sorry for her since she was the only colored girl in the class. Maybe she'd have a best friend. If she had a best friend, it was the outcast, the kid no one else liked, but it was better than playing alone.

She ran back to the empty house to take a long last look. The red ants, sensing their departure, were forming a two-lane highway along the baseboard next to the squeaky clean black and white linoleum floor.

Black Beauty emitted two solid 'clumps' as Lily and her grandmother climbed in and slammed their car doors. They were off, and the loud hum of the engine filled the car.

"I never liked that cracker woman I was working for," her grandmother said to Lily. "Can you imagine she wanted me to work more hours a day for the same pay? 'Lula, you just indispensable to me,'" her grandmother mimicked the white woman's nasal, high-pitched voice. "Can you believe she said that to me?"

Lily nodded, ever so slightly moving her head up and down in such a small way that only she and her grandmother understood.

"Now the way I see it, this time when I go looking for day work, I'm just gonna tell 'em they just gonna have to pay me what I'm worth!"

The hum of the motor drowned out the barely audible sound Lily made when she cleared her throat.

"The way those white folks treated me, it's just not right! I gotta take care of you and myself on only four dollars a day. Course now, when I was your age, Momma didn't have to do no day work. She stayed home with us."

Lily crossed her legs and stared down at her feet. *Oh boy, here we go*, she thought.

"Course, Poppa got sick, and we lost our place. It nearly killed Momma and Poppa too. Shoot, now they barely scraping by. And here I am, trying to make a life for you and me," she sniveled. "Ain't much work for colored folks. Just ain't much work."

The engine noise grew louder as they approached the treacherous Tehachapi Grapevine pass. Wildflowers were in deep bloom, and Guernsey cows and Jersey cattle grazed peacefully beside the hillside. A moment later, the tired engine coughed, and her grandmother shifted to second gear, merging the car beside the narrow highway so that faster cars could pass them by.

The motor sputtered again, and this time, grandmother pulled completely off the road and let the engine die. Lily and her grandmother rolled down their windows and sat in silence, watching the steam rise and quickly dissipate from Black Beauty's worn radiator into the warm desert air.

Pet heard the scream of diesel engines as the heavy trucks lumbered past: Willig Shaw Consolidated Freight Way, Pacific Intermountain Express. Almost an hour passed as they sat. A scent of cow manure wafted in, awakening both from their trance-like state.

CHAPTER 4

Wake Up, Lady!
No Vagrants Allowed!

The engine had cooled, and Pet refilled the radiator with water from the canvas canteen that had been hanging on Black Beauty's front bumper. She and her granddaughter continued on their journey.

By evening, they were both tired—Pet of talking and Lily from listening, and both of riding. Pet pulled the car off the road, then edged it into a local park just as an orange-yellow moon rose over the passenger side of Black Beauty.

Pet retrieved the basket. They ate sardines, crackers, and cheese in silence. A silver-haired couple with a brown Chihuahua strolled past the car, the Chihuahua in front, barking playfully and trying to speed the old couple's progress.

Pet started up the engine and eased the car into another area of the park to get away from the main walkway. Old eucalyptus trees stood stoically beside the park, wafting scents of eucalyptus leaves through Black Beauty's open windows.

Lily climbed over the front seat and pulled a pillow and thin blanket from the back window. She plopped onto her bed and was asleep when her brown face met the white starched pillowcase.

The harsh afternoon sun had set, followed by a damp coolness that appeared to envelop the park. Pet grabbed the thin bedding and, after several attempts at finding a comfortable position, slept.

Later, a loud tap on the car window and a bright white flashlight awakened Pet. "Ma'am, you can't sleep here tonight! Didn't you see the 'No Vagrants' sign?"

Pet shielded her eyes and looked up at the police officer dressed in a dark blue uniform and black hat with a blue county emblem. She sprang up from her slumped position and let the covers fall off her shoulders as if they were not there. She rolled the car window down.

"Officer," she whispered, "this girl is sick, and I'm taking her to her Momma. We got robbed at the cafe in that town down at the end of the grade, and we had to sleep here tonight."

The policeman did not seem convinced.

"Don't worry, officer, we'll be on our way by mornin.'"

"Well, humph, you make sure you do."

"Yes, Sir." She rolled up the window and eased back into her car seat, majestically selecting the covers. She leaned back down and quickly shut her eyes. The brightness of the flashlight filled her lids until the policeman shut it off. The officer slipped away as quietly as he had come.

CHAPTER 5

Desert Kids

The next morning, Lily and her grandmother visited the park bathroom. The park was deserted. Lily ran ahead of her grandmother because she really had to pee. Her lips were slightly parted as she ran, and she breathed through her mouth because she had learned a long time ago that if she didn't, the frigid air would make her nose burn. The burning sensation only happened in the morning, and she did not know why.

The cleaning crew had not arrived yet, and Lily knew that bathrooms this time of the morning were usually gross. This part of traveling was always difficult for her because she hated nasty bathrooms, and she hated brushing her teeth in icy water. It was never fun. It hurt her teeth.

After washing up, she and her grandmother continued on their journey, but this time her grandmother said nothing. She just drove and drove, downshifting to climb the hills and upshifting when reaching the flats.

Meanwhile, Lily counted telephone poles–154, 155, 156, which suddenly blurred into one long pole. The next thing she knew, she had stopped counting, fallen asleep, reawakened, and watched as her grandmother pulled Black Beauty into a Union 76 gas station to fill her canteen and purchase a dollar's worth of gas.

Lily quickly nodded off again, and when she awakened, she heard the distinct sound of rubber meeting gravel as the car pulled into a long driveway. At the end of the driveway was an old, white, dilapidated, clapboard house.

Remaining in her slumped sleeping position, Lily squeezed her eyes shut while leaving a tiny slit open so she could observe what her grandmother would do next. Her grandmother glanced in her direction, "Get up, girl, we here at Mayola's." With that, Grandmother walked up the steps and knocked on the door, which Mayola opened before Pet could finish.

"Girl, I'm sho' glad to see you," Mayola said. "I know you all tired after that long drive." Her grandmother entered first, followed by Lily. "Pet, you ain't never let no grass grow under you, Chile. You steady on the road, ain't you?"

Her grandmother appeared visibly tired from the long drive. She sat down on the couch and tossed the tattered old newspapers aside. A large black fly with thin, wispy wings landed on grandmother's forehead. Lily watched as she angrily slapped it away.

Mayola sat opposite her grandmother in a battered folding chair she had brought in from outside. Lily watched the two women from the edge of the couch. Next to Mayola, her grandmother looked ancient. Mayola was tall and light-skinned, with a stocky build like her grandmother, but there was something different about her. It took Lily a minute to realize that Mayola didn't look mean!

Lily's grandmother's dark brown face looked old, mean, and tired. Her grandmother's features, including the small brown eyes and broad nose with large heart-shaped lips, all appeared more pronounced than she had noticed before.

As Lily watched the two women, she thought about the two kids she had seen playing outside when they first pulled into the driveway. Maybe she could go play with them. Well, nothing to do but ease toward the door, real innocent-like, and see what happens. She walked toward the door as if it was the most natural thing to do. Not urgent, not too slow.

"Yeah, girl, go on outside with the rest of the kids," Mayola offered. Lily glanced at her grandmother, who said nothing. Her eyes said,

"Don't do anything to make me mad." Lily acknowledged her grandmother's warning with a small smile and ran outside.

"Where y'all come from?"

Lily said nothing, just stared at a lanky boy around her age with large brown eyes that reminded her of a baby deer. His lashes were thick and brown and slanted down, like the Spanish girl who used to be in her class last year. Or maybe it was this school year at John Swett Elementary in Palmdale. Anyway, he was kind of cute. They watched each other.

"Delhi," Lily finally answered.

Roger, Jamie's brother, rushed over to inspect Lily.

"Who are you?" he asked in his two-year-old voice.

Lily frowned at him. Even if she told him who she was, he'd just ask again. That's how two-year-old's were, the same question over and over.

"You going to our school? Jamie asked.

"Don't know."

"Gee whiz, you don't know nothing."

Lily said nothing.

Jamie stared at her. "Bet you can't even play ball."

"I got a rock collection," she said. "And my rocks are worth a lot of money."

"Liar!" Jamie said. "Why would anybody want to play with some dumb rocks?"

She went over to Black Beauty and retrieved the box from underneath the front seat.

Jamie and Roger followed her and stared at Black Beauty, her back-end sagging from the heavy weight. "I never seen so much stuff in one car. Where y'all going with all that stuff?"

Grabbing the box, Lily opened it. They all stared at the jewels inside the box. The amethyst sent a stream of colors streaking across Lily's face.

"Wow, what's that?" Jamie exclaimed. "What else you got in there?"

The boys stared intently at the rocks, but each time they tried to touch the precious stones, she eased the box away from them.

"I can play the violin, too," she offered.

"You really lying now; colored people don't play them funny things."

She pointed to the case. "See, it's in there."

"No kidding," Jamie said. This time he really looked at Lily. "You're neat. You gonna stay around for a while?"

She didn't know, so she didn't answer

"We got horny toads to play with; wanna see 'em?"

"Yes," Lily answered.

She wanted to stay; Jamie would be fun. They ran around to the backyard to find the horny toads. Roger started screaming because he couldn't keep up.

"Come on, ROGER," Jamie hollered. "I hate little brothers! You always gotta watch out for them, and they always cry."

"Yeah, I know," Lily answered.

"You got a baby brother?" Jamie asked.

"Yeah."

"Where's he at?"

Lily didn't answer. Jamie saw the look in her eyes and said nothing.

Jamie took Lily by the hand, "Come on, I'll show you how we get 'em to come out of their holes."

Lily let Jamie lead her to the backyard near the water hose that lay on the ground like a snake. Then, he let go of her hand.

"First," Jamie said as if explaining to a freshman biology class, "you gotta turn the hydrant on real slow, so Momma don't hear it from inside the house, 'cause she don't like us to play with water. Next, you bring it over here and put it in this hole."

It was hot outside, and the smell of hot rubber drifted through the air as Lily watched Jamie slide the hose over to the hole.

"I like to watch 'em come out at the other end—it's fun!" he said, pushing the hose into the small tunnel.

They waited in the warm afternoon sun for what seemed like forever.

"There one goes!" Jamie screamed. "There goes a lizard!"

All three kids ran toward the flitting lizard. He was gray with white spots, and his tail was almost as long as his body. When the children stopped, the lizard stopped dead in his tracks and seemed to be doing push-ups. It looked really silly to Lily. She kept watching as they silently crept towards him. The lizard cocked his diamond-shaped head from side to side and then scurried off.

This time the kids couldn't keep up, and he disappeared into the sand. The backyard was mostly sand dunes, with a few tufts of grass struggling in the arid climate. The kids scanned the yard in hopes of finding the lizard, but he was gone.

"We almost had 'em, huh?" said Jamie.

His brother Roger's petite brown face contorted into a woeful expression as he realized that the lizard was gone from sight.

"I never get to touch 'em," he cried. "It's no fair!"

"Quit your whinin' Roger," said Jamie, "I'm sick of you!"

After watching from the kitchen window, Mayola came outside with a tray filled with glasses of lemonade for the children.

Jamie, Lily, and Roger thanked her, took the lemonade, and sat on a piece of a weathered log in the backyard, each with the lemonade and a small twig in their hands. It seems as though desert kids always had a stick in their hands. They all felt comfortable sitting there, watching the sun work its way down in the western sky. It was still hot, but as the afternoon wore on, there was a hint of coolness to come.

"How old are you, Lily?" Jamie asked.

"Almost nine. I'm goin' in the fourth grade next year," she boasted.

"Me too," Jamie answered. "If you all stay, we might be in the same class 'cause there's only two fourth-grade classes at our school."

"Hmm," said Lily.

They both looked out over the backyard, each lost in thought. Roger had left the two of them on the log and was drawing figures in the sand with his stick and singing baby songs to himself.

As the daylight faded, the kids continued to sit on the log, mesmerized by the deep red/orange afternoon sun. The lizard returned, but they felt too lazy to bother trying to catch him. Roger had gone inside to take his afternoon nap which had been delayed by the excitement of Lily and her grandmother's arrival.

Suddenly, a rattlesnake appeared in the sand, inches from Lily's stick. "Look out, Lily, there's a snake!" Jamie screamed.

Lily jumped backward, almost knocking him down. Her blood-curdling scream sent Mayola and Pet running into the backyard. The snake coiled and waited. Jamie grabbed Lily's hand and steered her, walking backward, away from the snake.

When they were far enough away from the snake, Lily bowed her head, and with sweat glistening on her forehead, began whimpering, "I want my Momma, I want my Momma."

Large wet tears welled up from her sad brown eyes. Jamie and Mayola looked quizzically at Lily's grandmother, who said nothing.

After a long pause, Jamie said, "What's wrong with her?"

Lily did not look right. Her eyes held a far-off gaze, and she no longer seemed to notice Jamie or anyone else.

"Her Momma's dead, and when she gets scared, she gets a little crazy. That's all," her grandmother replied. "She's just scared. She'll be all right; I'll take her inside."

"Lay her in Jamie's bed, Pet. Jamie can sleep with Roger," Mayola offered.

They all followed Lily's grandmother back into the house. The screen door groaned loudly as her grandmother slammed it shut. She led the dazed girl into the boys' room and laid her down. She was still sobbing.

Jamie looked around the yard, but the snake that had caused all the commotion was nowhere around. He had wanted to kill it but was so absorbed with Lily that he had forgotten about what had frightened her.

Later that night, when the house was dark and quiet, Jamie crept out of his baby brother's bed and stood over Lily. Her grandmother had exchanged her play clothes for pajamas, and Lily lay curled up in a ball. The moon cast a ray of blue light upon her face, giving her the appearance of a dark blue angel. She slept peacefully, and her long black lashes lay still upon the white pillow.

"Lily," Jamie whispered, and her eyes opened immediately.

"What are you doing here?" she asked. Her voice sounded loud in the quiet house.

"Be quiet!" Jamie whispered loudly. "Momma will hear us."

"Okay," she whispered back.

She propped herself up in his bed and rubbed her eyes. "I guess I been 'sleep a long time; I gotta go pee."

"Down the hall on the left," Jamie whispered back.

When she returned, he was sitting on the edge of the bed. "How long ago did your mother die?" Jamie whispered as she sat on the bed beside him.

"Since the second week of school last year." She replied.

Jamie was at a loss for words. He didn't know anybody who didn't have a mother. Roger tossed his scrawny body around in the bed so that his head ended up at the foot of the bed and his short legs jutted to the side of the bed. They both watched in silence as he tossed and turned for what seemed like an eternity. When he was still again, they resumed whispering.

"My daddy died before I was born," Jamie offered. "I never met him."

"But I thought Jim was your daddy," Lily whispered.

"No, he ain't my daddy—no way!" Roger stirred again. They both fell silent.

"You don't like him?" Lily asked.

"We don't see him much," Jamie said simply. "Our Momma don't let him tell us what to do. She said we her children, not his. We glad 'cause we don't like him anyway. And he doesn't like us," Jamie said. "He never talks to us."

"Oh," Lily said.

At that very moment, she thought about her stepfather. He was tall and dark and very good-looking. She had never known her real father; her mother had never mentioned him. She just knew that Orville was not her real father.

She thought about the last fishing trip before her mother died. Lily got to go because she was the oldest. Her sister and brother were too young, so she accompanied Orville. Even her mother didn't go. It was fun. All day long, they had sat, pole anchored along the ditch bank, and waited for just one bite. Orville told stories about being in the Korean War. The battlefield he described was both exciting and scary.

His voice was warm and gentle, and he'd say things like, "Baby, you won't believe that old Sergeant we had, a real Okie. He treated us real nice, though, said he wasn't going to have no mess. If this man's Army is gonna be integrated—by God, he was gonna do his part. Made that cracker serve me and my buddies in the mess hall. Yeah, baby, it was real nice in the Army. First time I been treated like a decent man in my life."

When Lily and Orville would go fishing, it would be icy cold in the morning and burning up hot by mid-day. In the late afternoon, the mosquitoes would swarm around, and Lily would slap them as they'd gather around her face and bare legs.

Orville would dab the repellent onto her face and arms, and legs, saying, "Close your eyes, baby. You can't let this stuff get in your eyes."

When Lily and Orville arrived home in the late evening, Orville Jr. would run to her and grab her legs and pull her into their bedroom. At two, he wanted a blow-by-blow description of what happened on the fishing trip. She loved to tell. She felt so proud, being the oldest child.

"Hey, Lily," Jamie whispered. She had a faraway gaze in her eyes, and she looked at Jamie as if she didn't know him.

"Oh, I'm sorry. I guess I was thinking about my stepdad, Orville."

"You miss him, huh?"

"Yeah, I guess so. He moved to Merced. My sister and brother are staying with his sister, and I'm with my grandmother. I miss them."

A small tear rolled down her face. She looked at Jamie to see if he noticed her crying, but he looked away, picking at tiny cotton balls that were fiercely attached to the light woolen blanket.

They both jumped when they heard a loud thump. One of the grownups was up. They heard footsteps echoing down the hall. They scrambled to their beds and pulled the covers up to their faces.

Before they had a chance to resume their conversation, they were fast asleep.

"Here bend the black folks,
Hands to the soil–
Bosses of nothing.
Not even their toil."

—Langston Hughes

Inside, Mayola stood at the kitchen window, watching the kids playing outside. "Pet, you want some lemonade?" Before she could answer, Mayola continued, "I'm sho' glad y'all came down—uh—how long you all planning on staying? 'Course you know we got plenty of room here, and you can stay long as you like and uh ruh…"

Pet shifted her weight towards the edge of the couch and interrupted Mayola. "Mayola, damn the lemonade, gimme a beer. Shoot, I'm hot and tired, and I don't want to think about nothin' but coolin' off—like I told you on the phone, I had to get away. You know 'bout any work 'round here—I mean house cleaning or—what about any fieldwork?"

"Well, you know ain't never been much goin' on around here—they don't let nobody but them crackers work in the cannery up there in Delhi. I thought you had a real nice job working for the Nahas. Ain't they into produce or something?"

"Yeah, but me and that woman fell out. She expected me to work for less money. It's mighty hard for folks to get decent work anywhere nowadays. What they pay for day work now is hard to live off. Welfare gives me twenty-five dollars a month for that grandchild of mine, but that's just not enough money. The truth of the matter is I just needed to get away, try something different."

Mayola had returned with two cans of beer for Pet and herself. She joined Pet on the couch, and the newspapers rose and sank with the weight of both women.

"Well, Pet, let me ask my old man when he gets in tonight. They cutting and spreading grapes over in Firebaugh, and they payin' two dollars a row, course them some long damn rows!" Mayola laughed loudly, slapping her thighs with her hand as she laughed, almost spilling her beer. "Shoot, Jim said he was happy when they told him how much they paid till it took him nearly all morning to do just one row. They making it hard for us to make any decent money!"

Mayola returned to the kitchen window and smiled as she watched the children chasing the lizard.

CHAPTER 7

What? That Gal Ain't Got No Momma?

Orville was having a bad day. First, it was seven o'clock in the morning and already ninety degrees. He was sitting in his truck at a rest stop on the outskirts of Chowchilla. His truck was loaded with vine-ripened tomatoes, and because a refrigerator truck was unavailable, he knew he'd better get moving. He had to get them to Modesto Frozen Foods no later than 11:00 am.

But the worst part of Orville's day was remembering his Ellen's dreams. She had been haunting him since the day of her funeral. But today, got damn it, he was gonna have him some fun and shoot the shit with a few of his friends in town.

After unloading his produce, he headed to Bill's Barbershop in Merced, a quick hop from Modesto. Orville had known Bill since they were in grade school. He was the only black barber in town. Like Orville, Bill was a tall, dark-skinned man.

Orville chuckled to himself as he thought about how folks said Bill's long arms seemed to go past his knees. Folks also said that he was married to the whitest colored woman that he could find, and their kids have a honey-toned skin coloring that happens when you mix a lot of cream with black coffee.

Orville was looking forward to the rowdy conversations that can only happen at Bill's. He ambled down Thirteenth Street, the heart of the colored community. Bill was not there, and Orville didn't know any of the waiting patrons or the other two barbers. The shop was crowded, and Orville headed toward the back and sat in the only vacant chair in the shop.

He noticed that one barber had a chubby, brown-skinned two-year-old boy strapped into his chair like a prisoner. The child's hair was thick, black, and tangled, looking like a comb or brush had never touched it. Big crocodile tears were silently rolling down the child's fat cheeks.

Orville eased back in his chair and noticed the boy's mother, dressed in white shorts that she most likely purchased twenty pounds ago, and her pink, almost see-through blouse did not hide her ample cleavage. He grinned at her.

She stood next to the child, hands on her generous hips, glaring at her son with a-you-better-not-cry look. She was looking around to see who else besides Orville was checking her out. She gazed past Orville and seemed to be pursing her lips at another good-looking light-skinned man. Orville laughed; she was not his type.

The barbershop patrons were gossiping about Orville's stepdaughter, Lily, who had recently secured a finalist position in a state-wide spelling bee contest. Orville tried to look uninterested as he heard them discussing his stepdaughter.

"Who is that gal's Momma?"

"What, she ain't got one?"

"Well, I'll be damned!"

"Folks say her Momma killed herself?"

Orville tried to sink his tall frame lower into the chair. He squirmed, sweat trickling down his armpits. He was tempted to let himself be known but decided to sit it out.

"Well, how the hell did that happen? I ain't never heard of no colored man or woman killing themselves!"

"They say that it might've been her husband?"

"Now that makes mo' sense!"

"I mean, after all, we colored people ain't got no reason to kill ourselves, right?"

"Injustices, you say?"

"You mean like having a dollar-an-hour store clerk following you around the store to make sure you don't steal none of their fine merchandise?"

It relieved Orville that the conversation was veering away from him as the suspect in Ellen's death and toward the injustices that most coloreds felt were a part of their everyday lives.

"Or, how about all the white folks vacating the swimming pool when you and your friend arrive with your brand spanking new bathing suits you brought from J. J. Newberry?"

"Uh, huh!"

"You say we just paranoid?"

The crowd of patrons laughed, and Orville joined in, then stood up and walked towards the front door. Any moment now, someone would come in and recognize that he was the husband married to Ellen–and that Lily was his stepdaughter. He stopped at the barber's chair next to the sad-faced two-year-old.

"Hey man, Imma come back later when it ain't so crowded. What you think, maybe around three o'clock?"

"Yeah, man, this afternoon will be better." The barber clamped the child's head with his large hands, jerked the child's head at an odd angle, and shouted at Orville's retreating figure, "Say, man, you must be Bill's customer; he took off today, going to a funeral out of town. What's your name?"

Orville heard the child squealing, probably protesting the uncomfortable head angle, and noticed the fresh tears rolling down, covering the salty ones already there. He smiled, pretended he didn't hear the barber's question, and quietly closed the shop door. He was fuming. He didn't know if he should focus on the wife he no longer had or the fact that too many people knew too much about his business. What went on between him and his family was not their concern. And besides, hearing other folks talk about his Ellen was way too painful.

He'd parked a block away from the barbershop, and when he reached his car, he fumbled for his keys. He jumped into the car and tried his damnedest to will away the painful images of Ellen beginning to form–but he couldn't. Damn, them people in the barbershop, why did they have to bring up his Ellen?

As he sat in the car, he stared into the street in front of him and immediately saw an image of Ellen in their house. She was lying on the floor in a pool of her own blood that slowly meandered its way from the bedroom toward the entrance to their bedroom. He closed his eyes, again trying to will the images away.

Instead of the images disappearing, he saw a widening pool of blood coming directly from the large hole in Ellen's abdomen. As it congealed, the blood oozed its way like a winding river pulled by gravity toward Baby Lorna, who was screaming, with tears, snot and drool running down her puffy face. After several attempts at getting up, Ellen collapsed onto the floor, disturbing the path of the wandering pool of blood.

Baby Lorna let out a full-throated scream that jarred Orville from his frightening hallucination.

The imagery was vivid and terrifying, and for the life of him, Orville didn't know how the strange image of his dying Ellen came to him so clearly. Was he there? Did he shoot her? Was it a bad dream that came out of nowhere?

Orville shifted his lanky body in the car seat and looked around at the same street that had recently transformed itself into his Ellen nightmare. It was now just a quiet, nondescript street, one block from his barbershop in Merced.

The nightmare he had just had, happened on his last day with Ellen, one year ago in Sacramento. That day with Ellen had been like many other days with her. They'd have a heated argument; he'd leave in a huff. She would beg him not to leave, but he'd go anyway. It was a common fight that they had nearly every time he'd return from a three-day run, hauling hay and produce throughout the San Joaquin valley.

How was he to know that he'd never see her alive again? That day after their fight, he'd driven around for hours, playing their argument around in his head. Mad at himself, mad at her. She'd wanted to move back into town, away from her God-forsaken, lonely existence in the middle of nowhere, but he'd resisted. He'd wanted to save money–shit, their rent was only twenty dollars a month! He didn't make much money driving the truck. What did she expect from him?

He didn't remember leaving Ellen and driving back into town. But there he was, in the colored section of town on J Street in downtown Sacramento, twenty-two miles from home. He'd lost track of time, and out of nowhere, there appeared a set of neon lights from a cheap motel beckoning him and his Thunderbird to come inside. Before he knew it, he'd paid a disheveled night clerk for a one-night stay. He parked his car in front of Room 123. He wasn't hiding from anyone; he didn't have another woman with him.

The room was simple. A bed and nightstand. There was also a tiny sink, toilet, and shower stall in a corner of the room. Within minutes, his exhausted body drifted off to sleep.

A loud thump on his motel door awakened him. His truck-driver friend, Lonnie, dressed in wrinkled army fatigues and already sweating in the midday sun, screamed through the wide, splintered gap on his motel door frame, "Orville, is that you? Are you in there alone? What the hell you doing out here in this motel, man? Wake up, wake up!"

Lonnie went from tapping to banging on the motel room door, "Man, get up, Mr. Charlie is looking for you! They got an APB out on you, and they mean business!"

Orville, awakened by Lonnie's insistent banging, jumped up, turned the door handle, and peered sleepily through the crack in the door.

Lonnie barged past him, his eyes sweeping the area, looking all around the cramped room. "Look, man, I guess I'm the one gotta tell you before the police do. They found your wife, Ellen, dead at the house with the kids. Kids are fine, but Ellen is dead." Orville was wiping sleep from his eyes and staring intently into Lonnie's. "Look like somebody shot her, or she shot herself."

Orville stared at Lonnie, confused. He looked at his hands. He couldn't speak. His mouth felt like a bowl of dust had been suddenly dumped inside, with grit clinging to his teeth, tongue, and gums. He tried to swallow, but his mouth was way too dry. He felt panicked. How in the world was Lonnie telling him something that was not possible? His Ellen–dead?

"Man, look, I don't know nothin' about that. When I saw that girl, she was alive— I, I…don't even know how long I've been here. I was driving around, and then I ended up here!"

Orville noticed Lonnie inspecting his clothing, looking for something.

"Look, man, the cops ain't here yet. What the hell happened at that house? Did you have anything to do with that girl's death?"

"I don't know, Lonnie, I just don't know." I mean, we argued, yes, we argued, and I left the house after our argument. Yes, I left, but I don't remember much after that."

"Let me get this straight. You don't remember? I mean, look, Orville, somebody shot that girl. Was it you, her, or somebody else?"

Orville watched Lonnie pacing around the bed in the narrow room, hands thrust deep into his pockets, but the look on his face said that he wanted to grab Orville and choke the living daylights out of him.

Orville felt defeated and slumped down on the bed and began whimpering, "I don't know, man, I just don't know."

The fact was that a year later, sitting in his car on a side street one block from the barbershop, Orville still didn't remember much about what happened that day with Ellen either.

How in the world had he seen those bloody images? How could he have seen all that blood and Baby Lorna's face without having been there?

Orville remained in the car, his hands clutching the steering wheel with his head bowed. He raised his head, looked out into the street, and said to an audience of none, "I just don't remember what happened that day!"

CHAPTER 8

Is It All Right to Play With a Colored Girl?

The first day of school for Lily began with a familiar jolt. "Momma," yelled Roger. "Momma, I want to go to 'chool with Jamie. JAMIE, TAKE ME WITH YOU," he cried. "You promisssseeedddd!" As the morning flies danced lazily around his head, Roger sat in the doorway, bleating like a screeching baby goat who had lost its mother.

Mayola, standing in the doorway with her morning beer, just shook her head. The last thing Lily and Jamie saw as they ran to catch their bus was the sight of Roger, tugging furiously at his mother's blouse and pointing pitifully at the school bus.

"Lily, we'll have to test you to determine your grade level. You'll either be in Mrs. Morris's class or Mr. Swanson's."

They were seated in the registration office with dozens of kids with their parents, anxiously awaiting a room assignment. Pet, who had driven separately, was busy completing Lily's registration form, looking unnatural in the all-white surrounding. She was dressed in a faded blue skirt and a white blouse that had large yellow rings of sweat encircling the underarm area. She had combed her hair before she left Mayola's, but in an old-fashioned style that reminded Lily of a maid she saw on television. As each new parent and child arrived, they paused to look at her grandmother. Everyone knew there would be another colored child in school that year. Lily kept her head bowed. This was the most uncomfortable part of registering for school. Her grandmother just didn't fit in. The worst part was she didn't even realize it.

After registration, her first day of school was fun. Jamie accompanied her, holding hands with his new friend. She had never felt so safe. There were two other colored kids in the school, and they didn't waste any time finding each other.

After her test, Linda, the school aide, took her to the classroom. She was young and immediately liked Lily.

"Now, Mr. Swanson's hard, but he's an excellent teacher. They couldn't believe you did so well on your test, so they called your old school. You're smart, especially for a colored girl. Make sure you do all your homework, okay?"

They had arrived at the doorway to the classroom. Linda handed Lily her registration card and nudged her into the classroom.

"Well, well, look who we have here!"

Lily handed Mr. Swanson her card and looked around for an empty seat. Mr. Swanson was short and stocky, with a bulbous red nose and wispy blonde hair. He had a warm smile that immediately made her comfortable.

"Let's see…hmmm…why don't you sit next to Nancy," he said.

Feeling the eyes of every boy and girl in the classroom on her, Lily eased into her chair. Jamie was not in her class. She felt the disappointment of having to start school without Jamie at her side.

"Now, don't look so sad. Nancy won't bite," Mr. Swanson said. "She's really a nice girl."

Lily half-smiled and went to her seat. The morning went by quickly as he reviewed the class schedule. Before she knew it, the bell rang for the first recess. She bolted for the door, not wanting to know if someone in her class would want to talk to her or not.

"Lily!" She turned around. Nancy ran up to her and grabbed her hands. "We had a colored girl in our class two years ago. She moved away. She was so neat."

As the other kids ran for the playground, they made a wide space around them, avoiding eye contact. Nancy was a big girl with flushed red cheeks and bouncy red hair. She had green eyes. Well, Lily thought, she probably doesn't have any friends either, so I guess I'm stuck with her for the school year.

But Nancy seemed like she wanted very much to be her friend—it would be better than having no girlfriends at all. As they skipped to the playground, she looked again for Jamie.

Nancy asked, "You looking for Jamie?" Before Lily could answer, she continued, "Well, he's in Mrs. Morris's class, and they already had recess."

The screeching children filled the playground, awash with bright, bold reds and blues and yellows of this year's new school clothes. Even as they skipped onto the playground, both girls felt the uneasiness created by Lily's arrival. As they strolled around the schoolyard, many children paused and stared. Some spoke, most did not. For Lily, this was a crucial moment in time. If Nancy felt too ostracized by the other children, she would drop her. Fast.

Lily tried a technique she had learned at her previous school. She smiled and nodded at the other children as they skipped along. The children mostly smiled back; some kids even ran up to say hello to them. She noticed Nancy basking in the attention granted to someone brave enough to befriend a colored girl. Soon enough, the magic moment happened—the children acknowledged another brown face, and except for a few children determined to continue staring, the playground games resumed. Two girls ran up and invited them to play tetherball. They accepted. The lone grownup, the playground supervisor, sighed heavily and checked her watch. Three minutes until the end of recess.

The classroom was an interesting array of neatness and clutter. Neatness because children's books were properly stacked in the basket underneath each chair. One and only one yellow number two pencil sat inside the pencil well on the top of each desk. Some pencils were gnawed, some were not. Even though the school district was poor, the math, English, and history books looked new. Mr. Swanson saw that they kept all textbooks in perfect order. When a page ripped or a cover loosened from its binder, he painstakingly repaired each one. His students knew that he did not tolerate damaged textbooks.

The rest of the classroom was in disarray. Half-finished maps with stick figures of legendary people, crudely drawn by Mr. Swanson, adorned one wall. He had problems with spatial relationships, and Daniel Boone appeared to hold a beaver trap half the size of Virginia in his hands. When the children offered to create the legendary characters, Mr. Swanson adamantly refused. He wanted them to memorize dates, names, and places. He had the brightest kids in his class, and he didn't want them wasting time with art. He understood music, but he had no patience for artwork.

Another wall depicted a poor representation of the solar system with a bright yellow sun in the center and a complete set of planets rotating around it. It was impossible to distinguish one planet from another. Mr. Swanson's only concern was that the children knew the names of the planets. During open house season, he secretly watched and listened to the parents' comments. To his disappointment, it never impressed parents.

At the end of the first week of school, Lily sat at her desk, alternating between doodling and chewing her pencil, unaware that the recess bell had rung and the other children were outside playing. She and Mr. Swanson were alone in the classroom. She looked up as he ambled toward her. He grinned as he approached her desk. She noticed that he had small yellow teeth that needed brushing.

"Lily, why aren't you outside with the rest of the children?" Mr. Swanson asked.

"Dunno," she replied.

"What are you drawing?" She snatched the pencil from her mouth and followed his eyes to her crude drawing of a violin.

"I—I guess I was drawing a violin. I used to play at my old school," she stammered.

"That's a hard instrument to play. How d'you learn?"

For a moment, Lily panicked. Maybe he knew that she had a violin at home. Maybe he knew that she hadn't returned it from the last school year. But then she thought of Mr. Jensen. He'd let her take it home to practice during summer. He'd know that it wasn't her fault that she couldn't return it. She didn't know that was her last day at that school. Only her grandmother knew that. She relaxed.

"Yeah, I played at my old school. The viola and cello too, but I liked the violin best." She put her pencil back into her mouth and resumed chewing. Tiny specks of yellow paint surrounded her mouth, giving her face a speckled brown and yellow appearance.

Mr. Swanson sat a few desks away from her as they talked. He was too big for the student's desks. His pot belly bulged, filling the space between the chair and the edge of the desk. She stared at his eyes. The eyes, always the eyes. The eyes told her what to expect from the person. His eyes were like those of Mr. Jensen, her old violin teacher: kind. She craved kind eyes. Soft. That's what she looked for. Kind and soft. When she noticed him blushing, she quickly averted her eyes to his shoes. They were Penny Loafers.

"Well, Lily, I'm sure you will like your new school just fine."

He painstakingly extricated himself from the desk, inching his belly out first. "I'll talk to Mr. Sharp, the orchestra director, about you joining. I'm sure we can use a talented violin player."

"Thanks, Mr. Swanson." She ran outside to join the other children just as the recess bell rang for them to return to class.

By October, Lily was certain that they would remain in Tulare for a while. Mayola had cleared out a cluttered spare bedroom for her grandmother, and she and Jamie and Roger shared the kid's room. In the beginning, they all dressed together in the bedroom, but Lily had caught Jamie staring at her several times as she undressed. She had never felt self-conscious about her body before, but when Jamie looked too long, she felt uncomfortable. She was sure that he had never seen a girl undress before, and she wasn't certain if he should.

CHAPTER 9

Just a Little Pee-stained

"Pet, look what I found in the alleyway." Pet watched Mayola trudge into the living room, holding one end of a single bed frame with a pee-stained mattress. "You can use this for your granddaughter. That way, Jamie and Roger can go on back to their own beds. Pet watched Mayola's sly grin, knowing she was obviously proud of herself, having found a solution to the kid's sleeping arrangements.

Pet muttered a thank-you, but did not smile back. She was in a funk. She cut her eyes in Mayola's direction, and both she and Mayola silently dragged the cot into the boy's room.

Pet plopped down on the thin cot as she waited for Mayola to return with the sheets and blankets. She stared out into the backyard and thought, *I'm already tired of living with Mayola, but I don't have a backup plan. Yet, having the extra burden of this child is too much sometimes. I don't have a choice. Didn't I tell my daughter that if anything ever happened, I would take her child? It's just not fair. I never dreamed that one day I'd have to keep that promise.*

All of my life, taking care of my own and other people's children. It's just not fair. I remember the day of the welfare visit. It was early in the afternoon when Lily was still at school. I'd always tried to schedule the visit when she was away at school. Lily was just too nosy, trying to hang around while me and the welfare woman completed all the necessary forms: Full Name of Child; Birthdate: Mother's maiden name; Full Name of father; Occupation-Father; Occupation-mother; Guardian of child-Relationship to child; Current address; School attending...

Hell, that was the silly part of it— Lily's father was doing time for statutory rape. Do you tell that to the welfare people? Hell no. And Lily's Momma, she went crazy and took another route to her next life. Do you tell that to some nosy cracker trying to get into your business? Another hell no. I tell them what they needed to know, no more. They ask too many questions for the little bit of money they dole out. Lily is constantly growing and needing everything. Shoes. At nine years old, she wears a women's size seven-and a-half shoe. She's gonna be tall like her Momma. She's gonna be weak like her Momma, too. Not tough like you needed to be in this world. Every time I lie to the welfare people, Lily's face tells the truth. No, it's better when Lily is not around.

"Pet!"

Mayola's voice startled Pet, and she looked with surprise at her hands. She was in the middle of tucking the bottom sheet between the mattress and the rusty springs below.

"Girl, I been talking to you since I returned with the bedding, and you been in another world. Here, take the top sheet." Mayola threw the top sheet across the bed, and they continued making Lily's bed.

Lily and Jamie arrived home from school just as Pet and Mayola were leaving their room. The kids' foreheads and noses were shining with perspiration from their long walk from the bus stop. The sweet smell of young, warm bodies permeated the room. In another six months, Pet and Mayola would have to introduce the kids to deodorant, but for now, the smell was pleasant.

Mayola pointed to her underarms and winked at Pet, "It won't be long, girl."

Pet met her gaze and winked back at Mayola. "You know you right; get me another beer."

As the grownups left the room, Jamie and Lily exchanged quizzical glances. Lily walked over to the closet just as Roger ran in, exclaiming, "Lily got a new bed, Lily got a new bed!"

Lily dropped her book bag and looked around. Right in the middle of the floor sat her "new" bed. It was a narrow cot with a thin mattress that curled up at both ends. Unlike Jamie or Roger's bed, it had no pillow. The clean sheets on top did not hide the fact that the mattress had been peed upon many times. There were old spider webs attached to the springs underneath the bed. Upon closer inspection, she found dead flies attached to the web, apparently abandoned by their prey.

"That's not a new bed," Jamie said quietly, "I saw that bed in the alley on our way to school this morning."

Lily said nothing, but she let go of her bottom lip and frowned as she surveyed the bed and the rest of the room. She knew from experience that anything she changed would have to be done with the cooperation of the three of them in the room. Roger would be easy.

"Tell you what, Lily, we could help you clean it up." Jamie offered tentatively.

"Sure," she said. "You got any old rags?"

After dinner, Lily and Jamie spread their books on the kitchen table to perform the nightly ritual of homework and fun. She usually completed her homework during school, so she coached Jamie through the myriad rules for performing division. He hated word problems, so she presented him with the actual math exercise without the words. After he worked through the problem, she added the necessary words to complete his answers.

"Lily, you think I'll ever learn this stuff?" Jamie asked.

"I used to think math was hard too, but you'll get used to it," Lily responded. She had clasped a sharp number two pencil between her teeth so that when she spoke, her words lacked the "th" and "s" sounds. "You'll be used to it by Christmas." She liked Jamie and thought of him as her best friend. They didn't play together at school since they had separate recesses and lunch breaks. Besides, boys and girls their age did not play together anyway.

When Mayola put Little Roger to bed, she noted with surprise that the children had changed the room around. Lily's bed no longer sat in the middle of the room. Each bed in the room sat alongside a wall. The dresser sat on the remaining wall. Jamie, and Lily's beds were each placed next to a window. Roger's bed was on a wall that did not have a window. Lily and Roger's stuffed animals were mysteriously now all perched on Roger's bed. Mayola placed one of Lily's stuffed animals into the child's hand and tucked him into bed. He was dead asleep when his head touched the pillow.

CHAPTER 10

Strings, Oh Soulful Strings

Lily was finally in the school orchestra. What fun. Practice on Thursdays, all afternoon, in exchange for United States history. What a relief! She had dragged her old violin out and started practicing. Not in the house; she knew better.

The next day, Mayola and Pet sat inside the house, shucking corn for the evening's dinner. "Pet, that girl is pretty good. When did she learn to play that thing?"

Perched in the old, beat-up, abandoned car in the backyard, Lily used the dashboard as a music stand. They watched and listened to the sweet strings of the violin as the afternoon desert wind silently flapped her sheet music.

"She seems to be in a world all of her own."

"Yeah, you wanna laugh? You shoulda' seen her before she got that thing. Girl, I came home from work one day, and Lily was trudging from the bus stop with a tuba!" said Pet.

"A tuba?"

"Yeah, I looked up and saw this skinny, brown thing limping down the road with this big shiny tuba. It was all she could do to drag the thing in the house. I asked her what the hell she was doing with that instrument—hell, I didn't know what they called it until she told me. She said she wanted to play in the school orchestra. I told her to take that thing right back where she got it, and next thing I know, she's coming home with the violin. They made me sign saying that it was the school's property. Shoot, I ain't thought no more about it—it's hers now. Girl, if you'd 'a seen her coming down that road..."

They both laughed and watched and listened as the rich sound of the mournful violin reached the drab living room.

Lily practiced in the car as often as possible. Later at school, the director informed the children that he had scheduled a school performance for a day prior to the Thanksgiving school break.

She and Nancy had become fast friends since they were the only elementary children in the Junior High school band. Nancy had everything. She was redheaded with flashing green eyes and a cute heart-shaped mouth. Her mother was appalled that Lily attended her daughter's school. She knew because Nancy told her. It was after band practice one day. They were rubbing their violin strings with rosin, their feet dangling from the fold-up chairs as they watched the rest of the children file out of the auditorium. Practice was over, but they both seemed hesitant to leave. Nancy was curious, Lily pensive.

"Where'd you learn to play the violin?" Nancy asked.

"At Herbert Hoover last year," Lily answered.

They both sat, self-consciously snapping and plucking their violin strings. There appeared to be a rhythm to the plucking as if each had a part to play that depended on the other.

"I like to play," said Lily, "it makes me feel sad and happy."

"What do you mean?"

"Oh, I don't know—it's like the strings cry and laugh sometimes," Lily chuckled, both girls relaxed, simultaneously closing their violin cases.

"Is it...uhh...hard? I mean...," Nancy stammered, looking at Lily with pleading eyes.

Lily inched forward, scooting her fold-up chair closer to Nancy. "You mean about being colored, don't you?"

Nancy immediately nodded her head, grateful that Lily said it for her.

"Well, it's OK most of the time. I mean, sometimes kids are afraid to touch you, and sometimes they are mean to you—but sometimes it's OK."

"My mother told me not to play with you when I told her about you."

"Is your mother mean—I mean do you like your mother?"

"Oh, yes," Nancy replied. "She's really neat. I talk to her about everything." Nancy paused, not sure of what she should not tell Lily. "I mean, she likes almost everybody, except coloreds. She won't even let them clean our house. You see, one time I heard my uncle talking, that's my mother's brother, and he said that no one better find out about Sheila or we'd be kicked out of town."

"Who's Sheila?" Lily asked.

"That's my grandmother. She's half-colored," Nancy whispered, cupping her hands over Lily's ear so that no one else could possibly hear.

"You're kidding!" Lily exclaimed loudly.

"Shhh," Nancy whispered excitedly. "Promise you'll never tell anyone."

"I promise," Lily said solemnly but she looked at Nancy with renewed interest. Her mouth, that was it—her mouth, Lily thought. It was too big. But her skin—so pink and her hair—so red.

"If my mother found out that I told you, she would kill me. It's a secret. We never tell anyone. That's why mother moved here. Nobody knows. She met daddy here."

"Does your mother know that you know?" asked Lily.

"No, well, I don't think so. Even my dad doesn't know. I don't think mom knows that I know. Daddy hates colored people too. They both do. If he knew my mom had colored blood, he would kill her. I'm sure of it. Yes, he would kill her."

"Well, does your mother look colored?"

They both spoke in whispers, their voices echoing softly in the now vacant auditorium.

"No, she looks just like her father. He's white. My grandmother looked white too. Only people who knew she was colored would know."

"Why doesn't your mother want anybody to know?"

"'Cause kids at school teased her and my uncle. They called them names. She'll never go back to that town. I heard her and my uncle talking about it one day after grandmother's funeral. They thought I was taking a nap. I was six, but I remember that day. I'll never forget it."

The girls sat on the fold-up chairs, one leg tucked under the other swinging back and forth. Nancy seemed relieved to have someone to talk to about her secret grandmother, and Lily absorbed the confession with interest. She felt a sense of kinship with Nancy, but she also felt despair. They couldn't really be friends because the kids would become suspicious. Even now, Nancy's friends shunned her whenever she played too much with Lily. They felt like secret lovers. Keeping the friendship to themselves. Afraid to talk about the other for fear of ridicule: Lily for trying to be white, and Nancy for loving coloreds. They both sat swinging in their own private thoughts, but each knew what the other was thinking.

"Hey, girls!" said Mr. Sharp, "What are you still doing here? You're not practicing, are you?"

The girls jumped up and stumbled to the door of the auditorium, waving goodbye to Mr. Sharp on their way out.

"See you tomorrow," yelled Nancy, and she ran to catch her bus.

Lily ran in the opposite direction to get on her bus to go home.

As Mr. Sharp watched the two girls depart, he smiled, grateful to see their friendship developing.

CHAPTER 11

Another Day, Another Move

"Pet, girl, you ain't packing that car, are you?" Mayola met Pet in the doorway to the kitchen, perspiration dripping from her shiny forehead. "Girl, I thought you and your granddaughter was going to stay around for a while. What's wrong?"

"May, ain't nothin' wrong. I just got to move on, that's all. I can't let Lily finish out this week of school because we got to go. We'll be gone by Thursday," Pet said.

She had rearranged the car and pulled Lily's mattress from the tool shed and sat it in the dirt next to Black Beauty.

"But the kids were gettin' along so good. Why don't you stay awhile longer?" Mayola said.

She had gotten used to Pet and her granddaughter, and Jamie was doing so much better in school since Lily's arrival.

"Well, my youngest daughter had herself a baby, and I'm going up to Merced to help her. Lily can go to school there. She'll be able to help with the baby and all."

"Since when you worried about your baby girl. I thought you said you all weren't speaking. When did you talk to her?"

Pet didn't answer; she went inside to get a beer. *Ain't none of her business why I'm leaving. I'm just going, that's all. I don't have to tell her nothing. Everybody always worried about Lily. Shit, I know how to take care of that girl. She starting to like this place too much, anyhow. Gotta move before she gets too attached. Maybe I can catch up with Arthur in*

Merced. He always was sweet on me. Shit, I need me a man. Mayola got one; I need one too. To hell with Lily. She ain't no man. She just a child. It's time to move on.

Jamie and Lily saw the mattress at the same time. It leaned on its side next to the car. Jamie felt awful. He didn't know what to say.

Tears welled up in Lily's eyes before she could stop them. That old panicky feeling started up again. She knew all the signs. She felt sick to her stomach and scared. Scared of what, she did not know.

Her grandmother walked to Black Beauty, carrying a red plastic laundry basket full of clothes. "Girl, don't just stand there looking dumb; go on in the house and help me with this packing. You old enough to help now."

Without a word, Lily ran inside.

Jamie ran to Mayola. "Momma, why they got to leave!" he wailed. Tears rolled down his sweaty brown face.

"Now, Jamie, it's none of our business. Go on outside and play with Roger. He's in the backyard looking for some lizards to play with, help him find some lizards or horny toads," Mayola said as she steered Jamie outside.

The sadness on Lily's face could be seen by everyone. It all happened so soon. Lily could see that Mayola did not understand it herself. One minute she and Lily's grandmother were discussing the taste of wild mustard greens. Then, five minutes later, her grandmother was carrying a load of clothes to Black Beauty.

"Girl, I just don't understand you—you a real gypsy, ain't you?" Mayola said. She followed Pet from the house to the car, still not used to the idea that her finicky visitor was really leaving. She couldn't bring herself to help with the packing because she could not believe what was happening.

"May, I done told you, it's time for me to go. My daughter needs me there with her."

From what Lily could see, Mayola did not believe for one minute that Pet was worried about her youngest daughter. Why, even down here in Tulare, people knew that Pet's children were the last thing on her mind. Folks said that all her children had left home before they turned sixteen. Couldn't stand the woman. The boys joined the Army, and the girls got pregnant and left home. Just like that. No one was around. Lily knew that her aunts and uncles were young teens when they left home. Who did her grandmother think she was fooling? The only reason Lily was with her grandmother was because she had no mother. Strange woman, Lily's grandmother.

"Well, girl, I know you know what's best..." Mayola's voice trailed off when she looked up and saw Lily run back outside to the car.

Lily carried her rock collection and violin case as if they were the most precious things in her life. Lily could see the pitiful look on Mayola's face. Mayola offered, "Now, 'course, Lily could stay here while you get settled at your daughter's and uh..."

"May, look, we leavin'. That's it. You know I can't leave Lily here; she comes with me wherever I go. She'll be all right. We do this all the time. I told you she can help with the new baby."

Mayola gave up and went outside with her children.

Jamie fiercely threw rocks at a target he and Lily had set up in the backyard, sometimes barely missing Roger. "Boy, be careful! Don't you see Roger playing out here?" Mayola screamed.

Jamie looked up, not used to his mother using that tone of voice with him. Lily and her grandmother's departure seemed to upset the whole family.

"I'm sorry, Momma, I'll be more careful," Jamie said sadly. "It's just not fair—just when we were having so much fun, she's got to go. How come she's got to go, Momma?" he asked.

"Jamie, I done told you, that's not our business. They just got to go, that's all. Maybe they'll come back soon for a visit."

By late afternoon, the packing was almost done. Lily's forehead glistened with sweat as she helped carry the last of the staples to Black Beauty. She helped her grandmother with the mattress, but this time it wasn't as much fun. Leaving Ripon was easy; she hated it there. But here, it was fun. She had friends at home and at school. Jamie and Nancy were her best friends, and little Roger reminded her so much of her little brother that it would be like losing her family again. Lily couldn't shake the sadness. Why couldn't she have her mother and stepfather and brother and sister? Why did Momma have to die and leave her here with her grandmother? Why didn't Orville keep them all together? Where were her sister and brother now? It just wasn't fair. She was tired of moving from town to town. Why couldn't they just stay put for a change?

In the end, she didn't say goodbye to Roger or Jamie because she couldn't. Her grandmother rushed her to Black Beauty and waved to Mayola, who was standing on the front porch. "May, you know I don't like goodbyes—tell your children we said bye." With that, they were off.

CHAPTER 12

We've Got Enough of Them

Her grandmother started the car and eased out of the sandy driveway. Lily caught a glimpse of a sad Roger and Jamie peeking out from the living room window. She kept her head down, not wanting them to see her tears.

As they headed north on Highway 99, Lily watched the dusty oleanders swaying in the gusts of wind made by the cars and heavy trucks.

"It was about time for us to leave," her grandmother said. "Them kids were starting to get on my nerves."

Lily said nothing as she watched a fly scamper along the floorboard. "I bet you didn't forget your violin and rock collection, did you?" her grandmother said, trying to get Lily involved with the move.

"No, ma'am, it's under the seat." Lily smiled but averted her face, pretending to brush an insect away from her ankle. She couldn't stay mad at her grandmother. Besides, they would move whether she was mad or not. After several moves, Lily had already learned that hard lesson.

"Jamie was doing real good with his math," Lily said, "I hope he keeps studying after school."

Her grandmother rolled the window down slightly, allowing the wind to cool down the warm, stuffy car. Black Beauty smelled good to Lily. It had the familiar, comfortable smell that reminded her of all the other moves.

"You know, now that I'm thinking about it, I don't think I'm going to Merced," her grandmother said. "All that girl of mine wants is a permanent babysitter for her damn children. I got a sister in Ridgecrest; maybe we ought to go there."

When they got to Bakersfield, Pet pointed the car east on Highway 178 towards the great Mojave Desert. It was a two-lane road, and Black Beauty meandered along, sputtering and hissing as the car overheated in the early October evening. At the next turn-out, her grandmother pulled the car off the road. They both sat in silence. Lily, feeling anxious over their next move, and her grandmother, preoccupied with where she would find work.

The first day of school in Ridgecrest loomed heavy on Lily. She missed Jamie and Roger and her new-found friend, Nancy. In less than a month, Nancy and the other band members would be performing in the Autumn concert. Without her. Lily wondered who would play in her place. She had one solo piece. Two stanzas, but two important stanzas. She played the melody in her head and fantasized the movement of the bow. It was a Bach concerto that was slow and mournful. The piece sometimes made her feel melancholy. The sound reverberated over and over again until Lily thought she would cry aloud.

When getting ready for school, she examined each button of her dress as if seeing them for the first time. Her grandmother seemed to have more patience and appeared to not notice Lily's lazy, slow preparation for school. She even appeared to angle and re-angle the car in the school's parking lot, giving Lily time to adjust to the inevitable first day of school for the new colored girl.

"Take this registration card to your classroom; it's room 205," said a matronly woman with white hair and a large, sharply pointed nose. She didn't bother to look at Lily; she just shoved the card into her hand and walked back behind her desk as if the act of giving Lily the registration card had never taken place.

Red hair and blonde hair with green eyes and blue eyes and hazel eyes stared at Lily as she entered the classroom. She felt hot and prickly. Everything about her itched and stung in all the wrong places. Mrs. Kerr greeted Lily warmly as she entered the classroom.

"Welcome to Alta Mira," she said, with soft eyes that seemed to smile.

"Thank you," Lily said softly and sat at a desk near the front of the class. She busied herself with re-tying her shoelaces and tried to look as inconspicuous as possible. The hour and a half before recess dragged on and on.

Lily realized that sitting in the front of the classroom was not such a good idea. She had not thought about how many children were staring at her from behind. It felt as if the eyes of the entire classroom bored into the back of her head.

"Why don't you tell us a little about yourself and what school you attended before," Mrs. Kerr said a minute before the recess bell was scheduled to ring.

"Well, I…" Lily stammered, "I just came from uh…I mean…"

"Slow down, child; we won't bite. Did you like your other school?" Mrs. Kerr asked, sensing Lily's reluctance to speak in front of the class.

"Oh, yes," Lily answered, "The teacher and kids were real nice. Do you have an orchestra here?"

"Yes, child. You must have played an instrument before."

"Uh, huh," Lily answered, smiling sheepishly.

"Good. I think you will fit in nicely at your new school here."

The rest of the classroom visibly relaxed. Mrs. Kerr had a way of making uncomfortable situations seem comfortable, and the children relied on her for their cues. It was the first time most of the students had seen a colored child up close, so their stares were mostly curiosity.

The bell rang, and several girls ran up to Lily's desk before she had a chance to bolt out of the classroom for the safety of the outside. They all talked at once. Lily felt overwhelmed.

Mrs. Kerr stepped over to the excited children. "Children, Children! Why don't you girls show Lily where to find the bathroom and the lockers. Mellissa, also take her to Mr. Fine so she can sign up for the orchestra, and don't forget, girls, be back in class in fifteen minutes sharp!"

As the children ran for the door, Mrs. Kerr breathed a sigh of relief and leaned against the corner of her desk. She wiped the perspiration from her forehead and decided to make a brief visit to the school office.

"Bertha, where did that child come from?" Mrs. Kerr asked.

"You mean that Ne—"

Mrs. Kerr interrupted Bertha, annoyed that the other woman made her distaste of the colored race so obvious. "No, I mean that colored girl that started school today. She is such a lovely child. Reminds me of the children from Africa when I worked in the Peace Corps in Nigeria."

Several of the office clerks looked up with mild interest at the interchange taking place between Mrs. Kerr and Mrs. Versall, the office manager. They had all heard many times before about Mrs. Kerr's exploits in Africa, and most found her tales a bit outlandish and hard to believe.

"Well, you might like 'em, but I don't," Mrs. Versall replied haughtily. "They smell, and you have to watch your stuff around them."

Mrs. Versall had an unkind look about herself. She wore her hair pulled tightly back in a bun. She had thick glasses that made her eyes look twice their size, and her mouth was placed in a permanent downturn.

"Mrs. Versall!" Mrs. Kerr stammered. "How could you say such a thing? She is obviously a sweet child, and she does not smell! At least keep your prejudice to yourself." Mrs. Kerr was well aware of the ill feelings expressed by Mrs. Versall and other staff members and teachers in the school. No doubt, the child had been assigned to her class because the staff knew that the other teachers would object vehemently to having a colored child mar their classroom. Mrs. Kerr retrieved Lily's new folder and looked at the contents inside. There were no transfer papers in the folder, only a hastily completed application signed by the child's grandmother.

"She's going to have a hard time in your class. You have the upper-division fifth graders. You're going to have to slow down all the children because of that girl." Mrs. Versall continued, "You might want to place her in Mr. Scott's class…"

"But that's a fourth-grade class, and Lily's in the fifth!" Mrs. Kerr interrupted, feeling her face flush.

The entire office was silent except for the exchange taking place between Mrs. Versall and Mrs. Kerr. No clanky typewriter keys and no loud mimeographs echoed in the office. Most sided with Mrs. Versall, but no one joined to support either conversation. The recess bell rang, and Mrs. Kerr placed Lily's folder on Mrs. Versall's desk. She hurried back to her classroom. Mrs. Versall and the other staff members exchanged knowing looks and continued with their work.

The children were lined up, patiently awaiting Mrs. Kerr. Discipline was not a problem in her classroom. If her students noticed her flushed face and moist eyes, they said nothing. "Well, class," she said as they filed in behind her, quickly taking their seats, "The excitement is over. I'm sure you have all met our new student, Lily, and if you haven't, I know there's plenty of time. Mary, you were sharing your pen pal experience with the class; where did you say your pen pal was from?" To Lily, Mrs. Kerr winked and whispered, "See me at lunchtime about your pen pal."

Mary, obviously proud to have center stage, stood next to her desk and announced, "My pen pal is from Lexington, Kentucky. She said she likes the puzzles in the Weekly Reader, and she goes to her friend Amy's house to playhouse and trade comic books. She especially likes Buck Rogers." Mary had an elfish-looking face with large brown eyes on a tiny pink face.

A boy with short-cropped brown hair, sitting at the desk adjacent to Mary, kicked the side of her desk, "Girls shouldn't read Buck Rogers; why isn't she reading those Nancy Drew mysteries? Isn't that what all the girls like?

"I like to read Buck Rogers," protested Mary.

"Me too," several other girls chimed in.

"Oh brother," the boys groaned in unison. "Next, they'll want to play Army!"

CHAPTER 13

My Feet Hurt So Bad

That afternoon, Lily rode with her grandmother to look for work. It appeared that there was not a sister Grace in Ridgecrest. The colored part of town was easy enough to find, but Grace had since moved to another town. Mabel Browning, who kept house for Colonel Dickinson, the Commanding Officer of China Lake Air Force Base, let Lily's grandmother know as they sat on her front porch. It was warm and sticky, and Lily had knowingly sat in the car and waited.

"Now, there's plenty of work here," Mabel informed Lily's grandmother, "but these folks don't pay much. The most we make is around six dollars a day, eight if we work overtime, and I mean a lot of overtime."

The house, an old white structure with a flat roof, seemed to sink into the hot desert sand as Lily watched the conversation from the car. "We rent from the Nelsons, and the place Grace lived in around the corner is still vacant. Why I'll bet they'll let you stay there without a deposit."

As soon as they moved in, Lily understood why they didn't need a deposit. After her first day of school, she walked in to see her grandmother sitting on the worn couch, soaking her dusty feet in hot water, fanning her sweaty face, and looking mean. Without a word between them, Lily picked up the broom and mop and began the task of making their hole in the wall a decent place to live.

"Girl, my feet hurt so bad, Mabel wasn't kidding when she said they work you to death. Girl, I'm so tired."

As Lily cleaned, all she could think about was the refuge of school. At least there, she got to learn and play with kids. She did not have to listen to the old woman complain about how hard she worked or how nasty those white people's houses were. *Compared to this*, she thought *school was fun*.

CHAPTER 14

Imperialism! Humph!

During lunch recess, Mrs. Kerr had been called to the office by the Vice-Principal, Mr. Burns. When Mrs. Kerr arrived, he was trying unsuccessfully to transfer Lily to a neighboring school. The other Vice-Principal refused, saying he already had three, and one more was more than his district could take. Mrs. Kerr had listened to the exchange with the appropriate amount of concern for Mr. Burn's predicament.

Later, Mrs. Kerr sat at her desk, logging math grades in her ledger. She looked up and glanced thoughtfully at Lily who was working quietly at her desk. "Lily, I'm sorry I didn't get a chance to assign you a pen pal after lunch the other day, but sometimes it's pretty hectic around here. I don't quite know how to ask you this, but I'm wondering if you'd be interested in a pen pal from Africa?"

Lily stared blankly, not knowing what to say. Images of dark-skinned people wearing tribal warfare with grass skirts swaying among palm trees entered her thoughts. "Do they speak English?" Lily blurted before she had a chance to think.

"Why, of course. Nigeria, which is where I have in mind for your pen pal, has been taken over by the English for quite some time. I was a Peace Corps volunteer there, and I know lots of lovely young girls who would love to correspond with an American girl."

Lily sat speechless, staring at Mrs. Kerr. "Why, what's the matter, child? Did I say something wrong?"

"Well, I—I never..." Lily had never thought of herself as an American girl. But, of course, she was an American girl. She was born here, her mother was born here, and her grandmother and great-grandmother were born here. Why they were all American people! The realization hit Lily like a loud pistol shot going off in an empty auditorium. Why hadn't she ever felt like she was an American girl? Was it because she always felt like an outsider? Was it because most white kids did not play with colored kids? Why did her grandmother seem so out of place when she registered Lily at school? Why did people stare at them wherever they went? Why was there always a colored section of town where all the coloreds lived, apart from the white? Why did colored people have to work for white people, doing the jobs no one else wanted to do? Why didn't she feel American?

"I guess I never thought about an African pen pal," Lily said.

Mrs. Kerr noticed that Lily looked disappointed. "Lily, you don't have to have an African pen pal. I just thought that it would be a unique opportunity to meet a child who lives halfway around the world and..."

"Oh yes, Mrs. Kerr, I want to know about African kids, I mean, they do speak English, you say?" Lily asked

"Yes, child. They do speak English."

Later that evening, Lily spent hours locked in the bathroom writing to her pen pal. Once she had mailed her letter, it seemed as though years had passed since she received a reply.

Dear Lily,

I was so happy to hear from you and learn all about your country. My family remembers Mrs. Kerr and asks of her health and well-being. We are all grateful to her for her support during her stay here. I have so many questions to ask of you, I don't know where to start. My name is pronounced A-knee-ka and it is spelled Anika. This means goodness. My father tells me that when I was born, I looked like his mother, who he says is full of goodness and love, and he wanted to honor her. Yes, I learned English in school, it is a required subject, and because the schools in these rural villages are run by the English, we speak English. Our country is in turmoil right now. We are trying very hard to fight the colonization of our country. We hope to become free of the imperialists who are now running Nigeria. My mother is afraid for my father because he is very outspoken. In my next letter, I will tell you more about my family, my sister, and brother. They are younger. My regards to your family and schoolmates.

Sincerely,
Anika

Reading the letter from Anika, made Lily glow with joy. A big smile creeped across her face as she read the letter over and over. This was exactly what she needed, a new friend, a true friend. Lily grabbed a pen and paper and sat down right away to write Anika back. The next morning, she dropped the letter in the mailbox.

Every day, she looked for a return letter from her pen pal. As the days turned into weeks, she began to wonder if she would ever hear from her. One day, for reasons unknown to Lily, she knew the letter would be at home. She had pictured a miniature blue letter depicting a funny-looking stamp of an African lion or zebra. Mrs. Kerr received letters from Africa. She sometimes read passages to the class during the history lesson. Mrs. Kerr wanted the children to visualize people thousands of miles away. She felt by hearing the voices through the letters, the children would know and love the people of Nigeria. To most of the children, Nigeria and its people were too far away to be real. But for Lily, the pages of the letters suddenly came alive.

When she arrived home that day, the excitement of knowing the letter awaited her was as if God had returned her mother home. Because Lily knew that her mother knew everything that occurred in her life, she would, of course, know of the pen pal. She would know of Lily's loneliness. She would know that Lily longed for a friend who didn't care that her skin was brown. Who cherished friendships, no matter who knew of them. She would know that Lily wanted so much to be accepted by other kids. The not-yet-seen letter meant everything to Lily.

She stepped into the house, sighing from the cool relief offered inside. It was 110 degrees outside. The odor of string beans and ham hocks assailed her nostrils and seemed in contrast to the neatly folded letter with the unfamiliar postal stamp. It had already been opened and lay on the kitchen table, exposed to her grandmother's prying eyes. Lily's eyes followed her grandmother's—back and forth, from the letter to her grandmother and back to the letter. The letter lay exposed like an open wound.

"You read my letter?" Lily asked incredulously. Her grandmother shot her a look that meant she had overstepped the boundaries set by culture and time. Lily's heart sank. She didn't want to read the letter.

"Girl, go on and pick the letter up and read it. Some silly girl talking them big words, trying to show off. Them people still running around half-naked in them jungles. What do they know about IMPERIALISM? Humph!"

Lily walked over to the table and slowly picked up the letter. The paper felt different. Kind of like parchment paper. All of her excitement was gone. Silent tears rolled down her face as she took the letter to the bathroom. In this house, she didn't have her own bedroom. She turned on the water so that her grandmother couldn't hear her sobs. As she read the letter, her tears spattered onto the paper, turning one of the words into a black smear. Seeing the smear, Lily galvanized into immediate action. She placed the letter on the back of the toilet seat, washed and dried her face, then, began answering the second letter she had received from Anika.

Dear Anika,

Sometimes it's hard making friends in my new school. One day, I saw this girl on the playground. Her name is Latisha Kay. She's real light, and her hair is soft and fluffy. I tried to play with her, but she doesn't want to play with me. This is what happened on the playground. I ran up to her, all friendly and stuff, but she turned away before I got too close. When I told my grandmother, she asked if the girl was high yellow. I didn't know what that meant. She asked if the girl was light skinned, and I said yes. She told me light-skinned people don't like dark-skinned people like us, and I shouldn't play with her anyway. I never went to school with other colored kids before. So, I didn't know there were rules about dark and light kids not playing together. I noticed from the picture you sent me that your skin coloring is like mine. So, I guess it's all right for us to write each other and play if we ever meet. I wish you were here because we could play every day. Well, I've got to go and practice my violin, so I'll write you next time.

Sincerely,
Lily

CHAPTER 15

Light and dark Are Not the Same

This new school was really different. The kids were not as friendly as in her previous school. The hot nights of late summer turned into the cool nights of early fall. Lily's grandmother worked nights now. One day as Lily walked home from the bus stop, head down, looking for rocks to add to her collection, her grandmother greeted her.

"Put your books and violin in the house; we're going to meet the Broussards."

Lily's heart began to race, and fine beads of perspiration dotted her upper lip. She ran into the house and scooted her books and violin underneath her bed. She sat quietly in Black Beauty. As her grandmother eased the car onto the gravel road, Lily spied her grandmother out of the corner of her eyes. She didn't look angry. That was a good sign. She dared not ask where they were going or why, so she just sat and waited. She rolled her window part way down and stuck out her tongue to taste the sweet hot desert air. *I wonder who the Broussards are and where they live,* she thought. Her grandmother gunned Black Beauty onto the highway, keeping the car in the slow lane. They exited after about five miles. Cows grazed peacefully in the wide-open space, irrigated by the nearby canals. The green alfalfa next to the parched desert landscape reminded Lily of the new word she learned at school today. Oasis.

As they exited, her grandmother said, "You're going to stay with the Broussards while I work at this live-in job, and I'll come and get you on the weekends. They are pretty decent people, even if most of them are high yellow. They wanted to meet you before you start staying with them next week."

Lily was in such a state of shock, she hadn't noticed that they were parked in front of someone's house, presumable, the Broussards. Her narrow hands gripped the seat, and her arms hurt from pushing down in the seat cushions.

"Smile, girl, they ain't gonna bite you."

Lily peeked out of the car window and saw a flock of children, all shades of beige and brown encircling Black Beauty. From inside Black Beauty, it felt like a bunch of Indians encircling the wagon in an old western. Lily did a double-take when she noticed that one of the children was her classmate, Latisha Kay. For a brief second, their eyes locked, but Lily's moved on, marveling at the number of children surrounding her. Her grandmother stepped out and waded through the children like a sheep herder through a flock of sheep. Lily got out also. Her grandmother lumbered up to the front porch. A short, dark woman greeted her.

"Pet, girl, I'm glad you made it. You children, go on out back and play." She gestured to the children, shooing them into the backyard. "They act like they've never seen anybody that wasn't kin. Well, actually, they don't see too many coloreds around here." Lily hesitated, unsure if she should follow the flock of children or the two adults about to enter the house.

"Go on and play with the kids. I'll be inside," her grandmother said.

Latisha Kay had disappeared. All of the other eyes descended upon Lily.

"My grandmother said you gonna stay with us during the week. My name's Tony. What's yours?"

"Lily." She looked closely at Tony. He looked like a white child. He had thin, straight, brown hair and blue eyes. Some of his younger sisters were dark like Lily, but they all had either gray or green eyes. "Is this an orphanage?" Lily blurted. "Cause I'm not staying in no orphanage; I don't care what she says." And with that, Lily ran from the backyard and back to Black Beauty. She buried her head in the seat cushions, crying hysterically. The kids who looked like Indians followed her, but this time Latisha Kay came too.

"Hey, Lily," Tony hollered through the rolled-up window. "This ain't no orphanage, We all family."

Lily wailed even louder, trying to drown Tony out.

He cupped his hands to the car window, his pink lips grotesquely shaped by the glass. "Honest, these are all my sisters and brothers. We Creole. I'm colored, too, honest. Lily, look at my nose. It ain't like most white folks."

Lily eased up and stared at Tony. His nose was broader than any white person she'd seen, but his hair and eyes were different. She stared, confused.

Tony gently opened the car door and stepped back to allow Lily to get out. The Indians, ranging in age from about twelve to two, gathered round. Tony gestured to the kids, "This here's Latisha Kay. Come back, Latisha Kay." Latisha Kay had darted away again. "She tongue-tied, and she don't like to talk 'cause people make fun of her. This here's Randall." He squinted up at her, his hands shielding his chocolate brown face from the late afternoon sun.

"Hi, Lily," he said solemnly.

"This here's Stevie." He dropped his head down and started giggling.

Lily thought that Stevie looked like the Mexican kids that went to the new school.

Tony continued, "This one with the thumb in her mouth, she's Alicia. These two here are twins, May and Kay." The girls had on matching red and white outfits that contrasted sharply with their dark brown skin. "I got a big sister named Shirley, but she's in high school, and she's not home yet."

Lily looked from one to the other, raising and lowering her head as she eyed each child. They were so different, yet their resemblance was unmistakable. She was taller than all of the children except Tony and Latisha Kay.

Eyeing Lily defiantly, Latisha Kay knew that her brother had told Lily about her affliction. He always told everybody. Better for him to tell. She glared hard at Lily, her eyes saying, *I dare you to make fun of me.*

Lily did not; she just smiled at her.

Latisha Kay jerked her head down, but she didn't run away.

"You're going to sleepth in our room," Latisha Kay said. Lily looked puzzled at Tony for an interpretation because she only understood "our room."

"She said you're going to sleep in the girl's room. Don't worry, you'll get used to her; it's easy to understand her once you get to know her."

Just as the children were getting familiar with one another, Lily heard her grandmother call. She ran for Black Beauty, her Indians following in hot pursuit. When she got to the car, her grandmother gestured, "Mrs. Broussard, this here's Lily." Before Lily had a chance to acknowledge, her grandmother reprimanded her. "Didn't I teach you any manners? Say hello to Mrs. Broussard and her daughter, Lettie Contrale, but you call her Mrs. Contrale. Those were her children you met when we pulled up."

Mrs. Broussard's face lit up with a smile, but her daughter, Lettie, puckered her thin lips and glanced disdainfully in Lily's direction.

Lily answered quickly. She couldn't help but stare at the two women. Mrs. Contrale looked like a white woman, and Mrs. Broussard looked like her Mexican maid! On closer inspection, however, Lily noticed the same close family resemblance—just like the children with their varying degrees of light and dark.

"I'm sure we won't have any trouble out of Lily, Pet. After all, she seems like a nice, quiet girl. I just hope she can adjust to being around all my grandchildren."

Once on the highway, her grandmother said, "They some real nice people, them Broussards. She the one told me about that night job. When I told her about you, she offered to keep you during the week. Now her daughter, Mrs. Contrale, is kind of color struck. You watch out for her. Mrs. Broussard said she don't like none of her dark-skinned children. Funny how this world is. White against colored. Colored against colored. It ain't never been right. That oldest gal, Shirley, is passing for white. Mrs. Broussard says Shirley don't let nobody know who her people are. Her white boyfriend drops her off six blocks before her front door. Poor child. She don't know they gonna find out anyway. What she gonna do? Keep everybody but her Momma and the white-looking kids away from her? What about her black daddy? She gonna keep him away too?"

Lily answered a quiet "hmmm" to keep the conversation going. She never knew when or under what circumstances her grandmother would talk. Almost always, it was in the confines of Black Beauty. Lily wanted to ease the car window down, but she was afraid that her grandmother's talking spell would be broken. She played with her shoestrings and nodded and grunted at the appropriate moments.

"Way I see it, one day you won't have to work for white folks cleaning their dirty houses. You won't have to grin at them when they tell you they can only pay you seven dollars a day. Less than one dollar an hour. Lily, I want to live to see the day you don't have to live like I do."

Her voice startled Lily. Her grandmother was no longer talking to anyone in particular. She was talking to Lily.

"One day, light-skinned colored people won't look down on dark-skinned people, and we all won't be afraid to speak up. We'll tell white people what we think of them and how we hate to clean their nasty houses."

Lily almost fell to the floor as her grandmother slammed on the brakes, and Black Beauty barely avoided a truck full of chickens on their way to be slaughtered. She straightened up in her seat and gave Lily a stern look that meant she had ceased talking. Lily slumped back into her seat.

They were home. Black Beauty purred into the gravel drive, bouncing with each rut in the road. Lily began thinking about her part-time home. All those children. She felt both excited and afraid. Excited about having so many kids to play with. Afraid of what her life would be like living at the Broussards.

CHAPTER 16

I'll Have Some Cawn Fritters, Please

Friday arrived, last morning at the Broussards until Monday. The girl's bedroom was in disarray. Lily busied about trying to locate her blue sock. She had found all of her socks except the mate to the blue sock. It had blue and white ruffles on the cuff. Lily awakened early to gather her clothing. Last Friday's arrival home had been a nightmare. She had not known that her grandmother cataloged everything in the overnight bag.

"Lily, I packed you five pair of panties, two slips, three pair of socks, and your school shoes," her grandmother said. Lily watched as her grandmother pulled her dirty clothes from the bag. "And you're missing a pair of socks and two pair of panties." Lily started to tell her grandmother about the casual way the children exchanged their clothing but stopped short. She wouldn't understand.

"Now, we don't want them Broussards thinking I can't send you to school in decent clothes. Girl, are you listening to me?"

"Yes, ma'am," Lily replied.

All of a sudden, the cramped living room seemed even smaller. Seeing her week's clothing strewn on the lumpy living room couch made Lily feel vulnerable. Sort of like when her grandmother had opened her pen pal letter from Anika. Lily had managed to circumvent her grandmother's prying eyes by writing her pen pal using Mrs. Kerr's address. But there was nothing she could do about this weekly clothing inspection.

Now, as she located the missing sock underneath the bed she shared with Latisha Kay, Lily ran to the bathroom to wash up before breakfast.

Breakfast was so much fun at the Broussards. Old man Broussard, retired from chauffeuring and cooking for a well-to-do local family, delighted in preparing breakfast for his grandchildren. It was an elaborate affair that took an hour each morning.

Sometime during the previous evening, one of the children had deposited a slip of paper into a small paper bag located by the brightly lit kitchen window. The paper contained a request for a particular breakfast item.

Broussard had emerged at six in the morning and smiled as he read the scrawled note. It was from his five-year-old grandchild, Alicia. *Cawn fratters*, it read; He sat shucking the corn from its stalk. He lightly seasoned the shucked corn and dipped it into the batter.

Lily entered the kitchen just as Mrs. Broussard arrived.

"Morning Lily, morning mother," he said to his wife.

She nodded and gave Lily an inquisitive glance as the couple sat down at the kitchen table. Lily walked over and sat on a stool near the kitchen sink.

Mrs. Broussard never stayed in the kitchen long, just long enough to get her morning coffee. Lily sat watching them, feeling a bit chilled from the not-yet-warmed-up kitchen.

Mr. Broussard was tall and lanky with a full white beard that matched his extra curly, short white hair. When he beamed at his wife, she blushed. They were so different—he, very dark and handsome; she, very light and pretty. The love between them was evident.

"Morning, daughter," Mr. and Mrs. Broussard said as their only child, Lettie, entered the kitchen. Mrs. Broussard rose from the table and winked at Lily as she hurried from the kitchen. The pleasant feel of the kitchen suddenly changed for Lily. She no longer felt welcome.

Lily began looking down at her shoelaces, trying to become invisible to Mrs. Contrale's prying eyes.

"Mornin' daddy," Lettie said as she yawned and stretched like a lazy cat. She had a long, white, terry-cloth robe, and her face was flushed from her hot morning bath. Even though Lily had observed her many times since moving in, it still felt like an alien, white woman had entered the room.

Without another word between them, Mr. Broussard placed a hot cup of coffee on the kitchen table in front of his daughter. With a disapproving glance in Lily's direction, Lettie left, her hot coffee creating a cloud of mist behind her. She didn't thank her father.

Lily stayed in the kitchen. For this quiet hour before the children awakened, with Broussard's help, Lily managed to feel like she belonged to a family.

Since she had moved in, Lily had once overheard Mrs. Contrale talking to her cousin, anguishing over her dark-skinned children.

"Mother knew I hated dark skin and wondered why I married my husband. But his darkness makes me look even whiter, and I thought my kids would turn out light like me," she had said.

Lily thought God had other plans. Half of the kids had turned out dark like their father and grandfather. Lily realized that Mrs. Contrale didn't like her dark-skinned children because she thought dark people were beneath her. Maybe that's why she doesn't like me, Lily thought, I'm too dark.

"Hey, Lily, do you like corn fritters?"

"Oh yes, sir," Lily replied. "I mean, I've never had 'em before—I guess I like them," she stuttered.

"Of course, you do—you'll like mine anyway." He laughed. "If you don't, what else you gonna eat for breakfast?" He smiled down at Lily as she relaxed on the kitchen stool.

She was sleepy this morning, but she wouldn't miss the early mornings with Mr. Broussard for more sleeping with Latisha Kay breathing in her face.

"Now, girl, don't you pay my daughter no mind; she don't like children that much. She's half asleep when she comes in here in the morning. Don't worry about her," he advised.

Lily nodded.

"'Course now, you could have done a better job of washing your face this morning. We wash up before we come down for breakfast."

Lily nodded again.

Mr. Broussard placed a small plate of corn fritters on the kitchen table and gestured for Lily to join him. They smelled so good. He opened a mason jar of peach jam and placed a dollop of jam on the plate next to the corn fritters.

Lily was impressed, *I wonder how he knew not to put the jam on top of my fritters*, she thought.

Mr. Broussard and Lily ate the fritters, obviously enjoying the breakfast and each other's silent company.

As the clock inched toward seven, the younger children broke the quiet mood of the kitchen, and Lily departed into the bedroom to wash up and gather her books. She wanted to be alone.

As she left, she pondered about the Broussards. Such a different family from her grandmother. First of all, they had a mother and grandparents at home. The children's father was nowhere around. Lily had never thought about her mother being her grandmother's daughter. What a strange thought. Her grandmother rarely talked about Lily's mother. Except if Lily really begged her to.

It had all started with the kids at school teasing her about not having a mother. It seemed as though every child in school knew. When asked about her mother, Lily usually clammed up, and then the gossip began. It happened at every school she had attended since her mother's death. At her current school, they'd ask Tony or Latisha Kay, who would repeat what they'd overheard their parents discussing.

The children had heard the parents use the word "suicide," but not quite understanding it. They'd move on to embalming because at least one family would know the town's undertaker, and they always had children in school.

They knew that dead people got embalmed. They said that the undertaker had embalmed her mother. Lily asked her grandmother about embalming. Lily remembered that a painful look had crossed her grandmother's face. It seemed strange to Lily that her grandmother felt pain. She was so mean most of the time. Lily kept asking about the embalming until she got an answer.

The answer had come from her grandmother before Lily had moved in with the Broussards. She was sitting on the floor, between her grandmother's legs, getting her hair combed. Lily's back was to her grandmother, so she couldn't see her face.

"After your mother died…"

Lily smiled. Just hearing her mother mentioned felt good to her. She pictured her mother combing her hair instead of her grandmother.

"Her body was full of blood. The undertaker drained her blood and filled her body with fluid. It made her cheeks fill out, and her body could be kept until we finished with the funeral arrangements."

Her grandmother's voice seemed to be quavering, but Lily dared not turn around and look into her grandmother's face. Hearing her grandmother talk about the funeral had made Lily think back to a few months earlier when her mother was in the casket. She had wondered why her mother was laying there, appearing to be sleeping peacefully.

Every family member that Lily knew was there. Her mother's family, her stepfather's family, and kids from her school—they were all there.

She'd thought that she would be glad when the ceremony was over, and her mother could get up from sleeping, and they could all go home. But when it was over, they went to the cemetery, and she'd watched the cemetery men lower her mother's casket into the ground! That was the saddest day of her life, and she had just turned eight.

Now, she was eleven, and Lily was awakened from her musing by the faraway hum of her school bus. Finished with her hair, her grandmother tapped Lily's head to indicate that it was time for Lily to get up. Lily sat immobile and then jumped up, grabbed her schoolbooks and violin, and ran all the way to the bus stop.

Next morning at breakfast, Lily stumbled into the kitchen, rubbing her eyes as she walked. She had dreamt about her mother and a priest telling her that she would see her mother again soon. The kitchen was illuminated with the morning sun, contrasting sharply with Lily's dark thoughts.

"Girl, you didn't hear me talking to you?"

"Oh, I'm sorry," Lily replied. She looked up in time to see Mr. Broussard staring at her. He seemed to shake a thought out of his head the way her stepfather used to do when something puzzled him.

"What I was saying as you walked in the kitchen, child, is that you can start adding your request for breakfast in the bag we keep by the window here. What kind of food do you like?"

"Well, I…uhh…I like banana pancakes," Lily blurted. "My mother used to make them for me." That sad expression revisited Lily's face, the same look that Mr. Broussard had observed when she walked into the kitchen. Lily sat at the kitchen counter with elbows on the table, hands cupped to her face, her brown and white oxfords swinging rhythmically in time to the blues number belting from Mr. Broussard's old phonograph.

She enjoyed spending her mornings with Mr. Broussard. She always arose before the other children so she could watch him cook. Starting her day with the old man was the best.

"Hand me that wrapping that says 'link sausage' from the freezer so I can thaw it out for breakfast." Mr. Broussard said.

"Yes, sir."

CHAPTER 17

Duck Under the Covers

Lily had waited all week for Sunday to arrive, and finally, it was here. The Broussards went to the drive-in on Sundays, but this would be her first time. Latisha Kay had told her all about it. The early evening was quiet as Black Beauty coughed onto the highway, the yellow headlights illuminating the darkening asphalt. It seemed to her that they were the only ones on Highway 99. A large white-winged moth hit the windshield with a loud splat, and Lily and her grandmother watched its dead white wing flap silently in the dark night.

Lily unconsciously tried to hurry Black Beauty to the next exit by pressing down on the floor of the car. They finally pulled into the Broussard's driveway, and Lily, anxious to see Latisha Kay and the other children, jerked the car door partially open just as her grandmother stepped on the brakes.

"Hold on, girl, you want to fall out the car?"

"Sorry," Lily mumbled. She released the door handle and eased back into her seat.

"Go on, girl. I know you all going to the drive-in; what you seein' tonight?"

"I don't know," Lily blushed. She didn't want to appear too anxious, especially knowing that her grandmother didn't want her to have too much fun.

"Lily's here!" Tony roared.

As she walked in, the front porch screen slammed behind her, and Latisha Kay ran up. They grasped hands and began to swing back and forth in unison. Both girls were now fast friends.

"I got a new doll!" Latisha Kay exclaimed. Lily nodded. "Let's go look at her."

"Okay." The girls skipped, hand-in-hand, through the Broussard's living room that was filled with Mrs. Broussard's collection of odd trinkets from the local junk shops. They paused in the doorway to the kitchen, and Lily and Latisha Kay beamed up at old man Broussard.

"Evening, girls. "And where do you young 'uns think you're going?"

"I'm gonna show Lily my doll you and grandmother got me," Latisha Kay said.

"Well, well," Mr. Broussard said. "And where's your new doll, Lily?" Mr. Broussard winked slyly at his wife, who had just entered the kitchen.

Lily eyed Latisha Kay, who looked puzzled at her grandparents.

Mr. Broussard pulled a Woolworth bag from atop the kitchen counter and handed it to Lily. She solemnly accepted the package and looked inside. A beautiful doll with long black Shirley Temple curls was inside.

"Ooooh weeee," both girls exclaimed in unison. In the excitement, they dropped the empty doll package and ran to their bedroom with the dolls, forgetting to thank the couple.

As the sun marched toward its evening descent over the desert mountains, everyone climbed inside the Broussard's worn Ford station wagon. The station wagon smelled like a movie theater, and Lily followed her nose to the greasy brown paper bag filled with hot buttered popcorn stashed on the floorboard. Suddenly, Lily frowned and turned up her nose as she detected a whiff of the youngest girl's rotten-smelling thumb as she snatched it from her mouth. Lily was determined to enjoy this night, so she concentrated on the sweet aroma of the popcorn wafting through the air.

The boys got in first, followed by Lily, Latisha Kay, the twins, and Alicia. Everyone was already dressed in their pajamas, and the odor of warm, freshly bathed children intermingled with the popcorn.

"Muh Dear, are you gonna tell us when to get under the covers?" Alicia asked.

"Chile, don't start worrying me already; I'll let you all know. Sit back in your seat, girl."

Alicia dutifully followed her grandmother's direction and eased back onto the worn car seat. By hanging back as everyone else had piled into the station wagon, Lily had landed a seat next to the window. She watched the desert landscape whizz by as she counted the telephone poles alongside the highway.

Around pole number twenty-nine, they exited the highway and turned right, following a big DRIVE-IN sign. "OK, kids, duck under the covers!" As Lily watched in awe, all the children's heads, except hers, disappeared under two green, musty army blankets. Latisha Kay grabbed Lily's arm and pulled her under. The overwhelming smell of hot breath enveloped the blanket, and Lily created a hole to breathe through.

"Don't do that, Lily! They'll see us. Be still," Latisha Kay whispered.

"Who'll see us?" Lily whispered, clutching the blanket and not letting it go.

"The people that collect the money, that's who." Latisha Kay answered.

Lily closed her eyes and held her breath. She listened patiently as the Broussards paid the fare for two adults. The minute they drove through the entrance gates, all heads reappeared. Tony opened the bag of popcorn, and Mrs. Broussard passed the children a thermos of Kool-Aid. In the short drive to the drive-in, the late autumn sun had set, and the evening had turned cool. The Broussards simultaneously rolled down their windows, placed the speakers inside the car, and adjusted the volume. The screen completely filled the front window, and everyone sat back to watch the movie. Alicia was already asleep.

"Tony, you and Stevie put Alicia back there with you boys so she can spread out, and don't wake her," said Mrs. Broussard.

"Yes, Muh Dear," replied Tony. He gingerly scooped Alicia up in his arms and placed her in the rear seat.

As the darkening sky filled the station wagon, Lily tried to stay awake, but her eyelids kept closing. It was an action movie, and the more she followed the characters' movement across the screen, the sleepier she got. She finally gave in and joined the other girls who were already asleep. Only the boys and the Broussards remained awake throughout the movie.

CHAPTER 18

The Photograph

With Lily's help, the rented house had taken on a somewhat homey look. She had placed her mother's framed photograph on the living room wall, which made Lily feel her mother's presence every time she entered the house. She was coming home to her mother, who patiently waited for her daughter's daily arrival. The portrait was a black and white that her mother had taken at a photography studio. Lily remembered the day it was taken. Her brother had just had his first birthday, and Lily had accompanied her mother to the studio. Her mother was shy, and the photographer had to coax her into several poses that accentuated her beauty. She was a tall, large-boned woman with honey-colored skin that glowed under the hot studio lights. Her large, white teeth seemed to sparkle like the teeth of the toothpaste models that Lily saw on highway billboard signs.

Maybe her mother had known that Lily would need something tangible to hold onto. Maybe she had known that she would die. Maybe she had known that she would kill herself. Lily hadn't known. The smile in the photograph was warm and friendly, and the soft eyes seemed to follow her as she moved about the room.

The first time Lily remembered seeing the photograph was after her mother's death. She had first been sent to live with her stepfather's family. They were all mean, except for the grandmother. She had given Lily Ellen's picture. Lily cried when she first saw it because she remembered when it had been taken. Her heart started hurting again. It ached, and it felt like it was turning over in her chest. Her step-grandmother had hugged her and given Lily a cardboard box to place the framed photograph in. She was a quiet woman, and the photograph exchange had taken place in silence.

In the beginning, Lily had to fight to keep that photograph on the wall. The first fight began right after she moved in with her grandmother. She was mean too. "What you doin' with my daughter's picture?" she had asked.

"Grandma Jenkins gave it to me," Lily had answered.

"Well, how come they gave it to you? Them Jenkins had no right to be keepin' my daughter's stuff. They ain't right." Her grandmother had retorted.

When her grandmother had attempted to snatch Lily's picture, Lily screamed, clutched the picture to her chest, ran toward the front door, and cried, "This is all I got left, and you're not taking it from me." She stood near the front door, ready to bolt if her grandmother came after her, but her grandmother had just sighed heavily and left Lily alone. With each new move, the picture was the first thing Lily placed on the wall of the living room. If they stayed with other people, Lily would place it next to her bed. Everyone understood the sacredness of the photograph.

CHAPTER 19

Oh, Mother, You're Gone for Good

Lily wanted to see her sister and brother again. It had been many years since her mother's death, and she had not seen them. She knew that her stepfather's and grandmother's families did not get along. Living with the Broussards during the week was a constant reminder of the loss of her siblings. She had felt the same loss with Latisha Kay and Tony. It seemed that everyone she knew lived with their sisters and brothers.

Her sister was eight months old at the time of their mother's death, and her brother was two. She remembered their last day together. It was a hot, dusty day. Lily and her brother sat on the front porch gazing upon the fig tree outside. Her sister was inside in her crib, crying and banging on the railing as babies seemed to always do. Her sobbing and banging seemed to coincide with the same sound that the figs made as their syrupy juices dropped onto the ground. Plop, plop, splat, splat.

The next few days were a blur to Lily. A loud shot frightened the two children, the third child, baby Lorna, suddenly quiet in her crib. A police car in the driveway, an ambulance taking her mother away. A funeral, her mother lying in a coffin. The Jenkins family sitting as far apart as possible from her mother's family. Lots of wailing and crying from grownups. Eight-year-old Lily was screaming as loud as she could, everywhere she went, so that her mother would return. People staring. What is wrong with that girl? A hushed response, her mother's dead. Her stepfather's sudden need to be as far away as possible. The suicide word, what does it mean when a person takes their own life. For a man, can you believe it, she killed herself over that no-good man.

Afterward, Lily had nightmares for years, each time painfully awakening to no mother. But Lily was eleven now and finally knew that her mother would not return. And she knew that her stepfather didn't love her after all; if he did, wouldn't he have tried to see her by now? Wouldn't he bring her sister and brother to her? She had heard that her sister and brother were with their Aunt Mickey, his sister, the mean one.

As the scene slowly unfolded before Lily's eyes, she tried to picture what her sister and brother looked like now. Her sister would still be at home, and her brother in first grade. They wouldn't remember her. They were too young. But Lily would find a way; she had to see her sister and brother again. Grandpa Broussard, she would talk to him. He had to help her.

CHAPTER 20

Yes, Sir, Dew Drop Inn

Lily's stepfather pulled his 18-wheeler into the diner, Dew Drop Inn, along Highway 99. He jumped down from the cab and strolled into the restaurant. As a tall, brown-skinned man, he continued to wear his army uniform, even though he had been out of the service for over two years. He looked good in the sharp, highly starched khakis, and he knew it. He imagined that the uniform gave white people a sense that all was well, even though a colored man had just entered their diner. He sat down at the counter and picked up a menu that had been shoved into his hands by the waitress.

It was a cool morning, and the dew from the cotton field across the way was still clinging to the white cotton bolls. He smiled when he thought about not having to stoop over and pick that cotton. Truck driving was an occupation a colored man would gladly do over field-work. He smelled the ham, eggs, and biscuits and was suddenly hungry.

"What'll you have, sir?" the waitress asked, pencil in hand, ready to take his order. She was at least two paces further away from him than she would be for her regular customers—but for her, it was close enough. The colored man squinted at her and leaned forward to hear what she had said.

"I'll have some pancakes, bacon, and eggs, coffee, black. You're gonna have to come closer 'cause I can't hear too good. Did you ask me what I want to eat?"

She held her ground and shouted, "Yes, sir, I got your order, and it'll be up in a few minutes." She turned and scurried off to the kitchen to place his order with the cook.

The other diners watched with amusement as he walked over and placed a quarter in the jukebox. He selected three songs and walked back to the counter and sipped the coffee that had been delivered in his absence.

The sudden death of his young wife had left him with a complete sense of bewilderment. His life on the road was, thankfully, away from the prying eyes of the town, the questioning looks, the whispering—he had to get away. It was here, in these faraway places, that he could just be another human being. Colored, yes, but not the man whose wife had committed suicide. Not the man who had given his children away and couldn't bear to look at them and see their pain. For when he looked at them, he saw her. And the ache was still too raw. It would never go away; of that he was certain.

The snap of the jukebox turntable brought the smell of bacon to his senses. He hadn't noticed that the waitress had delivered his breakfast. He quickly ate, paid, and left. Highway 99 loomed ahead, and as he shifted the myriad gears, he thought of lovely Ellen, tipped his cap to the sky, smiled, and wiped the tears from his eyes.

CHAPTER 21

I'm Gonna Write Him Now

The next morning, Lily decided, was the morning to talk to Grandpa Broussard.

Old man Broussard knew something was bothering Lily. For one thing, her black and white Buster Brown oxfords were swinging furiously back and forth. She didn't look him in the eye when he walked into the kitchen, and she didn't smile. He decided to approach her directly. He sat down beside her, careful to avoid her long, swinging legs. She increased the pace. "Lily, girl, what's on your mind? You look like you 'bout to bust"

Lily flushed and swung her head downward, embarrassed that someone knew her inner thoughts. "I have a sister, she's in kindergarten, and my brother's in third grade."

The old man knew this, but he feigned surprise. "You don't say. Hey, I bet you miss them a lot."

With that, Lily burst into tears and looked like a frightened rabbit about to run off.

"Now look, Lily, we know you must miss your sister and brother, and they probably miss you too. Why don't you write them a letter? I betcha' they'd love to hear from you."

"But they can't read!"

"Oh yes, if your brother's in third grade, he can read, and he can read to your little sister." The swing in Lily's legs lessened considerably.

"I never thought about that, I'm gonna write him now!"

CHAPTER 22

Them Kids Can Take Care of Themselves

Little Orville Jr. had just turned seven. He was crying, without a sound, of course, because he knew the consequences of being caught crying.

The walk from school last week had been bad. As he was walking home, the sole on one of his shoes had come apart. FLAP, step, FLAP step, FLAP, step. Everyone had stopped in their tracks, and a crowd had formed. Boys and girls were laughing and pointing and having fun as he cringed each time the torn shoe hit the pavement. As soon as he arrived home, he threw the shoes in the trash can in the kitchen.

When his stepmother arrived home from work, she said, "Orville Jr., what the hell you doing putting these shoes in the trash for?"

"They broke"

"What you mean, 'they broke'? Boy, you better come get these shoes and clean them up and put them back in your room."

"Annie, the bottom came off," he whined. "The kids were laughing at me."

"You think we got money to buy you some more shoes just 'cause you done tore them up and put them in the trash?"

"No, ma'am," he mumbled.

CHAPTER 23

If Only I Could Take You Home

Years later, Lily would remember that day. That was the first day she had seen her brother since their mother died. Orville Jr. was walking as fast as his torn shoe would allow. Their little sister, hand clasped tightly to her big brother, was being pulled by the sheer force of his shame and frustration. She hurried along, taking what seemed like a dozen steps to his one.

Lily had cried for him, for them. Gone were the days when they were part of a real family. Now they were fractured, the gawked-at offspring of a woman who had managed to kill herself.

She had followed her brother and little sister home from school that day, hoping to get a glimpse of her sister and brother's life. She had caught up with them just as they had entered their empty house. Even though it was a warm day, it was cold, dark, and quiet inside. Her five-year-old sister ran into their bedroom and quickly changed into her play clothes. Her brother did the same. Lily was puzzled; these kids seemed to be taking care of themselves. They didn't play. They sat motionless on the couch in the living room and waited like zombies for their stepmother's arrival.

"Where's your dad?" Lily asked.

"Driving his truck, he won't be back till another day, huh, Deenie?" her sister answered.

"Yeah," her brother said, "He's gone a lot."

"Do you guys get to go fishing like we used to do?" Lily asked.

"Nah, he say he's too tired. He and Annie fight a lot, and we hide in our room," her brother responded. He looked so grown up; Lily wanted to cry.

They sat. There was so much that Lily wanted to say to them. How she missed them. She remembered their last night together in the tiny town of Clarksburg. Her mother had finished bathing her eight-month-old sister and had laid her on the bed to dry her silky brown body. Lily had seen how her mother had playfully slapped the side of her sister's face. Her sister loved it, so she rolled her over on the bed to slap her cheeks. Her baby sister giggled, showing her two new front teeth. Lily kept slapping, and the baby kept laughing until, in her enthusiasm, she slapped her too hard. The baby suddenly stopped laughing. Her smile had changed to a frown, looking as if she was about to start crying. Lily was scared. She'd never been in trouble before. But hurting the baby? Even accidentally? She gave her sister a *"please don't start crying"* look, and her sister, sensing her distress, broke into a raucous fit of new laughter.

How much they had grown. She had easily recognized her brother, even though she hadn't seen him in five years. He looked like her little two-year-old brother, just taller and without the baby fat. How she had wanted to take them home with her, but she didn't have a home to take them to.

As the time for the stepmother's arrival loomed, the kids seemed to get more and more fidgety. They'd look at Lily, then the door, and the ticking clock. Feeling their anxiety, she grabbed them both and hugged them close to her, taking in the sweet aroma that can only be found in the familiar smells of the ones you love. She slipped quietly out the back door. That hurtful feeling in her chest started up again as she walked down the alley and away from the prison those poor children had to call home. There was no love in that house, of that Lily was sure.

As the memories of that day raced through her mind, Lily began the letter to her sister and brother. It had been a year since that day, and she decided to make it a fun letter to tell them about the fun part of her life. She didn't write in cursive, but in large block letters that she hoped her brother could read.

She talked about her rock collection, her violin, and the fun of living with the Broussards. She ended the letter with a promise to ask her grandmother to take her to visit them. She put two of her most prized rocks, an amethyst and an opal, into the envelope Mr. Broussard had given her.

Lily felt such a feeling of accomplishment. She knew her grandmother well enough to know that there would be an opportunity to ask to see her sister and brother again. She just had to wait for a non-mean day.

CHAPTER 24

Waiting It Out

Lily's grandmother had wanted to arrive at the Broussards early. Getting there before the children arrived was important. She sat in the driver's seat of Black Beauty, fanning herself with an old newspaper and wiping the sweat from her brow with a yellowed handkerchief. She started the car and pressed down on the gas pedal and revved the engine before taking off on the short drive to the Broussards.

His phone call to her this morning was alarming. Who did he think he was? She knew how to raise children; after all, she had seven. And they hadn't turned out too badly. Her two sons had joined the army and traveled all over the world. Ellen married a good, hard-working man. The other girls were not doing too well, but that was because they hadn't listened to her, right?

The good thing about old man Broussard was that he seemed very fond of Lily. The bad thing was the questions that he was asking had nothing to do with him. How she raised her granddaughter was none of his business. On the phone this morning, she felt like he was chastising her. Asking her about Lily's sister and brother. Asking didn't she think it was time for Lily to go back and visit? Asking if she thought at all about how Lily needed to be in touch with the rest of her family?

The more she thought about his questions, the madder she got. She eased Black Beauty onto the exit and pulled into a 76 Station alongside the highway. The attendant, shading his eyes against the hot morning sun, approached the car just as she rolled down the window.

She looked into her handbag and saw two crumpled dollars at the bottom of her bag.

"Give me a dollar's worth of regular." Her tone was nasty, just like she felt. The attendant grabbed the dollar from her outstretched hand, pivoted, walked over to the gas pump, snatched the nozzle, and jammed it into Black Beauty. You could almost hear the gas splattering as it entered the bottom of the empty tank.

It didn't take long for four gallons to pump into the car, and she drove the few blocks to the Broussards. A block before the house, she stopped the car alongside the park and rolled down all the windows. She actually had to get out of the car because it was too difficult to position herself comfortably to roll down the back windows. With that task completed, she went back to the driver's side and just sat there, drumming her fingers on the hot steering wheel, feeling as hot as the car felt inside.

She had to ask herself, *why am I so mad?* She knew, but she hated being forced to think about it. Do you tell old man Broussard that you and your grown children were the laughingstock of the town? That you kept moving because you didn't want to look at them? Or for them to see you? That your poor dead daughter was hated by her husband's family. That his sisters and brothers thought he had made a big mistake marrying a woman who already had a child.

For Lily to see her sister and brother and step-aunts and uncles would be almost impossible. They wanted to pretend that Lily didn't exist. She was the reminder that their brother had married Ellen. He had remarried and had a new life. Lily was the old life.

The only reason that Lily saw them last year is she had to sneak over and visit when no grownup was around. Someone had said that upon hearing of Ellen's death, Orville's sister had proclaimed, "One less mouth to feed, good riddance." She had seen Lily's pain, and she knew it was because Lily missed her other life. Her mother, stepfather, sister, and brother were the family that Lily once had. That family was no more, and the only thing that she could do was to help Lily forget. Just forget.

A fire truck, horns blowing and alarms screeching, rushed past Lily's grandmother. She looked up and realized that she had been sitting in the car for a while as the sun was now shading the park at a different angle. Kindergarten-aged children were being walked home by young mothers, and she could hear two cats fighting in a sycamore tree near the playgrounds.

Lily's grandmother started the engine and drove the remaining block to the Broussards. He was sitting in a rickety chair on the front lawn with a blade of grass between his teeth. He rose to greet her as she exited the car.

"Sho' glad you could come early. I didn't want to talk in front of the kids."

Lily's grandmother said nothing, just nodded in his direction as he pulled up another lawn chair. This one looked sturdier than the one he sat in. She wondered if he intentionally saved it for her.

For some reason, all of the fight and anger she felt earlier had left her. She just felt tired. She had never talked to anyone about the painful situation that she and her granddaughter were in.

At first, no words were spoken between them; they just sat. He, flexed his long bony fingers in and out of a praying position, and she, found an interesting inchworm making its way along the tall, slender blades of grass near her feet. They were waiting each other out, and this made Pet think of when she was courting three men at the same time, most times during the same week.

Men's Pet, Women's Fret

It was back in the days of her three, no-good, married men, Arthur, Jesse, and Louis. They were all sweet on her, and she couldn't make up her mind which one she wanted. Arthur would come on Mondays, which worked well for her because he'd always give her money, thinking that it would persuade her to favor his advances. For Pet, it meant school lunch money for Lily and beer money for herself. Jesse was a handsome man (his nights were Wednesdays), but he tended to always be broke and in need of funding. She didn't understand it, but somehow, she'd end up slipping him a few dollars to tide him over 'till next week.' Her weakness for him was that he looked at her and saw her and still wanted her. It was a powerful connection. Louis was the dumb one. She could order him around, and he'd gladly do whatever was asked. She was not enthralled with him, but it gave her great pleasure to watch him jump to her commands. She also liked to dance, and Louis was good for taking them out on Fridays to the local Rhythm and Blues Club and dancing till the crack of dawn.

Ah, but the waiting game. It began with Arthur, who always came first, and sometimes not on his "allotted" night, but a night when the wife was playing pinochle and wouldn't miss him 'till midnight. He was a short, squat, dark man who knew that handsome was not a word that women thought of when thinking about him. He dressed rather plainly since he was aware that trying to look sharp instead of attracting women to him, actually turned them off. He was aware, of course, that money talked, and bullshit walked. Women responded to his money.

Jesse, on the other hand, was handsome, and he knew it. He arrived next and was surprised to find Arthur sitting in his spot on the couch. He sat next to him, and they both engaged in small talk, checking their watches and looking at Pet for some clue as to why the other man was sitting there.

Arthur sized up Jesse, aware that this light-skinned, obviously good-looking man was here for more than a friendly chat with Pet.

The small living room was getting darker as evening settled in. Pet turned on the two lamps sitting on the wobbly end tables and closed the curtains to keep the nosey neighbors from peering inside.

As the tension between the two men in the living room rose, everyone jumped slightly when they heard a light knock on the front door, and in walked Louis. Pet visibly scowled at him as he plopped down between the two other men. He smiled sheepishly at her, looking like a child who had just gotten caught snatching a cookie from a toddler.

Pet couldn't help herself. "Louis, what the hell you doing coming over here this time of the evening? You know you don't do my lawns this time of night!"

Louis looked confused, but eventually, the synapses fired in his brain and told him that he needed to play along with Pet's antics. "Well, Pet, I could come over tomorrow and do the front and back lawns if that's what you'd like."

"Yeah, Louis, you do that. As you can see, I'm busy." With that said, Pet coughed and lowered her head to shield her face from the piercing glances from Jesse and Arthur. She could barely quell the laughter that was about to bubble to the surface.

Louis rose and headed for the front door, but he couldn't help but wink at Pet on his way out.

Now Arthur and Jesse had stopped all pretenses of cordiality and sat glaring at each other.

Jesse, feeling the more entitled of the two, gave Pet a warm smile and began talking to her as if they were alone. He talked about how well his daughter was doing in her second year of college, the last fishing trip he and Pet had gone on, and as he leaned forward, he reached out to touch her knee, but Arthur cleared his throat and smiled at Pet also. Jesse's hand stopped mid-air.

Arthur knew his version of a warm smile did not match Jesse's, and it made him angry. He didn't have the courage to say anything, so he just sat there fuming. All three of them knew that Jesse had won and all but Arthur was pissed. The waiting game was over, and Arthur, with a half sigh, half groan, rose from the couch and left, not saying goodbye to anyone.

CHAPTER 26

Time to Reunite

Mr. Broussard watched Pet as she sat on the front lawn, seemingly lost in another world. The tension had left her body, and her face was lit up as if she was about to explode with laughter. It surprised him. He could never imagine that she laughed or had fun; she always seemed so serious. It appeared to be an opportune time to mention Lily. When he cleared his throat, she looked up at him, shaded her eyes from the afternoon sun, and leaned in his direction.

"So, Pet, what do you think of sending your granddaughter back to visit her sister and brother?"

Pet's brow furrowed, and a look of sorrow and distress swept across her face.

Mr. Broussard shifted his eyes downward and began folding and unfolding his fingers again.

Pet almost arose from the lawn chair, but the soft ground beneath the grass had slowly anchored the chair deeper into the soil. Getting up would take some effort, and she did not want to appear to be struggling.

Pet couldn't understand why she felt such pain, but she did. After all, having the responsibility of a child was not what she had expected—who could have guessed that it would ever happen? The "it" was the impossible thing for Pet to think about. Did her daughter really kill herself, or was it an accident, or did someone kill her? She would never know because investigating the death of a young colored woman in rural California in the 1950s was not high on any prosecutor's priority list.

When Ellen was alive, she had always said that if anything happened to her, she would want Pet to care for Lily. Pet had agreed but never imagined that it would happen so quickly. Pet wasn't sure why Ellen had insisted that they have a discussion regarding Lily's future. Was it because she sensed her impending death and those mean-spirited Jenkins could not be trusted to care for Lily in Ellen's absence?

Feeling Mr. Broussard's eyes upon her, Pet shifted in her chair. She tried to think of a diplomatic way to discuss the Jenkins family, herself, and Lily's predicament. It was far too complicated. Orville's family, like many other families, saw no reason for a man to marry a woman who already had a child. Orville had broken a community taboo, and for that, the fractured family had to be punished. As Pet had thought and said many times, Lily just had to forget about her past family life. There was no other way.

As she sat on the lawn beside Mr. Broussard, thoughts about her own family life began to surface. When she was nine, because the family felt the strain of too many children, she had been sent to live with an older sister, leaving her two remaining younger siblings, a brother and sister, behind. She had missed them and had wished that she could go back home but dared not complain to anyone. For a brief moment, Pet felt Lily's pain. She could still feel Mr. Broussard's eyes upon her. She didn't have to look up; they were there.

She maneuvered herself up from the lawn chair, stood next to Mr. Broussard, and locked eyes with him. The kindness she saw made her heart lurch. She leaned in and whispered to him, "I think it's a good idea." She began to formulate a plan of using Lucille, Orville's mother, as a bridge to communicate Lily's wishes to see her brother and sister. Lucille was a kind woman who truly cared for Lily. After all, hadn't she given Lily Ellen's portrait?

Mr. Broussard arose, and Pet, without knowing why, reached out and hugged him. He was tall and lanky, and she was short and round, the top of her head barely reaching his scrawny chest. Neither said a word. Mr. Broussard noticed her misty eyes, and tears formed in his also. They both looked up as they heard the piercing screech of the school bus's brakes as it rounded the corner.

CHAPTER 27

Nothing Like a sweet letter to chase the blues away

Lily, Tony, and Latisha Kay emerged along with a dozen other children, a few colored but mostly white.

"Well, Pet, looks like our children have arrived," he beamed. They both walked toward the children.

Lily, sensing danger, tensed. But then she looked into her grandmother's eyes and saw no anger, no pursed lips, none of the huffing and puffing that usually indicated that Pet was raring for a fight.

Lily visibly relaxed and, yearning for a soft touch, sidled up next to her grandmother—her head was already touching Pet's shoulder. The ache started in Lily's chest again, and she remembered for a brief moment what it was like to have her mother.

Pet gazed at her granddaughter and, in a haunting flashback, saw herself. She wondered for the hundredth time why she had been chosen to stay with her older sister. She would never know because folks just didn't talk about grownup decisions, even after the children were grownup themselves.

Old man Broussard observed this interchange between the grandmother and granddaughter. It was painful to witness. So much need and so little understanding between the two generations.

Lily felt like she was in heaven. After waiting what seemed like years, she had finally heard back from her little brother. His letter arrived on an unusually cool Saturday afternoon. She had been left alone at home while her grandmother shopped for groceries.

She could already hear her grandmother complaining about the price of eggs and milk and how she couldn't believe that the local grocers charged so much for ham hocks and chicken feet. And then there was the "They used to practically give pinto beans away, and now they cost nineteen cents a bag!"

Even though her grandmother had left her with a pile of clothes to fold because she didn't believe in Lily having nothing to do, Lily sat on the couch with her feet propped up on an ottoman like she had seen the grownups do. It was such a relief to be alone, even though Lily knew that her grandmother would not be gone long.

From the open living room window, she heard the familiar squeak of the mailbox hinge as the mail carrier inserted the letter. There was something about the spring in his step as he walked to the house next door that triggered her excitement. This had to be the day! She flung the front door open, ran to the mailbox, snatched the letter, and ran back inside. It was perfect—she was alone with a letter from her little brother. She knew it wouldn't be a long letter, 'cause after all, he was so young. But he had really tried, and she could tell.

Dear Lily,

Thank you for your letter.
Me and Lorna love you.
And we like the rocks.
Grandma Jenkins help me write you.
When will we see you again?

Love,
Deenie and Lorna

Within a few minutes, Lily had memorized the letter. Her fingers touched and retouched the boldly, printed words on the page as if she were reading braille. She saw and felt the words from her brother's lips to her very being. She hugged the letter to her chest, reached under her bed, opened the worn, velvet-lined cigar case that held her rock collection, and slipped the precious letter inside. She put it under the rocks in hope that her grandmother's prying eyes would never see it.

Lily wanted to show old man Broussard the letter, so on Sunday night, she slipped the letter into the pages of her history book. But then she began to have second thoughts. Her brother and sister were so precious. Would the old man understand that he should not mention the letter to Latisha Kay and Tony? Did he know of the pain she felt when she lost her whole family? Actually, would anybody understand?

The last time she had talked with anyone about her brother and sister was when she and Jamie had talked after the rattlesnake scare. And that was such a long time ago.

But she had to talk with someone, and old man Broussard would be the one. After all, hadn't he suggested that she write the letter? And hadn't he given her the postage stamp and an envelope?

Monday morning, Lily awakened early. She had thought about old man Broussard all night. Before the kid's bedtime, she had put in her request for Corn Fritters. She could already smell the corn frying in the skillet and was glad that she had awakened early enough to be alone with old man Broussard.

"Mornin' Lily, I see you put in your request. You like them fritters just like my granddaughter, Alicia, huh?"

"Yes, sir, they are so good."

Lily couldn't hold it another minute. As she sat on the kitchen stool beside Mr. Broussard, she thrust her brother's letter into his free hand. Lily noticed that he looked at her with heightened interest.

"Now look-a-here, what do we have? Looks like a letter from your brother?"

Lily watched as he looked at the envelope with her brother's bold, childlike handwriting.

Mr. Broussard broke into a wide smile. "Well, Lily, looks like our prayers have been answered. Your little brother wrote you back, huh?"

"Yes, sir, I can't believe it!"

"I know you miss them, and they miss you too. Since our prayers have been answered, I'm gonna talk to your grandmother about you going to mass with us on Sunday. Do you…uh, go to church with your grandmother?"

Lily was taken aback. She hadn't expected that question. It made her think. Why didn't her grandmother go to church like her real family did? She hadn't been to Sunday school since her mother died. But then that brought up another problem—where was God anyway? How could God have let this happen to her and her family? What happened to "God will answer your prayers?" She had prayed for years for her mother to come back, and still no mother!

"Lily, child, are you okay?"

Her head was woozy, she slipped off the stool and stood unsteady, grabbing tightly to his apron strings. She felt like she had unexpectedly been transported from Mr. Broussard's sunny, warm kitchen to some far-away place.

Are you alright, Lily? Mr. Broussard asked.

Lily couldn't answer. She was busy trying to process what was happening to her. Did she almost faint because she had questioned God? Images of Jesus with his long brown hair, dressed in a white robe swirled around her. Jesus wasn't laughing or mocking her, just looking at her with a small, quiet smile of love and understanding. She watched in awe as the image of Jesus twirling around her continued for one full turn around the kitchen. When it was over, she let go of Mr. Broussard's apron strings and slipped back onto the stool, exhausted.

CHAPTER 28

Hail Mary, Full of Grace, the Lord is With Thee

Lily's first visit to the Catholic Church left her in awe. They arrived early, like when Sunday school used to start, except there was no "children's church." No separation of children from adults. Everybody had beads in their hands as they prayed; Latisha Kay called them rosaries. Lily didn't have any, so she kept playing with her fingers as if a rosary would suddenly appear.

All of the windows were adorned with beautifully colored, muted glass that made Lily feel loved and protected. Latisha Kay called them stained glass windows. She and Latisha Kay, and Tony sat in the pews behind the grownups, and every few minutes, Mrs. Contrale, the Broussard's only daughter, would turn around and give them a stern, shut-your-mouth look. But to the children, the look made them giggly. It was all they could do to look politely quiet and reposed for as long as she stared at them. The moment Mrs. Contrale turned around; they'd burst into quiet laughter. It was a familiar game, and Mrs. Contrale and the children played it well. Lily wasn't used to it, and she felt a bit terrified knowing that Mrs. Contrale could, at any moment, get up and haul the three of them to the back for a real spanking.

There was an enormous organ near the front of the church, and the organist's fingers appeared to glide effortlessly among the black and white keys. The melodic sounds reverberated so loudly that Lily's temples seemed to be buzzing in a syncopated rhythm that matched the organist's tempo.

Lily couldn't understand what the priest was saying; he was speaking another language! Latisha Kay called it Latin.

Three altar boys, wearing waist-length cassocks, stood ready to assist with mass. One of them, the youngest and smallest, looked like he was about to faint. Latisha Kay said he fainted most Sundays. And she said Lily should watch 'cause another older altar boy would swoop him up, lead him to an adjacent room, and replace him at the altar. As Latisha Kay was describing the series of about-to-happen events, it was happening. Lily was dumbfounded. She looked around at the parishioners, who seemed unaware of the flurry of activities happening up front, right next to the priest!

In the pews, everyone was sitting, then kneeling, then sitting, then standing, interspersed with the loud screeches of the low wooden stools being moved as they knelt to pray and stood or sat to sing. Lily figured that all of this activity had to do with keeping the parishioners awake during the long service.

At her church, when the preacher dragged the sermon on and on, the adults just slept, snoring loudly until someone tapped them on the shoulder. Children slept too, but the parents felt grateful to lay them down on the hard benches, heads on their mother's laps. At least at her church, the children were resting, without the fidgeting or whining that accompanied too much time trying to be quiet and sit still.

When the service was over, Latisha Kay asked Lily, "What did you think? Did you like it?"

Lily wasn't sure how to respond. She had heard Mr. Broussard talking to her grandmother earlier about sending her to mass and how it would be good for her. Something about "reviving" her faith.

Lily wasn't sure what to make of it all. After all, the priest spoke Latin. Was she supposed to understand it? She did recognize the prayer, "Hail Mary, full of grace… pray for us sinners now and at the hour of our death," but not much else. And then there was the rosary thing, which looked kind of neat, especially as she watched two young women in the pew beside her kiss their rosaries and lightly touch each bead as they recited their prayers. The look of peace and contentment on their faces was enviable. Lily hadn't felt that sense of contentment since she had her baby sister Lorna in her arms.

Lily and Latisha Kay were holding hands as they exited the parish, and they both stopped and faced each other on the church lawn. Lily, feeling extra dark, looked around before she spoke. Many families, white, Mexican, and Creoles, were milling about, but no one was close to her color. Mr. Broussard, the only real dark one in the Broussard family, had stayed home to prepare Sunday dinner.

Watching the families, she noticed they were not self-segregating. There were hugs along with friendly greetings, no matter which color they were. Maybe Catholics were different. Only coloreds went to her church. And if there was any segregating, it was the dark skin versus the light. This was really different.

With a vision of the two girls clasping their rosaries in her mind, she answered Latisha Kay's question about whether or not she liked the service. "I think I'll ask grandmother if I can come next Sunday." Even though she had made the commitment to come again, she still felt uneasy, and she wasn't quite sure why.

"Hey, Lily, wanna come with me to the spooky house next door?" Latisha Kay said, running towards an old house with peeling white paint and a sagging front porch.

Lily wasn't sure and looked around to see where Mrs. Contrale and Mrs. Broussard had gone. The boys were nowhere to be found.

"Uh, I don't know. Why do you want to go there?" Lily's skin felt prickly, and the starch from her Sunday dress was beginning to irritate the area around her shoulders and neck.

"Don't worry about the grownups. They're having tea in the parish and won't be ready to go for a while. Come on, it'll be fun!"

Lily reluctantly followed Latisha Kay to the bottom of the stairs, but when her companion took the first step onto the porch, Lily noticed a large spider carefully spinning its web around a helpless fly that had landed there. She knew it was a black widow because of its red butt. She usually hated flies, but this one was struggling furiously to free itself. The more it struggled, the tighter the web became. Lily was perplexed. How could you hate something and feel sorry for it at the same time? In the next minute, the fly stopped moving, and the spider began to eat it, head first.

Latisha Kay, mesmerized by Lily's stoic attention to the spider and fly, had watched also. Both girls had lost interest in the spooky house and returned to the parish to join the adults.

CHAPTER 29

I Can't Help it if You Got Bad Hair!

On the ride home that morning, both girls were silent. Lily watched as Latisha Kay played with her long, shiny Shirley temple curls. All of the Broussard children had "good" hair.

Lily did not. Her hair had been pressed by her grandmother that morning but was not long enough and too full of grease to bounce as she turned her head from side to side. If she really jerked her head, her hair could manage a small sway, but no real bounce.

If anyone, especially Latisha Kay, who didn't have bad hair, saw Lily's in its washed, nappy state, Lily would be horrified. It took hours and lots of pain with plenty of moans and groans, gritting of her teeth, scrunching up her face, biting her lips—all to go through the ritual of getting her hair washed, straightened, and curled every two weeks.

This morning, Lily suffered the usual two extra tough tasks, getting her hair combed after washing it and having to bear the heat of the hot comb as her grandmother tried her best to get her hair as straight as possible. After washing, her hair shrank into a tight ball of extra curly, unruly, hard-to-comb hair. Every strand of black, coarse hair was tightly wound and completely covered Lily's scalp. Even though her grandmother used the widest-toothed comb and slapped plenty of Bergamot grease on her hair to soften it, it still hurt as her grandmother combed.

"You just tender-headed, Lily. You a big girl now, and you don't need to be crying and carrying on every time somebody try to comb your hair. Straighten up your face! I can't help it if you got bad hair—and it's so thick, too."

Lily sat on the floor between her grandmother's legs, and her grandmother sat on a low, soft-cushioned chair. Lily glanced sideways as her grandmother's hands brushed past her shoulder and blindly reached for the attack tools on the end-table adjacent to where they were seated. In addition to the wide-toothed comb, there was a long, skinny-handled comb that she used to part Lily's hair into sections. To Lily, it felt like a sharp knife was cutting into her scalp. She interspersed loud sighs and grunts and soft whimpers to let her grandmother know that everything she did hurt. Once parted, the wide-toothed comb was put to work by her grandmother, trying to comb out the super kinky hair. Eventually, by repeatedly running the comb through Lily's hair, she was satisfied that most of the kink was gone. She twisted each section, tied it into a knot, and moved on to repeat the process until Lily's whole head was done. At that point, Lily's scalp would be throbbing in so many places she didn't know where it hurt the most.

Next came the painful and satisfying part—getting her hair straightened. Her grandmother used a wooden-handled straightening comb, which sat atop the small hot plate at the end table with the rest of her tools. The painful part came about because most of the time, her grandmother put too much grease on Lily's hair while combing it, which led to the acrid smell of burning hair as the hot comb met Lily's greasy hair and scalp. The heat generated by this encounter seemed unbearable. Her grandmother's answer, of course, was to continually blow air onto Lily's scalp as she maneuvered the comb through her hair.

But then, the satisfying part came. Her tightly wound, kinky hair became straight, somewhat silky, and even long. She went from looking like a recently shorn French poodle to a charming, young, colored girl like the ones Lily saw in the Ebony Magazine ads. Her hair was shining from all the grease, and Lily could actually feel her scalp. She sat pensively, wondering if this would be the day that grandmother would let her wear her hair down. If she started parting her hair, Lily knew the answer. It meant it would be braided in some mammy-made style that she hated.

Today was her lucky day. Grandmother, when done with the straightening, actually put a few Shirley Temple curls in her hair, curled some cute bangs, and let her wear it down. It had way too much grease for it to bounce, but swaying did happen! Her scalp was, of course, throbbing and burning, but by the end of mass, her head felt normal.

Boy, Lily thought, Latisha Kay really is lucky. All her mother has to do is roll her hair with pink rollers before bedtime, and in the morning, wrap her hair around her fingers to create gorgeous Shirley temple curls!

When the girls arrived home, they both ran into the girl's bedroom.

"Wanna play with our dolls grandpa gave us?" Latisha Kay asked.

"Sure."

They both grabbed the dolls from their toy box and plopped onto their unmade bed, each engrossed in arranging their doll's clothes, shoes, and hair accessories.

"Lily, how long you gonna stay with us?"

Lily gave Latisha Kay a sidelong glance. She never knew how long she would be anywhere. She was about to panic but realized that Latisha Kay was just asking. "I don't know, but I really like the school and staying with you guys, and we had so much fun at the drive-in." Both girls had their dolls placed in between their legs as they smoothed their doll's hair with miniature brushes.

It was warm outside. The yellow hems of the curtains billowed in the window opening, created by the crosswind that kept the bedroom cool.

"I betcha can't guess who was sweet on me at school today?"

Lily had an idea, but she looked questioningly in Latisha Kay's direction. "Who"

"Rupert, Rupert Jones."

"You mean that skinny kid who still sucks his thumb during recess?" Lily asked incredulously.

"Yep."

CHAPTER 30

He Didn't Know He Was Colored

Rupert Jones was incredibly shy. The school bullies teased him incessantly because his mother still kissed him on the top of his head when she dropped him off at school. And he didn't walk to school or catch the school bus! Only the uppity white kids were dropped off by their parents. There weren't that many of them. The girls wore Mary Janes, and the boys wore dress shoes that other kids only wore to church on Sundays. Their parents owned the town's two banks, one Chevy dealership, the hardware, and grocery stores but lived too far away to place their children in more affluent schools. They wanted their children to appear to be more prosperous, and they were.

Rupert's parents also sent their only child to school sharply dressed, and he did get driven to and from school. The difference, of course, was that Rupert was colored. Except he didn't know it, and the other colored kids knew that he didn't know it.

The moment he first saw Latisha Kay, he latched onto her. She was so pretty. Everyone knew she was colored, but she didn't look it. She had long, beautiful, auburn hair, and rosy cheeks. Her skin looked almost as white as the white kids. Rupert was in love. Of course, he saw his brown face when he looked at himself in the mirror. And he saw his skinny brown arms and legs, but that didn't resonate with him. He was a white boy trapped in a colored boy's body. He had always felt like that. He didn't think about why he felt like that; he just knew that he did.

His parents were colored, but they didn't know it either. The few friends they had were white. His father was the only high-ranking officer assigned to the nearby Airbase. The brass had been getting flack about there being no commissioned officers of color assigned to the base, and Rupert's father was the right man at the right time.

He enjoyed being the "token Negro" invited to the gatherings held on and off base. Little Rupert accompanied them to all the events. Being an only child, his mother forced him to tag along. She knew he was too old to need a babysitter but too young to be in the company of grown-ups, so she'd encourage him to play with the other children.

At one such event, Rupert had been sent outside where the girls were sitting at a card table, cutting out paper dolls, and the boys were playing catch. When he emerged in the backyard, the girls saw him first and immediately bent their heads down, seemingly engrossed in penning colorful paper dresses to their cardboard dolls.

Rupert looked in the direction of the boys, and Jerrod, knowing that Rupert was not prepared, threw a ball in his direction. It hit him in the shoulder, and he grimaced and covered his injured shoulder with his hand. The boys all laughed.

One of the boys, Percy, felt sorry for him and said, "Come on guys, give him a chance." To Rupert, he said, "You want to use my glove? I brought an extra one." Percy handed the glove to Rupert, who was grateful but still recovering from his embarrassment.

"Thanks," was all Rupert could say. He shoved his hand into the glove and joined the circle of other boys in the yard.

For the hundredth time, he wondered how many times he would be forced to endure the interactions of being a white boy trapped in a colored boy's body. He wished they could see what he saw.

Being in school was torture for Rupert. He didn't "see" the colored kids, and they didn't see him either. The white kids were a different matter. At the pretend-that-a-colored-family-is-not–really-colored social events, the kids were forced to play with him. But at school, the uppity kids had their own cliques, of which Rupert was not a member. Latisha

Kay was the only person, colored or white, who talked to him, except, of course, his teachers.

Lily didn't know what to make of Rupert. She thought he was kind of cute, but there were only two-colored boys in the school close to her age—Tony and Rupert. Rupert didn't see her. When they passed in the hallways, he'd look straight ahead and seem to do so on purpose. But the way he looked at Latisha Kay—it was obvious that he saw her! Lily wanted a boy her age to look at her the way that Rupert looked at Latisha Kay. No matter how straight her hair or how broadly she smiled in Rupert's direction, it just didn't happen.

The afternoon had cooled off, and Lily got up, coached the curtains back inside the room, and slammed the window shut. She returned to their bed with her doll and eyed Latisha Kay. She didn't know what to say. She just wished she had a boy sweet on her that she could reject.

"I don't like Rupert; he's too square!" Latisha Kay said while her and Lily were still playing with their dolls.

"What do you mean, he's too square? He seems real shy, but what's wrong with that?" Lily inquired.

"Anybody who sucks their thumb when they think nobody's looking is not a boyfriend for me!" Latisha Kay threw her doll in the toy box and plopped back onto the bed, and began playing with her curls again. "I just think he's a queer or something."

Lily asked, "What's a queer?"

"You know, boys who like boys!"

"What?" Lily could not believe her ears. "There's no such thing! I've never heard of that. Besides, look how he looks at you, and he doesn't look at anyone else like that!"

"Yeah, you're probably right, but he is creepy."

The next morning brought a definite shift in the weather. As Lily headed for the front door, she peeped through the kitchen window and noticed that the usual bright blue sky was now beginning to show signs of rain. The clouds, though high in the sky, were dark and gloomy looking. The walk to the bus stop seemed longer than usual to the kids.

Lily, who didn't have a winter coat, clung tightly to her thin, woolen sweater and thought about how she hated it. The sweater was cheap and scratchy, and she knew by the time she got home, she'd have tiny red whelps all over her arms from wearing it.

When their bus arrived at the stop, she made a beeline for the fourth row back on the driver's side of the bus. It was her favorite place to sit. She didn't like sitting in the back because that's where the bad kids sat. She didn't want to be too near the front because it always looked as though the bus driver was going to collide with the cars in front of her. And she could also see the driver yelling at the kids in the first few rows. The fourth row was perfect, not too close, not too far away.

CHAPTER 31

Reflection Day

Today was Friday. It was one of those days when she wanted to sit alone…nobody bothering her…just quiet. It was her reflection day, and at least once a month, she set aside the whole day to remember her mother. No one else did.

Tonight, she'd start by taking her mother's picture off the wall and placing it under her pillow. That was to ensure that she had a "juicy" dream that, of course, starred her beautiful mother. Her mother would be smiling and happy and full of life. They'd both give each other lots of kisses and hugs in the dream because that's what Lily missed the most. And her whole family would be in the dream–Deenie, her little two-year-old brother, and baby sister Lorna. In the dream, no one got older. Lily thought about that a lot. Maybe no one got older because she couldn't imagine her mother being older.

The next day, on the bus ride home, sitting alone, Lily thought about the last time her mother's friend had visited. Her memory was sharp, and she could recall in vivid detail that last visit.

"Ellen, I canned some peaches and thought you and the kids would like some," said her mother's friend who lived about a mile away. She drove her light blue Chevy station wagon with wood trim over to their house frequently. She was white and a little older than Lily's mother, usually dressed in a light cotton drab-looking smock with a brightly colored apron tied around her waist. She had large bags under her eyes which made her look tired.

At first, Lily didn't understand the frequent visits, but by standing by the door to the living room, she could listen to their conversations.

"Thanks for the peaches. I think I'll make me and the kids a peach cobbler. You know, Orville's gone again, and he won't be back until next week."

"Yes, Ellen. Both our men are some truck-driving fools, ain't they?"

"I just wish he wasn't gone for so long." Ellen rose from the couch and ran to get baby Lorna whose screams jarred both women back to the reality that Ellen had three young children to care for.

As she returned with baby Lorna, Ellen and her friend resumed their conversation on the couch. Baby Lorna, content with her toys spread on the floor in front of them, was quiet again.

"Ellen, I don't understand why you and the kids are stuck out here in the boonies."

"Me neither, but I think it's 'cause he wants to keep me out here away from everybody. He's so damn jealous. I've read every book I can get a hold of; I watch these damn soap operas on TV, and if it wasn't for you coming over, I'd be all the way crazy."

"Look, honey, my husband drives a truck too, but I got a car, and I can go into town whenever I feel like it. Heck, sometimes we go out on the runs together. Our kids are grown, and we are free to hit the road anytime we feel like it. Our oldest boy just graduated from high school; shoot, this is a great time for us. You and the kids should be in town with the rest of your family. This is no life for a young girl like you to be out here with three young children. Why don't you just tell him that you and the kids want to move into town? Hey, let's go into the kitchen, and I'll help you with the pie crust."

The sudden beep of the school bus's horn awakened Lily from her daydream. She looked up, realizing that half of the kids had already been dropped off at their stops. She gathered her books, looked outside to get her bearings, and prepared to get off at the next stop. She smiled secretly to herself, knowing that tonight and all day tomorrow would be devoted to her mother.

CHAPTER 32

Death Hurts the Living

It was time for Pet to contact Lucille, her son-in-law's mother. She had been thinking about him and Lily for the past several weeks and was simultaneously looking forward to it and dreading it.

Looking forward because she knew how painful it was for Lily to not see her sister, brother, and stepfather. Old man Broussard had awakened that part of her own childhood that still remembered what it was like to lose your family. The poor child always looked so frightened, pretty much how she felt after being sent to live with her older sister, Margaret.

For Pet, there was the adjustment of living with cousins who were a lot younger and a lot needier. Of learning new family dynamics that included her sister, who was like a doormat to her domineering, full of fire, and brimstone preacher-husband Paul. Pet hated living there, especially because it was so different from her life with her mother and father. Her parents were dirt poor, but there were no small, snotty-nosed children to care for.

At her sister's house, there were six kids, ranging in age from ten to just over a year. And the house was filthy, not what she was used to. Dirty diapers from the two toddlers kept the small, cramped house smelling like a pigsty. Upon arrival, Pet had expected to be enrolled in school but was promptly told that there was too much work to be done around the house for her to go to school. It was not a nice place to be, and it never got better. Lily had it so much better than she did at that age, but Pet was certain that the home-sickness in Lily was real. Even though she had wanted to avoid it, talking to old man Broussard had helped her want to help Lily.

Pet was dreading the meeting with Lucille. There were a lot of reasons, but the main one was Lucille wanted to talk about Ellen, and that was too painful. Her last conversation with Lucille had been at the repast following Ellen's funeral. The repast was held at a Baptist church, which was full of what looked like every colored person in town. A sea of black suits and dresses and shoes milled about, and muted conversations could be heard, interspersed with small, quiet laughter. It seemed like everyone knew a funny story to tell about Ellen.

"That girl was scared of her own shadow. Why I remember one time I went to her house, and she had a towel thrown over her arm and was leaning back as far away from the stove as possible while she was turning over the chicken she was frying. I guess she thought if she got far enough away from the skillet and with the towel over her arm, she wouldn't get burnt!"

It was Lucille, laughing and crying at the same time. Several others joined in the quiet laughter.

"Yeah, well, the good thing is she could laugh at herself. She told me if she could wrap herself in a sheet while she was frying chicken, she would do that too."

Pet missed her daughter. Most times, it was too painful to think about, so she'd just play a game she called forget. Forget Ellen was born, forget how she played second mother to her younger sisters and brothers, forget how she'd always ask if there was anything Pet wanted her to help with, forget the love that always shone in her eyes, and forget the day the policeman knocked on her door to tell her that her daughter was dead.

Pet picked up the phone to call Lucille. Lily had fallen asleep early, and Pet sat sprawled on the couch, tightly clasping the black telephone to her ear. As the phone rang over and over, she began to hope that Lucille was not home. Just before she hung up, Pet mumbled to herself, "I guess she ain't home." Lucille answered.

"Hi, Pet. I recognized your voice. How you doing?"

Pet hesitated a moment, almost deciding to quietly put the phone in its cradle. But she didn't.

"Oh, I'm fine. I thought I'd call and see how everyone is fairing these days."

"Oh, we good, but we sho' miss your daughter, Ellen. I bet you do too."

Well, here it is, Pet thought. I knew this was coming. Tears rolled down her face, but she didn't wipe them away because no one could see them anyway. She reached for a roll of nearby toilet paper and wiped her nose.

"Well, speaking of Ellen, you know I got Lily here with me, and she wants to see Deenie and Lorna. I'm thinking about driving up that way next week. Are you and old man Henry gonna be around?"

"Well, we was gonna see my daughter, Nedra, next week but what you think about meeting us up in Sacramento? We could ask the rest of the kids to come up too, and she could see all of her other cousins, too."

"Okay, I'll let you know when we get ready to leave. Lily will be so happy."

After they hung up, Pet began to have second thoughts. Meeting up with the rest of the Jenkins would be hard. They didn't like Ellen, after all, didn't one of them have the nerve to say that with Ellen gone, there'd be one less mouth to feed?

She was going to have to rethink this visit.

CHAPTER 33

You Too Young to Understand

Traveling to Sacramento was going to be hard for Pet. For one thing, it was only twenty-two miles from the small town of Clarksburg. The town that took her daughter's life. That isolated hick town that drove her daughter to kill herself. What the hell was Orville thinking, forcing her daughter to live so far away from her family?

But Pet was drawn to Clarksburg. She couldn't go to Sacramento without stopping by that town, hick and all. Maybe she'd stop by to see the house. Maybe she'd stop and talk to the white lady who had made friends with her daughter. On the phone with Pet, Ellen had spoken of her often, saying if it wasn't for that cracker-woman, she'd, sure enough, be stir-crazy sitting all day in that lonely house with no one but the children to talk to.

As the week loomed ahead, Pet was anxious with worry on some days and relaxed and peaceful on others. On her anxious days, she dreaded the pain of seeing the house where her precious daughter had taken her last breath. On her relaxed, peaceful days, she could imagine that being near the place where her daughter had once been would give her a sense of closure. Up 'til now, the only closure Pet experienced was the fake, I'm-pretending-that-Ellen-didn't-exist closure. She had always known that one day she'd have to confront her Ellen-pain. That was one of the hard parts of keeping Lily. Lily was a constant reminder of the loss of her daughter Ellen.

It was time for Pet to decide whether or not she and Lily would visit Nedra. She had already made up her mind when she picked up the phone, but she hesitatingly reached for it and picked it up as it sat in its corner in the living room.

Nedra answered quickly, and Pet responded to her "Hello" almost immediately. "I called to let you know that we gonna be traveling to Sacramento, and I thought I'd swing by Clarksburg, too, before I head over to your place."

Nedra responded by shifting her bulky frame in a narrow armchair placed at the far end of a small, crowded living room. It was dark inside, helping to create a place of needed solitude for her. She leaned over the armchair to reach the end table where the black telephone sat. It had a knotted and twisted telephone cord that Nedra absentmindedly attempted to unravel as she spoke with Pet. The white numbers inside the black rotary dial seemed to blur as tears welled into her eyes.

"I don't think you want to go to Clarksburg, Pet. My brother Orville was so upset over Ellen's death that he done tore the house up. He's torn up all of her pictures and letters, and he won't let nobody go in there. I'm sure you don't want to go in there. And then, when the sheriff and his people were there, they tore it up too. I told my husband, Ray, we just need to burn that house down. It's been vacant since she died, and we can't rent it to nobody. Hell, her blood is still on the floor where the gun went off!"

A scratchy noise and a loud screech sounded on the phone line, and both women fell silent. Nedra and Pet were used to nosey people clicking in and out of their conversations, so both sat quietly, awaiting the tell-tale click that let them know someone had finally hung up the party line.

Nedra was grateful for the interruption because she could cry and mourn her sister-in-law's passing. She could not see any of the numbers on the telephone. It had gone from blurred numbers to no numbers. The telephone itself was one black blob. The thought that anyone had experienced such a violent death in the home she had raised her children in made her shudder with fear.

There had been talk of some farm worker lurking around the area before Ellen's death. There was talk of Ellen being depressed and begging Orville to move them into town. Of Orville being too stubborn and insisting that they stay out there and save money. And all Nedra felt was guilt. She knew that Ellen would have a hard time surviving in such remote surroundings with three young children. Nedra had also felt isolated when she first moved into the house in Clarksburg, but her children were old enough to keep her company, and her husband was home every night.

They had moved into town so that their oldest child could attend high school in Sacramento, and her brother Orville had jumped at the chance to rent the house for cheap. If only she had put her foot down. She couldn't understand why these domineering men didn't listen to their women folk. They thought they had all the answers. And now Ellen was gone.

Nedra had completely unraveled the phone, and she marveled at the extra length she had gained by untangling it. Both she and Pet noticed the loud click as the snooping party line neighbors slammed down the phone.

"Well, Nedra, you certainly convinced me that I don't need to go into Clarksburg to see the house. Maybe I'll just stop by the white woman's house who lived down the road from Ellen. Maybe she can tell me what my poor daughter was going through."

Both women hung up their phones. Nedra dragged the phone and the newly-lengthened cord into the far side of the living room and sat it next to the local phone book on another end table. She stared at it. The images of her damaged house where Ellen and her children had been was forever etched in her mind. Why didn't she see this coming? Why did no one see this coming?

Her youngest daughter, Tammy, approached. "Mamma, what's wrong?"

"Nothing, baby. I'm feeling sad, that's all." Nedra sat down on the couch and moved the newspaper aside to make room for Tammy to sit. "Come here, sit here with momma, baby."

Nedra always carried a handkerchief inside her dress pocket, and she used it now to quickly dab the tears from her eyes. She prayed that her daughter had not seen the gesture.

Tammy plopped down next to her mother. She was the same age as Lily but chubby with big, sparkling brown eyes. Today she was dressed in a red polka-dot dress with hair ribbons that matched her dress. She was Nedra's girly-girl and could always be found snuggling up next to her mother.

Nedra thought she had the best temperament of all of her children. Tammy inched closer to her mother on the couch. "Momma, why do you think Lily's mom killed herself?" Nedra tried to keep her face expressionless but could tell from the pained look on Tammy's young face that she had not succeeded.

"Baby, you too young to understand. I'll have to explain that to you when you're a lot older." Nedra thought about her husband, Ray. When the children asked him about Ellen, he refused to discuss her. He told the children that what happened to Ellen was grown-folks-business, and that was that.

"But momma, you remember how after it happened, you and daddy picked up the kids, and Lily just kept screaming? I felt so sorry for them."

"Yes, baby, that was hard. But her grandmother tells me that Lily is doing a lot better now. She's bringing Lily next week so that she can see Deenie and Lorna. Maybe that damn brother of mine will get off the road long enough to see all of his kids."

Nedra covered her mouth with her hands, realizing that she was saying too much to her ten-year-old daughter. She quickly got up from the couch and hurried to the kitchen.

"Tammy, you go on to your room, change into your play clothes and go outside with the rest of the kids. I gotta go start dinner."

CHAPTER 34

He Must be Hiding Something

The day to see her sister and brother had finally arrived. Usually, Lily was reluctant to leave the Broussards, but as soon as she got off the school bus on Friday, she ran into the girl's bedroom, quickly changed into her play clothes, and sat alone at the kitchen table, anxiously awaiting her grandmother's arrival. She absent-mindedly flipped the pages of her Nancy Drew book that she had tried to read but couldn't. She always kept her brother, Deenie's letter inside her history book, and she took it out now and reread it, even though she knew the contents by heart.

She sat near the kitchen window and could hear the Broussard children playing outside, and she knew that any minute now, an adult would come in to remind her that children were not allowed to play inside the house during the day. Unless, of course, old man Broussard saw her inside. He seemed to instinctively know that Lily needed her own quiet time. He never told her she had to go outside to play.

Not many cars wandered down the Broussard family's street, but with the ear of a keen Chihuahua, Lily listened for the sound of grandmother's Black Beauty. It had a low, gravelly hum that distinguished it from any other car that passed the house. Lily watched the kitchen clock slowly march its way from four to five o'clock. What was taking her grandmother so long?

She alternated between rereading her brother's letter and attempting to read Nancy Drew. She couldn't concentrate. Just as she was about to give up, the purr sounded. Before her grandmother could engage the parking brake, Lily was in the car, panting slightly from the quick run to gather her things from the girl's bedroom and jumped into the car.

"Slow down, girl. Where you think you're going so fast?"

Lily could tell from her grandmother's crooked smile that she didn't have to worry. Grandmother was happy too. Lily felt that there was something that passed between her and her grandmother that could not be described. For Lily, it felt like it might be love. Or a shared conspiracy to be happy for once.

Lily eased back in the front seat and waited for her grandmother to return from exchanging pleasantries with the Broussards before taking off.

Lily checked for the third time to make sure her rock collection was underneath the car seat. The worn cigar box with its velvet lining would be another great thing to show off to Deenie and Lorna. She might even let them touch the rocks. At first, she thought that she couldn't dare part with any more of her rocks but had brought along two new stones that she found last week on the way home from the bus stop. Not very fancy, but they wouldn't know the difference. It was settled; she'd give them at least two more rocks.

"You got your rock collection underneath the seat?"

"Yep, I remembered," Lily responded. I even got two more rocks I found last week to give them. But they're not getting the really pretty ones like I gave them last time. Have you seen my beautiful copper ore?" Before her grandmother could respond, Lily continued, "Well, they're not getting that one. I'll never give it away."

Lily and her grandmother were sitting comfortably in Black Beauty. Lily's long slender feet were propped up on the dashboard, and her grandmother sat hunched over the velvet-covered steering wheel, constantly checking her rearview mirror. Of course, Lily knew the reason for the constant surveillance—her grandmother did not carry a driver's license. Ever.

"Watch out," Lily screamed. Her grandmother was so engrossed in looking for Mr. Charlie in her rearview mirror that she almost ran into a couple of Mexican fieldhands who had just pulled out onto the main highway without looking to see if a car was coming.

"Just like them damn Mescuns, driving like they the only ones on the road," muttered her grandmother.

Lily knew immediately that she had to bring her grandmother back to a happy time. Letting the mean one take over now would make for a long, dreary journey to Sacramento.

"Remember that time when Louis came to visit, and Arthur and Jesse were already at the house?" Lily laughed nervously, hoping that this tale that her grandmother loved to repeat to any and everyone she visited would lighten her mood.

"Yes, I sure do."

Lily watched as her grandmother immediately belted out a raucous laugh.

"That damn Lewis didn't know what to say at first, but he finally got the message and got the hell outta my house."

"Pet, I can come back tomorrow to finish your lawn." Her grandmother mimicked Lewis's dumb, goofy response when he finally figured out that it was not his night to be there. "But you know," her grandmother continued, "Lewis was always nice to me, and them other two married fools were never there when I needed them. They were too busy with their wives and children. Yep, Lewis was a good man and fun to go out dancing with, too."

Lily visibly relaxed as she slid her feet from the dashboard to the floor. She positioned her head on the window and allowed the engine's low hum to lull her to sleep.

Pet watched her granddaughter as she drifted off to sleep. She was glad that Lily had fallen asleep because she wanted to think about their upcoming visit with the Jenkins family. Her son-in-law, Orville, would probably not be around when they arrived, heck she would not be surprised if he was hundreds of miles away with no way for family members to reach him. After all, that was the life of a trucker. If he had enough quarters to call home from a pay phone, he would not be using those quarters to call his children.

Pet could see the pain and yearning in Lily's eyes every time she watched a trucker pass them by. But how do you explain to a child that some dads can only be dads when there is a woman in their life? Once her daughter Ellen was gone, Orville ceased to be a father. He just didn't know how, and as far as Pet could tell, he had no intention of ever raising his children again. In the past year, those poor children had lived with Orville's sister, his brother, and their other grandmother, Lucille.

There was even talk that some spinster from church had wanted to adopt all three of the children. But Orville's mother stepped up to insist that Orville and his new wife, Annie, raise the children. But everyone knew that neither Orville nor Annie wanted to be bothered with children. Pet had even heard that his new wife had yelled at baby Lorna. The poor child thought her daddy's new wife was her momma but quickly learned to call her Annie.

There was so much talk going on in the small town of Merced that Pet felt that she was forced to leave her hometown. The entire colored community watched and gossiped about the drama of her daughter Ellen's apparent suicide. There were those who felt she had definitely killed herself; after all, wasn't she the timid one who was afraid of her own shadow? Living in that house by herself with her three young children probably drove the poor child crazy. There was, of course, the rumor surrounding the isolated town of Clarksburg and some crazed Mexican farm worker lurking about who was known to carry a pistol. Didn't someone say that he had just been released from that crazy house up in Napa? And there was even town folk who thought that maybe Orville killed her because of his known jealousy streak. After all, hadn't they fought about a letter she received from an old boyfriend? And after all, wasn't he the one who had forced the poor girl to live out in the middle of no-goddamn-where in the first place?

For those who thought Orville "did it," wasn't there proof in his absence, in his inability to look folk in the eyes? His mother having to force him to go get his own kids?

Pet didn't know and would probably never know what happened to her daughter. And the white folks didn't care. The death certificate she read said, "gunshot wound to the abdomen with severe blood loss." She bled to death. Pet had contacted the coroner, but he said he didn't find it necessary to do an autopsy. She remembered his every word as if it was yesterday, "Your daughter's gone, and no post-mortem examination I can do will bring her back. I'm sorry." And with that, a click and a dial tone. And a second click as the snooping party-line eavesdropper had also hung up.

Even the sheriff she had contacted offered no assistance. He had informed Pet that they were not investigating her daughter's death—she was dead, and they had no suspects, so she must have done it to herself. He'd let her know if anything else came up. And that was over a year ago. But the Merced gossip continued. One day, she would corner Orville and make him tell her everything. He must be hiding something.

CHAPTER 35

A Friend in Need

Lily's stepfather was feeling the pressure. His sister, Nedra, had called on one of his few off days to let him know that a family reunion of sorts was taking place soon. Lily and his kids would be there. What to do?

He was at the Dew Drop In's parking lot, trying to decide whether or not to go in. He parked the truck away from the entrance so that the owner wouldn't come out and ask him to move it. The small diners wanted truckers' business, but they didn't want their trucks parked too close.

As he sat there, the painful moments surrounding Ellen came flooding back. He and Ellen arguing about her feeling lonely… of desperately wanting to move them closer to town. She spoke to him of their young son, Deenie, almost picking up a snake in the yard just the other day… of her fear of being alone out in the boonies. Ellen couldn't stop crying. The more he put his foot down, the more she cried. Their argument finally ended when he brushed past her, slammed the front door, and gunned his old Buick out of the gravel driveway.

He could still see her puffy face and the tears streaming down her cheeks. Why did they have to have that argument anyway? He couldn't get her to understand that if they just stayed out there for a year or so, they could save enough money to buy a house. And all that new furniture she wanted too. But all she did was cry, and now she was gone. Period.

He couldn't go. No, he wouldn't go. Lily would be there, looking just like Ellen. The last time he saw her, she looked like she was still in shock.

And his two kids, they acted like they didn't know him. Well, then, when was the last time he'd seen them anyway? He couldn't remember. No wonder they didn't know him. But Lily would watch him and act like she couldn't take her eyes off of him. He could see the haunting look of love and pain in her eyes as she gazed in his direction, and it broke his heart.

He shifted in the truck's cab and stared out the window. It was beginning to rain outside. A loud tap on the window broke his reverie.

"Hey, man, you gonna come inside?" It was his friend, Lonnie.

They had met in Korea during the war when they found out they were both from the San Joaquin valley, Lonnie from Turlock, and Orville from Merced.

"Well, ain't you a sight for sore eyes, man; where you been?" Orville rolled the window up and stepped out of the truck's cab. Lonnie was tall and slender, with big, widely-spaced teeth that seemed too big for his mouth. His hair was close-cropped, and like Orville, he still wore his starched army khakis.

They both walked into the diner, immediately lowered their voices, and shuffled into a nearby booth. The hush that always follows two colored men entering a small-town diner was brief.

"Man, I haven't seen you since your wife, uh, died, but I want to offer my condolences to you and the family."

"Ah shucks, man, thanks." Orville took off his baseball cap and sat it on the empty seat next to him. He took out his handkerchief and mopped the sweat that was forming on his brow. "Man, to tell you the truth, I been having a hard time. " Orville thought about the long talks that he and Lonnie had when they were stuck doing KP duties together. They both loved to kill time talking about their family back home.

Lonnie was his best friend in the army, and once they were sitting in the booth at the diner, it was like they had never been apart. Orville didn't realize how much he needed to talk to someone until he and Lonnie sat down together. Orville tried to will the tears away, but they just wouldn't stop. He saw Lonnie glance away but was sure that he saw his tears. He had to brush them away as he saw the waitress approach. She took their order and hastily disappeared.

"Look, man, you been through a lot, and you know people are talking. I know you loved that girl, and she loved you too. Don't worry about them old busy-bodies. They always got something to say, even if they don't know what happened. "

Orville knew what Lonnie was talking about but decided he did not want to talk about it. Everybody wanted to know if he did it, or did she do it to herself.

"Yeah, well, my sister wants me to go to Sacramento and visit her and my kids. Pet's even bringing Lily up, too, but that's what I don't want to do. It's just too hard right now." Orville leaned back and moved his hands away to make room for the steaming hot plates being delivered by the waitress.

"Look, Orville, I got a girl I'm sweet on in Sacramento, why don't I go there with you? I could drop you off on my way to my girl's house, and you and I can talk on the way there. What do you say?"

"Man, you ain't hearing me. I can't see them kids, especially Lily!" Orville's voice had risen a few notches, and several customers looked up in their direction.

"Oh, I see, man. I'm sorry, Lonnie whispered. "Yeah, it's a hell of a thing, losing that poor child's momma like that. Lily's what, eight or nine, right?"

"Well, I think she's 'bout to turn ten. Man, to tell you the truth, I never saw it coming. Orville shifted his body in the narrow booth and stretched his long legs beyond the table to ease the cramp beginning to form in his thigh. He ducked his head down between bites and lowered his voice. "One day, we arguing just like any other married folk, and the next thing I know, they sending you to find me on my route to tell me she's gone!" Now, Orville's tears were flowing freely. He didn't care if Lonnie or any of the other diners saw him. He felt lucky to have run into Lonnie, and, knowing their crazy work schedules, he didn't know when they'd meet up again.

"Look, Orville, I tell you what—Uh, where you staying now?"

Lonnie, too, had hunched over the booth trying his best to keep their conversation as private as possible. "I'm stayin' in the rooming house over on Thirteenth Street." The tears had stopped, and Orville pulled a napkin from the dispenser sitting next to the ketchup and other condiments. More napkins came out than he needed, so he busied himself with trying to put the extra ones back in, all the while avoiding eye contact with Lonnie.

Lonnie sat up straight in his seat and spoke quietly and firmly in Orville's direction. "This is not the time for you to be by yourself. Shit, man, I'm a trucker, too, and I know. We always on the road alone, goddamn, man, you don't need to live alone, too! Lonnie looked around the diner to make sure no one was listening to their conversation. Satisfied that they weren't, he continued, "Two things you need, man— some poon-tang and a place to stay. My momma loves having me around, and since junior left, shit, you can have his room. Momma loves her some company, and between the two of us, we just what she needs. Junior done joined the Army, and I'm on the road a lot, just like you. At least when you come home, you can have home-cooked meals and someone to talk to. 'Course momma will talk you to death—I mean, she just can't stop talking. And you know she can cook, right?"

Lonnie slouched back in his seat and glanced in Orville's direction. Orville had finished replacing the napkins and began fidgeting with his hands, not sure what he should do next.

Orville jumped up quickly and strutted to the jukebox with a handful of quarters. He selected several songs, but after spying the diners' disapproving glances, shuffled back to the booth. He had momentarily forgotten that he was a colored man in a white man's diner.

In spite of the glances, his spirits had lifted.

"Lonnie, man, I sho do 'preciate your offer. I think I was gettin' a little stir crazy in that rooming house. I'm gonna take you up on that offer. You don't think your momma would mind?"

"What, to have someone else to cook for and another set of ears to listen to her talk? She'd be happy, man. I'm gonna talk to her about it tonight."

"Well, then it's settled," Orville said.

Both men rose and headed for the line of diners waiting to pay for their meals.

Once back in the diner's parking lot, Orville hesitated in front of his truck's cab. He wasn't ready for their chance meeting to end.

"Why don't you tell me about your girl. Is she the same one we talked about when we was overseas?" Orville let a toothpick dangle from his lips as he spoke.

"Nah, man, I had to let her go. I was hearing tales from lotta my friends saying that she was sleeping with half the men on post. You know, at the base, word gets around 'bout them loose girls." Lonnie's face took on a wistful expression as he continued, "She was fine as wine, but the girl had no morals. Even though I'm only twenty-two, I'm ready to settle down, maybe start a family. This girl in Sacramento might just be the one. She's a church-goer, but not too goody-two-shoes, you know what I mean?"

Orville nodded his head in agreement and self-consciously thrust his hands in his pockets.

"Matter of fact, you ought to come go to church with us this Sunday. You off, right? Shoot, you never know; you might meet you somebody too."

A warm sensation in his groin reminded Orville that he hadn't thought about a woman in that way in a long time. Down there mostly just felt empty. That familiar longing for Ellen swept over him, and he quickly pushed the feelings away. She was gone, and today would have to be the beginning of someone new. Maybe one of those loose girls could be a good place to start.

CHAPTER 36

Sweet Baby Brother

As her grandmother continued on her drive to Sacramento, Lily drifted in and out of one of her favorite pastimes—daydreaming about her mother. In one of her awake spells, she realized that finding a suitable, comfortable sitting or sleeping position in Black Beauty would be almost impossible.

Lily began nervously crossing her legs, then placing her feet on the dashboard, then scooting her butt around in the narrow car seat, all the while secretly watching for her grandmother's reaction. Her grandmother hated fidgeting and would surely see the opportunity to pull over at the next available town to use the bathroom and let Lily stretch her long, restless legs.

Lily saw a highway sign that showed the next town was three miles ahead. She stopped twitching, rolled down her window, and stuck out her tongue to taste the dry, desert air. That was another thing she liked to do. She could smell the outdoors better with the taste on her tongue of the passing cotton fields and over-ripened grapes languishing in the late afternoon sun. Her mother and Orville had picked that cotton and cut those very same grapes, and it wasn't that long ago.

Last week she had spent an entire day reminding herself of what her life had been like with her mother, stepfather, and her sister, and brother all in one place. Her brother was the best baby brother in the world. She was reminded of the time when they were visiting relatives in Merced, and her mother was changing Deenie's diaper, and he peed all over her. And her mother thought it was funny. Lily did, too, along with all of the cousins.

The best part was when surrounded by cousins that were strangers to him, Deenie would begin to cry. But as soon as he spied Lily, his face would light up, and he would crawl furiously towards her, dragging his baby rattle. He would be half-crying, half-laughing all the way until he was in her lap. She felt so proud, and she could see the look of envy on her cousins' faces. They were older cousins and didn't have a baby brother to play with.

For Lily, knowing that her baby brother was no longer a cute, chocolate butterball but a grownup little child was hard. The last time she saw him, he didn't look happy, but she would make it her business to see him smile and laugh again like he did when he was little.

Lily was wide awake now, and after stopping to use the bathroom and walk around a bit, she and her grandmother had both returned to the car for the final stretch of their journey. It had been a long day, and both were tired, but a feeling of anticipation had come over both of them.

CHAPTER 37

Nobody Want Them Kids

Just as the sun was about to set behind the faintly visible Sierra Nevada Mountain range, Lily and her grandmother pulled into the Jenkins dirt driveway. Nedra rushed out to greet them.

"Pet, I know you and the girl are awful tired, but I got everything ready for you two. First of all, you can put your stuff in the front bedroom, and as soon as y'all wash up and get ready to join us, I can finish up dinner. We got greens, cornbread, candied yams, and fried chicken. Poppa will be home soon, and we'll all eat then."

"Yep," Pet replied, "I could smell that food when I was pulling up into the driveway!" They both laughed as they walked toward the front porch.

Nedra had a beautiful, smooth, dark-skinned complexion that looked like silk. She wore a brightly colored floral dress and a matching apron. She had dainty floral thongs and brightly colored red nail polish on her toes. Next to her grandmother, Lily thought she looked gorgeous.

Like most houses in Sacramento in the summertime, the curtains were closed to keep out the harsh, penetrating sunlight. Once inside, both Lily and her grandmother had to adjust to the dimly-lit bedroom, almost having to feel their way toward the closet to place their things.

"Well, the sun's going down, so let me open up these curtains, so you can see." Nedra opened the curtains and led them back to the living room. It was the only room that had the curtains already pulled back, displaying the sunset with pink and purple streaks filling the evening sky.

"Why thank you, Nedra. Me and Lily sure are tired and…" Pet stopped talking, realizing that she and Lily were here so that Lily could see her brother and sister. Plus, Lily needed to be outside with the rest of the children. Looking in Nedra's direction, Pet inquired, "Nedra, where's the children?"

"Oh, Pet, don't worry. They out back, putting the chickens down for the night." Nedra walked toward the back door to show Lily where the children were. "Lily, go on outside and look for your cousins. Your brother and sister are both sleep. They been so excited since they found out you were coming that they done wore themselves out and had to take an early nap. They been waiting all day for you to arrive. But don't worry, we gonna wake them up in time for dinner."

"Yes, ma'am," Lily mumbled, trying her best not to show how excited she was. She wanted to go looking for Deenie and Lorna but knew better. Her grandmother would kill her for being disobedient.

As soon as Lily left, the two women walked back to the living room and sat on the couch.

"Now, Pet," Nedra began, "I'm not gonna lie to you about how your grandchildren are doing. They having a hard time. You know I got my hands full with my five children, and so does my sister Mickey with her six. Cecil only got two, but they way up in Washington state, and I don't think the children should be that far from California. The children have been going back and forth between me, my sister Bertha, and Mickey. I want to keep them here with me, but like I told you the last time we talked on the phone, my husband Ray said no. You know how these men are about raising other men's children."

Pet swatted at a fly and interrupted Nedra, "Girl, you got a fly swatter? I can't stand these damn flies!"

"Yeah, sure." Nedra sighed, got up, and went into the kitchen to retrieve the swatter from beside the kitchen counter.

"They been staying with Orville and that new wife of his. First, we hear tell that he sleeping with every tramp in Merced, colored and white. Next thing we know, he done went and married this woman named Annie. We think the only reason he got married was 'cause our momma was pushing him to come get his kids. They got married at the courthouse and didn't even invite anybody."

Nedra continued, "But them kids are miserable there. When we went to pick them up yesterday, Annie and Orville were fighting, and the poor kids were hiding in the closet in their room. And they look like orphans. Their hair ain't been combed, and their clothes look raggedy—looking at them just about broke my heart." She shifted on the couch and leaned in closer to Pet.

"My brother ought to be ashamed of himself, but when I look at him, it ain't really him. He's still grieving; I can see it in his eyes. Annie can see it too. She knows she can never take Ellen's place."

Tears had begun to roll down Nedra's pretty brown face, but she quickly wiped them away with a handkerchief that was in her apron pocket. Pet looked down at the floor and stared at Nedra's polished red toenails, willing herself to not look at Nedra's face. Hearing the plight of her other grandchildren was hard for Pet. Lily was more than Pet could handle, and she was not about to add more to her plate. Pet could see her daughter's pleading face looking down on her from heaven, but she couldn't do it. She just couldn't. Shit, damn that Orville, she needed a drink!

It was finally time for dinner, the children had washed up as instructed, and Nedra, her husband, Ray, and Pet all sat down to eat. The adults ate in the dining room, far enough away to not be heard by the children.

"Pet," Nedra said, as she sopped her cornbread in the steaming hot greens, "You oughta' think about what we gonna do with your other two grandchildren. You know Orville and Mariane don't want 'em."

Pet grabbed a fried chicken drumstick and immediately stuffed it in her mouth. She wasn't expecting Nedra to jump right in so soon after sitting down to eat. She bit into her drumstick and looked over at Ray. He averted his head, seeming to take a keen interest in slicing the cornbread and generously spreading butter onto each piece. He licked his lips and kept slicing.

"Look, Nedra, I just got here. Give me time to figure out what I need to do," Pet said. "Shit, I know just like you and Ray that them kids ain't been taken care of. That woman don't want them kids no more than Orville do. Seems to me like he shoulda got a woman who at least likes kids."

Nedra peeked at the kids in the kitchen to make sure they were not listening in on their conversation. Satisfied that they were not, she stood up to reach the far end of the table to scoop another helping of greens, "Since we picked the kids up yesterday, I been watching them. They so timid and scared. They don't even play like other kids. It's a damn shame!"

"Well," Pet said as she grabbed a piece of Ray's buttered cornbread, "Let's talk about this more tomorrow. Shoot, I wanna' enjoy my dinner you done fixed for us. You got any beer in the refrigerator?" She, too, peeked in the kitchen to see what the children were up to.

The children were spread out on the kitchen floor, sitting in a circle, Indian-style, with newspapers in front of their dinner plates. Lily's legs were too long to sit on the floor comfortably, so she sat on the edge of the circle and stretched her long limbs out toward the kitchen hallway. Each child was eyeing their vegetable portions to determine who was the least-favored child. It was a well-known fact that the child with the least amount of vegetables and the most mashed potatoes was the most favored among them.

Lily made sure that she and her brother and sister were sitting next to each other. She barely ate as she stared at them. They were so precious to her, and realizing that this was a short visit, she was already missing them. Nedra had combed and parted Lorna's hair into three cute braids, a single braid on top and one on each side of her head with colorful barrettes clipped onto the end of each braid. Her hair was shiny with Dixie Pomade, and her cheeks displayed the same round dimples as Orville's. Uncle Ray had recently cut Deenie's hair, making him look so handsome. Nedra had dressed him in Sunday dress pants and a shirt that her youngest son had outgrown.

Oh, if only they could all be together, Lily thought.

The weekend went by too quickly. Lily did not let her sister and brother out of her sight. She hugged them, kissed them, and smothered them with all the pent-up love that she had to give.

Sunday night, all of the children were outside playing just before dusk. Ray Jr, Nedra's oldest son, had rounded up the kids for a spooky night of storytelling. There were seven children, Ray Jr., Nettie, Rob, Cleotus, and Lily and her siblings. Ray had checked out a book from the library, and he was determined to scare the bejeezus out of the younger kids.

The kids sat in a shed behind the chicken coop, forming a circle with Ray Jr. in the middle. As the story unfolded, they clasped hands, afraid to let go of each other. Ray couldn't help himself and kept embellishing the tale with more and more gory details of an evil witch running through the forest, gobbling up little children as she crisscrossed among the thorny bushes and giant trees. In no time at all, the dusk had turned to dark, and twelve-year-old Ray Jr. had managed to scare even himself. By the time he heard his father calling him and the other children, he was too afraid to move.

When his father finally found them huddled in the shed beside the coop, Ray Jr. had never been more relieved to see his father's angry face.

"You children, get your butts in the house. We been looking all over for you!"

"Yes, sir."

The next morning, Pet decided they would stay another day. School was out, so there was no need to rush back to Palm Springs. Next to the parched desert, Sacramento seemed much cooler. It had always been a town with lots of trees which offered some relief from the scorching-hot, late-summer sun. She sat outside Nedra and Ray's house in a hammock underneath a huge eucalyptus tree.

She'd awakened earlier before anyone else was up. She was never comfortable inside, and as she sat there in the hammock, she contemplated her current situation with her three grandchildren.

She looked out over the expansive lawn and observed the other trees in the yard. A chinaberry tree with branches that stretched out to cover a good portion of the yard was, of course, not very tall but offered plenty of shade. Over the past two days, she had noticed that this was the favorite spot for the children to start their hide-and-seek games.

The eucalyptus trees, one on each side of the expansive lawn, served as a perfect place to hang a rope for the children to play tetherball. The two trees were also suitable for hanging a badminton net. When she was growing up, children were not allowed to play in the front yard, but here at Nedra's, the children could be seen playing in the front and backyards.

Pet looked up as she heard the front screen door open and saw Nedra approaching, still in her brightly colored nightgown and robe. Pet caught a whiff of coffee drifting toward her as Nedra plopped down on a bench next to the hammock. She could see the steam rising from Nedra's cup of hot coffee.

"Girl, what you doing up so early?" Nedra asked. Pet observed that Nedra's hair was secured tightly with a scarf that matched her robe. Her face was soft and round, and it appeared that she had gotten a good night's sleep.

"Well, you know me, Nedra, I never could sleep in," Pet answered, "When I heard the first rooster crowing this morning, I had to get up. I have to tell you, Nedra, I don't know how you can look so rested and calm with all them damn kids and that husband of yours to take care of. How do you do it?"

"Well, I think I made out good with my husband, Ray. He ain't like most men around here. He don't mind helping out around the house, and he don't mind helping with the kids. I think it was because he was the oldest and only boy in a house full of girls. His momma raised those kids by herself, and she had to depend on Ray for help. He's used to it."

"Humph, well, I ain't got no husband to help me, and I just don't see how in the hell I can take on more than Lily. I can't see no way!" Pet had sat up in the hammock and was unconsciously digging her bare feet into the grass moistened by the morning dew.

"And besides, you know welfare don't give me but thirty-five dollars a month to care for Lily!" I don't know how they expect me to feed, clothe, and shelter her on that little bit of money, it just ain't fair!!"

Nedra stood up from the hard bench, preparing to go inside to get the children's breakfast started. "Well, Pet, to hear you talk, Lily and your other grandchildren are like the cattle on my grandpa's farm. It ain't just the feeding and watering, it's the loving and caring about their well-being. That's what these children are missing, you know that, right?"

Pet rose from the hammock and lost her balance as her feet almost slipped on the wet grass. She was suddenly feeling that same sorrow and distress she felt when discussing Lily and her other grandchildren's predicament with old man Broussard. He was the one who talked her into this mess of bringing Lily to see her sister and brother.

She wondered if everyone saw her as someone who didn't care about her grandchildren. Frankly, she cared, but not enough to take on the responsibility of two more mouths to feed.

In the uncomfortable silence that followed Nedra's question, they walked back into the house, heads down, both unsure of how to finish the conversation.

The children were all up, and Ray was barking wash-your- face-brush-your-teeth-get-dressed orders to the children, who were quickly obeying his commands. Last night's scare was still fresh in their minds, and they were not about to get into more trouble with him.

As they sat down at the breakfast table before the children arrived, Ray asked Nedra and Pet, "What's with you two looking like you about to go to a funeral of a relative you never liked anyway?"

Pet smiled sheepishly and answered, "Well, your wife done put me in my place about my grandchildren. I know it ain't the best decision I could make, but I done decided that Lily is all I can handle. Nedra, you right, though. They ain't being taken care of by Orville and Annie, but I ain't got the help and support you two can provide for your kids."

Ray could see where the conversation was leading, and he immediately scraped his kitchen chair back, moved his plate aside, and put his hands on the table in front of him, his thumbs and forefingers arched in the shape of a church steeple, "Now like I told Nedra before—I ain't takin' care of no other man's children."

Ray got up from the table, threw his plate in the sink, and quickly walked toward the back door.

The children, returning to the kitchen with their freshly scrubbed faces, saw the scowl on Ray's face and allowed plenty of distance between themselves and their papa. They looked into the remaining grownup's faces, trying to gauge what had recently been discussed between Lily's grandmother, their mother, and papa.

Nedra rose, went to the stove, and spooned the steaming grits into their waiting bowls. She then placed a tall stack of warm, buttery toast straight from the oven onto the kitchen table. A jar of Nedra's strawberry jam had been opened, and the children eyed it greedily.

When all of the children were settled, including Lily, Deenie, and Lorna, their attention was diverted into figuring out who had the stomach for gross stories about mealy worms they had found in the grits last summer. Some of the children still couldn't stand the sight of grits and settled on just toast and milk. This, of course, left plenty of leftovers for the storytellers to eat the abandoned bowls of highly-sugared grits.

Pet and Nedra went out back to the chicken coop to feed the flock. The chickens rushed up to them as soon as Nedra opened their gate and reached for the small shovel. As she spread the chicken feed from a large gunny sack into the feeding troughs, the chickens went into a frenzy of loud cackling and screeching, feathers flying as they toppled over each other to get to the feed.

Pet had dragged a hose into the coop and was refilling their water stations. As they dispersed the feed and water, the chickens started to calm down. Both Nedra and Pet silently went through the hen's houses and gathered the eggs for tomorrow's breakfast.

One of the bantam hens would not leave her nest, but Nedra simply swung her arm toward the hen and coaxed, "Go on, Becky, it's time for you to eat your breakfast with the rest of 'em. As if on cue, the hen cocked her head from side to side and stared piercingly at Nedra then Pet as if she couldn't believe she was being forced to leave her nest. But as she did every morning and evening, she arose from her nest and strutted over to the feeding trough and joined the rest of the chickens.

"Pet," Nedra said as they left the chicken coop and headed for the backyard, "I know you feel like you between a rock and a hard place, and I do have sympathy for your predicament."

Even though it was still early in the morning, they could both tell that it was going to be a hot day. Pet was already perspiring in her long-sleeved, all-black muumuu, and Nedra had removed her shoes and was enjoying the freedom of a light, loose-fitting, colorful house dress. The two women were so different, but the kinship between them was evident.

Pet visibly relaxed. She felt that Nedra was not trying to judge her, just stating the facts. "Nedra, I know you understand what I'm going through, but to tell you the truth, not taking my other grandchildren hurts too. I want to, but I just can't."

"Pet," Nedra said as she sat on one of the lawn chairs in the back-yard, "I went to my brother's house, and I tell you, something strange was going on there. Remember I told you on the phone about Ellen's pictures being torn up, right?"

"Yes, Nedra, I do remember." Pet reached into her muumuu pocket and pulled out a wad of toilet paper, and wiped her brow.

"Well, it gets stranger than that. Turns out that my brother was messing with one of Ellen's cousins, and she 'bout to have a baby by Orville too! Well," Nedra continued, absentmindedly shooing a fly that was buzzing around her face, "I found a letter written to Ellen that she had hidden in her chest of drawers that he didn't know about. It was from Ellen's cousin telling her that she 'bout to have Orville's baby, and he oughta know she's expecting Orville to help her take care of it. I think that they must have been fighting about that, and it got out of hand."

Pet got up from the backyard bench she was sitting on and stared up at her.

"Wait a minute, you telling me that you think your brother Orville done shot my daughter?"

The dynamics of reflexes took over, and all of a sudden, Pet looked into Nedra's eyes and saw Orville. He was the enemy; she was the enemy. After all, Orville was Nedra's brother.

"Pet, I don't know. Nobody knows what happened to that poor girl. You know my brother is grief-stricken. Even though he's remarried, anybody that knows him know he ain't right. He ain't been right since that girl died. And them poor kids are suffering just like he is. It's a tragedy, plain and simple, and no one knows what really happened."

Nedra, too, reached into her house dress pocket and pulled out a handkerchief. She wasn't sweating; she was crying. "But why do some people say she killed herself? Pet whined. "That's a hard thing to hear about your own daughter."

"I don't know," Nedra answered, "The coroner never got back to us, and Orville don't want no part of talking to them people." Nedra wiped her tears and placed the handkerchief back into her pocket.

Pet looked at those high cheekbones and those Orville eyes again and had to look away. "Yeah, I contacted the coroner, too, and they said they didn't see a need to do an autopsy. Something about wasting the taxpayers' money."

They could both hear the children inside testing the boundaries of rowdiness with hoops of laughter (someone was the victim of incessant teasing), intermingled with petty fights over whose turn it was to do the breakfast dishes. Their increasing loudness was begging for grownup intervention.

"Pet, I know the worst part of all this is not knowing exactly what happened to your daughter." They both rose to answer the children's secret call for help.

Pet pulled her wad of toilet paper from her pocket again, but this time a chill had come over her, and she wiped her nose and dried her tears.

CHAPTER 38

A Walk in the Park, Chasing Little Girl Blues

Lily was enjoying the time spent with her cousins. They had decided that it was Ray Jr.'s turn to do dishes, and Lily convinced them to stop their playful teasing of Nettie, who, like Latisha Kay, had a lisp. Even though Nettie's brothers and sisters teased her, woe to any child at school who tried. Every kid at school knew that Nettie's brothers would meet them after class and beat the crap out of them if they even thought about teasing their younger sister.

Lily was oh so grateful to have her sister and brother here with her, which made it difficult for her to want to leave. She watched her grandmother like a hawk, looking for any signs that they might be leaving soon. If grandmother picked up her junky purse, or glanced outside at the weather, or asked Nedra if she could make a long-distance call, or acted in any way restless, Lily would break into a cold sweat.

Nettie, the cousin closest to Lily's age, had decided that it would be fun to go on a picnic. "Lily, I think you should ask my mamma if we can go to the park, it's only three blocks away, and mamma will say yes, if you ask." The girls were sitting on their beds, dressing their paper dolls, Nettie deftly folding the handles of her paper skirt onto the cardboard-paper doll, Lindy Lou.

"I don't know," Lily replied, sticking a paper shoe onto her twin paper doll, Cindy Sue, "Maybe you should ask MY grandmother, I don't think she will tell you no."

"Look," said Nettie, "I've watched your grandmother, and she's mean as you know what. You can tell she don't like kids!"

Lily was having a hard time getting her paper doll's shoe to stay on, so she licked the back of the paper shoe and pressed it hard onto her cardboard doll's foot.

"Yeah, you probably right, I'll ask Aunt Nedra—are you sure she'll say yes?"

"Girl, my mamma hardly ever says no to company, 'specially if they don't come around much. We haven't seen you since your mamma d—" Nettie blushed and reached down into her box of paper doll clothes, frantically searching for an appropriate new dress for Lindy Lou.

After tiring from their paper doll play, the girls cornered Pet and Nedra after they had fed the chickens and were leaving the chicken coop.

"Aunt Nedra," Lily timidly asked, "Is it okay if me and Nettie walk to the park, it's only three blocks away; maybe we could have a picnic lunch in the park?"

Out of the corner of her eyes, Lily noticed the frown and disapproving look that her grandmother gave her. She pretended not to notice, turned toward Nedra, and flashed a big smile. Nedra smiled back and marveled at how much Lily looked like her momma.

"Well, you girls can go to the park, but make sure you take your brother Ray Jr. with you. He's older and can look out for you two." With that said, Nedra pivoted around and headed for the back door.

Nettie stared at the back of her mother's head and shouted in disbelief, "Momma, I knew you wouldn't let me go by myself, but I thought you'd let us go together since it's the two..." Nettie stopped mid-sentence, realizing that now her mother knew that it was her idea, not Lilly's, that they go to the park.

What Nettie didn't realize is that Nedra, like most parents, already knew that it was Nettie's idea. From Nedra's point of view, since the beginning of time, kids always put other kids up to ask for parental favors based on the belief that parents didn't say no to children that were not their own.

Nedra turned back around and looked at Nettie. She didn't have to say a word. "Well, come on, Lily," Nettie said, "let's go pack our picnic lunch." She looked apprehensively in her mother's direction, hoping that Nedra had not nixed the whole idea of them going to the park.

Nedra laughed, "You two have a good time, and you know my rule about coming home after a couple of hours. Don't let me have to come get you, and you know you have to take your brother!" She laughed again, and Pet joined in with her own high-pitched giggle.

At the park, the girls spread out their brown, wool blanket onto the green-clover-leafed grass. Both Lily and Nettie noticed the tiny droplets of water clinging to the clover leaves. They found another spot on the lawn to spread their blanket and settled down in the park.

Ray Jr. had found a few boys his age who were playing catch within seeing distance of the girls, both of whom were wearing pedal-pushers, the latest rage of high fashion for summertime in the park.

"Lily, I been meaning to tell you I'm sorry about mentioning your mother earlier. I bet you miss her a lot."

They were both sprawled out on the blanket, even though their skin intensely felt the itch and sting caused by the scratchy, woolen blanket. Lily had scratched so much that small, red whelps were beginning to form on her legs and ankles. Nettie hadn't fared much better, but she was busy preening and smiling at the boys playing catch with her brother.

"It's okay, Nettie. I guess I feel kinda' funny 'cause kids don't know what to say to me. Everybody at school talks about it, but not to me. When I come around, everybody gets real quiet. I know they been talking about my momma. I am the only one at school without a momma."

Nettie stopped preening long enough to look into Lily's face. It was hard to pull herself away from staring at the boys because one of them had just caught her eye and winked.

"But Lily," Nettie said as she sat up straight on the blanket with her legs folded, "How do they even know? You say you hate it 'cause you change schools so much, so how do the kids know?"

Lily sat up also and tried softly caressing her painfully sore arms, trying hard not to scratch them. She was at a loss for words. How did everybody know? She shaded her eyes as she looked up at the sky, her mouth still clamped tightly shut. She finally spoke.

"I, I guess that it just comes up. Kids are always talking about their mothers, how strict they are, or what yucky vegetables they cooked and made them eat for dinner, or how they won't let them have sleepovers. But all I can talk about is my grandmother. And then they ask. And then I say my mother's dead. And then they don't know what to say. And the next thing I know, everybody's talking about it, but without me."

Tears were welling up in both girls' eyes, and Lily hastily jumped up and ran to the bathroom. Nettie watched her run away, then looked back over at her brother and the boys playing catch. The boy she had been eyeing didn't look cute anymore.

Walking back from the park, Ray Jr. walked ahead of the girls, tossing a baseball that he'd brought with him high in the air, and as it pummeled to the earth, slinging one cautionary hand out to his side as if blocking anyone else from catching it. He swooped in on each toss of the ball as if they were hard, fast fly-balls that only Roy Campanella could possibly catch.

Lily and Nettie had no interest in Ray Jr.'s athletics and were walking slowly behind him, swinging their clasped hands in unison.

Lily was regretting that she did not ask if her sister and brother could come along with them to the park. But Nettie had frowned when she mentioned bringing them along, and Lily now knew that it was because Nettie wanted to flirt with the boys, and having younger children around might slow down her fun.

As they approached the house, she could see her brother and sister peering behind the kitchen screen door. When they saw Lily, Deenie almost knocked Lorna down as he flung the door wide open. Lorna didn't seem to mind; she saw her big sister and ran behind her brother. The three of them embraced, and once again, Lily felt comfort in smelling and feeling the closeness of her sister and brother.

"Why'd you go off and leave us?" Deenie whined. "We were looking all over for you!"

Lily drank in the love and concern she heard in his young, timid voice. She stared back and forth between the two of them, trying to lock in the memory of their faces, hands, hair, and beautiful brown coloring. She noticed that both of them had big, brown sad-looking eyes, and she wondered if everyone could see what she saw. Lorna stuck her thumb in her mouth and eyed the two of them.

"I'm sorry, Deenie; you know you and Lorna still have to take naps every day. So, me and Nettie and Ray Jr. went to the park without you 'cause grandmother said," she added. The last part was not true, but Lily knew there was no way that they would question grandmother.

Later that evening, Lily saw her grandmother reach for her purse, and she was comforted to find that she was only looking for her nightly cigarette. It was such a relief for her to watch grandmother step out into the back yard, pull out a pack of Pall Malls, strike a long-stemmed match on the red and black Diamond matchbox, light her cigarette, and take a long drag as she relaxed in the low-hanging back-yard swing.

CHAPTER 39

You Mean to Tell Me the State Pay More for Foster Care

The house was quiet as the Jenkins family were early risers and were usually in bed as soon as it got dark. The kids, of course, were already asleep, and Lily sidled out to stand next to her grandmother's swing. They were the only ones still up.

"Girl, what you doing out here? You got on something to keep those mosquitoes off of you?"

"Yes, ma'am, Nettie gave me some of her insect repellant. It works, but it sure stings my eyes." Lily was attempting to wipe her eyes with the sleeve of her dress, but just touching in the area set off an intense stinging pain around her eyes, eyebrows, and lashes.

Her grandmother instinctively reached into her muumuu pocket, pulled out a strip of toilet paper, wet it with her saliva, and moistened Lily's eyes.

"There, now, keep your hands away from your face; you're just going to make it worse if you don't."

"Yes, ma'am."

Lily plopped down on the swing next to her grandmother and began to ease the swing into motion. She had decided that now would be the best time to talk to her grandmother about Deenie and Lorna. She had overheard her telling Nedra and Ray Sr. that she couldn't take on any more responsibility with kids, but Lily had a better idea. What if she, Lily, offered to do everything that needed to be done for them? Lily wasn't old enough to cook, and she knew her grandmother would never allow her in the kitchen to prepare meals, but she could do everything else, right? As the thoughts of how to approach her grandmother raced through Lily's mind, her grandmother interrupted her musings.

"Lily, I know you got something on your mind, so spit it out. You know I don't like kids sitting up under me anyway, so tell me. What, has the cat got your tongue?"

"Well," Lily stammered, holding onto the rod that secured the canopy swing, "I—I was wondering if we could keep the kids, I mean, I could help out a lot, and I know how to wash, and I could iron their clothes, and I could help them dress for school, and I could…"

"Stop, Lily. I know you been thinking about that; I been seeing it in your eyes ever since we got here. I ain't gonna answer you now, but I know what you want. If the state could help me, it's possible, but you know them welfare people. They'd rather give a lotta money to them white folks to be foster parents than give me a decent amount to keep my own grandchildren. At least it would be in the family. Shit, the system is all messed up."

Lily kept her head bowed and stuck out her lips. She didn't know what her grandmother was talking about but maybe if she looked sad enough…

Nedra, who had gotten up to pee, watched Lily and her grandmother from her darkened kitchen window. Coming back from the bathroom, she had heard voices, tiptoed up to the window, and listened to what sounded like the entire conversation. She felt a little guilty for not letting her presence be known.

She, too, felt that the children would all be better off in one house. But how to convince Pet, well, that was another matter. As she quietly slipped back into the room she shared with her husband Ray, he raised himself up on their bed, opened one eye, and asked, "Girl, what took you so long? I'm used to you going to the bathroom late at night, but you been gone a while."

Nedra half-heard what he was saying because his voice was muffled by the yawn emanating from his lips as he spoke. She knew the gist of his question, though. She removed her house shoes and slipped back into bed. The moon shined through their window and cast a blue-black coloring over both faces in the darkened room.

Nedra finally spoke, "I got an idea of how we can beat the system and get Pet the help she needs."

Ray, who had been only mildly interested in Pet and the children's predicament, shifted his eyes from gazing at the full moon to his wife. "Oh yeah," he said dryly. "What you got up your sleeve, woman?" He chuckled as he lightly placed his broad, strong hand on Nedra's stomach, just below her breast.

She placed one hand on top of his. "What if we petitioned to become foster parents for the kids and…"

"Whoa, whoa, woman, what you saying?"

"Now, Ray, hear me out. You don't even know what I'm about to say. "

Ray put his hand back on her waist, and she replaced her hand on top of his. He was praying that whatever she was about to say did not involve increasing his family size. He waited pensively, feeling a little bit of sweat trickling down his underarms.

"So, what I was saying, Ray, is we can be their foster parents 'cause we ain't got the same last names that they have. I know someone who's a janitor at the Welfare Office, and she said if we was foster parents, we could get four times as much as welfare pays to keep the kids."

Ray was sitting straight up in their bed now, one elbow leaning against his pillows, with one hand over his mouth to keep from talking.

Nedra continued, "She knows all about the paperwork 'cause their trash bins are always full, and she can't help looking at them applications. She'll help us fill out the paperwork, and once the money comes in, we can send it to Pet. The toughest part will be keeping up with her; she's such a Gypsy!"

Ray let out an audible sigh. His wife might have just thought about a way to beat the system. "Now, wait a minute," Ray's elbow was burning, so he shifted his weight to the other elbow, "You mean to tell me you wanna help Pet get foster-care money for her grandkids?"

"Shhh, Ray, you ain't gotta talk that loud." Nedra burrowed deeper into the pile of fluffy pillows on their bed and found another comfortable spot, still holding her hand on top of his.

"Look, it may not be legal, but them folks done set up a system where you can't take care of a family on the little money they call themselves giving you—don't make no sense. It outta not be legal to expect folks to live on that chump change they dole out!"

Ray shifted his weight again and put his hand on top of Nedra's. "Baby, you know I don't want no trouble with them folks at the welfare office. The other day, Junie told me that when his wife found out he was cheatin' on her with that hussy, Jessie Mae, why she called welfare and told them that his other woman had a man staying at the house with her. And you know she got all them kids with all them different daddies, and they all on welfare. And…" he sat up straight in bed to ease the crook forming on his neck, "...don't you know they sent somebody out and was threatening to cut her off. They don't play, baby, 'specially when it comes to our side of town."

"You got a point, Ray. But my friend that works there says she knows how to get around the system. Funny thing is they leave all that paperwork out, denial letters, acceptance letters, letters asking for more information, all of it out for the world to see. What they don't realize yet, is that Betty Lou is one nosey woman, and she can and does read whatever they leave out. She's probably a lot smarter than those nasty-ass white women they got working there. Betty said they filthy, most of 'em don't even wash their hands, leave toilet paper and unmentionable stuff on the bathroom floor…"

"Okay, baby, I get the picture."

"Ray, some of them don't dress any better than the folks on aid. She said it's sometimes hard to tell them apart."

They both chuckled at the image of poor white trash on either side of the welfare line, looking both poor and pitiful.

The moon, which had earlier brightened their room, had silently slipped out of sight, and both Ray and Nedra drifted in and out of sleep in the darkened room. When one of them awakened, they would softly touch the other and continue their conversations.

"Nedra, I tell you what, find out what Betty Lou knows, and let me know when y'all come up with a good plan. Orville's your brother, and I sure do hate to see them poor kids separated again."

"Ray, have you noticed Lily? She's like a mother hen, stuck to her brother and sister like white on rice."

"Yeah," Ray said, absent-mindedly stroking his chin with his index finger and thumb. "You wonder, baby, what them poor kids' mother was thinking when she shot herself to death."

"Well, I ain't convinced that she did it. One of these days, we'll find out what really happened."

"You think your brother did it?" Ray asked incredulously. All of a sudden, he was no longer sleepy.

"I don't know; I don't think so." The room suddenly grew more and more quiet. Neither of them could think of anything else to say.

The thought that Orville could harm Ellen was hard to picture. The thought that Ellen could kill herself was likewise difficult to comprehend.

As they sat in the silence, the sound of a far-away rooster crowing reminded them they had talked away most of the night.

The next morning, Nedra decided that now was a good time to approach Pet about her foster-parent idea. They were both in the chicken coop, soundlessly doing their morning chores, Pet with the hose at the watering troughs and Nedra spreading feed to the wildly frantic chickens.

"Pet, what you think about me and Ray applying to help you get foster-care aide for your grandkids?"

The noise from the rooster, hens, and baby chicks was thunderous, and Pet could barely hear what Nedra was saying. The hens were squawking, the roosters flapping their wings loudly, and the baby chicks peeping and wandering around aimlessly trying to avoid the chaos brought about from Nedra's spreading of their food at the feeding trough.

Pet waded through the chaos, feeling the chicken's feathers and beaks on her legs and feet as many of the flock tried to follow the food trail ahead of her. She reached Nedra just as she scattered the last of their food.

"Let's go outside, girl, I could barely hear what you said, "You wanna get my check for Lily?"

"No, girl."

As they walked toward the backyard swing, Nedra sat on a lawn chair, and Pet gravitated to the swing that she and Lily had sat on the previous night. Nedra spent the next few minutes telling Pet about the discussions that she and Ray had throughout the night. As she spoke, Pet nodded, mildly interested at first and then curiously attentive to Nedra's plan.

"Wait a minute, Nedra, let me see if I got this right. You telling me that the state pays more for foster care than regular welfare—well, I'll be damned. Shit, I wished I had known that before. Whenever I complained about it not being enough money to take care of Lily, they always told me there was nothing they could do."

"Yeah, that's why I'm saying that me and Ray can do it. They don't have to know we kin."

"So, you saying that y'all would turn the money over to me, why?"

"Pet, it's only right. These are my nieces and nephew, and I hate the way they being treated by Orville and Annie. If I could knock some sense into my brother's hard-ass head, I would, but I don't know what else we can do now."

Pet, against her will, was becoming teary-eyed. Having someone else care about the children's predicament made her heart hurt. She pulled out a wad of toilet paper and blew her nose.

"You ain't saying Orville had anything to do with Ellen's death, are you."

Nedra didn't hesitate, "Why no, Pet, why would you ask that?"

Pet stared suspiciously at Nedra, not sure if she should believe her. Those Jenkins' eyes looked back at her again, just like they had the other day when they were discussing another woman having Orville's baby. Pet decided to let it go. None of her pain or suspicions would bring her child back. Ellen was gone for good.

Maybe she needed to make this trip. She had tried so hard to not feel, to not think about her dead daughter and her other grandchildren.

Lily was enough, but seeing that Ray and Nedra wanted to help, made her feel less helpless.

Pet was about to follow Nedra back into the house through the back kitchen door, but thought better of it. She knew that Nedra had probably seen her swollen, tear-streaked eyes, and Pet didn't want to talk anymore.

She watched as a flock of red-winged blackbirds descended upon the cottonwood tree in the backyard. The sounds of their loud, squawking chirps seemed to fill the entire yard. One of them had a fat earthworm dangling from his beak, which reminded Pet that the top of her can of fishing worms was missing. She quickly replaced the top and went inside to see what Nedra was doing.

Nedra was standing at the kitchen sink, peeling potatoes for tonight's dinner. The kids had all followed Ray Jr. to the nearby park for a game of catch, and thankfully, Ray Sr. had to work again today.

It seemed to Pet that Ray's nose was so wide-open, and having him around reminded her that she didn't have a man who loved her like Ray obviously loved Nedra. Men who were that much in love didn't much like having anyone else around.

Sam Cooke's "You Send Me," a 'forty-five record, was softly playing on the phonograph in the living room. Mesmerized by the soulful sound, Pet followed the music as if in a trance, then stood next to the turntable, watching the forty-five's circular, bumpy spin. The record was scratchy but maintained enough of the song's quality to keep her listening.

A smile crept to her lips. That used to be her and Jesse's song, *"You ooh ooh ooh send me."* Yes, Jesse, she recalled, was the one who truly looked at her, saw her, and still wanted her. Their hot nights of passion together were memorable.

CHAPTER 40

I Gotta Have Me a Man Too

She began thinking that it was time for her and Lily to move on. Nedra had a man, and she needed a man, too—shoot, she wasn't that old! But having three kids and trying to find a man would certainly cramp her style. But then, she thought, Lily had been real persuasive about helping to take care of the kids.

There was a part of her that felt sad for Lily. Even though Lily had offered to care for her sister and brother, Pet knew how burdensome the task could be, especially for someone so young. Pet also thought back to how it felt for her to be stuck with caring for her sister's children. She hated it, hated them.

One thing was for sure, she wouldn't force Lily to quit school to take care of the children. That had happened to her, and even now, she resented everyone for that— her Momma, Papa, sister, the white folks she cleaned house for, and anyone else she could think of.

As she silently formulated her plan, she absentmindedly restacked the forty-fives on the turntable and listened again to Ray Charles, Sam Cooke, and Etta James. Just listening to the soulful sounds stirred that need in her. She had some long-distance calls to make when she got back home. A loud slapping sound and click announced the end of the last forty-five on the turntable.

Nedra stood in the doorway of the living room, smiling at Pet. "Girl, you look like you was a million miles away. You wouldn't 've been thinking about that hound dog Jesse, would you?"

Pet blushed, eyed a small clump of dirt that had been tracked by the children into the living room, and bent down to pick it up. "You know we always telling them children to wipe their feet before coming in the house, but they never do."

They both had decided to take a break from their morning chores and sit comfortably on the living room couch. Nedra wore a flowery sundress with green and red polka dots, her hair was pulled back in a ponytail, and Pet, in her usual style, had on a large, loose-fitting muumuu.

"Pet, I saw you looking all pitiful. Where's Jesse at these days anyway? Is he back in New Orleans? I have to tell you, when I last saw you and him together in Merced, I said to my sister, Bertha, 'Honey, that's one fine hunk of a man,' but he looked real slippery, even then."

"Well," Pet reminisced, "fine ones don't usually stay around too long." They both chuckled.

"When I met Ray," Nedra said, "I knew he wasn't fine, but I had given up on the fine ones. They good to party and dance with, but they ain't nowhere to be found when you need a man who'll stick around and help you raise his kids."

"Well," Pet said as she propped her feet up on the ottoman in front of her, "I ain't like most women; I can't stay in one place too long. And I don't want to be takin' care of no man. Every man I meet want somebody to cook and clean and take care of 'em. Your Ray is the exception. How'd you find him, anyway?"

Nedra, too, placed her dainty feet, with their brightly colored polish, on the ottoman. She had always admired Pet's free spirit, even though it wasn't a life she chose for herself.

"Well, my Momma told me as pretty as I was that I should make sure to marry a plain man. She said he'd be so grateful to have someone like me that he would go out of his way to be a good husband. Now, I have to tell you, at first, I wasn't attracted to Ray. As you can see, he's not good looking, but I've grown to love him for who he is, a good man and a good provider."

Pet looked down at her own fat, stubby toes, badly in need of clipping and a good polish, her loose-fitting muumuu, and felt her close-cropped "nappy" hair. She resolved to the fact that most men merely looked at her as someone who should take care of them. From a colored man's perspective, she was an easy lay who would cook and clean up after them. What else could she offer?

"Well, Nedra, like I told you many times before, the domestic life ain't for me, but I suppose I'm gonna have to settle down a little if I'm gonna take on all three of my grandchildren. Shoot, I been thinking, maybe, I'll see about hooking up with DH again," she continued.

Nedra had removed the rubber band from her ponytail and was beginning to loosen her hair by running her fingers through it. Her hand stopped midair.

"Wait, you ain't talking about Ellen's dad, are you? I thought that he married the other girl when he got both of you pregnant at the same time."

"Yeah, that's him alright, but I heard they done broke up. You know, he was my first love." Pet had a wimpy love-struck half-smile on her face that quickly turned sour. "He was the love of my life, and he never should've married that bitch anyway."

"Yeah, Pet, tell me how you really feel!" Nedra laughed. "You don't cuss much, so I know you must really hate her. 'Course I heard she's a drunk, and they tell me her kids were born with some kinda birth defect from all that drinkin' she was doing while she was pregnant."

"Yeah, I'm thinking if I do meet up with DH, it'll give him a chance to meet his grandchildren."

"Wait, you tellin' me Lily and the little one's never met their grand-father—Lordy be!"

"Yeah, well, he was a drunk too, most of his life, I think that's why he and that bitch got along so well. But they tell me he's sobered up and got himself together, and he's whining about being stuck with her. You know, once you sober up, it's hard to be around another drunk."

"Well," Nedra said as she stood up and walked back into the kitchen to finish dinner. Pet followed her in, the back screen door squeaking as the hinges cried from lack of 3-In-One Oil. "I lucked out with my Ray, his dad was a drunk, and Ray promised himself that he'd never touch the stuff. He saw how it ruined his family's life."

"Yeah," Pet responded, sitting at the kitchen table with a pile of green beans waiting to be snapped. "My brothers had the alcohol bug, and they never did straighten up. Seems like drunks run in every family I know."

Pet was in a talking mood, and with the kids gone and Ray at work, she swooped the green beans into her lap and set a large wooden bowl beside her on the kitchen table. As she snapped and placed the beans from her lap to the bowl, she spoke in a rhythm matching the snapping of the beans.

At the sink, Nedra was peeling onions and chopping garlic with a large, stainless-steel knife. The sting of the onions affected her eyes, and she constantly wiped them with her blue apron strings.

"You know, a colored man has a hard row to hoe in this white man's world. It's no wonder they turn to drinking. Even with a high school diploma, it's hard to find decent work around here."

Nedra responded with an occasional "hmmm" but otherwise listened as Pet continued.

"You know, DH told me a story one time about being in Los Angeles with a buddy, and they were looking hard for work. The only thing they could find was work nobody else wanted to do, like shoveling horse shit on a farm or picking cotton all day long for a few dollars. Half the time, it wasn't worth it when they thought about how much gas it took to actually find the fields in the first place. And DH always said he would never shine no grown man's shoes, white or colored.

Then they heard about a new ice-skating rink opening up downtown, and they were looking for clowns to entertain the crowds. People here weren't used to ice skating, and they were trying all kind of gimmicks to get people to get on the ice. They said they were recruiting colored folks. Why DH said he jumped at the chance—I mean, a white man actually looking to hire coloreds! Well, he and his buddy get there, and sure enough, they are hiring coloreds. Seems like the white folks were getting quite a kick out of watching them stumble and fall on the ice rink.

"But then, the colored boys they hired started getting real good. They were doing jumps and twirling around, doing all kind of tricks.

They were starting to look too much like that winter Olympics' champion—what's his name, yeah, Dick Button. The white folks were getting mad; who did these niggas think they were, anyway? Next thing you know, they was all fired. Fired, I tell you, for skating too good!"

Nedra giggled nervously, not sure how to respond to Pet's story. "Yeah, Pet, that's a sad and funny story. We trying so hard to make it, but they just won't give us a chance. What about you? Have you ever done anything besides day work and fieldwork?"

Both Nedra and Pet had finished preparing the vegetables. Ham hocks were boiling on the stove, seasoned with the onions and garlic chopped by Nedra. The kitchen windows were steaming, and the smells were beginning to make both women hungry.

They both looked up as the sounds of children's laughter could be heard coming from the backyard.

"It's not time to eat dinner yet," Nedra yelled to Ray Jr. and the rest of the children from the back screen porch. "Y'all know how long these greens take to cook, so you might as well come in here and get yourselves some bread, peanut butter, and jelly, and make yourselves some sandwiches."

The kids stumbled in, sweaty, laughing, and ready to eat.

"Now, first, go wash your hands," Pet instructed, trying not to look as mean as she felt.

Ray Jr. opened the big wide-mouthed jar of peanut butter and grimaced at the glob of strawberry jam that had been left behind the last time it was used. "Momma, look, I bet Monie left this strawberry jam here; she's always leaving stuff behind."

Nedra turned around just as Ray Jr began swinging the peanut butter jar in front of her nose as he laughed playfully. "Now stop, Ray Jr., you all ain't always got to be blaming stuff on your sister, Monie she ain't the only one leaving jelly in the peanut butter jar—shoot, your daddy do, too!"

"Yeah, but she sticks her finger in the jar when she thinks no one is looking, and…"

The back-screen door slammed shut, and Nedra and Ray Jr. looked up as Monie rushed in to defend herself. The other kids followed behind her. "Momma, that's not true. I heard Ray Jr. lying, even from out there! She pointed in the direction of the backyard. "I gotta have my peanut butter in a sandwich with jelly 'cause otherwise, the peanut butter be getting stuck to the roof of my mouth! Ray don't know what he's talking about!"

The other children had gathered around and let out hoots of laughter.

"Who wants to play jacks when we're done eating our sandwiches?" Lily inquired. She, Deenie, and baby Lorna were stuck together like glue—baby Lorna hanging on to Lily's leg with sheer ferocity befitting a child who had been left alone too long. They didn't know about the decision to keep them together.

Within ten minutes, all seven children were spread out on the kitchen floor, the boys playing marbles, and the girls playing jacks.

Long, brown skinny legs, shiny with Vaseline petroleum jelly, sat spread-eagle, dresses carefully pressed down as they leaned over to throw the jacks in between their legs. They quickly went from their onesies, twosies, and threesies, all the way to their tens and back to one again to move on to the harder tricks for the next go-round.

Meanwhile, the boys were in their corner, playing marbles. Kneeling on one knee, wearing colorful shorts with ashy legs (Nedra didn't worry her boys about "greasing their legs," they were intently staring at the marbles on the floor. One-by-one, they took turns with their thumb and index finger, trying to knock the encircled marbles out of the invisible ring. Ray Jr., of course, had the biggest shooter marble, and he mercilessly collected more marbles from the circle than his younger brothers and Deenie.

The boys usually played marbles outside but having Lily, and her siblings there seemed to change the family dynamics. Everyone seemed to want to stay physically closer together, especially since it was scorching hot outside by noontime.

Pet was sitting at the kitchen table, and Baby Lorna shyly climbed onto Pet's lap, solemnly turning her head from side to side, watching the boys, and then the girls as they played. Pet's dark brown hands encircled Lorna and held her tightly face-forward against her chest.

As she watched the boys and girls, Pet flashed back to her own nine-year-old childhood. All she could remember was dirty dishes, screaming babies, and shitty diapers that had to be dunked up and down in the toilet. She couldn't remember how she got tricked into leaving home and moving in with her older sister, but she knew it was a trick. She would never volunteer to be forced to stay home from school and be her older sister's slave.

And, of course, there was the pain of watching her younger nieces and nephews frolic off to catch the bus to a school that she couldn't attend. And all her older sister could say was, "I need you here to help me with all these babies. You so far behind in school now anyway, no need for you to try to go, you'll never catch up."

There was something about the way that Pet sat holding Baby Lorna that caught Nedra's eyes. She had a far-away look about herself, and it seemed as though she was crying!

Nedra was also sitting at the kitchen table, across from Pet and next to Tammy, her girly girl who seldom left her mother's side. Nedra was absent-mindedly twirling Tammy's hair. Nedra removed her hand from Tammy's hair and started to get up to comfort Pet, but stopped. Pet didn't have that "I need to be comforted look"—more like, as Nedra's brother Orville would say, "I need a whole lot of lettin' alone."

After dinner, Pet and Nedra supervised the children's nighttime rituals. Two girls got in the tub at a time, and when all the girls were done, they were followed by two boys in the tub at a time.

The girls were always pickier and wanted to go first because they said the boys never cleaned the tub well enough when they finished bathing.

By the time all seven kids were done, Ray Jr. got to bathe alone, both Pet and Nedra were exhausted from having to help bathe the little ones.

As they were leaving the steamy bathroom, Nedra grabbed Pet's arm. "Girl, when the kids were playing in the kitchen, you seemed like you were in a trance, a million miles away. What's going on?"

Without answering, Pet peered into Nedra's eyes as if looking for a sign and headed for the back porch swing. Nedra followed. Pet had a leftover towel around her neck and used it to mop the sweat from her forehead and the back of her neck. As she plopped down on the swing, Nedra stood beside her. It didn't feel like the right time to be facing her sister-in-law.

"You know, Nedra, I never had a childhood. Watching these kids today reminded me of what I lost. You know, I've always been the black sheep of the family. I'm the darkest, the shortest, and I never went past the third grade. Everybody else at least made it to eighth grade! I don't know why my mother never liked me. What did I do? I kept sending word to Momma that I wanted to come back home; I didn't want to stay with Toots, that sorry-assed sister of mine! But she never wrote me back, just left me there. What did I ever do?"

Nedra nodded, unsure of what to say. A mosquito buzzed around Pet's ear, and she slapped blindly at her face, trying to stop the sickening mosquito whine that pierced her ears. When she withdrew her hand, she felt but could not see the blood that the pesky mosquito had stolen from her.

"You know, Nedra, you asked me earlier had I ever done anything besides day work and fieldwork, and the answer is no. As soon as I got pregnant with my first child, Toots and her so-called good-for-nothing preacher husband put me out! He was more concerned about what his congregation thought about me being pregnant than he was about my well-being. And he wasn't worried about me having to stay home from school and keep his nasty-assed children neither! That's why you won't see me in anybody's church today—I know what them damn preachers really do when they think ain't nobody watching!"

Pet was, of course, thinking back to when she first arrived at her sister's. She had just celebrated her ninth birthday—without any presents, of course, but she had noticed that Toot's husband kept winking and smiling at her. She knew he was up to no good, and she immediately devised a plan just in case he showed up dallying around her small cot that had been set up in the hallway. Several times during the night, she would pretend to have nightmares that left her screaming and talking in tongues.

Toots would awaken and drag herself out of bed, wearing some big, floppy raggedy nightgown. When she'd arrive at Pet's cot, Pet would pretend to awaken from a dazed state, apologizing for disturbing everyone. That kept the bastard away.

The mosquitoes intensified their quest for blood as they swarmed around Pet and Nedra. "Pet, let's go inside; I think the mosquitoes have won this go-round. As soon as the sun goes down, here they come outta nowhere!" As they walked inside the house, Nedra lifted her hand in the air, groping for the hanging light switch that she knew was just inside the living room entrance. She grabbed the string and pulled down, but coming in from the dark, she and Pet winced at the light emitting from the bright 60-watt bulb. She turned it off instantly, and they plopped down on the nearby couch. Feeling the inside heat, Nedra walked over and propped the window to a higher level, using a longer stick that was sitting on the window sill. She pressed her face close to the window's screen, taking in the slight cool breeze coming from the west. She looked over at Pet, who was sitting pensively, eyes cast upward at the ceiling.

"Well, Pet, there you go again, looking like you talkin' to Jesus. What *do* them preachers do when they think nobody's watching?"

"Nedra, I don't want to talk about that right now, but getting back to your question about what kinda' work I've done—no, I have no skills. And even if I did, you know of many colored folks with decent jobs around here?"

Pet had worked herself up to a state of frustration that could not be willed away. Without realizing it, she began furiously stomping her feet on the floor and fanning herself, trying to keep the mosquitoes that had followed them inside away.

Pet wasn't nearly done talking, so she continued in the near-pitch dark room as if no time had passed since she had killed the mosquito.

"I guess it didn't help that I had two babies by the time I was fifteen, Veda, then Ellen. Next thing you know, I had four more…more mouths to feed than I could handle by myself."

Nedra could see the silhouette of Pet's face in the dimly-lit room. There was a moon tonight, but the trees in the backyard cast a shadow so deep that it was impossible to see anything other than the outline of her face.

It was perfect for the kinds of questions that Nedra wanted to ask.

"So, Pet, you said earlier that DH—by the way, what does DH stand for anyway?"

"His name is Daniel Hershel Jones, but he always hated that name. When kids at Sunday school learned about Daniel being thrown to the lions, they started teasing him, saying he was gonna get eaten by the lions. They never quit. If you want to make him mad, call him Daniel!"

Nedra slapped another mosquito. "Well, we never teased anybody about that, but then again, I don't think I remember any kids at school named Daniel," Nedra paused, "So, when DH married Cynthia, did you say that he knew you were pregnant with Ellen?"

"Yeah, he knew, but her family pressured him to marry her because I had already had a kid—I had Veda. I was already a tainted woman! He told me that he didn't love her, but he had no choice. You know, back then, if the girl's family knew the boy who got the girl pregnant, that man would be forced to marry her."

Nedra could imagine Pet's raised eyebrows and furrowed brow in the darkened room.

Pet kept opening and closing her mouth, not sure what she wanted to say and afraid that it would sound pitiful to Nedra. After several false attempts, she finally said, "If I had a family that cared about me back when I got pregnant with Veda, I would not've had to raise her and Ellen by myself."

Nedra couldn't see Pet, but she could hear the anguish in her voice. "But Pet, you did end up getting married. Wasn't his name Eugene?"

"Yeah, but he turned out to be one good-for-nothing Negro. Always slipping off to the next town, sleeping with other women. He seemed to show up just in time to get me knocked up again, but I was so stupid then, I didn't know that I could be treated better than that.

You know, nowadays, these doctors don't have no problem tying a colored woman's tubes. After my last child, Marie, they asked me if I wanted my tubes tied, and I said, hell yeah!"

Nedra and Pet let out a loud laugh that broke the sour mood that Pet was in. Their laughter echoed through the living room and down the hallway, and if anyone had been in the backyard, they would have heard it, too.

Nedra rose, walked to the window, looked out, and stretched her arms above her shoulders. She could hear the cricket's loud chirping racket coming from the grass and bushes in the backyard.

"It's kinda spooky looking out there, and I guess we should be turning in soon. I'm glad that we talked. Seems like I know you better now than I did when your daughter Ellen was alive!"

Nedra turned away from the window and faced Pet's silhouette, "My brother loved that girl. She was everything to him."

Pet whispered softly in the darkened room, "She was everything to me, too. I miss her so much."

CHAPTER 41

You Want to Find a Good Girl, Go to Church

Orville was missing her too. He was sitting in his truck outside of the diner where he and Lonnie had talked a few weeks ago.

It was early in the morning but already hot, so he had left the engine running so that he could keep the air conditioner on in the cab. He wanted to go inside, but he couldn't get Ellen off of his mind. So, he sat there, listening to the gentle roar of his truck's engine and the soft whirr of the cab's air conditioner.

He thought about the girl in church. Funny how the same way she'd smiled at him across the pews was the same way that he had caught Ellen smiling at him from across several rows of a San Joaquin County cotton field. If only he had kept attending church with Lonnie and his mother, he'd probably have that cute girl who kept smiling at him right now. But no, he'd let Annie talk him into getting married. She was a one-night stand who wouldn't go away. Seemed like once she decided that he was husband-material, he could not get rid of her. Next thing he knew, he was standing in front of the Merced County Courthouse with a marriage certificate in his hand.

He thought back to that time when he had accompanied Lonnie and his mother to church. He hadn't been to church in such a long time that he chuckled thinking about his papa saying he ought to throw his hat in the church doorway before entering!

Lonnie's mother, Coretta, and Lonnie had sat beside him, each with their shoulders tucked in, hands clasped in their lap, trying to accommodate the overcrowded pews in the stifling hot church.

At that time, Orville had been rethinking his promise to attend church with Lonnie and his mother. They said that good, Christian girls could be found here, but all he saw were old ladies with big, swollen feet tucked into tightly pointed shoes, wearing outlandishly colored headgear that seemed to have every peacock feather between Merced and Fresno sitting atop their heads.

As he glanced around the pews, he saw a few pretty girls here and there, but they were either sitting closely guarded between an ever-watchful mother and father or an obvious husband with his wedding-ringed hand lightly resting on her thigh. Finding a girl in church was not going to be easy.

One of the girls flashed a bright smile in his direction, but her mother caught the smile in time to elbow her and produce a nasty scowl in her direction. The girl blushed and looked away. Orville smiled back at the mother too.

After the last selection by the choir, everyone stood up from their seats. Orville was trying to sneak another peek at the girl but jumped up when he found he was the only person still sitting. The minister, followed by the congregation, chanted, "May the Lord watch, between me and thee while we're absent one from another."

Orville's reverie was broken by a low growl from his stomach. A couple of truckers emerged from the diner, followed by the tantalizing smell of hickory-smoked bacon. He turned off the truck's engine and rushed inside.

CHAPTER 42

Where's the Towel?

Lily could hear a rooster crowing in a field next to a ditch bank where she and her stepfather Orville were fishing. It crowed again, but she awakened to realize that the sound of the rooster crowing was actually coming from the backyard near the window of the bedroom she was sharing with her cousin, Monie.

As she slowly opened her eyes, she saw that the sun did not appear to be up yet, and it was still cold in the room. She had to pee and was mad that the rooster had awakened her from a beautiful dream. In it, her mother, baby Lorna, and Deenie were at home, and she was with Orville, her long skinny fishing pole bobbing wildly with a fish she was about to catch.

She scooted down towards the foot of the bed so that her toes could touch the railing. She used her toes and the railing to gently rock herself back and forth. This was a trick she often used to keep warm under the covers while trying to stall that first-morning walk on the cold floor to the bathroom. Sometimes, she could stall for hours, and oftentimes she actually went back to sleep.

But this wasn't the morning for going back to sleep. The rocking didn't seem to be working, so she jumped up, ran down the hall, and made it to the bathroom just in time. She kept her feet in the air to avoid the cold floor while she peed.

As she quickly walked back to the bedroom, an image of a deck of cards flashed in front of her, and she just knew that this was the day they were leaving. She felt it. Lily tried to think back over the past five days, wondering what her grandmother said or did that made Lily know the time was near. Maybe it was when she noticed grandmother playing solitaire for two nights straight. When she played solitaire, it meant she was bored. And when she was bored, they would be on the road within a day or two.

When Lily returned to bed, Monie was propped up on her elbow, with her head in her hand, rubbing the sleep from her eyes with the back of her other hand. "Lily, what you doing up so early?"

"I had to go pee. What you doing woke?" Monie had on her flowery red and green flannel girly-girl pajamas, while Lily had on an oversized white tee shirt that hung down to her knees. It was soft from many washes. Both Lily and Monie had multi-colored scarves tightly wound around their heads to keep their braids in place.

Lily plopped on the bed beside Monie. "I think we going home today," Lily said matter-of-factly.

"Aww," Monie whined. "You can't be leaving now; we just getting to know you better!" She sat up in bed and tightened her scarf that was beginning to loosen.

Deenie and Lorna, who were in the cot on the other side of the room, stirred restlessly.

Lily put her index finger to her lips and whispered to Monie, "I know we leaving, and it would work better if you don't say nothing to the other kids. My grandmother gets mad when people make a fuss when we get ready to leave. She'll probably wait for Deenie and Lorna to take their nap so she don't have to see them cry. She funny like that."

Monie stared intently at Lily. She didn't know what to say and began removing her nightgown and putting on her play clothes. "Wait a minute, you mean, y'all just gonna leave, just like that?" Monie got up. "I never heard of anything like that. I'm gonna tell my Momma!"

Lily broke out in a cold sweat. She, too, began changing into her play clothes.

"Look, Monie, you don't know my grandmother. She's mean. If she knew I told on her, she would beat the mess out of me. I just know her, and I know what she gonna do, but please don't say anything! Besides," Lily continued, "I overheard her say that she's thinking about us keeping Lorna and Deenie. If she gets mad, she could change her mind, and then…"

The girls looked up and saw Nedra in the doorway.

"What you girls doing up and dressed so early? The sun ain't even up yet."

"Good morning, Momma," Monie said with a big goofy grin on her face.

Nedra laughed. "You ain't fooling me, girl. What you two girls up to?"

"Nothing, Momma," Monie replied. "We just couldn't sleep, so we thought we'd get up."

"Okay," Nedra said as she cinched her blue satin robe tighter. "You make sure you two don't wake anybody, and keep the door closed."

Nedra padded back to the bedroom she shared with her husband, Ray.

"Baby, I'm glad you're back. What them children doing?"

Nedra slipped off her robe and tossed it on a chair as she slid into the bed beside Ray.

"Lily thinks that Pet is leaving, and I got a feeling she's right. Pet has seemed mighty restless lately, and I ain't too sure she's planning on taking the two little ones with her."

Ray eased into a sitting position with his back resting on the headboard. Nedra scooted over and laid her head in his lap. It was still cold in the room, and they folded the covers around each other.

Nedra spoke softly into the covers without looking at Ray, "Pet's been making hints over the past few days that make me think that she's changing her mind about taking her other grandkids. You know," she continued, "she's not what I call a domestic woman. You're more likely to see her in a juke joint trying to talk one of the men into buying her a drink than to see her making a home-cooked meal for them kids. She done talked herself outta taking them kids, you watch!"

Ray lifted Nedra's head and shifted one leg over the other to get into a more comfortable position. She snuggled closer.

Ray said, "Honey, I hope you're wrong because them kids need to be out of Orville and Annie's house. He never should've married that floozy. Everybody know she wanted him, but she didn't want his kids. They tell me that Lonnie had him going to church and was hoping that he'd meet up with one of them Christian girls, but Annie put a stop to all of that."

Nedra sat up in bed and nuzzled next to Ray. "Yes, you right, Ray. When Annie met Orville, the kids were with his sister, and I guess Annie didn't figure on him getting his kids back. But Orville's mother told him he should be ashamed of himself having his sister raise his children!"

"I think," Nedra said as she rose to prepare for the morning breakfast, "that Annie is hoping that she can talk Orville into giving the kids to someone else. Anyone else. It's a shame."

Ray got up, too, sorry that the conversation had strayed so far away from his desire to have Nedra back in bed with him.

"Now, Nedra, don't you go thinking again about us taking these kids; we got our own to raise." He intentionally added some extra gruffness to his voice in case she was thinking of reaching for his soft spot again.

"I know, Ray. Let's just see what happens. We could be all wrong about Pet."

Pet was dreaming, too. Arthur, Jesse, and Louis were sitting on the couch in her living room, drinking cheap gin, laughing, and pointing at each other's shoes.

Jesse, being the suave and debonair one in the group, had on a fine pair of black Stacy Adams; Arthur, being practical, had on a pair of black and white lace-up oxfords; and Louis, the country bumpkin, was barefoot. All of them were naked. That's when she knew it was a dream, and Pet willed herself out of the fog and into the reality that she had to get the hell out of dodge. She needed a man, and she needed one now.

Pet decided to call Arthur. Of all of her men, he was the most dependable. She lifted the sheet and thin blanket, tossed them aside, and sat on the edge of her bed.

Even though it was early, she was beginning to sweat under her flannel nightgown. What to do next? It didn't sound like anyone else was up yet, so she slipped into her black house shoes and walked as quietly as possible to the kitchen phone. Then she remembered that they also had a phone in the living room. She had brought her neatly-written address book with her, and she flipped through it to find Arthur's number.

The sound of his phone ringing seemed loud, and she placed her hand over the earpiece to muffle the sound. He answered on the fourth ring, his gruff voice sounding sleepy. "Yeah," was all he said.

"Hey, Arthur, you woke?"

"I am now. Who is this? Pet? Why you whispering?"

"I'm at my sister-in-law Nedra's house, and everybody still sleep. I don't want to wake anyone. How you been?" The living room was on the shady side of the house, and Pet hugged her robe closer as a chill ran through her body. The wall heater had just clicked on, and she sidled over to it to get a blast of warm air.

"Hey, baby, I ain't heard from you in a while, I tried to call you, but you didn't answer your phone. What you doin' up in Sacramento?" Arthur was waking up, and thankfully, from Pet's perspective, was sounding happy to hear from her.

"Well, my granddaughter, Lily, been bugging me to see her sister and brother, so me and Nedra arranged to meet here so the kids could see each other. Her and Ray want me to take all the kids back with me, but I don't know about that. Shit, my hands are full with Lily!" Pet was getting hot again and shook her robe from her shoulders and tip-toed through the living room toward the kitchen to see if anyone was up yet. The phone cord stopped her at the kitchen doorway, so she turned back around to sit on the couch.

Arthur didn't quite know what to say. Pet having three kids instead of one would certainly cramp their style. She could send Lily to the store when they wanted to get busy, but two other younger ones, that would be hard!

"Pet, I tell you what, I'm gonna stay outta what you do with your grandkids. But you ain't gotta decide right now, do you?" Arthur had already decided that it was a bad idea. Her kids were grown now, and what did she need with more kids anyway? But, of course, he wasn't going to tell her that over the phone. He'd wait 'til she showed up at his place. Once he gave her what he knew she needed, she'd know what to do 'bout them damn kids. Shit, nowadays, it was hard to find a woman past forty who didn't have a bunch of mouths to feed!

Arthur licked his lips and turned on his charm, "Pet, you come on by after you get home, and we'll talk. You know I'm dying to see you—when you say you coming home?"

Pet was feeling warm and achy and wet, and she crossed and uncrossed her legs, hoping the sensation would go away. "I'm gonna talk with Nedra and Ray, so I'll probably head out sometime tomorrow. You still working out at the Nahas ranch during the week and home on the weekends?"

"Yeah, baby, I'll be here for you all weekend long. See you." With that, Arthur hung up, knowing that she would make a beeline for him as soon as she returned.

Pet got up from the living room and slipped back into bed. Her mind was spinning with images of her daughter Ellen and her grandchildren. The guilt was there, but so were her thoughts of freedom. More children meant less freedom, and hadn't she already paid the price? Hadn't she already kept everyone's children? Hers? Her sister's? Her grandchild? When would it all end? Ellen's image faded away, replaced by Arthur's.

Lily had heard the entire conversation between her grandmother and Arthur. Arthur's voice was loud and deep and could be easily heard from the phone line to the nearby hallway where Lily sat crouched on the floor. She didn't understand. Her grandmother looked so weak sitting on the sofa, clutching the phone cord as if it were her only lifeline to the outside world. Where was the mean one?

When her grandmother rose from the couch after Arthur hung up, Lily ran back to the bedroom that she and Monie were sharing.

"Where you been?" Monie whispered, "I thought you said you were going to the bathroom, but you been gone a long time. Is Momma up?"

"No," Lily whispered back, settling onto the bed again. "Looks like for sure my grandmother is not bringing my sister and brother with us."

She laid down, her face pressed into the pillow with Monie looking on, not knowing what to say.

Nedra was indeed up. The wheels of justice for Lily's siblings were turning ever so slowly, but Nedra had a plan. Several furtive trips to the Welfare department by Nedra had proven to be challenging. Ray would be easy. He wanted her to be happy. And she was, but she couldn't let the kids down.

She started with Ray. "Now, Ray, I know you done told me that you didn't want more mouths to feed, but they my niece and nephew. I know if Ellen was in my shoes, she would do the same thing for us."

It had been a week since Pet and her grandchildren had left Sacramento. She had at least agreed to drop the younger two off in Merced, but Pet was adamant that she wasn't ready to take on all three. Maybe later, she had said, but not now.

Ray and Nedra lay in their usual positions on the bed: he partially sitting up, and she with her head in his lap. It was very early, and the children were still asleep—not one rooster crow had been heard. Even the morning birds hadn't stirred. The sun would be up any minute now, and there was a hint of fall in the air, even though the wall calendar was stuck on August.

Ray gently stroked her head, playing with the fine baby hairs near her temple. It tickled. "Stop, Ray, you tickling me," Nedra laughed. Nedra shifted to a more comfortable position and placed the soft comforter closer to her neck and shoulders. She turned on her back and looked directly up at Ray. From this position, she could see the fine hairs in his nose and his short, stubby black eyelashes.

She continued with her plea on the children's behalf, trying to sound sweet and firm but not too syrupy or demanding. "Baby, I know I'm asking a lot, but I think I'm making headway with them Welfare folks. They at least agreed to hear my case." She turned on her side again, not wanting to be influenced by the stern expression on Ray's face. "I laid it on thick with the worker, and she seemed to cave in a little. I had brought pictures of baby Lorna and Deenie with me, and she kept looking at Lorna's picture. You know she was such a cute baby, looking like a chocolate Gerber baby. I think that's what softened the Welfare worker up a bit! Who knows, they might let us be the foster parents."

While she was talking, she tried to gauge Ray's reaction without looking directly at him. He wasn't frowning, which was a good sign. Nedra felt emboldened. "We could take the stuff out of the little pantry off the kitchen and …"

Ray sat straight up in the bed. "Hold it, girl, don't go thinking that I'm that easy," Ray laughed, patting the top of Nedra's head and pointing his index finger in her direction. "Don't get the shit twisted! I know what you doing, but at least gimme a chance to take this all in. Shit, my goddamned brother-in-law is totally off the hook. You and I both know that those kids are his responsibility, but he ain't being responsible." Ray's voice had taken on a more conciliatory tone. What kind of place we live in where kids like these can just fall between the cracks? Ellen's got sisters and brothers—five of them, right? And where are they now? Have we heard about any of them stepping up?"

Nedra sat up in the bed and slid over next to Ray. The rooster had begun a series of crowing that broke the morning stillness. The sun was up, and they could both hear the children jumping up and down on their beds, probably having pillow fights.

"Ray, I'm afraid that Ellen was the cream of Pet's crop. Except for her two boys away in the Army, the four girls put together wouldn't make one decent pot of greens," Nedra slipped out of bed, laughing, trying to keep their mood light.

Ray put on a mocked face of protest, "Come here, woman, you trying to slip out of bed with me?"

Nedra quickly slipped back under the covers and snuggled next to Ray. His body was warm and rock solid. She circled her thighs around his and pressed her breast into his chest. He immediately responded by placing light kisses all over her face and neck. "How much time we got?" he whispered in her ear.

"Not much," she panted, "the kids will be knocking on the door any minute!"

Ray was good. He made every minute count as he and Nedra found all the right places to touch and hold and feel. When they were done, they both lay on their backs, sweat glistening on their foreheads with sheepish grins on their faces.

Nedra spoke first, "Ray, where's my towel?"

"Under the pillow where we always keep it."

Ray felt for the towel under Nedra's pillow, snatched it up, and placed it between her warm, soft legs.

"Momma, we hungry!"

The kids were at the door.

CHAPTER 43

She Had a Way of Making Mean Look Meaner

Pet's grandchildren were at the front door of Orville's house. After the long drive from Ray and Nedra's, they had all reluctantly, silently filed out of Black Beauty and trudged up to the screen porch. After trying the doorknob and finding it unlocked, Pet entered and looked back at the children as they stepped into the entryway. She didn't look happy.

Lorna was too young to know what to say or do, but she was taking her cue from her siblings. She stuck out her heart-shaped lips and whined that she had to pee. Deenie grabbed her hand and said, "Come on, Lorna, I'll take you to the bathroom."

Pet had watched the exchange between Lorna and Deenie. "She's big enough to take herself to the bathroom," Pet growled. Deenie quickly let go of Lorna's hand and pushed her toward the bathroom. Lily and Deenie exchanged glances. Grandmother had a way of making mean look meaner.

It was at that moment that Lily's heart sank. Having to leave her sister and brother would be hard. Driving the rest of the journey to Palm Springs would be harder, especially with grandmother in a foul mood. And seeing the sadness and distress on her brother and sister's faces was just too much.

Why did our mother have to die? Lily thought. *What if she'd only been injured? What if Orville had kept them all together?* The "what-ifs" were painful because none of them seemed possible.

But then, Lily thought about the conversation she'd overheard with her grandmother and Arthur. It was clear that having two more children was not part of his plan.

Maybe Nedra and Ray? What about the Broussards? They were a nice family, especially old man Broussard, and she loved Latisha Kay and her brother Tony. Lily thought that if she had a choice, she'd choose to live with the Broussards.

When Lorna returned from the bathroom, all three children lined up on the sofa waiting pensively, their brown thighs touching each other. No one spoke, but they were all thinking the same thing. They kept stealing quick glances at their grandmother, who was in the kitchen talking on the phone with her hand covering the mouthpiece.

They couldn't hear a word she was saying, but her face had softened. She let out a loud laugh and turned in their direction to see if they had heard her. All three suddenly found an interest in looking down, tying and re-tying their shoes in unison, except for Lorna, who untied her shoe and looked to her brother for help.

Lily spoke first, "Look, Deenie, I'm gonna try to find a way to keep us together, don't worry."

Deenie scooted to the edge of the couch and placed a hand on Lily's thigh. He stared at her and said solemnly, "Lily, there ain't nothing nobody can do. Momma's gone bye-bye, and ain't nothing we can do."

Big tears were rolling down his petite brown face, and he looked so old to Lily. She knew her little brother was only eight; why did he look so old?

Lorna put her thumb in her mouth and began sucking noisily, glancing back and forth between her big sister and brother.

Pet was off the phone and stood in the hallway between the small kitchen and living room.

"You children need to go outside and play, I'm going to wait here for Orville and Annie to get home," Pet said.

"But we ain't allowed to go outside if Orville's not here!" Deenie exclaimed. A row of tiny beads of sweat suddenly covered his forehead.

"Why you call him Orville?" Pet questioned, "That's your daddy."

"He don't like us to call him daddy, Orville said he just Orville to us."

"Oh." Pet sat down on the narrow chair opposite the children. "I'll tell Orville and Annie that I told you kids to go outside; now, go on outside!"

Pet heard them before they even got to the door. Annie was screaming at Orville, and Pet suddenly heard a loud *platt* sound from the driveway as Orville slapped Annie. Pet jumped up and went to the front door. The children flew past everyone and headed to their bedroom, fear evident across all of their faces.

"Annie, I done told you to stop flirting. Every time I turn my head, you grinning at some nigga like you 'bout to drop yo panties. What's the matter with you?"

Before Annie could answer, they both noticed Pet at their front door. Orville formed a sheepish grin on his face, and Annie, feeling ashamed of Orville's behavior, looked down at the gravel driveway.

"Hey, Pet, I didn't know you were here. Did you bring the kids back with you?" The tone of his voice said I hope you didn't.

"Now, Orville, you know I brought them back, but I guess you and Annie were so busy fighting you didn't see them run right past you!"

"Nah, well, let me go and say hi to them; ain't seen 'em for a week."

Annie watched as Orville sauntered through the narrow hallway leading to the kid's bedroom. Their door was closed, which made the hallway look even dimmer than usual. As he opened the door, a skinny beam of light illuminated the hallway. She watched him duck into their tiny bedroom. She could hear his loud, booming voice and their timid responses to his questions.

Annie's face was still burning from Orville's stinging slap across her cheeks. She touched it. It felt warm. She glanced at Pet, who had busied herself on their couch, reading obituaries from the *Merced Sun Star*.

Pet looked up from the newspaper, "I think I'll go on outside to the back porch and rest awhile. I know Lily wants to stay and play with the kids, and I'm too tired to get back on the road so soon. You think

Orville would mind if me and Lily spent the night?" Pet had turned to the second page of the Obituaries and was obviously enjoying herself. "Look like old man Carter done finally passed away—I say good riddance to that old bastard, never did like him anyway!" Pet continued, "They tell me that old man done had four or five children that he never claimed, running around Merced with his old ass self plantin' seeds that he had no intention of watering. They say one of his sons, I think his name is JC, looks just like him, and that poor boy's Momma been on welfare from day one. That's one man for sure ain't nobody gonna miss, 'specially them poor young girls left to raise them children all by themselves!"

Annie had stopped halfway on her way to prepare dinner and was nervously looking between Pet and the kitchen. "Well, Pet, that's some interesting news. I'd heard he was paying them to have sex with him, then dumping them as soon as he got them pregnant!" Annie continued, "When he got low sick, everybody said he had it coming, but I gotta go cook before Orville come back. I'm sure he won't mind if y'all spend the night. Can I get you some cold water from the fridge?"

Pet opened the back porch screen door. "No, Annie, I'll be out back. Let me know if you need me to help you cook."

Alone in the kitchen, Annie again touched her face. She could feel the welt forming on her cheek where Orville had slapped her. And knowing that the children's grandmother had observed the slap made her feel ashamed. How in the world had she gotten herself in this predicament? She pulled out two onions to peel and chop. She had discovered long ago that Orville had no tolerance for a crying woman. So, when she needed to cry, she chopped onions, lots of them. She cried for her own children, the twins she left behind with her ex-husband—Bonnie and Donnie, left behind with an abusive husband who dared her to fight for their custody. He'd kill her, and she knew it.

Now, here she was with another abusive husband who also wanted to control her every move. A husband who was jealous to the core. Who couldn't stand to see her look at another man, let alone smile at him! She was just going to have to learn to keep her head down at all times. Don't even think about looking at any man, young or old, cripple or blind—it didn't seem to matter with Orville. Just don't look! Annie jumped as she heard the screen door slam and Pet's footsteps as she walked back toward the kitchen.

"Girl, I finished reading the newspaper. You want me to help you snap these peas you got in the bowl over here?" Before Annie could answer, Pet plopped down onto the kitchen stool and began snapping the peas. "Look, Annie, ain't no need in you trying to sugar-coat it. Everybody knows that Orville likes to fight his women. And you takin' it is no help to you or my grandkids. They scared stiff." Pet paused mid-air with a pea in her hand, using them to point at Annie, "I think he so mad that you ain't Ellen that he can't help himself. Sooner or later, you gonna have to leave him 'cause he's going to continue to hit you until you can't take no more."

Big tears rolled down Annie's face, and she tried to brush them away with her apron. "Pet, you don't know what it's like," Annie wailed.

Pet thought about the Merced rumors she'd heard over the years. Today, she had witnessed for herself the abuse that Annie encountered, at least with this new husband.

"Yes, I do," Pet continued snapping the peas, "Everybody in town knows your ex beat you, and now Orville's beating you, so what you gonna do, Annie? Girl, you need a plan!"

"I want my girls back," Annie cried, "and that son-of-a-bitch won't even let me see my kids, and now I gotta take care of Orville's damn kids!"

Pet got up, slammed the bowl of beans into the kitchen sink, and turned to face Annie. "I don't care about your damn kids, but I do care about the way you treatin' mine. My grandkids deserve better."

Annie had finished peeling the onions and garlic, and she was finished crying too. As Pet stared at her, Annie deliberately sat back down on the kitchen stool and braced herself. She felt her body swell with new energy. She wasn't sure where the energy was coming from, but it was there. Pet didn't look as mean or as tough as she usually did.

Annie had buckled under enough in her life. She was finally ready to stand up for herself, and Pet would be the perfect sparring partner for Annie's newly-found strength. Annie's keen features took on a fierceness Pet had never seen before. That made Pet sit up on her stool and take notice. Annie's small, perfect heart-shaped lips were parted slightly, and Pet could see the tenseness in Annie's furrowed brow.

"Pet, let me tell you something about my life. You don't know me, except that I'm Orville's new wife. I've seen pictures of Ellen, and I've heard people say that I look like her. But I'm not her, and believe me, Orville reminds me of that every time he hits me. He never hit her, she was perfect, and I'm not!"

Annie had gotten up from the kitchen and walked into the living room, sat on the couch, and watched as Pet stood by the window, looking out, watching the sunset over the backyard.

"Don't let Orville fool you," Pet said. He'd been beating up on Ellen, too, 'til she had enough. Next thing we know, Nedra called and said Orville had to go to the hospital to get his head stitched." Pet laughed. "I ain't heard no more about him laying a hand on her. You know them Merriman women don't play; even my shy Ellen did not take to no man hitting on her!"

Suddenly, Annie felt a kinship with Ellen that she had never felt before. Another woman married to Orville and unhappy. But she had killed herself, or so they said.

"Pet, what do you know about what happened to Ellen? Do you really think she killed herself?"

Pet had joined Annie on the couch, and both women sat in the semi-darkness created when the sun goes down, and no lights have been turned on yet. Dinner was ready, and the table was set, but since Orville and the children were still in their room, they had not called them to dinner.

"You know, Annie, I don't really know. I just don't believe that Ellen would shoot herself with them children there with her. She loved them, and I can't think of any woman intentionally killing herself, especially with baby Lorna in the crib in the bedroom when it happened. It just don't sound like something Ellen would do."

"I don't think she did it, I think Orville…" Even as the statement came out of Annie's mouth, she stopped mid-sentence. Her boldness was taking over, her inhibitions gone, but there was a part of Annie that was still a part of Annie.

"Pet, you know that Orville is a coward, right?" Before Pet could answer, Annie continued, "He's scared of his own daddy. Every time we visit, old man Henry just glares at him like he hates him. That old fart don't talk to none of his children, and they all scared to death of him." Annie stood up from the couch and began pacing, "Cowards always trying to find someone that they can beat up on, right? The one thing Orville can do is beat up on women. Ellen was the first woman he beat up on that fought back. And now she's dead. I just don't think that's a coincidence."

"Annie, let's go out to my car and talk. The mosquitoes might not be so bad with the windows down since the wind seems to have picked up. We don't have to worry about Orville hearing our conversation from the car."

Once settled in Black Beauty, Annie continued, she was happy to have someone to talk to about her relationship with Orville. Pet had witnessed what no other woman had witnessed, the humiliating slap from the man she married.

"Me and my family, we all just took the abuse. First, there was my domineering father, who beat my mother and scared me and my sisters and brothers. Next, it was the teachers at school who tolerated the colored children but refused to step in when the white kids bullied and taunted us. Next, was my first husband, always beating up on me, and now there's Orville."

Pet was sitting in the driver's seat of Black Beauty, looking straight ahead as Annie spoke from the passenger's side. The evening grew darker, and Pet watched as the light in the children's room went out, and the kitchen light went on. Orville and the children were most likely eating the food that she and Annie had prepared.

The chirping noise from the crickets seemed to flood the inside of the car, and plenty of moths could be seen flying around the lone yellow porch light.

Pet turned away from the house and spoke to the silhouette that was Annie's face. "Annie, don't you know that I know that the colored men in Merced, and hell, probably every other county 'round here, got us women so scared that we just take whatever shit or abuse they dish out—No questions asked." Pet heard the sickening whine of a lone mosquito and swatted blindly at the air in front of her. "Look, Annie, the only difference between me and the other women in this town is I'm not afraid to be by myself."

Annie turned toward Pet. "You right, Pet; most of us are too scared to tell our husbands that we too tired to lay with them. Tell them we ain't cooking tonight 'cause it's too hot to turn on the stove? And we sho ain't gonna take the chance of sleeping around like they do!"

"But you know Annie, I pay a price for being like I am. There's a lot of nights when I wished I had a husband to take care of me and my children. Someone to be with all the time, but these men want too much, and I ain't never been one to let no man tell me what to do. I just as soon be by myself!"

Annie had never thought about being without a man, but staring at Pet over what seemed like several minutes gave her something to think about. Taking in a deep breath, Annie continued, "Pet, I sure appreciate you talking with me like this. My Momma never said anything. Shit, she was beat up on all the time and never dreamed about leaving. That's just how it was growing up. I couldn't wait to be grown and leave home. It didn't occur to me that I'd end up in the same situation as my Momma!"

Several more mosquitoes joined the lone one, and soon they were both swatting wildly at the mosquitoes.

"Let's go in, Pet. These mosquitoes are just going to get worse now that it's really dark out here."

As they were opening the front door, they both heard a whimper coming from the children's room. Pet ran down the hallway and entered the room first, with Annie at her heels. Deenie, Lorna, and Lily were all lined up next to the tiny closet with their hands stuck out and their eyes closed. Orville was by the doorway and had pulled off his belt, and was walking toward them. All of the children were crying, and Lorna peed on herself.

Orville was sweating. "These kids trying to tell me that Ray gave them each a dollar. I know damn well he ain't gave them no dollar. They must've took it from the dresser drawer in my room!"

Pet stood in front of Orville and angrily pointed a finger in his face, "You leave these poor kids alone! Ray DID give them each a dollar before we left. Why didn't you come and ask me? I coulda' told you what happened."

Orville grinned sheepishly and looped his belt back into his pants.

Annie stared defiantly at Orville.

He began unbuckling his belt again and walked menacingly toward Annie. "You got something to say, woman?"

Annie did not flinch. "Orville," she said quietly, walking toward him, "just leave us alone. Go on back out there to your other bitches, lord knows you got plenty of them!"

Orville glanced at Annie with a puzzled look on his face. This was not the Annie he knew. "Well, you know how these kids are, always stealing and lying about it." He turned to the children, "Y'all go on to the bathroom, wash up, and get ready for bed," he demanded. All three children bolted for the bathroom, making sure not to have eye contact with any of the adults. Orville stalked out, ducking his head to keep from getting it bumped at the doorway.

Pet and Annie returned to the living room just as they heard Orville's Thunderbird spinning out of the gravel driveway.

"He must be headed down to the juke joint to find one of his bitches," Annie said as she sat down on the couch.

Pet joined her and said, "Annie, what you got in the refrigerator to drink? I could use a beer."

Annie quickly walked to the refrigerator and pulled out two beers. "Pet, I wish I had your nerves. Orville just scares me; I'm afraid to say anything when he starts going off. But talking to you today gave me hope," Annie continued. "And watching the way you talked to Orville—that gave me hope too. I'm tired of being pushed around and bullied, but I never learned how to fight back. How do you think I did tonight?"

Pet wrestled with opening her beer bottle, and after successfully freeing the cap from the bottle, said, "Girl, you are on the right path, that's for sure. All you gotta do is keep letting yourself get mad enough. You see how he had those kids so scared? There was no call for that. He's just picking on them 'cause he knows they can't fight back. Orville is just like any other colored man in this town," Pet continued. "They need us. So, all you gotta do is let him know that you don't need him—you don't. You need to keep on fighting back too. Shit, do like Ellen, get a cast iron skillet, and slap him upside his head. Matter-of-fact, if you just pick up the skillet, he'll get the message.

"Let him know that you ain't scared. Did you see that look on his face when you didn't back down? Once you start fighting back, he'll stop hitting you, but as long as you scared and he know it, he will keep on hitting you. But like I said, you on the right track!"

"Yeah, but what if he tries to kill me?" Annie's strength seemed to vanish as she pictured Ellen's dead body in the casket of the Stratford Funeral Home.

"He can't, Annie. Too many people are already suspicious over Ellen's death. He wouldn't dare!"

CHAPTER 44

Say Fella, You Got a Light?

Orville balled his fist and angrily slammed it against the Thunderbird's steering wheel. "Got damned them bitches," he cursed. The car swerved from the impact, and he quickly grabbed the wheel with his left hand and steadied the coupé.

He was heading south on Thirteenth Street, once a vibrant community on the colored side of Merced. The colored grocery store, liquor store, and blues club had all moved to Childs Avenue, where most of the poorer, rural coloreds lived.

Orville's part of town had been torn apart to make way for Highway 99. The streetlights were few and far between, and along with the colored businesses, most folks had moved too.

But Orville and Annie and several others had held onto their property in Merced. "Got damned peckerwoods have tried to take everything from us," he said as he positioned the rearview mirror so that he could watch his lips as he talked to himself. It was dark outside, so the only thing he could really see was his pearly-white teeth.

All of a sudden, a calico cat, legs outstretched, streaked in front of his car and quickly disappeared into the black night. He slammed on his brakes to avoid hitting it.

Orville pulled his car over to the side of the road, slumped over the wheel, and began sobbing. Before he could stop them, big hot tears rushed down his dark brown face. He happened to have stopped under a dim streetlight, and he looked around self-consciously to see if anyone could see or hear him. He again repositioned the rearview mirror and began talking to himself, closely watching the movement of his lips.

"Ellen, I'm so sorry. I didn't mean to keep you out there against your will. I was just trying to save some money. You know, just save and save until we had enough to buy us a decent place to stay. Hell, I had no idea you was so miserable out there. Shit, you had the kids; I thought they would keep you company. How was I supposed to know? I'm just a man!"

Orville stopped talking when he heard the faint sound of someone walking on the broken sidewalk. There was no pattern to the footsteps, so he crouched down in his seat and peered out through the darkness to see who was coming. He saw a man swaying back and forth on the narrow walkway. The wino stopped on the passenger side of Orville's car, and Orville leaned over to roll down the window.

"Say, buddy, you got a light?" The sour smell of cheap Gallo wine instantly flooded the car, and Orville looked up at the pale, washed-out, blue eyes of Pear, one of the town drunks.

Orville rolled down the window on the driver's side of the car to get a crosswind going. "Pear, man, you know I done quit smoking. Why don't you get on out of here and take your drunk ass on home? Can't you see when a man wants to be alone?"

Pear stepped back from the car window and almost fell into the bushes along the sidewalk. He regained his balance, snatched open the car door, and plopped onto the seat before Orville could stop him. Now the stench of wine and sweat and a musty order completely filled the car.

Orville began taking short, shallow breaths through his mouth to lessen his exposure to the stench emanating from Pear's body and clothing. "Man, now what you doin' in my car? I thought I told you to go on home." Orville leaned back into the back seat and began rolling down the back passenger-side window.

Pear belched and cleared his throat. "Look, Orville, don't think 'cause I'm drunk that I didn't hear you crying back there. What's going on? You and Annie fighting again, or are you crying over Ellen?"

Pear was Orville's Sargent when they were both stationed in Korea, and they had remained friends since their return home. Orville had often bragged to his friends that Pear was one of the few peckerwoods who stood up for coloreds when they integrated the Army. Unfortunately, Pear had been exposed to one-too-many pieces of shrapnel flying too close to his skull to ever be able to sleep without his Gallo.

Orville adjusted the car seat back so he could stretch out his long legs. They could both hear the "high-pitched buzzing" sound emanating from the almost-dead streetlight from above.

"Look, man, you know how it goes. For me, if I ain't thinking about my poor Ellen, I'm thinking about them Koreans and the stinking fox holes and the bad food, and wishin' I could just forget about everything." You know Ellen's mother, Pet?"

Pear was staring straight ahead, but before he could answer, Orville continued talking.

"She and everybody else want me to just admit that I killed Ellen, but I didn't!" The tears began again, and Orville did not attempt to brush them away. "I'll admit that I should have listened to her and got her out of that house in the middle of no-got-damned-where, but I didn't kill her!"

Pear pretended to be interested in a lone white moth that had landed on the car's windshield. He appeared to be more sober than Orville had seen in a long time.

"Look, Orville, I believe that you didn't, but who did? I think you know."

"Pear, go home, I gotta go!" Orville held his breath, leaned over, and unlocked the car door to let Pear out. Without a word, Pear pushed the door open and extricated himself from the car. With his lips tightly sealed, Orville watched as Pear ambled unsteadily along the sidewalk. His gait was much more balanced than when he had first sat down in the car.

CHAPTER 45

Tell Me About my Mother

The next morning, Pet awakened and stared at the living room curtains. Sometime during the night, she found herself drenched and had opened the window in the hopes of getting a draft of cool air. During that time of night, no wind was blowing, and she tossed and turned but didn't remember going to sleep.

She propped herself up on her pillow, rubbed her eyes, and kept staring at the curtains to get her bearings. There seemed to be a hypnotic sway to the white curtains as the wind continued to blow them to and fro. Then, Pet remembered that she and Lily were in Merced, and it was time to go. The house was quiet, and Pet didn't recall what had awakened her. It wasn't the chickens because there were no chickens, at least not here in town. She padded to the children's room and stood over the bed Lily was sharing with Lorna. Lily immediately opened her eyes.

"Get up, girl! Here's your toothbrush and washcloth. Let's go now before everybody wakes up," she whispered.

"Yes, ma'am." Lily jumped up from the bed and stumbled into the bathroom down the hall. As she stared at herself in the mirror, she noticed that two small buds were beginning to form on her chest and could be seen through her thin pajamas. She placed her hand on the left bud and touched it. It felt funny. She heard her grandmother's footsteps, and she quickly put the Pepsodent toothpaste on her toothbrush and began furiously brushing her teeth. The radio commercial for the toothpaste sang in her head: *"You'll wonder where the yellow went when you brush your teeth with Pepsodent."*

When she returned to the bedroom, Lily quietly dressed and met her grandmother in the gravel driveway. She didn't dare to look at her sister and brother, who were still sleeping. Lily said a quiet goodbye and closed the door behind her. Tears were running down Deenie's cheeks as he watched his sister depart, but he said nothing. Lorna continued to sleep.

Pet released the emergency brake on Black Beauty and quietly slipped out of the driveway without turning over the engine. They said nothing as they turned onto Highway 99. Pet was lost in her thoughts, and Lily was lost in hers.

Lily savored the week that she had spent with her sister and brother by making a mental movie of everything they had done together—Hugging Deenie, sitting Lorna in her lap, walking to the park with Tony, eating breakfast on the kitchen floor, and helping Lorna dress every morning. When Lily ran out of memories, she re-played them.

Around noontime, they stopped in a rest area. There were not many people around. It was over 100 degrees, and there were several cars with their hoods up with sweaty men slowly pouring water from canteens into hissing radiators.

Lily and her grandmother sat on a picnic bench and ate the ever-present cheese, crackers, and sardines. The roll-up sardine can almost slipped out of Lily's hand, spilling the oily juice onto her dress.

"Girl, I done told you to be more careful. Watch what you doing!" That was the first time either of them had spoken since they left Merced.

Before Lily could respond, her grandmother grabbed a washcloth and stabbed at Lily's dress to remove the greasy stain. The force almost made Lily fall backward from the bench. Now Lily had a grease and water stain on her dress.

"I'm sorry, grandmother," was all Lily could think to say.

"You just need to learn to watch what you're doing," her grandmother repeated. . "You always was careless!"

"Yes, ma'am," Lily said.

Lily threw the empty box of crackers in the trash and walked back to Black Beauty. She couldn't wait for school to start. At least she'd be around nice teachers and could spend her day learning new stuff and not have to be around her grouchy old grandmother.

When grandmother re-started Black Beauty and drifted back to Highway 99, Lily decided it was time to daydream again. The dry desert air was hot, and they both had their windows cracked to let in the moving air. The annoying loud whistle generated by the open window meant that Lily did not have to worry that her grandmother would continue her fussing.

Lily thought again about her new buds and realized that the first day of school was less than one month away, and this time when the girls looked each other over, Lily would have something to show off too!

"You thinking about school, Lily?" her grandmother shouted above the loud roar generated by their cracked windows.

Okay, here we go, Lily thought. Her mood has changed again. She smiled. She couldn't stay mad at her grandmother for very long.

"Yes, ma'am," Lily shouted back. For a brief second, Ellen's face appeared as a halo above her grandmother's head, and Lily, startled by what she saw, gasped. The brief appearance of Ellen emboldened Lily, and she secretly smiled back at her mother's image and said, "Tell me about my mother, grandmother."

Without a word of explanation between them, both Lily and her grandmother rolled up their windows in unison so that their conversation could be heard above the roar of the outside wind.

Her grandmother sighed heavily and said, "Lily, you always asking me about your Momma, but I don't know why."

Black Beauty was warming up again, and Pet pulled a yellowed handkerchief from the front pocket of her dress and furiously wiped her forehead, neck, and chest.

"Your Momma was the best daughter I ever had," she laughed. "Your Aunt Cozetta, Veda, Dorothy, and Marie couldn't hold a candle to Ellen and they knew it.

Lily nodded slightly and spoke a very quiet, "Uh-huh." She wanted to keep grandmother talking, but she knew any minute now, grandmother would remember Lily was a child who ought not be listening to grown folk's conversations.

They both saw steam rising and heard hissing from the car's radiator. Lily watched as grandmother shifted Black Beauty into third gear to slow the car down. She pulled off the highway into a rest stop to let the steaming engine cool.

The smell of hot rubber filled the car, and Pet handed Lily a can opener and a small glass bottle of Coca-Cola. "Here, open this for me while I go pee."

"Yes, grandmother," Lily replied. She slumped down in the car seat, disappointed that her grandmother had not finished their conversation about her mother.

A few minutes later, as her grandmother approached the car, Lily sat up straight in the car seat and placed a grownup smile on her face. Then she realized that her grandmother had opened the hood and was pouring water into Black Beauty. The car had cooled down enough to allow grandmother to remove the radiator cap, and the car was greedily drinking the water from the canteen.

It was hot inside and outside the car, and Lily fell into a desert trance. As grandmother slammed the hood, a loud *plop* awakened her, and Lily watched as she refilled the canteen at the air and water station.

Lily again placed the I'm-older-than-I-look smile on her face as grandmother approached the driver's seat. Sometimes she could be fooled into talking to Lily as she would another grown-up. Grandmother pushed the starter button, and Black Beauty let out a low growl, sputtered, and they slowly eased onto the highway.

Lily didn't hesitate to start up the conversation again. "Was my mother your oldest girl, grandmother?" Like a good lawyer, Lily already knew the answer to her question, but she was convinced that her grandmother liked and needed to talk.

"No, Veda is the oldest, but Ellen was my favorite, and I told anybody who would listen. She was a good girl, and when my other girls turned on me when I was fooling with C. C., Ellen told them to leave me alone, and she apologized when they said they hated him."

Pet paused; there was a part of her that wanted to keep talking and another part that said, *"Lily ain't grown."* Pet's mention of C. C.

made Lily cringe. She forgot all about hearing stories of her mother. The night of the pots and pans came back to her as if it had happened a few hours before.

It had started with one pot that Lily had not cleaned to C. C.'s specifications. She was inside doing her nightly kitchen chores, while her grandmother and her pretend-husband, C. C., were listening to a San Francisco Giants game. Lily could hear the sound of the crickets chirping outside and Lon Simmons duly announcing a home run by one of the Giants' opponents. There was no roar from the crowd.

Grandmother's dinner consisted of a casserole that had stuck to the bottom of the pan. Lily knew better than to leave it soaking in the sink because she was not allowed to leave anything in the sink. After several attempts at cleaning the pan, Lily gave up. She rinsed it and turned it over to dry, hoping that no one would notice.

Lily's heart skipped a beat as she recalled being awakened in the middle of the night to clean the roasting pan. C. C. had stood over her, screaming and snatching her out of the bed at the same time. As Lily stood at the sink, half asleep, she began crying while washing the pan. She found a steel-wool scrubber and was using all of her strength to loosen the dried-on food. She could barely see the pan through her tears.

When she was just about done with the pan, she ran her fingers across the bottom and sides of the pan to make sure she had left nothing behind. But then C. C. came up from behind her with more pans. And insisted that all of them needed to be scrubbed. Lily recalled being forced to wash pans all night long. Maybe it wasn't all night, but it felt like all night. And where was grandmother? Lily could not recall. That painful memory did not include grandmother's whereabouts.

"Girl, have you heard one word that I've said over the past ten minutes?"

Lily stared at her grandmother as if she had never seen her before. "Sorry, grandmother, I guess I must've fallen asleep in all this heat." She wiped the dampness off of her forehead with the back of her long, slender-brown arm and held her forearm out for her grandmother to see the sweat.

Her grandmother looked but said nothing. Lily sat back in her car seat and stared out at the telephone poles whizzing by in the hot desert air. Lily still hated him. And at that moment, she hated her mother for leaving her in this mess. Why did she have to go and die anyway?

"Grandmother, why did Marie and them run away from home?" Like the question earlier about who was the oldest, Lily already knew the answer.

"Well, them fast girls of mine just wouldn't stay put. They was always slipping out, chasing after one boy or another, and I wasn't about to be raising no grandkids when they got pregnant. They did the right thing to get out of my house!"

Just what I thought she'd say, Lily thought. Jesse, Louis, and Arthur looked really good next to C. C. But at least grandmother had left him. It had taken several more nasty incidents, like the pots and pans, but she had finally left. Lily already knew why grandmother had no children at home. They had all left because of him.

The needle on the gas tank was holding steady on the dash's red mark, and Black Beauty was beginning to cough and sputter. Pet had hoped that they had enough gas to make it to Palm Springs, but Black Beauty had other ideas. Pet was feverishly looking for a gas station and finally saw a red and white 76 sign up ahead. The sweat on her brow was more about finding a station than the heat inside the car.

Lily decided that this would be a perfect time to have a good daydream. When grandmother stopped at the gas station, Lily stayed put in her seat and thought again about their visit with her cousins.

Nedra and Ray would be sleeping in and making all kinds of goo-goo noises in the bedroom, and the kids would be super quiet so they could hear the secret lovemaking. Later in the day, Monie would be walking to the park, flirting with the boys playing basketball. And just before dark, Ray Jr. would have all the kids in the shed behind the chicken coop, telling tales so wild that they'd all be too afraid to walk back to the house.

Lily smiled again; life wasn't too bad after all.

CHAPTER 46

I Thought You Were a Cold-Hearted Woman

After stopping at the gas station, the last fifty miles of the trip went quickly. Lily couldn't wait to see her friend Latisha Kay again, but who she really missed was old man Broussard. She missed her morning breakfast with him, especially rising early and sitting quietly with him while he prepared the family's breakfast.

As they pulled into the driveway, Mr. Broussard was the first person she saw standing on the front porch. His beard seemed longer and whiter, and he flashed a big smile in her direction.

Lily grabbed the car's door handle, then paused, glanced at her grandmother, who was looking mean again, slowly sat back in her seat, and let go of the handle.

"Go on, girl; I know you can't wait to get out of the car. Shoot, I'm tired too." Pet pulled up the emergency brake and stepped outside in the hot, dry air. "Lily, after you go to the bathroom, you come back here and help me unpack this car. I'm tired!"

"Yes, ma'am," Lily replied. She ran at break-neck speed and jumped into Mr. Broussard's arms. He was startled by the force of her jump against his tall, lanky frame, and he fell back a few steps. It seemed that Lily had grown so much, and her long legs were dangling near his ankles.

He gently put her down and said, "Lily, I can't believe you've grown so much. You've only been gone a few weeks. How was your trip?"

Before she could answer, he inquired, "And how was it visiting with your sister and brother?"

"Oh, Grandpa Broussard, I had fun and…" Lily paused. She had accidentally called him Grandpa Broussard. What was she thinking? She immediately began sweating and itching, and stinging in all the wrong places. She glanced in her grandmother's direction, but grandmother was busy grabbing things from the trunk of the car. She hadn't heard.

Old man Broussard, on the other hand, had heard her, and he was pleased. He had missed Lily. He loved all of his grandchildren, but Lily had a kind, comforting presence that seemed to bring peace to the house even when it was full of rambunctious children.

"Ooh, Wee!" Latisha Kay came running to Lily. "Lily, you back! We missed you!"

Lily grinned and watched as Latisha Kay rushed up from the backyard. Her shiny Shirley Temple curls bounced playfully, and she had a doll in each hand. She stopped short just as she reached Lily. "You're tall," Latisha Kay pouted. "You're too tall!" She crossed her arms and looked defiantly at Lily.

"But I still like to play dolls," Lily responded. She reached for one of the dolls, and Latisha Kay, without hesitating, handed her one.

Mr. Broussard had watched the exchange between the two girls and smiled. He stepped down from the porch and greeted Lily's grandmother. "Hey, Pet, it's good to see you. You need some help with your things?"

"Shit, you know I need help," she laughed. "Here, grab these." She handed him several bags from the car. "By the way, you got a beer? That was a long trip, and I'm sho' glad to be back, but I need a drink. Where's everybody at? I don't see the rest of the kids."

Mr. Broussard grabbed her bags and chuckled to himself. The difference between the greeting from Lily and Pet was like night and day. "Well, the wife has gone into town to start buying school clothes for the children, and she decided she couldn't take them all at one time."

He and Pet walked into the house, and he placed her bags on the kitchen counter. They both gravitated toward the living room, and she sat on the couch. He sat opposite of her on an armchair.

"Pet, tell me, how was your trip? I was worried about Lily; she seemed hell-bent on seeing her sister and brother. Did everything work out all right?"

Mr. Broussard had stepped into the kitchen and brought back a beer for each of them. The swamp cooler was working overtime to keep the house cool in the late summer heat. The air blowing from the cooler made the room smell like a fishpond. It was noisy, and both of them had to speak loudly to be heard.

"Look, you asking a lot of questions. Give me a minute to catch my breath." Pet picked up a newspaper from the coffee table and began fanning herself.

"You right. Sorry, it's just that I been thinking a lot about you two since you've been gone, and I'm just nosy, that's all." He laughed and pulled out his handkerchief to wipe his sweaty brow.

"Well, Broussard, let's just say that you were right. Lily did need to see her brother and sister. I haven't seen Lily that happy since before her mother died.

"Nedra and Ray want me to take all of Ellen's children, and I've thought about it, but I'm just not sure. There's no doubt that they'll be better off 'cause the way Orville and Annie are raising them is not right."

Pet looked at the sweat dripping from the cold bottle of beer, picked it up, and took a long swig.

"Fact of the matter is, either I'll take them, or I'll let Ray and Nedra take them. But whatever I do, them kids need to all be together. They've got a special bond that only kids that have suffered as much as they have could understand."

Mr. Broussard stared at Pet. He didn't realize that she had thought that much about the children. The trip, especially the long drive, must have given her time to reflect. He scratched his beard and ran his fingers through his curly, silver-grey hair.

Pet stared back at him. Drinking the cold beer had cooled her down, both physically and mentally.

"What would you do in my situation, Broussard? Would you take all the kids?" She took another swig of the beer, which was no longer as cold as her first sip.

Mr. Broussard leaned forward on the armchair, squinted from the stream of sunlight coming through one of the living room windows, and raised one eyebrow in Pet's direction.

"You know, Pet, when I first met you, I thought you were a cold-hearted woman." He leaned back into the armchair cushions, laughing, "but now I see you in a different light. You do care about your grand-kids, don't you?"

Before answering, Pet also sat back and thought about how to respond. Her beer no longer looked appealing; since all of the beads of moisture were gone, it now looked like a hot bottle of beer. Pet gazed thoughtfully at the no-longer-appealing silver and blue-labeled bottle of beer. She knew that she saw her children and the nieces and nephews that she had helped raise as no more than bur-dens. A burden to feed, a burden to clothe, a burden to find decent housing for, just plain burdens. Having her daughter die and leave her with three more burdens most times just felt unfair. And if she let herself, she could justify not taking on the new, forced-upon-her burdens.

As Broussard sat there, he watched Pet's face turn from anger to indignation to despair. He wanted to help her. He scooted forward on the armchair again and said, "Don't beat yourself up, Pet. Taking on three kids after all of yours are grown and left home has gotta be hard. Why don't you do what I tell my wife to do when she's trying to make a tough decision? Write down the pros and cons of taking on the grand-kids or letting Nedra and Ray have them. Then think about it, at least for a couple of days."

Pet visibly relaxed and smiled for the first time since returning to Palm Springs. "That's a damn good idea! Now bring me a new beer, I need a cold one!"

As Broussard returned with the second beer, Pet smacked her lips together, anxiously reaching for the bottle. Her mouth was beyond dry, and she moistened her lips by flicking her tongue back and forth across them. She placed the cold bottle of beer against her lips and savored the coolness that she felt. She placed the beer on the back of her neck and sighed with pleasure. She was finally cooling down.

She gazed in Broussard's direction, feeling completely at ease. He was again sitting opposite her in his armchair, looking pleased. He had, after all, discovered a Pet that he liked to spend time with.

"You know, Broussard, you Creoles are different than other colored folks." She looked at his fine, dark features, whose keen appearance could be mistaken for a white man except for his ebony complexion.

"Why, Pet, what do you mean?" He shifted in his chair, not sure where Pet was taking the conversation. He self-consciously stroked his beard, making sure it was still there.

"Oh, I don't know, just look at the way your family is. I mean, you got dark-skinned children and light-skinned children, and children that could pass for white and children that look like Mexicans. And, of course, your daughter looks every bit as colored as me. Matter of fact, she the only one who seems worried about her color."

Broussard visibly relaxed and sat back in his chair. "Well, Pet, we Creoles are different. We got all them races you talkin' about in us. We ain't ashamed of who we are. We know we ain't colored, and we know we ain't white; we mixed. But the white man sees all of us as colored, and we done come to terms with that too." Broussard was beginning to get restless and stood up and walked over to the window. Pet's gaze followed him.

"But I know what you mean, Pet. I've seen too many colored men and women ashamed of their colored blood. But the biggest problem I see is how they treat each other! They always talking about light and dark, but as you can see, we Creoles got it all, and we proud!

Now, you know my daughter is very prejudiced, she can't stand her dark-skinned children, and she cherishes the light ones, especially my oldest granddaughter, Shirley, 'cause she looks white.

All of my daughter's beliefs come from self-hatred. Fact of the matter is, I think she married her husband 'cause he looks like a white man with dark skin. She knew she couldn't marry no white man, but a colored man who looks like her wouldn't give her a second look. You know why? 'Cause she looks too colored!"

Pet was also getting restless, but she chose to stay put on the couch. She could feel her body warming up again, but it had nothing to do with the heat in the living room; it had to do with the subject. She thought about the men in her life and how rarely they saw her as attractive. She had been told at an early age that she was not pretty and she should be grateful for any man who paid attention to her.

And she knew what it meant to not be pretty. It meant she had no white features. None. Her hair was short and nappy, her nose broad, her lips thick, and she had a high forehead. Jesse's image loomed in front of her, and she immediately recognized that he was attracted to her, and he was Creole. Creole men accepted all forms of colored women, and Jesse adored her. He didn't seem to mind her "colored-ness."

Pet suddenly looked up and saw Broussard staring down at her. She didn't know how long he had been standing there. He had an odd expression on his face that she didn't recognize.

"Pet, my wish is that in my lifetime, folks won't be so worried about color and features. We all God's children, and the sooner we figure that out, the sooner we'll all be better off. You've suffered a major tragedy in your life with the death of your daughter. And I'm here to tell you that I'm an old man, and I've seen pain and suffering before. Why don't you start by trying to love yourself?" Before she could answer, he leaned over and kissed the top of her head. She blushed and furiously began fanning herself with the newspaper again.

Pet and Broussard both looked up as they heard a loud creak from the front-screen door opening. Latisha Kay and Lily rushed in, the perfect picture of dark and light. Both had beads of perspiration on their foreheads and laughter in their eyes.

"Grandpa," Latisha Kay said, still breathless and sweaty from playing in the backyard with Lily, "since it's the weekend and we don't have homework, can you teach us how to make oatmeal cookies?"

She and Lily's hands were clasped together, their arms swinging rhythmically to a beat no one else heard.

Lily's mouth began watering at the thought of eating a homemade dessert. Baking, or cooking for that matter, was not high on her grandmother's list of things she enjoyed doing. The last time Lily had homemade dessert was when she and her mother had made shortbread cookies, and she got to eat some of the raw dough—yum!

Lily glanced furtively in her grandmother's direction. She seemed to be in an okay mood.

Pet, a little annoyed by the children's interruption, rose from the couch, gathered some of the bags from her car, and said to Broussard, "Well, I'll go on and finish unpacking. She mumbled something to herself as she padded down the hallway to her tiny bedroom.

Before she and Lily left for the trip to Sacramento, she had reluctantly agreed with Broussard that it would be cheaper for her to move in with them. This way, Lily would not have to go home every weekend; they'd already be together in one house. Money-wise, it was a good move. But on days like today, Pet was annoyed with herself 'cause she would have liked to have been alone in her own quiet place to think about their heavy conversation. And it was heavy.

She put her things down in the middle of the floor. Her narrow cot sat alongside the wall, next to the window, which was propped open with a sturdy block of wood from the scrap lumber left over from the chicken coop. The thin, brightly-colored curtains swayed listlessly with the faint breeze blowing in from the west.

Walking up to a narrow wall mirror that was placed near the entryway to her room, Pet studied her face. The dark face looked back at her. She inched closer. She could see the blackheads dotting her chin and the deep crease that extended from each side of her wide nostrils to just below her lips. Her face didn't look happy. No wonder Lily always seemed frightened whenever she looked at her.

The sun was setting, and it cast a golden hue that lit up her skin. It seemed to miraculously look lighter. Pet smiled at her face, and it smiled back. The dark shadows were gone, and she saw that her eyes were sparkling and her teeth pretty and white. The furrowed brow was also gone, and her nose didn't seem so wide or her lips so big. Why, her lips were shaped like a heart! The same shape that white women drew when applying cosmetics to their thin, straight mouths! Could it be that she determined how pretty or not pretty she was? Is this what the Creole men saw when they looked at her?

Just then, the bright, orange-yellow sun slipped from the horizon and plunged into nothingness. The room grew darker, and so did she. The shadows reappeared and her broad nose and big lips were back again. Her mood shifted, and she decided to call for Lily. She cracked the door open and shouted down the narrow hallway, "Lily, get in here and bring me a foot tub and fill it with hot water. My feet are killing me!"

Lily came from the kitchen, dragging her feet and pouting. She squinted her eyes in her grandmother's direction, trying to quickly gauge her mood. With the foot tub in hand, she cautiously approached her grandmother.

"Grandmother, when I'm done filling this pail with your hot water, can I go back to the kitchen? I think Mr. Broussard is gonna let me and Latisha Kay make cookies." Lily's question was spoken rapidly, her eyes downcast, bracing for the "no" which was most likely coming.

But her grandmother surprised her. Peeking out from her downcast, squinty eyes, Lily felt a glimmer of hope. The old woman was smiling. "Yeah, Lily, I remember making oatmeal cookies with my papa. He was a cook, you know, and he loved him some oatmeal cookies, especially with lots of raisins in them. You go on and have yourself a good time."

CHAPTER 47

Just Thinking About My Sister and Brother

Without hesitation, Lily bolted from her grandmother's small bedroom and raced to the bathroom in the hallway. She tried filling the pail from the sink, but it wouldn't fit, so she placed it in the tub, filled it with hot water, and clumsily brought it back to her grandmother. There was a trail of water splattered on the floor, but before her grandmother could complain, she grabbed a towel, placed it on the floor, planted her feet far apart, and skated across the floor, following the trail of water back to the bathroom.

Her grandmother eased her swollen feet into the pail of steaming hot water and smiled at Lily. At that moment, Lily looked so much like her Ellen that Pet wanted to cry.

Lily quickly dropped the wet towel in the dank washroom near the back porch, which was adjacent to the kitchen. Latisha Kay and Mr. Broussard were gathering the ingredients from the kitchen pantry. Lily noticed that they both had on matching multi-colored aprons, and her heart immediately sank. Why didn't she have an apron to wear?

Just when she was about to pout and look as pitiful as possible, she spied another apron on the back of one of the kitchen chairs. Her mood lifted immediately, and she beamed at both of them as she entered the pantry. As long as she had been living with the Broussards, she had never entered the pantry before. The smell of spices, sweet and savory, enveloped the room. One wall of the pantry was filled with colorful mason jars of jams and jellies, pickle relish, green beans, snap peas, peaches, stewed tomatoes. Why, to Lily, it looked like an old-fashioned grocery store! Another wall, shaded from the sunlight, was filled with brightly-labeled, white-tin canisters of flour, sugar, baking powder, baking soda, and cornmeal.

When Mr. Broussard removed the top from the canister of flour, Lily saw two green leaves sitting on top of the flour and frowned.

"What's the leaves doing in the flour?" she asked, looking at both Latisha Kay and Mr. Broussard with a puzzled expression. Latisha Kay knew the answer, but instead of answering Lily, she giggled.

"Well, you see, Lily," Mr. Broussard answered with a wise grin on his face, "there's no way to keep these darn weevil eggs out of flour and other dry goods. But them eggs won't hatch with a bay leaf or two added to the flour. My pappy taught me that one a long time ago, and it saves a lot of squeamish women from abandoning their baking chores." He looked at Lily, and they both joined in laughing with Latisha Kay.

"But is that going to make the cookies taste funny?" Lily asked.

"Of course not. Just wait; you'll see."

After placing all the ingredients on the kitchen countertop, Lily and Latisha Kay carefully measured the flour, baking powder, and salt, placing each ingredient in the wire sifter.

"Let me sift, I want to sift," Latisha Kay shouted.

"Hold your horses, girl. You'll all get a chance to make these cookies. Why don't we divide up the work? Lily, you can mix the sugar, eggs, and butter." He handed her a small glass mixing bowl. "And Latisha Kay, go ahead and sift the dry ingredients. Where's the raisins? You know we gotta have raisins!"

He clapped his hands together and surveyed the kitchen. Both girls' aprons were covered in flour, and one of the eggs Lily had placed on the counter rolled off and splattered onto the floor. Lily stopped, shocked, and looked from the floor to the counter to Mr. Broussard. "I'm sorry," she stammered, "I didn't know…"

"Don't worry, Lily," Mr. Broussard chuckled. "We got plenty of hens out there laying as many eggs as you want to break." He laughed again. "Just wet a kitchen cloth, and clean it up. Make sure to wash your hands with soap when you're done."

"Yes, sir," Lily replied. She could not believe that she was not going to be in a world of trouble. If that had been her grandmother, she would most likely have been scolded again and again for being so careless.

A half-hour later, the cookies were beginning to rise in the oven. The fresh-baked cookie smell wafted throughout the house, and the Broussard grandchildren, like zombies on the prowl for humans, gravitated toward the kitchen in droves. Playing outside seemed to take a back seat to the delicious smells coming from the kitchen.

As they lined up, Lily was again reminded of the first time she met the Broussards. She had thought that her grandmother was taking her to an orphanage. Seven kids, and none of them the same shade of brown. One could actually pass for white, Shirley the oldest one, who was rarely seen at home, two or three looked Mexican, and the rest looked colored but with keen features. This was her family now, and not surprisingly, she thought of them as much as she did her own sister and brother.

Lily was shocked to admit to herself that her sister and brother were no longer part of her everyday life, but the Broussards were. Was this God's way of telling her to forget them? She hoped not.

She tried to garner up images of Deenie and Lorna, the happy times they spent together in Sacramento. But now, all she could see were the images of their sad faces when she last saw them as she and grandmother were leaving Merced. Tears began welling up in her eyes just as Mr. Broussard re-entered the kitchen. She couldn't and didn't want to stop them. This was her time to be sad.

As he opened the oven door, the grandchildren let out a collective "Ooh wee," and took their places at the kitchen table.

They all knew grandpa's "no sweets before dinner" rule, but they knew that those rules were sometimes broken, especially if they sat down and quietly waited at the kitchen table.

Mr. Broussard had noticed Lily sitting by herself on the stool when he first entered the kitchen. "Why, what's the matter, Lily?" he inquired. He placed his white chef hat on the counter next to her and pulled up another stool alongside hers. Suddenly, a loud, deafening screech silenced the children's quiet-table talk. They all looked up in surprise. Mr. Broussard also looked at the stool, puzzled that he and the stool had caused so much noise. He lifted it and sat it as close to Lily as possible

Lily couldn't help herself. She quickly wiped her tears as he sat down. He was the epitome of the tall, dark, southern gentleman, and she wanted to answer his question. "Oh, nothing, just thinking about my sister and brother."

She could see the wiry white hairs on the back of his long, bony brown hands.

Broussard began his mesmerizing trick of flexing his fingers, separating his ring and pinky finger from his middle and index fingers, then putting his middle and ring fingers together as he stretched out his pinky and index fingers. It was an exercise he learned to do when preparing for piano lessons. It was also a perfect way to get his grandchildren to talk to him, especially when he felt they needed to talk.

He looked up at his oldest grandson, "Tony, grab the spatula and give your sisters and brothers one cookie each." (He paused between the last three words to emphasize his one-cookie-each rule). "And don't forget to come over here and give me and Lily one too!" He laughed gleefully, stroking his silver-white curly beard again.

The kitchen table was loud with the bantering of children swinging their feet and kicking each other under the table. Of course, they were all very happy to have a snack before dinner.

Both Latisha Kay and Tony were nibbling tiny pieces of their cookies, secretly eyeing each other to make sure that they were not the last one with nothing left to eat of their cookie.

When they were each down to one bite left, Latisha Kay got distracted and bit into her last bite. Tony immediately began his singsong, "Don't you wish you had some?" taunting her with his last bite of cookie. His arm swayed in front of her face with the cookie as if he were a maestro directing their school glee club.

Latisha Kay was furious and stalked out of the kitchen. Her brother had done it again. He was the only one at the table with any cookie left to eat! Tony savored the moment by sucking on each of the chocolate bits as he slowly eyed each cookie-less child at the kitchen table. There was a foul mood at the table as each child rose from the kitchen and ran outside to play.

Lily and Mr. Broussard remained seated after the other children left. She watched, mesmerized, as he continued his piano finger exercises. She became even more fascinated when he held up both hands and continued the exercise. She focused on his left hand and then his right hand. She felt like she was in a trance!

As Mr. Broussard continued flexing his fingers, he said, "Lily, you know we're your family, and your brother and sister are your family too. You CAN have both. He never took his eyes off of his flexing fingers or Lily. "You're gonna miss them, but believe me, you won't forget them. Between you and me, we're gonna keep reminding your grandmother that you need to see them – and they need to see you."

Just hearing his melodic, deep-baritone voice and watching his eyes dart from her to his fingers made Lily cry again. This time, she wasn't ashamed of crying; she knew Grandpa Broussard understood her sadness.

"But I don't understand why grandmother just doesn't keep us all together. It's just not fair!"

Mr. Broussard had never seen anger in Lily's eyes, but this time he did. Her heart-shaped lips, which were too big for her narrow face, seemed to swell up along with her woe-be-gone-looking brown eyes. He noticed that the tiny brown dot on her iris seemed even larger than he remembered.

"Lily, honey," he said as he covered his hands with her long slender ones, "You just wait. We'll make sure you regularly see your sister and brother. Maybe next time, we'll see if we can bring them here to visit you!"

The anger in Lily's eyes melted immediately. "You mean it, you really mean it?" she exclaimed. She was beside herself, already planning to ask if she could bring the cot that was stored in the wash house to the girl's room. She jumped up from her stool, encircled her arms around Mr. Broussard, and said, "Thank you! Thank you! You are gonna talk to my grandmother, right?"

"Whoa, slow down, girl. Let's take one day at a time. Like I said, I think between me and you, we can get her to our way of thinking. She really does want what's best for you, Lily. We just have to catch her at the right time."

CHAPTER 48

At Last, My Love Has Come Along

After Lily ran out to play with the rest of the children, Broussard sat back down on the stool, cupping his hands in his chin. He massaged his forehead with his thumb, index, and middle fingers, trying hard to rub the anxiety he felt from his throbbing head. One young mother's death had created a quagmire that even he didn't have all the answers for.

He heard footsteps and looked up as Pet entered his kitchen. She was dressed in her usual, brightly colored muumuu but had a scowl on her face that didn't match her festive attire. She didn't return Mr. Broussard's tentative smile, so he rose, and before she could stop him, gave her a big bear hug, swinging her body back and forth with his strong grasp. Involuntarily, she relaxed in his arms.

"Pet, you looked like you needed a hug. Hope you don't mind." Before she could answer, he continued, "You know, Pet, I want what's best for you and your grandchildren, right?"

She sat down heavily on the stool next to him, picked up a toothpick from the countertop, and jabbed it between her bottom middle teeth. She began sucking noisily on the toothpick, staring intently at his hands which were clasped together on the counter.

She finally answered him, "Why do I have a feeling that I know where this conversation is going?" She laughed, erasing the scowl that had been present just a few minutes before.

"Look, I overheard a little bit of what you and Lily were talking about earlier, and I don't want us to get her hopes up. I've told you before that dealing with them Jenkins ain't no joke! Them some evil people."

She stood up and peered out through the kitchen window as she watched and listened to a flock of red-winged blackbirds chattering away in the cottonwood tree in the backyard.

Mr. Broussard followed her gaze.

She turned back around and said, "Now, Nedra and Ray, they good people, don't get me wrong, but I also got to deal with Annie, Orville, Bertha, and their evil-assed sister, Bobbie. They been calling Nedra and Ray, saying Deenie and Lorna are Orville's children, and they don't want them raised by me or anyone else in my family. Can you believe that? And on top of that, they know their brother and Annie don't care nothing about them kids. And Ray been back-sliding 'cause he ain't happy about Nedra wanting them to raise Orville's children."

Pet's scowl was reappearing, and her face was flushed with the rising anger she felt at her and Lily's current predicament.

Broussard sat quietly and listened. He maintained eye contact with Pet as he crossed and uncrossed his long legs, but finally, he stretched out both legs and looked down at his brown loafers. He was at a loss as to how to comfort Pet.

"The trouble with the Jenkins is that they know their brother doesn't want them kids, they don't want the responsibility, and they don't want me to have them. The last thing on their mind is the well-being of Ellen's poor children."

Mrs. Contrale, Mr. Broussard's daughter, also entered the kitchen. As usual, she was dressed to the nines in a long, silk, emerald-green dress that looked out of place in the informal kitchen. She was usually holed up in her room, trying hard to isolate herself from her children and any other members of the family, but she was hungry, and no one had informed her that dinner was about to be served. She gave Pet a haughty look and smiled sweetly at her father.

"Daddy, when we gonna eat?"

"Well, Lettie, why don't you call your children in and have them set the table? Everything is ready, so me and Pet will go into the living room and finish our conversation."

As he was talking, he and Pet left the kitchen.

Lettie, astonished at being so summarily dismissed, snarled in Pet's direction. She stomped to the kitchen's screen door and screamed for her children to wash up for supper.

As Broussard and Pet settled in the living room, Pet managed to calm herself down a bit. She pulled out a handkerchief from her muu-muu pocket and dabbed at the sweat on her forehead.

Mr. Broussard could feel the pain radiating from Pet's heart to his. "Pet, there's got to be a feasible solution that will make everybody…"

Before he could finish, Pet interrupted him, "Like I said, you don't know them Jenkins—most of 'em are evil incarnate! I have a mind to give them Lily too, but I know they would mistreat her, just like they mistreated my Ellen. If any three kids should be together, it's them three!"

Lettie overheard the conversation from the kitchen. She sidled slyly into the living room and sat in the armchair next to her father.

"Why don't y'all just put them kids up for adoption, with the stipulation that they be kept together?" Lettie smiled and winked at Pet as she inched even closer to her father.

Pet felt a chill run up her spine, and she looked at Lettie as if a boa constrictor had just entered the room. The high-yellow, white-looking, scrawny bitch had just hit her last nerve.

Mr. Broussard saw Pet's reaction and knew that he needed to intervene immediately. "Daughter, why don't you go back to the kitchen and tend to your children's dinner," he pleaded. "Didn't you say you were hungry?" He quickly got up and ushered her back to the kitchen.

"I'll be back, Pet; just sit tight."

Pet sat tight, but she was fuming. A vision of Ellen's face loomed directly in front of her. It was replaced by another image of Ellen and Orville on their wedding day. Thinking about it automatically put a smile on Pet's face. She could erase any anger she felt when she played the Ellen and Orville wedding movie in her head. The movie now playing in front of her eyes was sharp and in vivid color!

Pet had to give Ellen credit; she'd snared a good-looking young man who made most of Ellen's contemporaries wet their panties just thinking about him. Shit, everyone who attended the small ceremony described him as Merced's finest colored catch.

Her Ellen was no slouch either. She had her father's honey-brown skin, tall stature, and the sweetest smile. Thinking of Ellen's father immediately brought DH to Pet's mind, and again in her mind's eye, she could see him standing proud at the make-shift altar at the downtown Merced County courthouse.

Orville had been drafted into the Korean War, and fearing that he would not be able to tie the knot before his deployment, had rushed the family into a quick ceremony.

When Pet had called DH to see if he would come, he was still married to Cynthia. She had hoped that if he did, Cynthia would not accompany him. To her pleasant surprise, when she met him at the bus station, he had arrived on time, and he had come alone!

Pet had dressed carefully for DH. No muumuu that day. And oh, how DH had looked so fine. He had stepped off the bus, grabbed his bag from the porter, and hopped into Black Beauty before she could bat an eye. He eased back in the car seat, grinned at her as she sat down, and reached over to give her an awkward hug.

"Sorry, Pet, I should have hugged you on the platform, but shucks, you know how you women are. Cynthia is so jealous, and I saw that colored porter looking at us. Next thing you know, the whole town will say we getting back together." He laughed. "How's my daughter doing? You like that scoundrel she calling herself marrying?"

Pet continued to stare at him, taking in his face as if seeing it for the first time. She wanted to memorize it. His thinning brown hair was cut short in the popular covadis hairstyle that colored men wore. He had, of course, left it long enough to show off the waves on the top of his head. His piercing, hazel eyes still had that effect on her. She tightened her thighs to try to stave off the warm feeling down there. He wore his ever-present brown khaki pants and expensive Stacy Adams loafers that looked like he had just left the shoeshine boy.

Pet looked down at her starched blue dress and simple black pumps and wished she had tried harder to pick out something a little more sexy to wear, but truth be told, her wardrobe was limited. She had at least put on red lipstick and powdered her face and neck. Her skin felt prickly, but she dared not scratch and ruin her makeup.

DH laughed again, breaking her spell, "Did you hear me, woman?"

"Oh, sorry, yes, I don't know much about him, Ellen's crazy about him, though, and he's a good-looking man." She started the car and headed straight to the courthouse. As they drove down Thirteenth Street, DH rolled his window down and swung his hand back and forth, spreading his fingers apart as the wind rushed through them. Pet watched and said nothing, pleased to observe that DH's habits had not changed.

"Well," DH said, "how is he taking to the fact that Ellen's already got a child? Lily's what, 'bout two years old now?"

Pet had driven in front of the courthouse and noticed several other couples standing outside. The men wore Air Force or Army dress uniforms, and the brides-to-be wore simple, short white dresses with no accompanying hats or veils. Orville and Ellen stood out because they were the only colored couple milling about.

Pet eased off of the clutch and pulled up on the parking brake, and turned to face the handsome man that she had once almost married. "Believe it or not, he didn't say one word, seems to take to Lily as if she was his own. Course folks tell me he was so strung on Ellen that it wouldn't have mattered if she had a pet chimpanzee for a daughter!"

Their laughter echoed out into the street, and Orville and Ellen looked up and ran to the car to greet them. Pet and DH jumped out of the car, and all four of them embraced in a group hug. The whites looked on with mild interest

The ceremony was over in less than five minutes, and as the young couple embraced with a long, haunting kiss, Pet and DH, sitting in the middle pews, sighed and looked at each other and grinned sheepishly.

There was no doubt in DH or Pet's mind that they were thinking about what their life would have been like had they been married. DH knew that he did not love Cynthia, and Pet knew that no man, not Louis, or Jesse, or Arthur, could replace DH.

The kitchen screen door slammed, jolting Pet from her memory movie.

Mr. Broussard was surprised to see Pet sitting in the same spot with an odd, faraway look in her eyes.

"Pet, you in the same spot, and I been gone longer than I expected." He sat next to her in the armchair, continuing his habit of rubbing his hands through his curly hair.

"Look, Pet, I'm sorry about my daughter. She don't know nothing about nothing but always got something negative to say. It ain't just your grandkids; the only person she cares about is herself. Hell, she don't care nothing about her own children. Me and the Mrs. always said we should've had more children, and maybe she wouldn't have turned out so selfish!"

Pet couldn't help but notice the anger and frustration creeping into his voice.

It had never occurred to her before, but now Pet realized that both, Mr. and Mrs. Broussard, tip-toed around their daughter as if they thought she was a time bomb about to explode.

Lettie stayed in her room, ignored by her parents and children, except for the youngest one, Alicia, who had not quite gotten the message that her mother did not want to be bothered. Later, she ventured out to accompany her other almost-white friend to a card party hosted by a local bridge club who allowed lighter-skinned "coloreds" to attend their monthly events.

"My daughter," Mr. Broussard said as he rose from the chair and stood over Pet, "is the meanest, most selfish person I know. I can't believe that she told you to put them kids up for adoption! And I can't wait for my wife to return from visiting her ailing mother. She been gone almost a month, and the first thing I'm gonna tell her is we need to get our daughter up out of here!"

His voice rose to a high pitch, and Pet looked up at him, alarmed.

"Now, Broussard, you don't mean that. Hell, I don't pay her no attention. You ain't got to do or say nothin' on my account."

Pet rose from the couch, walked slowly toward the phonograph, selected a '78 Etta James album, and placed the needle on the third groove to her favorite song, "At Last."

"Now, look here, Broussard, you missing your wife, and you need a break. Why don't you sit back, relax, and call her on the phone? She probably has put her mother down for the night and waiting for you to call."

"Pet, you know how much Central charges for long-distance calls, and rates don't go down 'till 10:00 o'clock tonight!"

The thought of his wife, along with the soulful sound of Etta flooding his ears and heart, had immediately lightened Broussard's mood.

Pet grabbed the black desk phone, whipping the cord to unravel it, and handed the phone to Mr. Broussard.

He grinned, "Girl, you'd talk a dog off a meat wagon if he gave you half the chance!" He grabbed the phone, and without hesitating, dialed his wife's number.

Pet smiled and left him and Etta and the Mrs. in the living room and sauntered back to her bedroom. She marveled at how good she felt even though the evening had started off with a nasty comment from Mr. Broussard's daughter.

Once in her room, she'd wished there was another phone in the house. Without hesitating, she grabbed her car keys and headed for the nearest payphone, which was just one exit away on Highway 395. She didn't say anything to anyone as she was leaving

It was a warm evening, and the phone booth was full of moths and other insects drawn to the lone lightbulb. Pet dialed the operator, holding tightly to a fistful of quarters that she had brought along. The buzzing from the insects was loud, but she was on a mission to call DH and temporarily could not hear them.

His wife would be at choir practice, and she knew he was waiting for her call. At the operator's instructions, she dropped in the $3.75 for the first three minutes. As she dropped the quarters into the slot, each ding brought her closer to talking to the only man she had really loved.

He answered on the first ring, "Pet, girl, I'm sho' glad you called. What took you so long? Well, never mind, give me the phone booth number so when our time is up, I can call you right back."

She saw a trucker walking toward the phone booth, and Pet turned her back so she wouldn't have to see his face. This was her time to talk to her man.

"Guess what song I was listening to just before I called?"

The trucker circled the phone booth, noticed that Pet was ignoring him, and finally walked away.

The phone lines had begun their snapping and crackling sounds, and Pet and DH paused, waiting for the noise to dissipate.

When the lines were clear again, Pet could see DH's smile floating through the phone lines.

"At Last," he said.

After DH quietly slipped the phone back into its cradle, he put his head down between his knees. He could hear his two boys studying quietly in the other room, and he was grateful that he had one night a week to escape from his wife. Talking with Pet was such a welcome relief from the constant on-edge feeling he experienced living with Cynthia.

In his mind, his face was a dead giveaway to the love he felt for Pet. If his sons saw him now, they'd know; after all, they were teenagers and had a knack for picking up his moods.

His other son, Leonard, was five years older and had joined the Army. He had asked DH to sign the army papers so that he could enlist early. DH knew that the constant tension was a strain on all of his children, especially Leonard, because of his sensitive nature.

And what would they think if they knew they had a sister who had killed herself? Those were two facts that DH hoped would never reach their ears, even though every time DH spoke with Pet, he'd hang up the phone, knowing they should have at least known that their sister, Ellen, existed.

Ellen and Leonard were born within weeks of each other, and DH suspected that his wife, Cynthia, knew but chose to never speak of his bastard child, who was born in the same hospital as their son.

DH also suspected that his wife knew of the Thursday evening telephone calls, even though he always managed to get home early enough before the postman delivered their monthly phone bill. It was a cat-and-mouse game they had played for many years, and each, in turn, knew their part.

DH unraveled the phone cord and tip-toed it back to the living room.

Pet placed her phone back into the metal cradle just as the trucker returned, glaring menacingly in her direction. She avoided eye contact and stepped out of the phone booth, hurrying to her car.

As Pet approached her car door, she heard the trucker's booming voice from the phone booth, "Can you believe a nigger taking her sweet time, making *me* wait."

Pet slammed her car door, grinned to herself, and gunned Black Beauty's motor out of the parking lot. When she got on the road, she said to herself, "Serves that cracker right. Shoot, I was there first, and I ain't gotta hurry my conversation for his white ass!"

Broussard was just hanging up the phone when Pet came into the living room.

"How's Mrs. Broussard doing? I sure do miss that old gal."

Mr. Broussard grinned sheepishly, got up, and placed the phone back on the end table. He noticed a deep scratch that marred the dark, brown-stained table and the accumulated dust sitting atop the table. Without hesitation, he grabbed the handkerchief from his flannel shirt and dusted it.

"Oh, she's fine. She'll be back next week. I can't wait to see her, hell, if nothing else, to clean up this place!"

Pet and Mr. Broussard laughed.

"Shoot, Pet, to tell you the truth, my wife has never been away from me that long, and I sure do appreciate your company while she's been gone. Hell, I remember the last time she left me here with these grandkids by myself—'specially since my daughter is mighty useless. Shit, I didn't know whether to shit or go blind with all that responsibility. Washing clothes, cooking, cleaning, helping with homework—I don't know how you women do it."

Pet laughed, "Hell, I don't do none of that. I got Lily trained, she do everything I tell her to do, and she know better than to give me any mouth, and I…" Pet stopped mid-sentence when she saw Mr. Broussard's jaw drop. He was no longer laughing with her.

"Look, Broussard, I raised my children different than you Broussards do. We a different kinda colored from you Creoles. We don't believe in coddling our children. As soon as they old enough, shoot, they out in the field, cutting grapes, pitching watermelon, chopping and picking cotton. Even though Lily worked alongside me every day, I sho' put my hand out at the end of the day to get what she earned to help put food on our table!"

Pet had worked herself into a fit of self-righteousness borne out of embarrassment and shame. She wiped the sweat accumulating on her brow. Ever since Pet had moved in with the Broussards, she had witnessed a different way of raising children that was far removed from her own experience.

Broussard's gentle ways of interacting with his grandchildren, the delight he took in preparing meals for them, and the interest he expressed in their young lives was implausible. Pet couldn't fathom how not to treat children badly. Where do you start?

Broussard sat watching Pet, seeing the mixed emotions cross her face. "Look, Pet, a colored child has a hard row to hoe in this life. We in 1959; we ain't got a lotta money, and no decent jobs. Hell, we can't even apply for welfare without them visiting our house once a week to check in on us and make sure ain't no man living in the house!

"We Creoles, as you call us, do spoil our children, but we do so intentionally. Don't you see how Lily has blossomed since she's been here? I actually see her smile and laugh every day, and she wasn't doing that when you all first arrived. That girl has lost her whole family, and I think it's up to all of us to give her all the love she can stand!"

Pet hadn't said a word since Broussard began his lecture. She just sat and allowed the tears to roll down her creased face, not even trying to wipe them away.

Broussard shook the dust from his handkerchief and handed it to Pet.

She took it, but instead of blowing her nose, she got up, and without saying a word, walked to the back screen door, opened it, and stared out into the pitch-black backyard.

The next morning, a lone dragonfly with its brightly colored, long, thin body landed on a dry blade of grass in the backyard. Pet, who was sitting outside with her morning cup of coffee, recognized it as a Desert Firetail. The thin, wispy wings were almost invisible against its bright, long, red body. She watched it in silence. It took off again, this time hovering over the cottonwood tree, then zig-zagging among the few flowering cacti in the yard. Another dragonfly joined it, and the two of them flew side by side and disappeared above the cottonwood trees. If only life could be that simple, she thought. She pulled Broussard's handkerchief from her pocket and wiped her nose, and went back inside.

After breakfast, Broussard retired to the living room and sat in the same chair he had sat in the evening before, listening to Etta again, and missing the Mrs. again.

Yesterday, he had seen Pet stuff his handkerchief in her muumuu pocket and walk away, and he had started to follow her but thought better of it. Pet and her grandchild situation was much too complicated for him to resolve.

Why not plan a party, he thought? Well, actually, Thanksgiving was next month. Why not talk to Pet about bringing Ellen's children here for Thanksgiving?

He couldn't help himself; he ran to Pet's tiny bedroom and knocked on her door. "Hey, girl, I got a proposition for you, and you're gonna love it," he shouted to her closed door.

Pet rose and opened her door. She was smiling, seeming to already be in a good mood. "What you want now?" she laughed. "You bringing me some money or something?"

"Pet, you know I'm broke. Hell, I'm so broke I can't even pay attention!"

"Well, if it makes you feel any better, if it was raining soup, I'd only have a fork in my hands!" They both laughed and walked toward the kitchen and sat at the table together.

"Say, Pet," Broussard continued in a more serious tone. "Most of our family is still in Louisiana, and we normally have a simple Thanksgiving meal here with just us. But I been thinking, why don't you bring Deenie and baby Lorna here for Thanksgiving and invite Nedra, Ray, and their children?"

Pet's squinty brown eyes lit up, and she broke into an infectious smile. "Really? Shit, are you serious?"

She rose from the kitchen stool and started pacing. Today's muumuu had been exchanged for a dark blue corduroy skirt and a wool sweater. A chill was in the air, and a draft of cool air was drifting through the usually hot kitchen. She crossed her arms and rubbed her hands up and down her forearms.

"The way I see it, this is the perfect time for us all to get together."

Broussard, seeing Pet's reaction to the chilly kitchen, stepped over to the door to make sure that it was closed tightly.

"Tell you what, you call them, and I'll work on the menu. You know I love to cook, and this will give me a good excuse to throw down a damn good Thanksgiving meal!"

Lily had overslept and walked into the kitchen later than usual. She was surprised to see her grandmother there and more surprised to see that old man Broussard had not started breakfast yet. She immediately stuck out her bottom lip and glanced at the slip of paper in Mr. Broussard's hand containing her request for today's breakfast menu.

Seeing her expression, Mr. Broussard said, "Oh, Lily, me and your grandmother were so busy planning Thanksgiving dinner that I forgot to cook breakfast." He laughed and looked at the slip of paper with Lily's scrawny handwriting. "Oh, I see you want banana pancakes again. You never get tired of them, huh?"

"No, sir," she responded. She sat on her favorite kitchen stool next to Mr. Broussard, looking jealously at her grandmother, and wondering again why SHE was here in her and Mr. Broussard's morning kitchen!

Mr. Broussard chuckled again, slipped on his apron, and pulled the flour from the pantry. Lily dutifully reached for the eggs and milk from the refrigerator. She glanced at her grandmother, giving her the "this-is-what-we do-in-the-morning look" and resettled herself on the kitchen stool.

Mr. Broussard saw the fire light up in Pet's eyes as she stared at Lily and decided he'd better diffuse the situation fast.

"Lily, what your grandmother and I were talking about was her bringing Nedra, Ray, your cousins, and your sister and brother here for Thanksgiving. What do you think of that?"

Lily almost fell off the stool, "You mean it? You really mean it?" Before she could stop them, huge, wet tears spilled out onto her face. She was grinning and crying at the same time. She ran over and hugged her grandmother, who almost fell from her perch on the kitchen stool.

Pet involuntarily hugged Lily back and looked puzzled that her hands were actually completely enveloping Lily. She was embarrassed. She wasn't sure why, but holding Lily felt strange. She could smell the pomade that she had applied to Lily's hair before she combed it, and it reminded her of earlier days, of holding Ellen as a young girl...

CHAPTER 49

Do You Have Any Sweet Milk?

Thanksgiving Day had finally arrived. At the first rooster's crow, Lily's eyes blinked open, and for once, she didn't have to think twice about jumping out of bed. Some mornings, she played a five-minute-more game with herself that consisted of snoozing every five minutes as she watched Big Ben quickly move from having plenty of time to get up and sit with Mr. Broussard, to barely having enough time to rush to the school bus, hungry, with Latisha Kay and Tony running behind her with sticky lips from the pancakes or French toast they'd had with Grandpa Broussard.

But this week, there was no school, and everyone was sleeping in except Grandpa Broussard. Lily could smell the fresh yeast rolls rising in the warm kitchen, and as she peeked inside the kitchen doorway (she couldn't let Grandpa see her unwashed face), she saw him slide the turkey out and moisten it with the turkey baster.

She hastily ran back to the bedroom she was sharing with Latisha Kay. Her brother Deenie and sister Lorna were still fast asleep on the cot that had been set up for them. Lorna had returned to sucking her thumb, and Lily watched as Lorna's thumb slowly slipped from her grasp and Lorna noisily sucked it back into her mouth. She could watch her sister all day long, but today was a big day, and she had been given a long list of chores by her grandmother. It seemed that every time she "got her way," her grandmother made sure she had so many chores that she couldn't really enjoy herself.

But Lily had a plan, sort of like the plan she concocted when she was forced to eat vegetables that she didn't like. She ate them first, then sat back and enjoyed the rest of her meal. She never understood kids who stared at their unwanted vegetables for hours. Two minutes of chewing and swallowing gross vegetables was nothing compared to the alternative chosen by most kids.

Pet stood in the doorway of her tiny bedroom, already sweating, already in a grumpy mood. "Lily!"

"Yes, ma'am," replied Lily. She snatched sleeping Lorna's thumb from her mouth and watched as Lorna squirmed in her cot and replaced it without waking. Lily smiled; having a baby sister was so much fun!

Before Lily could reach her grandmother's bedroom doorway, her grandmother hollered down the hallway, "Lily, I want you to go down to the corner store and see if they got any sweet milk." Her grandmother reached inside her bra to retrieve five dollars. "I need to make some eggnog for dinner; so see if they got any nutmeg 'cause old man Broussard say he don't have any more. And don't be long. I want you to come right back— wait a minute. Have you washed your face and brushed your teeth yet?"

Lily was stunned. She hadn't washed up, but she didn't know what to say. If she told the truth, she'd get in trouble because she was up and should have already taken care of it. And, of course, it would take her longer to be ready to go to the store.

But if she lied and said she washed up, her grandmother would scrutinize her face to see if it was clean enough. If it wasn't clean enough, her grandmother would accuse her of lying about having washed up. Lily figured that the odds that her face was clean enough, washed or not, were against her, and she decided to tell the truth.

"I'll go wash up now," and before her grandmother could chastise her, Lily sprinted in the direction of the bathroom and turned on the faucet, hoping that it would drown out any nagging coming from her grandmother's lips. It worked, because by the time Lily returned from the bathroom, her grandmother was in the kitchen, joking with Grandpa Broussard.

Lily snatched grandmother's money from the kitchen table and hurried out through the back door to the corner store. Another crisis averted!

At the corner store, Lily eyed the refrigerated section, looking for sweet milk. There was homogenized milk, buttermilk, half and half milk, and whipping cream, but no sweet milk. She went over to the canned milk section and saw evaporated milk and Borden's sweetened condensed milk, but no plain sweet milk.

Lily began to panic. If she came back with the wrong milk, she'd be in big trouble, especially since she was already skating on thin ice from not having washed her face this morning. She decided to ask the grocery clerk.

The clerk was a young girl, not much older than Lily. She was tall and thin with large blue eyes and wore her blond hair pulled back into a skinny ponytail. She was heavily made up with dark mascara and had on shiny pink lipstick.

"Do you have any sweet milk?" Lily asked.

The girl's jaw dropped, and she gave Lily a puzzled look. "Sweet milk? I never heard of it; we got all kinda milk, though." She laughed and turned around just as another man, older, probably her grandfather, stepped up to the counter. He, too, was laughing. He had the same thin, blond hair, but it was cut short, like a crew cut.

"Oh, you're looking for homogenized milk. It's on the middle shelf." When he saw Lily's puzzled look, he said, "Don't worry, homogenized milk and sweet milk are the same thing. In the old days, a lotta people drank buttermilk, but nowadays, people mostly use it for cooking. When somebody asks for sweet milk, they're really saying, they don't want buttermilk!"

"Okay," Lily said.

"Say, you must be related to that old colored woman that I see around here sometime. What's her name?"

"Oh, Pet, I mean, that's my grandmother," Lily replied.

"Yeah, girl, you don't have to worry; she just wants good, old-homogenized milk."

Shortly after Lily returned from her errand, dinner was served, and the house seemed to be bursting at the seams. Old man Broussard was dressed in his finest chef attire from his days as a cook for a well-to-do New Orleans family. The dining room table was set for fourteen with an exquisite white embroidered tablecloth, pink and blue flowered-China plates, their best silverware, white cloth napkins, and a large crystal punch bowl filled with Pet's frothy eggnog.

There were two red-lit candles, one on each end of the table, and as the children filed into the dining room, they each echoed oohs and ahhhs at the beautiful table setting.

Broussard stood at the head of the table, smiling and nodding to each person, young or old, as they entered the room. When his wife entered the dining room, a warm smile quickly spread across his face as his eyes locked with hers. He was so excited to have his wife back home, he could hardly contain himself. When she arrived home yesterday, she told him she couldn't wait to get back home to him because there was no place she'd rather be than home with him and the family during the holidays. He exhaled a long sigh, as he recalled she would have to leave again soon for at least a few more months to continue taking care of her ailing mother. But for now, he smiled as he glanced across the table at the love of his life.

Mrs. Broussard looked up and smiled as she felt her husband's eyes upon her. She looked around the table, taking in the presence and love of family. Her daughter, Lettie, sat next to her. Ray, Nedra, Pet, and the remaining children encircled the table. What a joyous occasion! Everyone seemed so happy, even Lettie, who had a smile on her face and seemed to be enjoying the guests.

The aromas of yeast rolls, candied yams, and turkey with dressing, and greens with ham hocks commingled and drifted through the air, seeming to lift everyone's spirit.

Mr. Broussard cleared his throat and stretched out both of his arms in a gesture meant to encourage all to clasp their hands together in prayer for the Thanksgiving feast they were about to devour. He said a silent prayer to God asking that his wife's upcoming departure to again care for her mother be brief. He missed her so.

After dinner, Lily quickly retreated to the backyard, hiding behind the tool shed beside the house. Departures were so hard for her. She watched as Nedra, Ray, their children, and her siblings packed into their old Buick. Her heart felt like it was breaking because she didn't know when she would see her brother and sister again. She couldn't stop the tears that slowly streamed down her face.

Once Lorna and Deenie were seated in the car, they craned their necks around looking for their sister as the car slowly drove away. *Where is she? We didn't get to say goodbye*, they thought.

CHAPTER 50

If Only Life Was Fair

The Thanksgiving holiday was over all too quickly. Lily sat on the back porch steps, pouting. It was warm out, especially for late November, and beads of perspiration dotted her forehead. She wiped her brow with the hem of her dress and muffled a sob that was threatening to become a loud wail. Lily busied herself with tying the shoelaces on her black and white Buster Brown's. She hated the shoes because no matter how hard she tried, she could not wear them out. The best that she could hope for was to outgrow them, but that would take forever.

If shoes could last so long, why couldn't families? What about her mother, stepfather, brother, and sister? Why couldn't they all be together and last for a long time in one house as one family? Then Lily remembered that her mother was dead; she certainly didn't last a long time. Her friends here at the Broussard's and at school had their whole family—they lasted a long time. It just wasn't fair!

Lily watched Latisha Kay playing a lone game of tetherball. She could feel Latisha Kay's eyes on her as she sat, continuing to pout at or to no one in particular. Latisha Kay would hit the ball, and as it swung around the pole, she'd shade her eyes from the bright morning sun and stare in Lily's direction. Lily kept her head down and refused to make eye contact.

Finally, Latisha Kay pushed the ball hard with both hands and, as it intertwined around the pole, walked away in frustration. She'd seen Lily like this before, and she was not about to let her continue pouting.

She ran over and stood over Lily, smacking hard on a big, pink, glob of Double Bubble gum. As Lily looked up, Latisha Kay thrust a wrapped piece of gum into her hands. Without speaking, Lily slowly unwrapped the piece of gum, glanced at the comic strip, and placed the gum into her mouth.

As the flavors burst onto her tongue, she swallowed, and slowly began chewing the sweet, juicy gum. Without pausing, she stretched the gum around her tongue and began blowing bubbles. Latisha Kay, not to be outdone, began chewing even more vigorously to create her own bubble. Both girls were facing each other and couldn't help but laugh at how each of them looked, having to use the back of their hands to wipe the excess drool gathering at the corners of their mouths.

Latisha Kay swallowed again, noticing that her friend's mood had lightened. "Look, Lily, why don't we go inside and play with our paper dolls?"

"We can't, my grandmother's here, and she don't like kids to play inside during the day—I just wish she wasn't so mean."

"Well, at least she talks to you. My Momma hates all of us kids, especially the dark ones. Don't you notice, Lily, that she don't have nothing to do with any of us, except, of course, my oldest sister, Shirley? But then again, Shirley can pass for white."

Both girls were now sitting on the back porch, the bubble gum stuck on the back of each hand, awaiting their next bubble gum-blowing contest.

"Yeah, I do notice that she's usually in her room or out with her friends. Looks like your grandparents are your real parents," Lily acknowledged.

This time it was Latisha Kay's turn to pout, "She doesn't come to our PTA, or our games, or holiday school events. Shoot, she hardly ever comes to mass with us on Sundays. I wish I had met your mother, Lily. it sounds like she was really neat, and I know she loved you a lot!"

From the porch, they watched Lily's grandmother leave in Black Beauty without saying a word to the girls. Both slipped inside as soon as her car rounded the corner. Latisha Kay pulled the paper dolls and scissors from a box in the closet, and both plopped onto their bed, one pulling out the paper outfits to dress the dolls, and the other carefully cutting out new shorts and dresses. They didn't talk; they were comfortable with the silence that had fallen on their bedroom.

They both jumped as they heard the back -screen-door close with a loud bang. It was Grandpa Broussard peeking inside their partially opened bedroom door with his hands behind his back.

"And what are you two young ladies doing inside this morning? It's your last free day before school tomorrow, right?"

"Yes, sir," they replied in unison.

Neither Lily nor Latisha Kay were worried about Grandpa Broussard. He didn't care if they played inside or not.

"I brought you something back from Woolworth's. Are you ready?"

Without hesitation, they both closed their eyes.

"You can open your eyes now, girls!" He had placed a dainty handkerchief doll in each of their outstretched hands.

Immediately the girls abandoned their paper dolls to examine their new, unique dolls. Lily's was pink with blue ribbons sewn into the hem, while Latisha Kay's was white with pink ribbons.

Mr. Broussard sat on the edge of the cot that had been left in the room for baby Lorna. "Now, when I peeped into your room, I noticed you both had some sad-looking faces. What's going on?"

"Oh, nothing, grandpa," Latisha Kay said. "I mean, we were both talking about our mothers, Lily's is dead, and my mother doesn't love me."

Grandpa Broussard was speechless at first, but after a brief pause, blurted out without thinking, "Why Latisha Kay, why would you say such a thing? Of course, your mother loves you; she loves all of her children!"

"Grandpa," Latisha Kay responded patiently as if speaking to a child. "Haven't you noticed she doesn't hug us or kiss us or tell us she loves us? When I visit my friends from school, their mothers are always loving on them. We just don't have that kinda mother!"

Grandpa Broussard knew what his grandchild was saying was true, but he didn't know that the children knew that it was true. He was at a loss for words, and he rose awkwardly from the cot. "You two enjoy your dolls."

As Broussard walked into the living room, he saw Pet sitting on the edge of the couch reading a newspaper. The room was dimly lit, and she was squinting at the fine print, sucking loudly on a toothpick.

"Play me some Etta again, Broussard. Shoot, I can use a taste of blues right now."

"You ain't said nothing but the word," he said solemnly. Broussard walked over to the shelf next to the record player, scanned the album covers, and pulled up Etta and Otis. "She sho' know how to wear them blonde wigs; look at her," he grumbled.

He placed the Etta James and Otis Redding albums onto the spindle, put the arm in place, and pushed the play lever. The phonograph automatically dropped the Etta album onto the turntable, and Broussard eased into the chair next to Pet.

It was getting close to noon time, and they could both hear the older kids in the kitchen making peanut butter and jelly sandwiches for the younger kids.

Pet grabbed the album cover, gazing at Etta's picture. She looked up at Broussard. "You got some kinda look on your face. What's the matter?"

Broussard quickly responded, "Funny you should ask, Pet. I just got through talking to the kids. You ever watch Art Linkletter's 'Kids Say the Darndest Thing' show?" Before Pet could answer, he continued, "Well, my granddaughter and your granddaughter know way more about life than we give them credit for. And the stuff that comes out of their mouths sure do make you wonder." Etta was wailing in the background, and he decided that now was not the time to listen to her.

He got up from the couch and put both albums at the top of the spindle but did not push the lever again. He absently ran his fingers through his curly hair and sat back down on the couch.

Pet was on the edge of her seat, wondering where this conversation was headed. "You see, Pet, we adults been thinking that kids are just that, kids. But in fact, they little people. We thought they didn't think like us, that they just had kid thoughts."

Pet had a puzzled expression on her face and interrupted him, "Broussard, what you talking about? Of course, they just kids!"

"No, I'm telling you that kids talk about death and life and love, just like we do. My granddaughter told me that her mother doesn't love her. Well, you know, me and the Mrs. know that our daughter is incapable of loving anyone but herself, but we didn't know that her children knew that too!"

Pet carefully placed the newspaper on the sofa beside her and leaned back into the couch. "Broussard, are you sure that you're not just imagining this?"

As Pet asked Broussard the question, she thought back upon her own childhood and the pain she felt when her mother sent her to live with her oldest sister, Hattie. Hattie was much older than Pet and had left home before Pet had even started grammar school. Pet never forgave her mother for sending her away, and even up to the day of her mother's passing, she and her mother had continued to have a strained relationship.

Not being able to live at home with her mother and other sisters and brothers was heartbreaking. Especially because the sister she was sent to live with treated Pet as her slave. Whenever Pet thought of her sister Hattie, all she could see were piles of shitty diapers and not being able to play with other kids her age. The feeling that she was not wanted stayed with her, even now. And, of course, she was Lily's age when that had happened to her.

"Pet, you there?" Broussard was standing by the phonograph, about to push the lever to start the turntable again. "Look like you deep in thought. What's on your mind?"

Pet laughed, "Yeah, I was just thinking you right—they are little people. Shit, I can remember being Lily's age, and yeah, we did think grownup thoughts. Like I was telling you the other day, you Creoles do raise your children differently."

Pet pushed the newspaper even further away from where she was sitting and spread her bulky frame further into the couch. She pointed her finger in Broussard's direction, "When we were growing up, I was way too scared to say grownup thoughts out loud. It was unheard of to even think about saying what was on our minds. We were taught to respect our elders with no talk back. Of course, the problem with our way of life is that as a grownup, you forget that children are much wiser than we give them credit for. You forget how you felt as a child when things were happening around you that you couldn't control."

A tear escaped, and Pet quickly wiped it away.

Except for the sound of the children in the kitchen, both sat silently in the living room, lost in their own thoughts.

Broussard carefully watched Pet's expressions. If he offered her unsolicited advice, she might not respond well. She was, no doubt, a woman who had experienced a hard life. She was dark, and in their colored world, both she and Broussard knew that along with her darkness came the scorn attributed to what her color represented.

In the several months that she and her granddaughter had been living with them, it was clear to Broussard that Pet was a thinking woman, but a woman who had been ignored as a child. She had no sympathy for children because no sympathy had been shown to her.

No matter how well she carried herself, she would be judged first by the darkness of her skin. To Broussard, Pet had already bought into that story and carried herself as a woman who was not well respected and not attractive.

To Pet, Lily was a burden that had been forced upon her because of her daughter's death—not a delightful child, but full of energy and the potential to succeed and be happy.

Broussard broke the silence, "So Pet, knowing as a child that you couldn't control the world around you, what you think is best, the Creole way or your family's way?"

He watched as Pet's facial expression went from curious to feisty to maybe even a flash of anger in her eyes.

"Look, Broussard. I guess I gotta' shoot for somewhere in between. We real heavy on respect, and sometimes when I watch you and your grandkids, it don't look like they respect you. For me," she continued as she nervously got up and began pacing, "I don't think I'm ready to hear how Lily really feels about everything, especially thinking out loud in a grownup way.

"She don't think I know, but she got her slick little ways of trying to get what she wants. And she lets me know when I've gone too far. Don't get the shit twisted, Broussard. She knows what she's doing, and there's plenty of times that Lily gets her way with me. I guess what I'm saying is she probably doesn't respect me any more than your grandkids do you. She just knows not to say what she feels." Pet looked in Broussard's direction with an odd expression on her face. "She's probably afraid of me."

To Broussard, Pet's statement almost sounded like a question. "Well, Pet, uh, we Creoles, as you put it, do give our children lots of leniency, but that's because we don't want them to be afraid to speak their mind, even if another adult is involved. We were able to stop a parish priest in his tracks from harming little girls because our children felt empowered enough to tell their parents what was going on in the Catholic schools. Kids who are afraid of grownups wouldn't have been able to do that."

Pet immediately sat up on the couch. What Broussard said had struck a nerve, a very tender nerve. The memories that flashed in front of her eyes were too painful to think about. Pet knew from her own experience that once a girl's mother is no longer part of her everyday life, her main protector in life is gone, and the predators come out of the woodwork. They know vulnerability when they see it.

The silence that followed Broussard's last statement was thunderous. With each pulsing temple, both Pet and Broussard heard his voice reverberating around the living room. His voice was high, it was low, it was shrill, it was silent, and both of their eyes followed the sound that was so profound.

Finally, Broussard broke the not-so-silent silence, "Pet, I seem to have hit a sore spot for you; you wanna' talk about it?"

He began subconsciously playing with his curly, silver mane again, this time pulling on strands of hair and twisting them between his thumb and index finger. Pet watched, mesmerized, unable to speak right away.

Pet rose from the couch and stepped backward to the corner wall joining the kitchen and living room, and began scratching her back, using a rhythmic, back-and-forth motion. "Oh, Jesus, this feels good. My back itch was driving me crazy!" She continued scratching, adding an up-and-down motion to the back-and-forth scratch.

Broussard rose from the couch and began laughing, "Pet, I've seen a lot of people scratch their backs, but most of them reach their backs the best way they can. Then, they use their fingernails or a wooden back-scratcher, but I've never seen anyone move like they making love to the wall to scratch their back!"

Pet joined in his laughter and hoped that their conversation was over. Broussard took the hint and went to the phonograph and put Etta on again.

CHAPTER 51

Send Her a Greyhound Ticket

The next day when Pet awakened, she lay still on her bed, letting the morning ease into her bones. It had been a chilly night, and she wasn't ready to get up and pad down the hallway to the cold bathroom. Usually, one of them fifty-eleven children would be in the bathroom, and she'd have to stand there, waiting for one of them to come out. There were at least two or three of them in the bathroom at the same time, and she wasn't about to wait them out, not today. Her bladder said she needed to go now, so she slipped on her thin, cotton robe and flip-flops and padded out the back door to the side of the chicken coop.

The lone rooster was the only one up, and he cocked his head to one side as she spread her legs and let her pee flow freely. He strutted to the edge of the coop, flapped his wings, and belted out a loud cock-a-doodle-do. She laughed and quickly wiped herself with the toilet paper she'd brought with her and tip-toed back into the house. The same ones were still in the bathroom, giggling away as she heard good water being wasted down the sink. *Kids*, she thought.

On her way back to the bedroom, she could smell Broussard's coffee and heard Broussard and Lily talking in the kitchen. She started to join them but thought better of it. Here I go again, she thought, catering to Lily's needs. *But like Broussard regularly tells me, Lily's had a hard life, let her have some of life's pleasures. Broussard is like a grandfather to her—shit, she doesn't know her real grandfather. They've never even met!*

As she sat up in bed with her back against the headboard, Pet began formulating a plan of how to introduce Lily to her grandfather, a plan that would separate DH from his current wife. Why she could kill two birds with one stone—a grandfather for Lily and a man for herself!

She decided to start with Lily. Christmas was less than a month away, and if she hurried, she could write to DH, introduce Lily, and make him want to see her. Lily looked so much like her mother that he'd have to fall for her. Ellen had always been a daddy's girl, and Pet knew that her death had hit DH in his most tender spot. What he needed, she decided, was a granddaughter. Lily. What he also needed was Pet, and Lord knows she wanted him.

Pet knew DH's wife, Cynthia, was aware that Ellen had existed, and she probably knew that Ellen had children. As far as Pet was concerned, it was time to acknowledge to Cynthia and DH's children that their father had another daughter who had died, who was indeed their half-sister. And that they had a niece about to turn ten years old.

She began with a letter; she dared not pick up the phone to call him. It wasn't Thursday night, and Cynthia was sure to be home:

Dear DH,

How are you? Fine, I hope. Forgive me for sending this letter to your house. I know you're married, and I respect your wife, but Lily is getting more and more curious as she continues to get older. She's almost ten and wants to know about her mother's father, you, of course!

I suggested that maybe she could come and spend the Christmas holiday with you and your family. She's anxious to meet you, and I think there's no better time than Christmas since she will be out of school for two weeks anyhow.

If you could send her a Greyhound ticket, she would be glad to meet you and your family. She has cousins that she's never met, and I think it would be a shame for her not to get to know her mother's people.

*Please give my regards to your wife and let her know I have
no ill feelings toward her, I just want Lily to get to know her
grandfather and cousins.*

Yours truly,
Pet

Knowing the letter would cause a shit-load of strife in the Jones's residence, didn't make Pet any difference. She didn't care. She had a plan to take DH from Cynthia, and nothing was going to get in her way.

Pet was getting hot sitting up in the bed, so she tossed the covers aside, slipped off her robe, and got dressed. Today was already warm and felt like a muumuu day.

She propped her tiny bedroom window open with a short two-by-four and immediately felt the cool breeze coming in from the west. From the backyard, she could see the old rooster chasing one of his hens around and another hen gathering her chicks and corralling them to a corner of the yard, out of harm's way. With the flapping wings, squawking hens, and peeping chicks, the morning yard was quite noisy.

She leaned on the windowsill and continued watching the yard action, deep in thought. She wasn't sure why she couldn't get DH off of her mind. Maybe it was because she knew that Broussard's wife had returned from taking care of her mother, so Broussard would have less time for her. Over the past several weeks, she and Broussard had become closer, and she would miss their thought-provoking talks. But Pet knew that since Mrs. Broussard had returned, her husband would surely devote his free time to her.

She again thought back to the phone calls over the years that she'd had with DH. She wasn't sure how they'd begun, but once he made it clear that he looked forward to their conversations, she'd kept it up. She smiled to herself as she remembered their last phone-booth conversation. That peckerwood was sure mad at her for hogging that phone line!

However good the conversations with Broussard were, spending quality time with him only made her wish for more than phone time with DH. She needed her own man, and she needed him full-time!

She had to admit to herself, though, that Broussard was a different kind of man. Not one that she could fall for; he was just too nice. She was more attracted to men who were a little rougher around the edges, like DH.

CHAPTER 52

She's Always Been Like That

Somehow, the day turned into mid-morning, and Pet had not left her room. Inside the house was pretty quiet, the kids were in school. Broussard had gone on an early morning errand, and his daughter, as usual, was holed up in her room.

She heard a knock on the door, and hearing no one else answer, she went to the door, and opened it. Standing in the doorway was a tall, skinny, young White man wearing a shiny, navy-blue suit with pants that were obviously too short and too tight. His brown hair was long, and it dangled across his forehead in an Elvis sort of style.

Pet was dumbfounded. Usually, the only white person ringing their doorbell was the milkman or mailman, and they generally dropped off their goods before anyone even answered the door. His presence created an unease that she felt throughout her body.

"Mornin', ma'am. I, uh, was wondering if you'd be interested in purchasing a set of our wonderful Encyclopedia Britannica's?"

He gestured toward the ground, and Pet followed his washed-out blue eyes to his feet where the box set of encyclopedias sat. Before she had a chance to say no and shut the door, he grabbed the encyclopedias, and stepped inside the entryway, almost pushing Pet aside.

"If you'd just give me fifteen minutes of your time, I will show you how having a set of these fine reference books can change you and your family's life." The young man nervously flicked his tongue to moisten his parched lips, and looking over his shoulder to make sure the lady of the house was following him, as he headed for the couch in the living room.

Pet padded after him, angry and surprised that he had managed to get past her so quickly. When they both arrived at the living room entrance, she sighed and reluctantly gestured for him to take a seat at the far end of the couch.

He sat down and busied himself with arranging the boxed set on the coffee table, stretching his long legs beside the couch. When he was satisfied with his arrangement, he motioned for Pet, who was fuming and still standing, to sit down beside him.

"Now, as I was saying, ma'am," again moistening his lips with his tongue and flipping his bangs back in place, "you will not find a better set of references for your family. I saw the kids' bikes outside. How many children do you have?" He managed a weak smile as he waited for her to answer.

"Them ain't my children," Pet grumbled, "I only have one granddaughter." She glared in his direction to let him know that she didn't like how he had managed to barge his way in.

"I see." The salesman pulled one of the encyclopedias from the set and flipped it open to a page that had a marked slip of paper between the pages. "Now, this book is from the letter T, and it includes a detailed description of the tiger, also known as the Panthera Tigris. Look here," he said, as he thrust the encyclopedia into Pet's lap and continued, "at this picture. Isn't that a fine specimen of an animal? I bet your granddaughter is studying these animals in school right now, and imagine how prepared she'll be when she has to write her report on tigers!"

Pet raised her eyebrows as if somewhat interested in what the salesman was selling while hoping that she could figure out a way to get him back to wherever he had come from. She rose from the couch. "Well, look…"

"Now, for only five dollars per week, you could own this entire twenty-four-volume collection of encyclopedias," the salesman said quickly after seeing the newly formed scowl on her face. You won't even have to send us a check. We'll stop by every week to collect your money and drop off an encyclopedia with a new letter of the alphabet. You can't ask for a better deal than this!"

The salesman had gotten past his nervousness and confidently stood up, blank receipt in hand, ready to fill it out on Pet's behalf.

Pet's confidence in the presence of a white man had returned, and she, too, asserted herself. "No, I ain't interested."

He nodded, frowned, and like any good salesman, said, "Well, if you change your mind, here's my card. You can get in touch with me anytime. I'll be checking back in with you next week."

As soon as she shooed him out the front door, she went back to her room and resumed plotting to get her man.

She heard the screech of the mailman's brakes and ran outside to hand him DH's letter. She saw the encyclopedia salesman two doors down. The neighbor. was standing in the doorway with the front door closed. She had obviously been visited by salesmen before.

Pet made a mental note of the tactic should the need arise again. She looked up again as a different screeching brake sound assaulted her ears, but this time it was Lily's school bus.

Lily, Tony, and Latisha Kay got off the bus. Pet looked up at the sky, and judging from the sun's angle, she knew it was too early for them to be home. Matter of fact, hell, she knew that it wasn't even past noon!

"What y'all doing home so early?" Pet wasn't ready for the kids to be home so soon, and the children could feel her agitation.

"School let out early; we only had a half-day today. I gave you the note from school last week," Lily responded in a monotone voice.

"Oh, now you not sassing me, are you?"

Lily could see the sweat forming on her grandmother's brow. She quickly responded, "No, ma'am!"

"Well, you kids need to go change your school clothes, and remember, play outside!"

"Yes, ma'am," they replied in unison.

When they reached the back door, Latisha Kay paused and whispered into Lily's ear, "Why your grandmother gotta be so darn mean?"

"Beats me," Lily replied. "She always been like that!"

Even though Latisha Kay thought she was whispering, Pet had heard both children. Pet left her bedroom door slightly cracked and stood just inside the room to hear if anything else was being said, but they were quiet. Next thing she heard was the screeching of children playing in the backyard. Seeing her door cracked, they must have tip-toed to the backyard.

She plopped down on the bed, and the springs groaned from the weight of her bulky frame. Her feet were puffed-up from too many days cleaning them nasty white folks' houses. Lately, ironing had been added to her daily chores, and the prolonged standing was not helping her swollen feet.

As she stared down at her feet, she sighed deeply, and a feeling of sorrow came over her. For Pet, the time had come to look deep. She could see herself in a multi-dimensional way—the way the children saw her, the way DH saw her, the way the white salesman saw her, and the way she saw herself.

When Pet looked deep, her heart felt as though it was about to burst. She knew she had an exterior that looked tough. It looked tough to the children, and it looked tough to Broussard, and yes, it even looked tough to DH. But that white salesman had barged into the house, and she had felt helpless to stop him. What did he see? Did he see the side of her that was not so tough?

In the end, she was a woman who had nothing, a woman whose daughter had committed suicide. A woman left with the burden of caring for a child about to turn eleven years old. A child who, like herself, was forced to grow up without her mother.

Pet could lament the fact that she was without a man. She could even lament the fact that she had contemplated stealing another woman's husband. And lament the fact that Broussard was a man lucky enough to have a wife who adored him.

But what did she actually have for herself? Nothing. The children were either afraid of her or hated her. Her other grown children rarely sought her out unless they wanted something. Tears rolled down her dark face as she continued to wallow in her own self-pity. She grabbed the end of her bedsheet and dabbed at her hot tears.

Why was it so hard to raise her grandchild, and what about the other two? Nedra and Ray had thought that she should take them and keep all of Ellen's children together.

Even as these thoughts raced through her mind, she knew the answers. She didn't want Lily, Deenie, and Lorna—they could not replace Ellen. Pet wanted Ellen, her real daughter. And why was she trying so hard to connect with DH? Because he was Ellen's father.

And speaking of her Ellen, what thought was constantly nagging in the back of her mind? Playing tough could not hide the fact that the tape that never stopped playing in her head was what the hell happened to her daughter? Did she actually kill herself? Was she killed? And if that answer was yes, who the hell did it, and why? Was it her son-in-law, Orville? Or was it one of those Mexican farm workers someone said they saw loitering around their isolated, rented farmhouse? Why couldn't God just answer her questions? Where the hell was he? And where was he when this happened to her daughter?

A light tap on her bedroom door broke the deep spell that she had allowed to envelop her. She looked up and saw Broussard standing in the doorway. He had been outside playing with the children, and she saw large sweat stains on his shirt and trousers. His canvas tennis shoes were dusty, and he had obviously tracked dirt in from the outside.

"The children are hungry, and I'm about to make lunch for them. Do you care for anything?"

"No, thank you." Pet so wanted to stay deep within her funk, and she quickly spun off the bed and pretended to be looking for a thimble that presumably had fallen under the dresser.

Broussard took the hint and sauntered into the kitchen, where all the grandchildren were hanging out in the dining area, waiting for him to prepare a quick lunch.

As soon as he left, Pet reclaimed her spot on the bed and allowed more tears to fall. She thought back to Ellen's funeral and how DH had come without Cynthia. How is it when they saw each other, they instinctively knew that the other was thinking about their daughter's wedding and how much joy they felt then. And now, how much more pain they felt than from just a few short years before. Oh, what a difference a few years can make!

The wails coming from that funeral home had been enough to break anyone's heart. A young mother of three small children, laying solidly in a casket with the smell of fear and death and mortuary flowers permeating the air, clinging to children's clothing and grownup suits and dresses—so much so that women would later spend hours and days trying to wash and dry-clean the stench out of them.

Pet dabbed her eyes again with the bedsheets, and this time, she got up and quietly shut her bedroom door. She didn't want any more interruptions, just peace and quiet, no one to stop her gloomy thoughts. Her Ellen was gone, and there was no turning back the clock.

CHAPTER 53

We Could Make Us a Beautiful Mother Who Loved Us

Lily was thinking about Ellen too. It had been several months since she had dreamed of her mother or dedicated an entire day replaying the memories of her mother in her head.

She sat alone, with her legs folded, on a small patch of Bermuda grass fighting for its life in the sandy, almost-barren backyard. One-by-one, she plucked a blade of grass, crumbled it between her index finger and thumb, then smelled it and closed her eyes. The aroma brought back the memories of living in Clarksburg, the last place her family had been a family.

With her eyes closed, a vivid image emerged of Orville mowing the lawn, the scent of Bermuda grass drifting from the front yard into the living room, where she sat crossed-legged, playing a game of jacks by herself. She saw her mother sitting on the couch with baby Lorna in her lap, laughing and cooing, and then there was her brother Deenie, driving his imaginary toy car over their shiny wooden floor. Lily had many times watched her mother on all fours scrubbing and polishing the floors, and she had heard her mother proudly say that the floors were clean enough for the children to lick them if they wanted to.

The Broussard children, even though they were also in the back-yard, knew better than to disturb Lily. The trance-like look on Lily's face told them everything they needed to know. She was in her own world and wanted to be left alone.

The movie continued to play but was interrupted by a stinging sensation caused by a blade of Bermuda grass poking into Lily's leg. She pulled the offending blades of grass and continued her ritual by smelling and closing her eyes to her next set of memories.

Latisha Kay, observing Lily's behavior from across the backyard, used the opportunity to run over to Lily's spot. "Whatcha doing?"

Lily was about to muster up her meanest, grandmother-like grouchy face when she noticed Latisha Kay's pitiful facial expression. She relaxed her frown muscles, smiled up at Latisha Kay and patted the narrow piece of grass left for her friend to sit.

"Bet I know what you were thinking," Latisha Kay offered as she plopped down beside her. "Or even better, as Grandpa says, a penny for your thoughts?" She, too began pulling up blades of grass, trying to avoid eye contact with Lily and hoping that she would not shoo her away.

Lily was not about to shoo Latisha Kay away, but she couldn't help but think about an idea that continually played in her mind about Latisha Kay and other friends and family that she knew. How come they seemed to sometimes be happy and sometimes be sad, just like her? Didn't having a mother and father and sisters and brothers kind of guarantee that you'd always be happy?

Lily had thought that when her precious mother died, she'd never be happy again. But she had found that there were days of happiness and that those days had been increasing, much to her dismay. Somehow or another, she'd have to come to terms with the idea that even without her mother, she could be happy. After all, look at the Broussards. The children weren't always happy, and yet, they had a mother, grandparents, sisters, and brothers. Go figure.

Lily found a small twig and began drawing in the sand adjacent to her patch of grass. Without looking up, she said, "I've always been jealous of everybody who has a mother and father."

Latisha Kay picked up a twig and began drawing also. "I know."

"How did you know?"

"'Cause everybody's hurting for something. Just like you wish you had a mother, right? Well, we wish we had a mother who loved us, who liked to spend time with us, who didn't treat our daddy so mean that he had to leave us. I know it's hard to believe, Lily, but we wish we had the mother that you used to have!"

Lily bolted up from her spot on the grass. "You mean that Latisha Kay? You really mean that?"

"Of course, Lily, all Mommas ain't good. We've told you about ours before."

"Yeah, but my Momma is never coming back; she's dead!" Lily sat back down on the grass, careful to arrange her pedal pushers to protect her from the stinging Bermuda grass.

Kay continued, "Well, I see how you go into your spells and don't want to be bothered with us. I betcha spend all that time just thinking about your mother, don't you?"

"Well, yeah, but I'd much rather have her here than dead!"

"Lily, me and my brother, Tony, talked about how you go into a trance or something, and we're jealous. You look calm and happy, and we don't know how to do that. Can you teach us how? If we knew how, we could make us a beautiful mother who loves us, and we could make us a family that has a daddy in it. We love Grandpa Broussard, but sometimes we wish we had our own papa too."

Lily looked at Latisha Kay with a puzzled expression. She thought everyone knew how to make an imaginary world. She had been doing it long before her mother died. Why, the first time she had done it was when they first moved to Clarksburg. She was lonely, away from the family and friends she knew. She'd sometimes daydream for hours, especially on the days when there was no school. How could you not know how to go into another world?

Lily absentmindedly reached for another bunch of Bermuda grass and brought it to her nose. Latisha Kay watched Lily deeply inhale the aroma of the grass, again traveling to her other mystical world.

Disappointed that her conversation with Lily was over, she plunged her twig deeply into the sand, arose from their Bermuda oasis, and dejectedly trudged to her spot on the opposite end of the backyard. Her Shirley Temple curls were no longer bouncing. They lay as flat on her head as she felt.

Latisha Kay, like Lily, was soon to be twelve years old, but she felt that she might as well be an old woman like Lily's grandmother. She looked for another twig, and when she found it, drew a few stick figures in the sand, but her heart was not actually interested.

Next, she tried shoving her way into her brothers' marble game, but they were not having it. Each place in the circle that she tried to insert herself was met with spreading elbows and knees. She finally gave up.

She remembered the tether ball and ran over to hit it. She punched the ball into the air with ferocity, but no aim, and watched as it swung wildly around the pole. She listened to the pinging sound as each chain rotation hit the steel pole. But it was no fun playing by herself, and she continued staring, mesmerized, as the ball began to gradually return to an inert position.

She was bored, as only eleven-year-olds can be bored. She decided to go deeper into the backyard near the duck pond. If Lily could have imaginary people in her life, so could she, except that for Latisha Kay, it would be the ducks.

"Hello, Daphney," she shouted as she neared the murky, green pond. "Ready for your daily bread?"

Daphney, standing on the edge of the pond, cocked her head to one side, took a step toward the water, and waited. The rest of the flock rushed to the pond and began squawking loudly. Daphney was the only silver-white duck among the flock. The rest were a dull, dishwasher color with bright orange beaks.

Latisha Kay pulled a handful of breadcrumbs from her pocket and began spreading it gingerly around the pond. As the ducks skirted across the water, plunging for the bread cubes, chaos ensued.

The smell from the algae-laden pond drifted up and assaulted her nose so much so that she placed her index finger across her nose and began to breathe through her mouth.

As the cubes of bread disappeared, the noise from the ducks was reduced to an occasional squawk as they smoothly glided around the pond. Daphney waited patiently. She was LaTisha Kay's pet, and she knew her special treats were coming.

Latisha Kay squatted at the edge of the pond near Daphney, who sidled up close to her hand. "All I want," Latisha Kay explained patiently, "is for my mother to pay attention to me. I wanna be like my other friends at school and be able to talk to my mother about all kinds of things. Like how come I get such bad cramps when I get my period, and why come boys don't have periods. I just don't think it's fair. God should have made them suffer too! And then, too, I wanna learn how to knit and crochet. Shoot all my friend's mothers taught them how to sew and everything. A girl can't learn stuff without a mother who cares!"

Daphney nuzzled her beak into Latisha Kay's balled-up fist, looking for her treat. Latisha Kay unfolded her fist and opened her palms. The duck pecked greedily at the breadcrumbs, and when they were gone, looked up expectantly at her friend, who had large hot tears rolling down her flushed cheeks.

"Now, to tell you the truth, Daphney, sometimes I wish my mother was dead; then we could find my father and go live with him."

As she spoke, Latisha Kay used her dress sleeves to wipe her tears away. Daphney, seeing no more breadcrumbs, quietly slipped away into the water, creating a ripple effect as she swam across the pond.

"Latisha Kay, what are you doing way out here?" It was Lily, her hands shielding her eyes from the intense afternoon sun. "I been looking all over for you!"

"Oh, I thought I'd come out here and play with Daphney." Latisha Kay hoped she had done a good job of wiping the tears away. She did not feel like telling Lily why she'd been crying.

Lily, keen on her friend's moods, could tell she'd been crying. Her face was dry, but her eyes were puffy, and she looked sad, and being her friend, she knew the reason for Latisha Kay's sadness.

"You know, Latisha Kay, I can help you learn how to be in a make-believe world. I go there as often as I need to, and in my world, everybody loves me, and nobody is mean to me. I have pretty dresses that are not hand-me-downs, and I don't change schools three times a year.

"And another thing, my mother is alive—me and Orville and my sister and brother are all together; I don't have to live with my mean-old grandmother. I am happy; no one calls me skinny, and I'm light-skinned, and I have good hair."

Latisha Kay frowned at Lily, then shaded her eyes as she walked toward the edge of the pond near a lone weeping willow tree. Lily followed her.

When they reached the tree, both girls immediately felt relief from the sun's unusually hot November weather. "Lily, you never said you didn't like being dark. I wish I was dark like you. Your skin is perfect like my father's. Shoot, the white kids at school call me half-breed, and the coloreds say I'm too white looking. Everybody's always got something to say to make us feel bad."

It hadn't occurred to Lily that there was a downside to being light. She didn't respond to Latisha Kay because she didn't know what to say.

Both girls noticed that a small section of the almost-black bark of the weeping willow had been shedding, exposing a smoother, lighter brown inner layer. Lily began picking at the bark near the tree's trunk, exposing more of the lighter inner layer. A small piece of the bark got stuck under her fingernail, and she quickly cried out as she snatched her hand away.

Latisha Kay laughed as she watched Lily furiously sucking on her injured finger.

"Not funny, Latisha Kay. That hurt."

Latisha Kay's laughter was infectious, and Lily began to laugh too.

"Guess that was kinda dumb, 'specially since I'd have to do a lot of peeling to get all that bark off!"

"Lily and Latisha Kay!"

Both girls jumped and ran towards the house as they heard Lily's grandmother screaming from the backyard.

CHAPTER 54

I Regret to Inform You

It was too late in the year to be this hot, but grandmother was hot. She was hot because it was hot outside, and she was hot because, from what she could see from the backyard, the two girls were having too much fun. The closer she saw Lily and Latisha Kay become, the more she felt the need to hit the road.

She and Lily could have a good life here, she knew it, but she also was not about to let any grass grow under her feet. The Broussards were good people, especially old man Broussard, but shit, it was time to go. There was, of course, the little nagging voice that spoke for Lily, but she had ignored it before, and she was planning to ignore it now. Kids don't dictate what grown folks do. That's just not how the world works.

And besides, there was DH. She hadn't heard back from him since she had written the letter, but she knew he'd reply. How could he not? He loved her; he had never stopped loving her!

DH was thinking about Pet too, but more importantly, he had been thinking about their daughter, Ellen. He had gotten the letter, and thankfully it was delivered on Saturday as he sat on the front porch, wiping his sweaty brow. He quickly slipped it into his coveralls, his eyes darting around to make sure Cynthia hadn't seen him, but she was inside preparing the afternoon lunch.

He sauntered over to his tool shed as if it were the most natural thing to do on a Saturday afternoon. It was not hot in the shed because he always kept a fan going to keep his tools cool. He could hear his boys playing catch in the backyard, and from his vantage point in the shed, he occasionally peered out at them through a slit in the wooden blinds. He locked the door from the inside.

He chuckled as he read the letter. That Pet had a lot of nerve, that was for sure. She wanted him to get to know their granddaughter, but he wanted to know what happened to their daughter. That subject came up almost every time they talked on the phone, but he knew that Pet didn't know any more than he did.

He thought again about the courthouse ceremony that he and Pet had attended together in 1951. Was her death his punishment for marrying Cynthia instead of Pet?

Like Pet, DH wondered, was Orville who everyone thought he was, an innocent man who lost his young wife to suicide? Or did he kill her? But unlike Pet, DH was determined to get to the truth. And he was going to start with the coroner. That damn peckerwood was going to tell him what happened to his daughter. If nothing else, he wanted to be able to let Lily know that her mother did not abandon her children to take the coward's way out of life. Something must have happened to his poor Ellen!

He finished reading the letter and folded it until it was small enough to fit into his large, rough hands. Then he placed it back into his coveralls and unlocked the shed door. At that moment, he saw Cynthia at the kitchen door.

"You all come on in before the food gets cold," she warned. She glanced in DH's direction.

He suddenly became interested in a tiny orange and black caterpillar slowly making its way across the lawn. To recover, he glanced behind him and yelled at their boys to put their baseball and gloves away and come eat. The boys looked up because his voice sounded gruffer than usual.

"Beat 'cha to the back door," he yelled, and both boys bolted past him. *Ah, youth, it's wasted on the young*, he thought.

As they sat at the kitchen table eating lunch, DH could feel Pet's letter rubbing against his thigh through his coverall pocket. Each brush against his skin felt like an announcement that he was cheating.

The kitchen curtains had been drawn to keep out today's intense rays of desert sunshine. It was dark inside, but a cool breeze was wafting in from the shady side of the house. The boys, sensing the tension in the room, hurriedly wolfed down their food and bolted for the back door.

"Come back here and clear your plates from the table and wash your face and hands," Cynthia yelled to the back of their heads.

Both boys spun around and did as they were told.

DH, never the disciplinarian, noticed his son's "Why-don't-you-ever-speak up dad?" expression and moved the canned peas around on his plate, at that moment more interested in his plate than his boys.

How was he going to break the news to Cynthia that he would be traveling to Sacramento? That's where he would meet up with Pet. The boys' issues with their domineering mother could wait. Hell, he was suffering under her spell too!

Sitting alone at the now-abandoned kitchen table, DH recalled in great detail the story that Pet had first told him of hearing the news of their daughter's death. He could clearly imagine everything through her eyes. He placed his fork beside his plate, leaned back on the hard kitchen stool, and let the movie begin.

It had been a chaotic day, starting with an early morning, loud, urgent knock at Pet's front door. As she padded to the window, she parted the thin, yellow curtains and peered out into the Tule-fog-filled morning. It was so white out that it looked like snow.

A chill crept through her body as she cautiously opened the door. She suddenly realized that she hadn't bothered putting on her robe. Standing in front of her was an imposing, flushed-faced young policeman with a stern look on his face. He was dressed in a dark blue uniform with a gold-embroidered county emblem on his left shoulder. He had his arms folded in front of him, fig leaf fashion. He didn't look her in the eyes as she greeted him with a nod and questioning look; instead, he looked down at his black leather loafers.

"Are you Lula Martha…?"

Before he could finish saying her full name, Pet interrupted him, "Yeah?"

At the same time, a weakness overcame her, and she was having a difficult time staying upright. The room suddenly began to spin. Seeing her shaky stance, the policeman grabbed her elbow to keep her from falling.

"I regret to inform you…"

Still feeling woozy, Pet interrupted him again, "It's Ellen, my Ellen, right?"

He led her to a nearby sofa, "Yes, ma'am, it's your daughter, Ellen Jenkins. I'm so sorry."

The tips of the man's ears looked hot, and she could almost see steam rising in the air around him. He looked as though he were about to flee from a grass fire gone wild. She saw him look around the small living room, seeming to gain a sudden interest in the yellow and white crocheted doilies that adorned both armrests of the tweed blue and gold sofa. His eyes darted to the linoleum black and white floor, which was sparkling clean, and then to her small, brown, wiener dog sitting silently, looking up at him with soulful eyes.

Plopping down on the sofa, her legs spread apart, exposing her plump thighs and breast. She was in shock, unaware that the age-old tradition of keeping her private parts private had abandoned her.

The young officer quickly sat beside her and began rubbing her arm and shoulder.

Pet noticed him averting his eyes away from her thin nightgown that left nothing to the imagination. She could tell that this was the officer's first death call to a family member, and he had no idea what was expected of him. It was also obvious to Pet that he had never seen a half-naked colored woman before. He appeared mesmerized by the contrast of her honey-brown breast with the almost black areolas. He didn't say anything, but she could tell that he had seen more than he could ever imagine.

And who knew that colored people had so many color contrasts in their skin coloring? Her face, neck, and arms had a rich, dark brown complexion, almost as dark as the areolas, but her chest and upper thighs were a honey-brown skin tone. Except for her nipple area, it was clear which areas of her skin had prolonged exposure to the sun and which had not.

"What happened to my baby?" Pet sat there wailing softly, rocking back and forth in slow motion, letting the tears roll down her face without wiping them.

The officer let go of her arm and shoulder and scooted toward the edge of the couch.

To Pet, it appeared he was putting on what he believed was his best sympathetic facial expression.

"We're not sure, ma'am," he said quietly. "The coroner said she died of a gunshot wound to the abdomen, but he's not sure what happened. They've been trying to contact her husband, but he can't be reached. We found your name in her address book. We may need you to come in to identify her."

Pet's wails increased in intensity, and she turned away from the officer. "Ooh Wee," she wailed, "I knew something was gonna happen to my baby. I just knew it!"

"Ma'am, is there anybody you want me to call? I've gotten permission to take you to Sacramento where her body…"

Pet quickly stood up, and shot her hand out in front of the officer's face. "Stop it! Stop it! I can't hear anymore!"

CHAPTER 55

First, I Want to Extend My Condolences

The movie playing in DH's head stopped, and he looked up to see Cynthia walk back into the dining room and snatch his plate from him.

"There you go, in your other world." Cynthia glared in his direction and stomped back to the kitchen, throwing his plate into the sink.

DH heard the clink as it, along with a water glass, broke. To avoid being in the line of Cynthia's wrath, DH retreated into his tool shed and sat on a small stool near the window overlooking the backyard. He returned to thinking about Pet and the officer.

"Look, ma'am, if you don't have anywhere else to go, let me drive you to Sacramento. It's less than two hours away, and you can have a chance to get ahold…"

Pet interrupted him again. "Okay, okay, let me go get dressed." Before he could answer, Pet disappeared into another room.

The officer sat up and paced around the small space in the living room. This was most likely the toughest job he'd had since joining the force. He pulled a handkerchief from his back pocket and wiped the cold sweat from his brow.

Forest Monroe had been the Yolo County sheriff and coroner for the past eighteen years. He, too, was pacing, because until today, he hadn't realized how tough his job would become. He looked up from his old, wooden, school-teacher-style desk in time to see his young rookie escort a short, dark, heavy-set, mean-looking, colored woman to one of the hard benches outside of his makeshift office. He felt a sudden chill, and a feeling of foreboding swept through the core of each one of his bones.

It was an unusually warm October day, and even though he had turned the tiny morgue's air conditioning to its coldest setpoint, the slight odor of death drifted slowly down the hallway, causing his innards to flip-flop uncontrollably.

Death wasn't something his office encountered very much, especially the death of a twenty-two-year-old colored girl, apparently dead from a gunshot wound to the abdomen. An occasional, horrific, drunk-driver-induced car crash, his office was accustomed to, but a young girl, dead, for what reason? Unlike most of his car crash victims, this girl wasn't banged up beyond recognition. She appeared to be sleeping peacefully in his morgue!

His rookie tapped on the glass-paned door and let himself into Forest's office. The rookie stole a furtive glance in the sheriff's direction, then looked around the cramped space as if seeing the office for the first time. The largest piece of furniture was the wooden desk, and on one wall, a plethora of wanted posters had been scattered about. Mostly white men, a few smatterings of Mexicans and coloreds, and all scruffy-looking. The linoleum floor was littered with old coffee stains and was sticky from the crumbs of countless glazed donuts consumed over the years.

The rookie dragged a wooden chair across the tiny space in Forest's office and plopped down beside Forest. "Sarge, I uh, brought in that dead girl's Momma, thought maybe you could talk to her? She didn't say a word all the way in; that was one hell of a ride from Merced. Though, before we left, she kept asking why her baby would want to kill herself and leave them three children all alone?"

Sheriff Monroe leaned back in his worn, peeling, black leather chair and cocked his boots high upon the wooden desk. The boots were practically in the rookie's face. The rookie cocked his head to one side, avoiding the pointy-toed cowboy boots.

The sheriff formed a steeple with his two hands, pressed both index fingers against his thin lips, and glanced at the colored woman sitting outside of his office. He let out a long, troubled sigh. "I'm going to rule that young girl's death a suicide."

The shock on the rookie's face was evident. He didn't try to mask his disapproval. "But there hasn't even been a preliminary autopsy report!" His face was beet red, and even though it was a mild, sunny day, he was sweating profusely. "Boss, let's find out what happened to this girl. Shoot, she left behind three young children. For Christ's sake, sheriff, the baby was in the crib and must've seen the whole darn thing!"

The sheriff's face remained impassive. He repeated, "I'm going to rule the girl's death a suicide, 'cause if I don't, this whole county will be in an uproar. The husband claims he was driving a truck over 200 miles away, and his sidekick is vouching for him. We got no one else to pin this on, and we can't have folks scared of a killer on the loose!" Forest abruptly bolted from his chair and began pacing, but there wasn't enough room to walk back and forth in the cramped office.

"What the hell was that colored girl doing way out there on Old County Road by herself with those three little ones while her husband was away? Geez, if we can't put the husband at the scene, what the hell we gonna do? Like I said, we've got to rule this a suicide!"

The sheriff looked up in time to see the dead girl's mother peering at them through the pane-glass door.

"Come on in, ma'am. We were just about to talk to you about your daughter. First, I want to extend my condolences to you and your family."

The rookie got up from his small chair and gestured for her to sit down. She looked from the rookie to the sheriff and reluctantly sat in the chair that was offered to her. She dropped her head down and placed one hand on her forehead and began nodding her head back and forth. She didn't look up at either of them.

"What I was saying, ma'am, was that we're sorry for your loss. Did you know that your daughter was depressed? I mean, we didn't find any note, and we can't find any evidence of anyone but the children being there." The sheriff was looking down and speaking to the top of Pet's head. He was glad that he couldn't see her face. The rookie was leaning into a corner of the office, arms folded, glaring in the sheriff's direction with his mouth clenched shut.

Pet began wailing again. Her body shook uncontrollably.

CHAPTER 56

If Wishes Were Horses

Lily was wailing. Hours after her grandmother had called Latisha Kay and Lily inside for the evening, Lily was having another nightmare. It was a recurring dream, one in which she was sitting on the other side of a priest's confessional, listening as a priest spoke in a low, menacing tone. He was admonishing her for being a bad girl, but Lily didn't understand what she had done wrong. He said she waited too long to get help for her mother.

From within the confessional, Lily could see the skies opening up, with billowy, white clouds and angry, dark ones encircling her entire body and sucking her up into the vast empty space called heaven. The priest's voice seemed to be getting louder, echoing from within the clouds, which were pushed along with each gust of wind. She tried to escape, to get away from the priest's angry voice.

She awakened to see Latisha Kay leaning over her, so close that their noses almost touched.

"Wow, you musta really been dreaming. You were crying and running in bed!"

Latisha Kay was sitting on her twin bed opposite Lily. She rose from the bed and sat back down again at the head of Lily's bed. "Pappa used to say if you dream that hard, the devil is trying to get in. I sure hope you didn't let him in!"

Lily sat up in bed. The last thing she remembered was Latisha Kay and her running into the house after grandmother had called them.

"You know, Lily, when we went in the house earlier, you kinda' went into a trance. Next thing I know, you sleep. When your grandmother came in our room, she took one look at you and left. She told me to leave you alone, too. Next thing I know, you running in bed. What happened to you?"

Latisha Kay was wearing her brightly-colored painting frock with pedal pushers with a t-shirt underneath. Her long plaits were braided Indian style, and as far as Lily was concerned, she could have passed for Pocahontas.

Lily's dress was permanently wrinkled from the battle with her priest demon. "I don't know what happens to me; I just know that I hate that dream. I didn't know how to get help when my mother was dying. There was nobody around to help me and Deenie and baby Lorna!"

Latisha Kay knew this story and remained silent.

"And that darn priest keeps showing up in my dreams!"

"Lily, let's go for a walk. Remember the pond you met me at the other day?" Before Lily could answer, Latisha Kay continued, "I go there when I'm sad, and I know it will make you feel better too."

Without another word, both girls simultaneously reached into the closet for their muddy, white canvas tennis shoes and slipped them on. Lily, as usual, sloppily tied her shoestrings, and Latisha Kay squatted down and re-tied them.

"Your strings always come apart, so I might as well tie them for you. What would you do without me?" Their mood abruptly transformed into a simple camaraderie that both girls felt.

Down at the pond, Daphne the duck quickly swam to the edge of the water, cocked her head from side to side, and stared intently at Latisha Kay's hand. Seeing no breadcrumbs, she swam away in disgust, greedily eying the insects in the murky water below.

"Lily, you know how the other day we talked about me and my brothers wishing we could go into another world like you do?"

Lily first looked puzzled, then remembering their past conversation, used the most authoritative voice that she could muster. "Well, I can't always make it happen, but sometimes it works. I just try going to another place by reading, you know, like *Alice in Wonderland* or *The Little Maid of Vermont* before putting myself in a trance. Like I said, it works sometimes."

"Wait a minute, did you just say you put yourself in a trance? How in the world—I mean, I wish I could do that!"

"Yeah, I'm not sure how I do that part. I just shut my eyes really tight and think of my mother, and sometimes she comes to me, and then we're somewhere else. I…I don't know how to explain it." Lily sported an embarrassed grin and ducked her head down, avoiding Tish's dumbfounded gaze.

Turning away from Tish, Lily plopped down onto the pond's sandy beach, laid back, and cupped both of her hands into the back of her neck to keep from getting sand in her hair. Tish followed suit. As they looked up into the sky above, Lily offered her sobering advice to Latisha Kay. "Tish, my stepdad used to say, 'if wishes were horses, beggars would ride.'"

Latisha Kay quickly sat up. "What the heck does that mean?"

"That means," Lily said in her most patient voice, "I don't always get to choose what I dream about; it just happens! Besides, if I had my way, I wouldn't have to dream about my mother being alive anyway; she would be!"

La Tisha Kay continued lying in the sand, cupping her hands just like Lily. "Oh, I get it, and if I had my way, I'd have the mother I've always dreamed about." She continued, "Maybe we could start a club and invite mothers and grandmothers who want kids to join." The idea started to take hold, "And we could invite kids who want or need a real mother to join too. Think of it, Lily, everybody would be happy!"

Lily sat back up, grasping her knees with her arms, "Well, that will never happen, not as long as grownups are in charge."

"Lily, wait, yes, this could happen." A small smile crept onto her face as she sat up. "I think we should talk to Grandpa Broussard about this and see what he thinks. We *could* start a club! I think it's a great idea. Do you know any kids at school who'd want to join?"

"No, I don't. I still don't think it could happen. There are too many people that don't want kids to be happy." Lily jabbed a stick into the loose sand, then tossed it aside.

The piercing sunlight was shining directly in Lily's eyes, and she attempted to shield the sun by squinting and covering her eyes with her hands. Streaks of sun still got in, so she closed her eyes and marveled at the blood-red color she could "see" through her lids. She reopened her eyes, "Who do you think would want to join?"

Latisha Kay responded to Lily, "Well, for one thing, me and all my sisters and brothers. In our own way, we all miss having a real mother. Our oldest sister, Shirley, is the only one who wouldn't join. She's too busy passing for white."

Lily looked puzzled.

"Oh, Lily, don't look so surprised. I told you about her a long time ago. The kids at her high school think her Momma is her Mexican maid; can you believe that? And she has a white boyfriend who doesn't know we Creole with lots of mixed blood. Boy, if he ever finds out!"

Lily reflected on what Latisha Kay just said and thought no one in her family could pass for white. Maybe that was a good thing, she wasn't sure.

She and Latisha Kay laid back on the warm, sandy beach and let the sun's rays lull them into a light, dream-like state. Both girls were partially conscious and could hear the wind causing a quiet lapping sound on the water. In the distance, they could also hear a noisy group of red-winged blackbirds landing on the willow tree near the pond and Daphne and friends swimming back to visit.

Under the warm, late autumn sun, Lily's frequent dream began, but this time it was the terrifying dream of her mother's last day on earth three years ago.

CHAPTER 57

Just Tell Me What Happened

Sheriff Forest Monroe was thinking about that day too. It was the day that he had first met the dead girl's mother. The rookie and the dead girl's mother were gone, and he had just sat there in his office, staring into space. He remembered that his boots had not moved one inch from their perch atop his desk. The clock above his head ticked loudly as the black second hand jerked from one space of time to another.

His office had turned dark, but he hadn't bothered to get up and turn on the lights. He had gone over in his mind the scene he had first encountered at the dead girl's home three years ago. There was blood everywhere, and the floor was sticky from the ambulance driver and two police officers' shoes carelessly walking in and out of her blood. They had been there earlier in the day when she was first discovered.

Two of the laborers, who had been summoned from their nearby fields by the dead mother's children to get help, were in shock. The sheriff had driven them into town for questioning, and even though they knew very little English, making it difficult to communicate, it was obvious from their glazed, sheet-white faces that they were not involved in this crime.

Seeing the children was the hardest. The baby was still in her crib when he arrived, exhausted from having been left alone crying for too long. Her face was puffy, and her diaper was sagging from the weight of too much pee over too long a period of time. And the other two children, looking about two and eight or nine years old, were huddled together on their parents' bed, heads down, unable to grasp the horrible scene around them. They were hanging onto each other for dear life.

It was the most heartbreaking scene that Forest had ever encountered. Up until that day, he hadn't thought too much about coloreds and their lot in life. But this colored family would never be the same after what they had just witnessed.

When Sheriff Monroe sat in his chair in his almost pitch-black office, he acknowledged to himself that he'd have to do more investigation into this poor woman's death, even though he had told his rookie that he was going to rule her death a suicide.

He had again methodically gone through what he'd observed when he arrived on the scene. There were the two Mexican field hands who'd been dragged by the children to witness this horror. Then there were the two ambulance drivers who had driven the young woman to the hospital. She'd been pronounced dead on arrival, but Forest Monroe was not clear if she'd been dead when they arrived. Had they tried to stop the bleeding? Had she had any chance of surviving? Were there any witnesses besides the children? Should he start with his medical examiner?

Several weeks after her death, as Forest had anxiously awaited news, he looked up in time to see the mail delivery girl slide a thick, yellow manila envelope under his door. She paused long enough to make sure that he had seen her place it there. He nodded with acknowledgment and hurriedly got up and snatched it from the floor. It was a preliminary autopsy report from his medical examiner.

He sat back down at his desk, propped his cowboy boots in their usual position, and jammed a cigar into his mouth. He couldn't help but notice that his hands were trembling. He stared at the envelope, focusing and refocusing on the official return address stamp from the Medical Examiner's office.

It was common knowledge that this particular ME was a hopeless alcoholic who had, many years ago, abandoned his life-long curiosity of letting the dead tell their stories. Usually, the only story he was telling was how quickly he could leave work and get to his bottle of Jack Daniels. But this time, Forest thought, it might be different. Of all of the coroners who could have gotten his case, it had to be Albert Johnson, ME, who was the only colored examiner for the entire state of California.

Forest leaned back in his chair, spun around, and planted his pointy-toed cowboy boots firmly on the sticky linoleum floor. He leaned over, put his head down between his knees, and clasped his hands together as if in prayer.

What was in that damn report? The clock's second hand answered back, saying, "O-pen-it, o-pen-it-and-find-out-Sheriff!" Each tick of the clock sounded like a thunderous roar that traveled from the morgue holding Ellen's remains to Forest's throbbing eardrums. The roaring ticking continued, and Forest, feeling as if his eardrums were about to burst, gave in and ripped the envelope open.

He couldn't focus. His eyes were burning and stinging simultaneously. He closed his eyes and pressed his thumb and index fingers into both eyelids. The stinging stopped. He wiped both eyes and tried to refocus.

Even though he knew he should take his time to read the full report, he skipped to the last page of the bulky document to focus on the cause of death.

1. **Exsanguination caused by**
2. **Gunshot wound to the abdomen**

Forest was perplexed. How did this happen? He went back to the beginning of the report, combing through, page by page. There was no mention of whether or not the ME found gunshot residue on Ellen's hands or arms. There wasn't even mention of how she could have shot herself with a twelve-gauge shotgun. He was at the crime scene and saw the shotgun. The only way the gun could have discharged was if she was barefoot. He had learned about that in the Police Academy. He was taught that there is too much distance between the barrel of the gun and the trigger, making it impossible to shoot yourself unless the trigger is pulled with the big toe. Or was there another way?

The first page of the autopsy report had the ME's contact number. Forest cocked his boots on the desk again, leaned back in his chair, and dialed the number.

"Albert, is that you, Albert?" Forest heard paper rustling and the sound of an old Bessie Smith number faintly coming through the phone line.

"Hold on," Albert answered. Forest could hear the clunk as Albert dropped the phone handset onto his desk and a loud scratch as he clumsily lifted the needle from the LP record. When Albert returned, he said, "You calling 'bout that colored gal they said shot herself?"

"Who said she shot herself?" Forest asked, "'Cause I thought you were supposed to determine the cause of death!"

After a short pause, the ME started mumbling about being short-staffed and how no diener, a morgue worker, wanted to work with him. Forest slammed the phone down with such force that it bounced off the desk and onto the linoleum floor. Well, he thought, it was a preliminary report. Maybe that nigger will get to work and do a real report.

Forest replaced the phone back onto his desk and looked up in time to see his rookie at the door.

"Sorry to bother you, Sheriff, but guess who's back?"

Forest placed his elbow on the desk, leaned over, and cupped his hand onto his forehead. Without looking up, he said dryly, "Send her in."

She sat down in the chair next to his desk, but neither of them made eye contact. She looked at the floor, and he continued looking down at his desk.

"I just wanna know what happened to my baby. They say the Medical Examiner was writing some kind of report—what did he say?" She leaned into his desk

Forest slowly lifted his head and looked at the woman. They were almost eye-to eye. She looked a lot calmer than three weeks ago. Before, she looked weepy and pitiful;

now, she looked angry.

"Ma'am…"

"Stop right there. Don't ma'am me, just tell me what happened. Did my son-in-law do it? 'Cause if he did, I'm gonna kill that nigga myself. Don't make no sense to leave three children without a Momma. What am I supposed to do?"

Forest cleared his throat and attempted to answer her, but she kept going.

"I tell you what, your little flunky that brought me in here say you ain't heard nothing from that medical examiner yet, but I'm coming back next week, and you all are gonna tell me something, or I'm gonna come up here every day raising all kind of hell!"

She pushed back her chair and was about to leave when she spotted the stack of papers containing her daughter's preliminary report. She saw, "Name of decedent, Ellen Jenkins," in huge, bold letters.

Forest watched as beads of perspiration instantly appeared on her forehead as she grabbed the back of her chair to steady herself. She spun around and plopped down onto the chair. Her eyes turned from smoldering to glassy, and her parted lips looked parched like all of the moisture had mysteriously left her body.

Forest grabbed her hand and squeezed it and watched as tears flooded down her dark brown cheeks. He regretted not hiding the autopsy report under the myriad of other papers on his desk.

Will We Ever Know What Happened?

DH had heard about Pet's visit to the Sheriff's office. Too many times. It had been several months since Pet had glanced at the stack of papers that held the secrets to their daughter's death. The sheriff had said it was a preliminary report that did not answer all of his questions. It would take months, he said, before they'd have the final report. As soon as he had more information, he'd be in touch. She had left his office unsatisfied. Dejected. Frustrated. Broken. Sad. Helpless.

In her most recent Thursday conversation with DH, Pet spent an exhausting, grief-stricken thirty minutes reliving her frustration with having no closure to their daughter's death. The one thing that tied them together was their Ellen. Over the past months, as their chance meetings became fewer and fewer, and as more and more Thursday phone calls were missed, either Pet or DH would find a way to rekindle the love they felt for each other. Strange as it was, Ellen was the glue that held them together.

He decided to get in touch with the coroner and send for a copy of his daughter's death certificate. He had actually made an appointment to meet him in Sacramento next week!

DH was now back to planning how to tell his wife, Cynthia. After several false starts and countless sleepless nights, he decided, why not tell her the truth? She knew he had a daughter who had died under mysterious circumstances. But of course, he wouldn't tell her the whole truth. It wasn't Cynthia's business that Pet was meeting him there.

Pet and DH had numerous conversations about why he was still with Cynthia. He felt her slipping away from him. He hoped the visit to the ME's office would bring them closer together again.

He figured the perfect time to tell Cynthia was the day Ellen's death certificate arrived in the mail. It was on a Thursday, his wife's choir practice, and Pet's calling day. It was late afternoon, sunny and breezy outside, the perfect day; DH hoped the death certificate would arrive.

Cynthia had watched DH from the front porch as he quickly ran out to greet the mailman. DH was dressed in his usual gray coveralls, high-top boots, and a baseball cap covering his prematurely balding head. Cynthia was dressed in a too-tight-for-her-breast size, lime-green halter top with mid-calf length shorts. Her thighs were already showing the tell-tell pockmarks of cellulite, and her head was covered with bright, pink hair rollers, with wisps of straight hair that had escaped the rollers.

Before he could close the mailbox door, Cynthia ran up to him and stuck out her hand, gesturing for him to hand her the mail. He shrugged and tried to step past her. She blocked his way and stuck out her hand again. He kept the mail in one hand and firmly grabbed her arm with his free hand and steered her towards the front steps. She tried to resist, but he held her firmly, and they walked together and sat down on the steps.

He let go of Cynthia's arm and opened the folder that held his daughter's death certificate. He smoothed out the document and placed it in his lap. They silently leaned over and read each line. What was most surprising was how little demographic information was there: Ellen's Father was listed as unknown. Maiden name of mother—instead of Pet's name, it had Ellen's maiden name! And Pet had apparently not given Ellen her father's last name of Jones, but Pet's maiden name of Merriman! It did have her correct date of birth and death, but both Ellen and Orville's last names were incorrectly spelled. The coroner's signature was not legible. Thankfully, below the signature was a typed spelling of his first and last name. The worst part was reading the cause of death. Gunshot wound to the abdomen, apparently due to suicide. That was it. DH folded the certificate, and folded it, and folded it until it was a thick wad of paper with very sharp creases. For once, Cynthia kept quiet

They both rose and walked away, Cynthia to the kitchen to pre-pare a quick meal before choir practice and DH to his private tool shed hideaway. As they departed from each other, DH said, "I'm going to Sacramento next week to see the coroner." He didn't wait for a response. Cynthia simply cleared her throat to acknowledge that she had heard him

Sitting in his toolshed, DH heard a car horn and knew that one of the women was there to pick up his wife. He visibly relaxed, knowing that he'd have a few hours to himself. The boys, both talented tenors, were meeting their Mom at church.

DH ran back into the kitchen to grab the phone and pull the 25-foot cord into the shed. He stared at the black rotary-dial phone, willing it to ring. It did.

"Pet, is that you?"

"Of course, it's me, you old, damn fool!" she laughed.

DH laughed, and his spirit lifted, but he quickly sobered as he unfolded the death certificate that he had thrust into his pocket.

"Pet, I got our daughter's certificate today." He propped his feet up against the corrugated wall of the tool shed and spread the death notice out on his workbench. He spent several minutes detailing the sloppy way that Ellen's death had been recorded. He didn't mention to Pet that Cynthia had seen it with him.

"We gonna have a long row to hoe when it comes to dealing with these white folks at the county offices about our daughter. If they didn't care enough to properly fill out her death certificate, they don't give a damn whether she killed herself or not," Pet sighed.

DH shifted his weight on the workshop stool. The pain of knowing that those in power did not give much value to his daughter's life but were able to make decisions about how much time and money could be spent investigating her death hurt him to the core. "I don't think they care, do you, Pet?

Pet nodded but said nothing.

"Did you hear me, Pet?"

"Sorry, DH, yes, I heard you." She was again in her favorite phone booth, but this time there was no one around waiting to use the phone. The temperature outside had dropped, and the cool wind was coming in through gaps in the door and sides of the booth. It was a rare evening with a static-free line; it sounded like DH could have been in the phone booth with her.

"Dee, you know another thing we gotta think about is Orville. He was the one who provided them the information. Shit, I heard that fool can barely even read and write! Maybe he didn't have sense enough to tell them people what to fill out!"

DH was absent-mindedly twirling the white cord around his fingers. "Well, Pet, maybe he was guilty and too scared to give them her information. We gonna have to plan our strategy to get the most we can outta them folks and make sure they investigate everything and everyone! If Orville did it, I want him to pay!"

Across the parking lot from the phone booth, Pet watched as a lone California Highway patrolman searched inside her car by pointing his bulky black flashlight into the front and back windows. He was walking all around the car as if he was looking for something or someone.

"I gotta go, Dee. We'll talk about this more later. Look like Mr. Charlie's checking out my car!" She hurriedly hung up the phone, listening as her precious quarters clanged to the bottom of the pay phone's empty coin box.

CHAPTER 59

They Bake in the Sun and Turn into Raisins

When Pet arrived home, frustrated from her encounter with the patrolman, Lily and Latisha Kay were sitting on the kitchen floor, enjoying their never-ending pastime of dressing paper dolls.

Latisha Kay was using her newest make-shift tool, Scotch tape, to independently stand each dressed doll up on the linoleum floor. Just as she was about to brag to Lily about her successful venture, one of the dolls' bodies bent over in an awkward pose that made Lily laugh.

Latisha Kay pouted, "What's so funny, Lily?"

Lily, laughing so hard she could hardly speak, stuttered, "She reminds me of grandmother when we used to go out in the fields cuttin' grapes and knocking down almonds!"

"You did fieldwork?" Latisha Kay asked, doubtful that Lily ever did hard work like that. Two more dolls toppled completely over, and Lily was beside herself with laughter.

"Yep, and that's how me and grandmother looked by quittin' time," Lily said pointing to the falling doll. "Phew, that was some hard-darn work!"

Latisha Kay began picking up her sticky-footed dolls from the floor and gingerly placing them in their toy box. "So, Lily, tell me, what was it like, I mean, working in the field all day?"

Lily, sitting with her knees folded under her legs, leaned toward Latisha Kay. "That's not a job I would wish on anybody." First, they make you get up when it's still dark outside. Then you gotta wash up and put on the oldest, raggediest clothes you got. Then you gotta find some farm out in the middle of nowhere and start working."

Latisha Kay, who had never been on a farm, sat on the floor with her legs folded, mesmerized as Lily continued recounting her field-work tales.

"And the people working there—there's mostly Mexicans, some coloreds, and white trash. And everybody looked tired, even when we first got there! Most of the time, I tried to tell grandmother that I didn't feel good, but she didn't care!"

"Last time we did fieldwork, we were living in Tulare with Mayola and them. Grandmother heard Mayola talking about cutting grapes in Firebaugh, and next thing I know, we spent all day on a Saturday cuttin' and spreadin' grapes!"

Latisha Kay had finished putting up her paper dolls, and Lily, noticing that she was enjoying hearing about her work in the fields, continued, "When I told grandmother I wasn't feeling good, she handed me a bucket and marched me out to a row of grapevines so long, I thought it would go from here to China!"

Both girls laughed. "When I stood there like I didn't know what to do, she gave me a two-minute lesson. She cut a bucket full of Thompson grapes, pushed 'em towards me, and said, 'Here, spread these out on these brown-paper sheets. 'Just so you know, I did what I was told. I spread the grapes out on the sheets, and then she said, "No, spread them evenly and work with both hands!"

"By noon time, I was hungry, thirsty, tired, and feeling kinda' woozy. When grandmother saw how I was looking, she fussed at me for not drinking water from the canteen she brought along. How was I supposed to know to drink a lot of water?"

Now, both girls were well into the story, Lily from the telling perspective and Tish from the hearing. They could hear the boys outside playing catch and the shuffling and stacking sounds from grandmother's playing cards coming from her bedroom. She and Solitaire were at it again.

Lily continued, "Grandmother had fixed us some baloney sandwiches, and we even had a bag of Laura Scudder potato chips—that was the best part of my day!"

Latisha Kay frowned, "You got to eat while you were out in the field? Did they ring a cowbell or something? Where did you sit?"

"Of course, we got to eat, silly. You can't do that kind of hard work without eating and drinking plenty of water. I learned my lesson that day. The field boss kept a big barrel of water for us, and we kept filling our canteens all day long.

"For lunch, we sat wherever we could find shade. Grandmother was smart; she staked out our shade tree when we first got there. She put our cooler under there and gave everybody that look, like, don't mess with my stuff. And they didn't!"

Latisha Kay burst out laughing again, Lily joined her. "Well, I still don't understand the spreading part. Why were you spreading grapes on brown paper sheets?"

Lily, shaking her head, gazed at Tish with a look of stark amazement. "They bake in the sun and turn into raisins!"

Latisha Kay responded with a soft, "Oh."

When the girls abandoned their paper-doll play, they decided it was time to engage in another fun pastime, sneaking up to spy on grandmother. It was an enjoyable activity because they liked to see how grownups behave when they think no one is looking.

CHAPTER 60

Time to Watch the Grownups

Pet's bedroom was near a small alcove near the stairway leading up to the upstairs bedrooms. If the girls positioned themselves just right, they could see her entire tiny bedroom and not, in turn, be seen from their hide-a-way across the hall.

As they suspected, she was sitting up in bed, with the top of a TV tray in her lap, ready to play her game of Solitaire. She had not yet begun selecting her third card from the remaining cards in the deck to commence playing when 'Tish and Lily slipped into their cubby hole to watch.

Pet placed a row of seven cards on the tray, each card's stack containing from one to seven cards. The evenly spaced cards barely fit across the dark, severely-scratched wooden TV tray. Pet flipped over the third card in her hand and waved it across the rows of cards, scanning for a place to match the card. Seeing none, she selected her next third card and repeated the scanning process. Again, finding no matches for any of her remaining cards in the deck, she frowned, gathered all of her cards, and began reshuffling them. "You got me that time, Solitaire, but don't think that'll ever happen again!"

She was about to start a new game when the phone rang. Both Latisha Kay and Lily quickly slipped back into their room.

No other adult was at home, so Pet begrudgingly padded to the living room to pick up the phone. The volume was set too high, and both girls plugged their ears to muffle the shrill ringing noise that was reverberating throughout the house. They tiptoed into the hallway near the living room entrance.

"Hello, DH, is that you? It ain't Thursday, and you callin' me. Is everything all right?"

Both girls settled in; this was going to be juicy. They weren't close enough to hear what Lily's grandfather was saying, but they were both good at figuring out most of the conversation.

"Yeah, Yeah, of course, I remember what we talked about last time. You say the sheriff and coroner are gonna meet with us? What you say!"

Both Lily and 'Tish were almost falling over themselves trying to get into the best position to hear grandmother's conversation.

Pet lowered her voice, and all they could hear was, "Yeah, I think I'll leave Lily here with the Broussards; she's too young. Them poor kids will never get over losing their mother like this. Her voice got even lower, "Orville…involved…jealous?"

The next thing they heard was the phone being softly placed back into its cradle. They both tensed, knowing that any moment, grandmother would come charging out of her room. But it was really quiet. Then they heard her sobbing. Lily stood up and quickly ran to their room, 'Latisha Kay following close behind her. When they reached their room, Lily sat in the middle of her narrow bed and could not stop the tears from spilling down her face. She absentmindedly grabbed a corner of her white ribbed bedspread and dabbed at her tears.

"What's the matter, Lily?" It was Latisha Kay's turn to cry; she wasn't sure why, but Lily looked so sad that it was contagious.

A flock of red-wing blackbirds landed on the willow tree outside their bedroom window and began loudly squawking, making it hard for them to hear each other. The shadow created by the flock darkened the room, and neither of them attempted to speak. After a few minutes, the birds flew away, and the room brightened and became quiet again.

"Lily, I know I'm not supposed to ask, but can you talk about what happened to your mother?" Latisha Kay's voice was barely above a whisper, and she did not make eye contact with Lily.

"No," Lily replied, and a fresh set of tears spilled down her cheeks. "I just wished it had never happened. Everybody I know has a mother but me!" She stretched out on the bed, face down into her pillow.

Latisha Kay sat on the bed next to her and gently rubbed her shoulders. She didn't know what to say; she just rubbed and squeezed. Within a few minutes, Lily had cried herself to sleep. She arose from the bed and slipped out of the room.

She went looking for Grandpa and found him in the kitchen, preparing for tonight's dinner. As she approached, Broussard noticed her puffy face and became alarmed. "What's wrong, Latisha Kay? You look like you just lost your best friend?"

Latisha Kay propped up on the kitchen stool closest to her grandfather, and cried, "Oh, Grandpa, Lily is so sad, and I don't know how to help her!"

Broussard grabbed her around her waist, placed her in his lap, and kissed her neck. "Oh, chile, everything is gonna be alright. Now, what's happening with Lily? She seemed okay when she helped me with breakfast this morning."

"Well," 'Tish sobbed, "I think Lily's grandmother and grandfather are going to see the cronna. I don't know who that is, but Lily's grandmother started crying. I've never seen grownups cry. Grandpa, what's a cronna?"

"Chile, you mean *coroner*; that's the man who examines dead bodies to find out what happened to them."

"Oh, grandpa, that's awful!"

CHAPTER 61

When Death Comes Calling

The awful truth was that DH did not relish the trip to the Sacramento County coroner's office. During his phone conversation with Pet, her voice had become quieter and quieter. At one point, he could have sworn that she was crying. In all of their years of having their on-again, off-again relationship, he always knew when life was getting the best of her, and it certainly was now.

When a woman like Pet, with a half-dozen mostly ne'er-do-well children, loses the cream of her crop, pain and misery follow her around like an orphaned lamb, painfully looking for a surrogate mother when none are to be found. DH noticed that the loss of Ellen appeared to negate the one thing Pet thought represented her success as a mother. And her cream, Ellen, was his child too, the only child that they'd had together!

As DH mulled over the tragedy that had brought him and Pet closer together, he stood up from his stool in the toolshed, grabbed the envelope holding his child's death certificate, found a blank piece of paper, and began to write out a series of questions for the coroner. He wanted to be prepared. A tear dropped onto the paper, and he quickly dabbed it with his handkerchief as he looked over the questions.

1. Did the ambulance drivers try to revive her in any way?

2. How long did it take them to get her to the hospital?

3. Was she able to talk to them on the way?

4. Did they look for a suicide note?

5. Was she barefoot when they put her in the ambulance?

6. Could he and Pet talk to the drivers?

The shed was getting more and more stuffy, and DH, beginning to feel faint, rose to open the door. All he could think about was Ellen's lonely, twenty-two-mile ride in the ambulance to the county hospital, surely a bumpy ride with a couple of two-bit EMT drivers who didn't give a damn about his daughter.

Ellen had taken her last breath alone, probably while hearing the mournful siren wail from the back section of an ambulance with no one around who cared about her. Did they even attempt to save her?

A waft of dusty air blew into the shed, causing the paper with the list of questions to flitter about and finally land on the floor, in the dirt, just like his Ellen's final resting place. DH couldn't shake the sorrowful state he was currently in, but he knew it was of his own making. He retrieved the coroner's list, folded it neatly into his coverall pocket, and tried to concentrate on his new-found mission: finding out what happened before, during, and after that fatal gunshot wound that killed his daughter.

Pet was also thinking about their daughter, but she was recalling her conversation with Lily about her mother's embalming. Apparently, the children in school knew about embalming, and told Lily that's what happened to her mother. They actually teased her about it! Every day after that, she had begged Pet to tell her about her mother's embalming. All Pet could think about was how much Lily wanted to hear about her mother; what the poor child didn't realize was that Ellen was Pet's daughter. And talking about Ellen was just too painful.

After hanging up the phone from DH, she couldn't stop herself from crying. It was the first time she had cried since Ellen's funeral. The longer she cried, the better she felt. For reasons she couldn't understand, she needed to call her mother. They didn't talk much, but now seemed like the perfect time.

She swung around in the bed, letting her feet dangle to the side, and plopped the phone on the tiny, rickety nightstand beside her bed. Her mother answered on the first ring. "Hi, Momma, how you doing?"

"Pet, is that you? My, oh my, I ain't heard from you in a month of Sundays!" Her voice was loud, and the scratchy phone lines made it painful for Pet to place the earpiece too close to her ears. She pulled the phone further away and answered.

"Oh, I'm doing fair to middling…"

Her mother interrupted her as Pet moved the earpiece even further away.

"Pet, you don't sound right. You been crying?" Before Pet could answer, she continued, "You ain't got to tell me no story, baby. Remember, I birthed you—I can tell when you been cryin.'"

Pet could feel the large, wet tears gushing down her face, and because she was alone in her bedroom, she made no attempt to hide them. Pet had never known her mother to exhibit kindness or sympathy towards her, but Pet could hear an unfamiliar concern in her mother's voice. *Where the hell was she when she sent me to live with Toots*, Pet thought.

"Well, me and DH are going to visit the coroner in Sacramento next week about Ellen's death, and I was feeling kinda low." Pet was nervously fidgeting, not used to confiding in her mother. She scooted to the edge of the bed and planted her feet flat on the linoleum floor to keep the bed from squeaking.

"Well, baby," her mother responded quickly, "as you know, I haven't lost a child yet, and I can't imagine what it feels like, but I'll be home all next week, and you and DH can come and see me afterwards. Maybe I'll make us some chicken and dumplings, and we'll have us a good old cryin' session, you hear?"

"Yes, Momma."

CHAPTER 62

But That Don't Make Him Guilty

The appointment date with the coroner had arrived, and Pet and DH were about to travel together in his brand-new Volkswagen Beetle. Ellen's death lay heavy on their hearts, and they were both in a somber mood.

They had met on the outskirts of town in a dingy, smoke-filled restaurant called the Dew Drop In. It was the same restaurant that many truckers, including Orville, frequented. Pet had arrived first and found the cook, Henry, outside sucking on a stubby cigarette butt. She walked up on him just as he was about to burn his mustache, trying to drag the last bit of tobacco from it.

As all colored folks do when greeting one another as strangers, she nodded in his direction, then struck up a conversation. "I didn't know they had a colored cook. How long you been working here?"

Henry, not surprised by the question, responded, "Oh, I used to be a cook in Uncle Sam's army, so they gave this ol' colored boy a chance. Been here since I left Korea in '53, damn near four years!"

Henry was a proud man with honey-brown skin, a large, protruding forehead, piercing black eyes, and wavy, black hair. He looked like he could have been part Korean, but his unmistakable Cajun twang gave his birthplace away.

Today he wore an all-white uniform, complete with a tall chef's hat. Pet, wearing her usual loose-fitting colorful muumuu, wished that she had worn something else. He was a fine piece of manhood to look at!

"Say, do you think your boss would mind if I left my Black Beauty here for a few days while I travel to Sacramento with a friend?"

"'Course not, just park it behind the restrooms near the back alley," Henry said without hesitating.

"Thanks! What you say your name is, Henry, right?"

"Yep, I'm Henry, alright, and it's mighty nice to meet you." He allowed his eyes to freely roam over Pet's body and looked as though he saw something of interest.

Pet blushed and hustled inside to meet DH.

He was sitting at a table, puffing on a Camel cigarette, and after each drag, allowing the ashes to hang over the ashtray. He enjoyed watching the ashes burn and made a game out of seeing how long the ashes would remain on the cigarette before falling into the ashtray.

DH always sat where he could see his car from the window.

Pet joined him. "DH, what in the world made you decide to buy that funny-ass looking car? I mean, look at it."

"Now, Pet, you know I'm cheap, and for three dollars I can fill up that tank and the spare tank that comes with it," DH chuckled.

Pet joined in the laughter, "Yeah, but it's still an ugly car!"

Several diners at nearby tables joined in the laughter, and for once, the normal tension that ensues when one or more colored diners enter the restaurant was absent. Having a colored man cook for you was one thing, but sitting at a table next to you, not so good!

They continued their bantering until the sun was beginning to make a rapid descent in the western sky. Each of them had made scooting noises with their chairs as if they were about to get up and leave, but Pet finally did get up, seized her purse, and headed for the door. DH grabbed the check and stood behind the cash register to pay.

When they were finally in the car together, their somber mood began in earnest. "Now look, Pet, I made up a list of questions for the coroner. You can look and see if you want to add any more, okay?"

DH had placed the list of questions on the top of the gear shift between their two seats, and Pet watched as the paper fell from the shaking gear shift and floated onto the floor. She was already crying.

"Look, Pet, our daughter's gone, but our job is to find out why. These white folks have not spent any time investigating what happened to her, and that's why we're going to do this."

DH was speaking in a tone so soft and caring, that Pet felt even worse. But she stifled her grief and wiped her tears so she could read the list. For the remaining drive, Pet kept imagining Ellen gazing at the expansive blue sky with patches of white billowy clouds above as she took her last breath alone in the back seat of a county ambulance, aware that she was on her way to heaven.

They reached Sacramento before nightfall and decided to stay with Nedra and Ray. Both Pet and DH felt that being rested was an important aspect of visiting the coroner. It had been several months since Lily and Pet had visited, but she and DH had decided that it would be better to stay there than at a cheap motel. Besides, Ray and Nedra were one of the last family members to have seen Ellen alive, except, of course, Orville.

Nedra greeted them at the door. "Hey, you two! You all come on in; I know you tired after that long drive. You got any bags you bringing in?"

Nedra looked the same: still pretty in her fashionable, one-piece, teal jumpsuit with fancy, matching, fake-rhinestone sandals. Again, Pet was sorry she was wearing her loose-fitting, loudly colored muumuu.

Looking around and seeing no one else, Pet asked, "Where's Ray and the children?"

Nedra helped them move their bags to the spare bedroom and answered, "The kids are all on punishment in their rooms, and Ray's on his way back from feeding the chickens in the hen house. Come on in the living room and rest yourselves."

They all heard the back-screen door slam as Ray entered the house and made his way into the living room. "Hey, DH, man! I think the last time I saw you was at Ell…"

"Yeah, man, it's been a while," DH interrupted him.

Glancing over to the couch, Ray spotted Pet sitting quietly. "Hey, Pet, I didn't see you sitting over here. How you doing?"

"I'm doing fine, Ray."

Ray and Nedra hadn't discussed Nedra's idea of raising Pet's grandchildren, and from his conversation with his wife before Pet and DH's arrival, he was relieved that this visit had nothing to do with the children. He'd hoped that it was a closed decision that he and Nedra would not be discussing anytime soon.

They were all sitting on the couch, except for Nedra. She was leaning on the arm of the large, overstuffed chair facing them.

"We have an appointment with the coroner in the morning," said Pet. "We hoping he can help us figure out what happened to our Ellen."

Both Ray and Nedra glanced nervously at each other. They weren't sure where this conversation was heading.

"Did Ellen seem depressed the last time you saw her?" DH asked, trying very hard not to sound accusatory. "I know it's been almost three years since she died, but we just don't think she killed herself. I mean, there were three children in that house, and baby Lorna was in her crib and saw the whole thing! I wish she could tell us what she saw." DH's voice was almost a whisper, and the rest of them had to strain to hear what was being said.

Without speaking, Ray and Nedra gazed into each other's eyes, inched closer together, and began holding hands. Nedra was the first to speak. "We been thinking the same thing, but Pet, we don't know how to tell you or what to say." She paused. The room became eerily quiet. "Orville's my brother, and I love him, but something seems suspicious to us too." She paused again. Silence.

"Well, what do you think?" DH's voice rose to a high pitch. He pursed his thin lips together and waited.

"Well," Nedra began, "after they took Ellen away," Ray pulled out a clean white handkerchief from his shirt pocket and handed it to her, "we went to the house, and he was standing there with all that blood, and he was leaning over the kitchen sink, tearing up and burning all of her pictures!" Nedra dabbed at her eyes and continued, "I didn't think about it then 'cause we were there to help him clean up the place. He looked so guilty; he wouldn't even look us in the eye!"

Nedra was shamelessly crying now, not even attempting to wipe the large tears rolling down her cheeks. Ray looked from his wife to his handkerchief and decided to let her be.

Pet, sitting on the edge of the couch, got up, and began pacing. "Well, was he?" She had broken into a cold sweat, and the scent coming from her underarms was not pleasant.

"We don't know, but God help us all," Nedra continued. "We think he had something to do with her death."

Pet almost lost her balance as her foot stopped in midair, nearly frozen in place. She regained her composure and rushed over to Nedra, "Well, what do you think happened?"

Pet was having a hard time remaining upright, and she plopped down on a smaller chair next to Nedra. Pet tried not to imagine what must have been a frightening end to her daughter's precious life. The more she tried, the more blood she could see and smell and feel. Even the floor underneath her shoes felt sticky.

DH and Ray looked on as if they were watching an intense movie drama unfolding in front of their eyes. Like most men they knew, they felt helpless in the face of two vocally grieving women. It was hard for them not to join in.

Ray rose from the couch and faced the two women and DH. "Look, me and Nedra ain't for sure. I mean, we don't have no proof. Why don't we wait and see what the coroner says? I mean…"

Nedra got up from the couch and interrupted him, "Ray, now don't you go making me mad! You always said you thought my brother was too jealous-hearted, and you agreed that he looked guilty!"

"Yeah, but that don't make him guilty." Ray's voice had an edge to it that was not missed by Nedra. Ray hated disagreeing with his wife, especially in front of DH and Pet, but he felt it his duty to talk some sense into her. He touched the top of Nedra's shoulder, his voice softening, "I'm sorry, baby, that poor girl's been dead for a while now, and it's hard for all of us to talk about her death. Let's wait 'til DH and Pet have visited the coroner and see what he says."

Ray and Nedra exchanged glances, and her eyes let Ray know that they were back on even footing. Ray relaxed back into the couch again, "I hear tell it's that colored drunk Albert that performed Ellen's autopsy. They tell me he might've sobered up for this one, though. Ain't too many coloreds that have the privilege of getting the county to pay for an autopsy."

DH, who had been watching the three of them, got up from the couch. "Ray, let's put on some music. What you got here?" He strolled over to the phonograph, went through Ray's stacks of '78s, and carefully pulled out Billie Holiday's Gloomy Sunday from its jacket. They all watched in silence as the phonograph's turntable accepted the shiny, black vinyl record, and DH placed the needle onto the first groove. Billie's soft melodic voice filled the living room with the lyrics from her song, Gloomy Sunday.

Pet stood up, "No, no, no, this is the wrong kind of music. Shit, let's play something else!"

Nedra joined her, "Yes, I wanna dance, let's have some fun!"

Hearing Billie's sorrowful tune had snapped the two of them out of their mood, and they couldn't wait to break the spell that had fallen over all of them.

From her perch on the couch, Pet spied a Chuck Berry '45, and soon "Maybelline" filled the void previously occupied by Billie.

All four of them hurriedly scooted the furniture to the corner of the room and began dancing. Next, Ray found an Etta James song, "At Last," and the two couples held onto each other tightly. While they danced, Nedra and Pet's eyes locked, and an unspoken thought between them said, yes, we are in love with our men, and this is good.

Nedra and Ray's children could hear the music emanating from the thin walls next to their adjacent bedrooms. They tiptoed into the hallway and crept toward the living room entrance.

Nettie, the youngest and prettiest, who looked just like Nedra, was pushed into the living room by Ray Jr., the oldest. Hearing no reprimands or protest from the grownups, the rest of the children sheepishly joined Nettie in the living room, all beaming at the adults, knowing that their punishment was officially over. Ray, Nedra, Pet, and DH beamed back, unofficially deciding that all talk about Orville and Ellen was over.

The next morning, DH had awakened before Pet and decided not to disturb her. He wandered toward the kitchen, thinking about Pet and how he enjoyed his coffee as he liked his women, very dark. Most mornings at home, his wife made his coffee, but today, here in Sacramento with Pet, he decided he'd make his own coffee, if no one else was up.

The aroma of coffee greeted him when he entered the kitchen and discovered that Ray was already there, drinking coffee and adjusting the rabbit ears on a shiny, new silver transistor radio that was sitting on the countertop. Ray turned the radio volume down as he heard DH enter. "Say, man, you up too?"

DH glanced at the phone book sitting atop the refrigerator before answering, "Yeah, couldn't sleep, so I thought, might as well get up!"

He helped himself to a cup of coffee and grabbed the Yellow Pages, flipping the pages until he reached the white government section. There he saw that the coroner's office would open at 9:00 am. His appointment was at 10:00 am, but he hoped that he could be seen earlier.

As DH drank his coffee and perused the phone book, Ray kept adjusting his staticky radio, trying desperately to hear an old Bessie Smith tune blasting noisily through the speakers. He kept turning the knob slightly to the left and then to the right, attempting to hone in on a nearby station that aired colored music from midnight to early morning. Every few seconds, he'd hear Bessie loud and clear, and then a piercing blast of static would penetrate into his inner ears.

Neither man wanted to continue last night's conversation about DH and Pet visiting the coroner's office today. And they certainly didn't want to talk about Orville's possible involvement in Ellen's death. Ray continued to adjust his radio, and DH read and re-read the coroner's office hours from the White Pages.

Albert arrived early to the coroner's office. He had planned his day carefully. No alcohol last night. He'd wanted to be as sober as possible in preparation for his meeting with the dead girl's parents and the county sheriff.

As he opened the door to his outer office, he paused abruptly. He didn't expect his secretary to be there, but there she was, at least thirty minutes early! Both looked at each other, shocked. Albert was dressed in his usual starched white shirt and black bow tie, accompanied with his white doctor's jacket and khaki trousers. He hadn't shaved, and his gray whiskers poked out around his chin and upper lip, contrasting sharply with his medium-brown skin. He subconsciously covered his mouth, greeted the surprised Mary gruffly, and hurried into his tiny bathroom to shave.

Mary, wearing her usual cotton dress, suddenly remembered that she hadn't removed all of her pink foam rollers, and she, too, rushed out into the hallway bathroom to finish her morning grooming. In the mirror, her pink face was flushed beet red, and the pores on her skin were larger than she could ever remember. But she had good eyes; she knew it. They were clear and blue as the sky on a beautiful spring day, matching perfectly with her blue and white dress.

By a quarter to nine, both Mary and Albert were in their respective places: Albert with his office door shut, reviewing his hand-written preliminary autopsy documents, and Mary sitting in an alcove adjacent to his office, typing one of his final post-mortem reports.

Albert opened his office door and motioned to Mary, "Can you find the autopsy report for that colored, uh, colored girl who was killed a couple of years ago?"

Mary rose from her desk, "You mean that gal who killed herself— humph?" From Mary's perspective, it was a suicide, no question, and her voice betrayed her contempt for the dead girl. "I don't know why we have to waste our taxpayer's money." With one cutting stare from Albert, Mary ceased talking.

Albert knew that when Mary said "our," she was not talking about him. He returned to his desk, and Mary began searching for the dead girl's files. The coroner's office had never performed an autopsy on a colored girl, so there was no question which file she would be searching for.

When she found the file, she tossed it on his desk with such force that the photographs of the dead girl taken from the bedroom floor where she had fallen, along with two newspaper articles, dropped onto the floor at Albert's feet. Mary stepped back, shocked at the dead eyes, wide-open, staring back at her.

"I'm so sorry, Dr. Johnson." She scooped up the file with the pictures and autopsy report and took them back to her desk.

Before Mary saw Ellen's picture, she was just a dead-colored girl who no one cared about. Now, as Mary sat, staring at the pictures and reading the newspaper reports, she saw a young mother and wife, and somebody's daughter.

She gingerly placed the file back onto Albert's desk, and with a quivering voice, whispered, "Do you mind if I take the day off today? I am feeling very sick to my stomach."

Before Albert could answer, she grabbed her purse, ran out heading for the bathroom, while cupping her hands over her mouth.

Pet and DH were about to stop the girl running toward the bathroom, but the wild look in her eyes changed their minds.

They saw an elderly, colored gentleman slowly swiping the floor with a mop and holding a handle that seemed taller than he was. They were about to stop and ask him for directions to the coroner's office, but saw the sign ahead, Albert Johnson, ME, Sacramento County Coroner's Office.

Shaven and sober, with his starched white shirt and black bow tie, Albert looked quite handsome and competent. He gestured for DH and Pet to have a seat in his tiny office.

DH stared at Albert. He never dreamed that the medical examiner would be colored. He looked from Albert to the framed diploma from the Armed Forces Institute of Pathology, where Albert had graduated.

Albert smiled coyly. He enjoyed this part when visitors took in the shock of being in the company of a colored medical examiner. There was also a photograph of President Dwight David Eisenhower shaking his hand as he handed Albert his diploma at his graduation ceremony. Even more of a shock.

DH and Pet visibly relaxed in their assigned chairs. Maybe they'd find out what really happened to their daughter.

DH rose and spoke first, "Now, my wife," he didn't want to complicate the meeting with details of his relationship with Pet, "tells me that she met with Sheriff Monroe a while back, and he said that he was the sheriff and coroner. Last time Pet saw him, he had just received a copy of the autopsy report that you signed."

Albert leaned forward in his chair, keenly focused on maintaining eye contact with DH.

Ellen's father continued, "Doctor, you got me confused here. Pet saw a copy of our gal's autopsy report, and your signature was on it. Is it you or the sheriff who's gonna tell us what really happened to Ellen?"

Pet, dressed more formal than usual in a starched white blouse and navy skirt, glanced nervously back and forth between DH and the ME. She was already sweating, and a large jagged, yellow ring appeared on underarms of her shirt.

Albert cleared his throat, stood up, and began pacing around his desk, keeping an eye on both Pet and DH.

"Your daughter died in Clarksburg, which is an unincorporated, rural area. The way it works out there is Monroe is both the sheriff and coroner. His official duty, when it comes to your daughter, is to identify the body, notify the next of kin, return belongings to the family and sign the death certificate. He's not a doctor or a medical examiner."

Albert returned to his chair, leaned back, and his chest appeared to inflate as he spoke. His voice seemed to take on a booming, professor-like quality.

Pet and DH exchanged somber glances.

"When the sheriff arrived at her home, the ambulance had already transported her to the hospital, where she was pronounced dead on arrival. They call that DOA, and that's what's on her death certificate."

Albert leaned over his desk and buried his nose in Ellen's files and thoughtfully glanced at each page as he spoke, "Says here in the sheriff's report that…"

The ME looked up just as Sheriff Monroe walked into the office, not bothering to knock. All three looked up in surprise.

Pet and DH watched in shock as Albert's demeanor immediately changed in the face of a white man entering their domain. All eyes were immediately downcast, and the ME timidly glanced in the sheriff's direction.

"Hello, uh, I mean, how can I help you, sheriff?" Albert stood and offered his chair to Monroe.

"Oh, Albert, sit back down. I just came to see how I can help." Pet's body immediately puffed up, and she glared in his direction. The last time she had seen Monroe, he had made it clear that he was not planning to waste taxpayer money investigating her daughter's death.

What Pet didn't know was during his last visit with her, he had changed. Watching Pet cry in his office had affected him in ways that even he didn't understand. He'd had nightmares and an unexplained guilt from having turned her away. He'd tried to rationalize his decision to ignore her and her plight, but couldn't. He'd thought about retiring early or changing jobs—anything to get that damn girl and her children out of his mind.

In the end, he'd settled on working with Albert, and today was his first step. The sheriff found a chair in the hallway and dragged it into the crowded office. He shook DH's hand, nodded to Albert and Pet, and sat down. They stared in disbelief.

When a white man like Forrest Monroe, a staunch conservative with lifelong, deeply embedded prejudices, takes a stand for the little man, it is a thing to behold. Pet, DH, and Albert stared at him in wonderment.

To Albert, who had had many unpleasant encounters with Monroe, everything about Forrest had changed.

Before anyone could speak, Monroe said, "I tracked down the ambulance drivers and have some good news. Now, you may be wondering," he focused his gaze upon Pet, "why all of a sudden, I want to help you, folks." He broadened his gaze to include Albert and DH. "Well, I tell you, the day after I last met with you," he said, gesturing to Pet, "I had a talking to myself."

Pet was so mesmerized by this changed sheriff that she sat, legs crossed, mouth agape, purse clutched tightly to her chest, staring at him intently.

Everyone's attention was focused on Monroe.

"And I said to myself, Forrest, you were born white, and Ellen and her family were born colored." And then I said, "None of us gets to choose which race we're gonna be born into. It's an accident of birth, that's all! You all didn't ask to be born colored. It was already preordained by God. And the day I saw your daughter, when she was brought to the morgue, I knew right then and there that when we're dead, we all look the same—not breathing."

He felt all eyes upon him as he once again stared intently at the dead girl's mother. "I saw your grandchildren when I got to the house, all three of them. Looking at those poor children broke my heart, and since I'm looking at this colored problem in a different light, I vowed to myself that we gonna find out what happened to that poor girl, and I don't care who done it, colored or white, they are gonna be punished! And if nobody did it, I mean, if she did it to herself, we're gonna find that out too, right Albert?"

Albert, DH, and Pet grinned sheepishly as they nodded affirmatively in Sheriff Monroe's direction. Albert had yet to regain his composure since Monroe had first arrived, so he didn't speak, just kept nodding.

Monroe rose from his chair and opened the tiny window in the corner of Albert's office. The small cubby hole, with four people occupying it, had rapidly become unbearably stuffy.

Forrest continued, "Now, back to the ambulance drivers; I interviewed them last week."

All three listeners were on the edges of their chairs, holding on to Monroe's every word.

"Your daughter died on the way to the hospital," he said in a monotonous, somber tone.

Pet gasped and cried out, "Oooh weee, my baby!"

DH said nothing but squeezed Pet's hand while rubbing her thigh with his other hand. Albert sat stone-faced.

"They think someone else was in the house besides your daughter and the children."

Before Monroe could continue, DH rose from his chair and practically shouting, "Who else?"

"They said it was hard to understand her, but it sounded like she kept saying, 'I tried to stop him!'"

"Well, who was it? And stop him from what?" Pet wailed as she attempted to stand, but was unsteady. DH grabbed her around the waist to keep her from collapsing on the floor.

"They say that's all she said," Monroe responded. "I'm sorry. But the good news is I don't think she killed herself!"

Monroe gestured to Albert, "You've done the final autopsy report. What else did you find?" Forrest had, in fact, read Albert's preliminary report months ago and knew that Ellen actually killing herself was a longshot.

Albert stood up and cleared his throat. "I, uh, I concur with you, sir. That girl had defensive wounds all over her arms and hands. She really fought for her life..."

Pet let out another long, painful wail.

Albert continued, "She bled to death, sir, and there's no question about it. The shotgun wound to her abdomen could not have been done by her, not unless she was barefoot, and we know from the police report that she was not."

DH eased himself and Pet back into their respective chairs. "But I don't understand. What does our daughter being barefoot have to do with it?"

"Well, Mr. Jones, that's a good question." Albert patiently began explaining the science of forensics. "A twelve-gauge shotgun cannot be readily used to kill oneself. There's too much length between the gun's trigger and the human body. The barrel is just too long. The only possible way is for a person to use their toe to activate the trigger, and it's very unlikely that this young girl would be trained enough in firearms to pull off that stunt!"

Pet stood up again, but this time she was steady on her feet, "So the good news is that she didn't kill herself?" she asked incredulously.

"That's the good news? I thought you were going to tell us you knew who did it?" She plopped back down in her chair, reacquainting herself with the anger directed toward Sheriff Monroe.

The sheriff shrugged, returned to the window, and slammed it shut, drowning out the rumbling noise generated by a cement truck passing.

"Mrs. Jones, we thought you and your husband would feel relieved to know that your daughter most likely did not intentionally leave this world. Why her son was turning two the very next day. We find it inconceivable that she would have intentionally harmed herself. It was her plan to continue to provide the children and her family with her love and support."

For the first time since the meeting began, DH smiled. Knowing his daughter did not take her own life was comforting to him.

Sheriff Monroe stood next to Albert, their shoulders almost touching. "Now, I want you folks to know that even though your daughter has been dead for over two years, our highest priority is to determine who did this to her. I have one detective who has been assigned to the case, and he will be interviewing everyone who came in contact with your daughter that day, including Lily. Wasn't she only eight at the time of her mother's death?"

"Wait a minute," Pet interrupted with a wave of her hand. "You can't ask that child any more questions. She couldn't take it!"

DH rose in Pet's defense. "Yeah, Pet tells me that the poor girl couldn't stop screaming after she lost her mother. She couldn't even go to school because she'd spend all day crying and moaning. We can't expose her to any more questions about her Momma."

Both Pet and DH closely scrutinized the sheriff, each revealing their same tightly sealed lips.

Monroe, in turn, responded by walking over and placing his hands on DH's shoulders. "With all due respect, Mr. and Mrs. Jones, sometimes talking about pain may actually help your granddaughter to heal. She won't be the first child that we've interviewed as a witness. I won't push you, but do think about it. Lily's probably stronger than you think, and talking about it might help her."

On The drive back to Nedra's, DH and Pet were silent. The only sound was the low hum of his four-cylinder Volkswagen bug. DH's long frame hunched over the tiny instrument panel while his oversized hands tightly gripped the steering wheel. A Camel cigarette dangled from his thin lips, and Pet watched curiously as the smoke swirled around the front dashboard and exited quickly through a small opening in the driver's window.

DH cleared his throat while skillfully pursing his lips to hold the cigarette steady. "What you think, Pet, about Lily being interviewed by the detectives again?" he said as he casually flicked the ashes through the crack in the window. "You know, I've never met my granddaughter, but the picture you sent me with your letter is a spitting image of Ellen."

Pet shifted uncomfortably in the narrow car seat. She stared down at her feet and did not look in DH's direction as she spoke, "Well, that sheriff really got me to thinking. Lily's always asking about her Momma, 'What did she like to eat? What was she like when she was growing up? Who were her best friends?' She can't stop asking questions!"

She leaned back in the seat and continued, "In the three years since Ellen's been gone, I been trying my best to get that child to forget about her Momma. But it ain't working, DH. Pet willed her eyes from her feet and met his gaze just as he was taking a deep drag on his cigarette.

Momentarily taking his eyes off the road, DH locked eyes with Pet, then flicked

the burning ashes through the window, "I think the sheriff's right. My Momma's still alive, and so is yours. We don't have a clue what it is like for Lily to lose her mother at such a young age. And I want to help that poor girl."

Pet squirmed, trying to find a comfortable position in the narrow seat. "Now, DH, I don't want you to go on about feeling sorry for her. She see that, and she gonna start up with that crying again. I had to put a stop to that for her own good!"

DH let out a low groan and quickly pulled the car to the side of the road, causing the driver behind them to swerve and slam on their brakes to avoid hitting them. He rolled his window all the way down and lit another cigarette. "Pet, you been a hard woman all your life. You ever wonder why I chose Cynthia over you?"

Pet's face contorted into an ugly frown.

"No, you probably haven't thought about it much, but you a hard woman to love!" He chuckled. "Now, I don't mean to hurt your feelings; you know me. But one day, you gonna have to let go of the mean, hard woman and show that other side. Me and you been sweethearts since we was in the third grade!

"Remember, I've known you most of my life since before you got sent away to live with your older sister Peggy. Times were even harder back then, and people made decisions they shouldn't have made. You ain't been the same since. Shoot, you used to be the cutest, sweetest girl in the world!"

Tears were flowing freely down Pet's cheeks. DH handed her a handkerchief to mop them away. Her face changed from a hateful grimace into a smile, and for a second, she was that sweet, innocent girl whose life had transformed in one day, just like their Lily. Gone was the worried frown and the tenseness that seemed to embody her presence.

He turned to face Pet and intertwined his long, bony fingers into her short, plump ones. "Pet, it's okay to feel for Lily. That girl has had a rough three years. Give her a break!"

Pet stopped crying and rolled down her window. She peered into the onion field beside the highway. She could see a few onion stalks that had survived last summer's pickings. The pungent smell of fried onions awakening in the unusually warm December sunshine permeated the car, making her realize that she was hungry.

"Here's what we gonna do," DH continued, "in your last letter, you asked about Lily coming to visit me, right?"

Pet nodded as she extricated her intertwined fingers from his firm grip.

"Well, that's a good thing. I'll get to know her and feel her out. I betcha' anything that girl is dying to talk about her Momma."

Pet began fidgeting, already anticipating how difficult it would be to imagine Lily meeting her grandfather for the first time. Why did she send DH that letter anyway—did she really want him to meet Lily?

It was late evening now. They had said their goodbyes to Nedra and Ray in Sacramento, then driven back to their rendezvous, the Dew Drop In. The restaurant was already closed and the parking lot was pitch black, except for DH's headlights.

Pet leaned over and kissed him, fumbled for her keys, and quickly left the warm VW bug. She walked slowly back to Black Beauty. She turned the key and started Black Beauty's cold engine. The only lights that could be seen were the red flame of DH's Camel cigarette and the four headlights shining into the darkness. Pet gunned the engine and took off with a jerky start as Black Beauty sputtered and struggled to get going in the cold night air.

The next morning, Pet finally arrived in Palm Springs before sunrise. She was tired, thirsty, and had to pee. She had stopped at several rest stops along the way to "cat nap," but they were dark, and she was afraid to step outside her car to pee.

Finally, she arrived at the Broussards. She quietly slipped inside, felt her way along the wall through the house, and plopped down onto the toilet seat, sighing heavily as she emptied the contents of her bladder. Her mouth felt dry, but she was too tired to do anything about it. She stumbled quietly to her tiny bed, and in two minutes, she was asleep, fully clothed, with her comfortable loafers still on.

CHAPTER 63

I Do Remember Everything

Lily had heard her grandmother come in, and she tried to stay awake to hear if she called anyone, but within a few minutes, grandmother was snoring.

Lily crept from her bed, slipped into her grandmother's room, and quietly unzipped her bulky black purse. She was looking for receipts—grandmother threw nothing away. There was a pause in grandmother's snoring, and Lily froze, but within seconds, grandmother's snore made a double-clutching sound and resumed. Lily smiled and continued her search.

There was really nothing there, three gas receipts and nothing else. Lily thought, *grandmother did not take any snacks with her, so she must have met up with my grandfather.* She rummaged through the purse again, finding no more receipts. The snoring suddenly stopped, and she heard grandmother stirring. This time she quickly tiptoed from the room, never taking her eyes from grandmother's closed eyelids.

Lily climbed back into bed, and soon fell asleep with lots of questions dancing through her mind. She slept fitfully the rest of the night and was up with the first rooster crow. She remembered to wash her face and brush her teeth before meeting Grandpa Broussard in the kitchen.

"Morning, Lily. You up mighty early today."

"Yes, sir."

Broussard had not started breakfast and was busy brewing his morning coffee. He hadn't combed his hair, and his silver-gray curls were knotted tighter than usual.

"Looks like you got a haircut, Grandpa Broussard."

He smiled, pleased to spend the first part of his morning with his new granddaughter. "You doing okay? I'm not used to seeing you this early."

Lily didn't hesitate, "I couldn't sleep." She frowned and began her habit of vigorously swinging her legs while grasping the kitchen stool with both hands.

"Well, now, what's on your mind this time?"

Lily blurted out, "I think grandmother went to see grandfather, and I think they went to see what happened to my mother." Lily's eyes followed the kitchen walls, and focused on the mason jars lined up on the countertop, then stopped at the black and white linoleum floors. She couldn't bring herself to look at Grandpa Broussard in case he didn't approve of her nosiness.

"Lily," he said in a nonchalant manner, "I think you want to know what your grandmother is up to, right?"

"Yes, sir." She resumed looking at the floor.

"Lily, everybody wants to know what happened to your mother the day she died." He crossed the room, pulled up a chair beside her, and grasped her knees to keep them from swinging.

"What do you remember, Lily?"

"Oh, Grandpa," she cried, "No one ever asked me that, but I do remember everything!"

"Good, now tell me."

"Well, me and my brother were sitting on the porch outside. He saw a snake crawling along the outside wall and tried to catch it. My mother was screaming bloody murder. The next thing I know, they started to fight, and Orville got mad and left.

"Then, I heard a loud noise like a gun going off, and when I ran inside, I found my mother on the floor with blood going everywhere." Lily's legs were swinging so forcefully the kitchen stool was began to wobble.

The noise from the percolating coffee seemed to flood Broussard's ears as he wiped the sweat that was forming on his brow. Envisioning eight-year-old Lily discovering her dying mother made him light-headed. He leaned over Lily's chair, keeping his head down as the blood rushed to his face.

Lily looked alarmed, "Grandpa, are you alright?" He shook his head back and forth a few times to regain his composure. He felt embarrassed and ashamed. Just hearing the initial telling of Lily's ordeal was tough. He did not want to imagine what it had been like for her.

Broussard felt Lily's eyes boring into the top of his head, and he willed his face into composure. When he looked up again, Lily saw a concerned Grandpa Broussard who had the kindest eyes ever.

Broussard yearned to lay his head on Lily's lap and allow the tears held back by sheer will to spill down his face. What he wanted more than anything was relief from the cold ache that had overtaken his heart. He wanted Lily to know that he, too, understood the anguish that she must have felt as she watched her mother's life ebb away in that lonely farmhouse.

He stood up, sat back down in the chair, and Lily crawled onto his lap. He'd never seen her suck her thumb, but there she was, rubbing the top of her nose with her index finger while noisily sucking her thumb like a seasoned thumb-sucker.

"Lily, I'm ready now; you can tell me the rest."

"Oh, Grandpa, it was awful! I ran to the kitchen and got some water, and sprinkled it on her face to wake her up. She shook her head and tried to get up, but then she just fell down again. I started crying, and I couldn't stop 'cause I didn't know what to do! Oh, Grandpa, I don't know how long I cried, but she wouldn't wake up!

"And then I told Deenie that we had to get some help. And we went out to the beet field out back, and it was hard to walk 'cause they had just plowed the dirt, and Deenie got stuck, so I told him to wait. I begged the men working in the field to come help us! They called the ambulance and the police. I keep thinking that I must've cried too long 'cause I couldn't save her. Oh, Grandpa Broussard, do you think I cried too long?

Lily couldn't remember how long she cried that day. What she could remember was feeling guilty that she was unable to revive her mother. She snuggled closer to Grandpa Broussard, wishing she could intertwine her body into his.

Broussard said nothing, just held her close to his chest. She could hear his heart thumping, and he could smell the pomade in her hair. He kissed the top of her head and looked down at her long, dangling legs entangled with his.

He gently placed Lily back onto the kitchen stool.

"Here's what we're gonna do, Lily."

She looked at him, puzzled, with a sad, questioning look on her face.

"Every day, you're gonna tell me a little bit more about what happened, and every day, you're gonna feel better. You've been through more in one day than most people have experienced in a lifetime."

He paused and firmly pressed his index and middle fingers into his eyelids to stop the tears from flowing..." So, why don't we stop now and start back tomorrow morning?"

Lily withdrew her thumb from her mouth and released her grip from Broussard, "Ok, Grandpa."

But she couldn't stop the movie. It played on as she got dressed for school, ate breakfast, accepted her lunch pail from Grandpa Broussard, slowly walked to the school bus, boarded, and sat by herself in the back. God, she missed her family! It was not just her mother; it was her step-father and little Deenie, and baby Lorna.

Her head began throbbing, and by lunchtime, she went to the office to see the school nurse.

Lunch was in full swing: kids lined up for meal tickets because they forgot their lunch money, tired mothers arrived to pick up their half-day kindergarteners, and first-period lunch kids screamed from the playground. Lily sat alone on a bench outside the nurse's small office.

"What is it, Lily?" The nurse was young and had the fresh, eager look of the candy stripers Lily had seen at the county hospital when visiting with Grandmother.

Lily put on her most sorrowful, woe-be-gone expression and grabbed her forehead, "I don't feel good. Can I go home?"

"Well, what's the matter? Do you have a headache?" The nurse gestured for Lily to enter her small office. She reached for the thermometer sitting in an alcohol-filled glass.

Lily momentarily panicked as the nurse motioned for her to open her mouth. "Well, uh, I don't know if I have a fever or not, but my head really hurts," she whimpered.

"Okay, well, then, let's call your Mom. Is she home?"

The thermometer was stuck in Lily's mouth, so she nodded her head, then thinking quickly, took it out and added, "You can call my Grandpa Broussard. He's always home," Lily exhaled with relief. Calling grandmother was never a good idea. She didn't believe in sickness, and hopefully, Lily thought, she wouldn't be home until the weekend anyway.

The candy striper removed the thermometer. "Well, Lily, you do have a slight fever, ninety-nine degrees. Come lay down on the cot until your grandfather arrives." She shook the instrument with a few quick snaps of her wrist, returned it to the glass container, and quickly left the room.

As Lily lay on the cot, the faint sounds of the children playing outside filled the room. Then, the rest of her horrific movie continued. As she was going to see about her mother, hadn't she heard a car gunning out of the driveway again? Had he come back? If he did, why didn't he stay? Did something happen that she couldn't remember? Why did she have so many holes in her memory of that painful day? Is that why Orville avoided her now? Did he kill her mother?

Every time she thought about her last day with her mother, she'd get a splitting headache. Grandmother said it was all in her mind 'cause kids didn't get headaches.

Maybe Grandpa Broussard was right; talking about what happened would make her feel better. Maybe she would remember everything that happened. Perhaps, the headaches would stop.

CHAPTER 64

Don't Kids Have Rights?

Nobody cares. As she sat alone on her bed, windows rattling from the howling wind outside, Pet propped the pillows behind her back. The images of her mother dangled around in her head. She hadn't wanted to be shipped off to live with her older sister, Margaret, but there she was. She'd written back home. Hell, she'd even snuck in a call after the 11 o'clock rates kicked in.

"No, you can't come back," Pet recalled her mother saying. *"We done rented out the room you and Jean slept in, now she sleeps with me. Does my daughter know you making long-distance calls?"*

Her daughter, Pet thought. Hell, I'm your daughter too! What about that trick you all played on me, convincing me to live with her? Having Uncle Joe give me candy and telling me how great it would be to live with them in Arizona. Humph, they lured me into the trap of a lifetime. Why didn't I get to protest? Why couldn't I get to change my mind?

Pet's mother had told her that times were hard back then. Folks were doing the best they could, and who was she to question her mother's decision?

Pet was in the dumps, and she didn't want to get out. It felt good to wallow. Hell, it was refreshing. No worries about what people would think. She could just wallow.

And how did she get stuck with Lily? Was it that vague promise she made to her daughter that if anything happened to her, that she would take over? But she didn't know her daughter would die, certainly not so soon.

Was this how my mother felt when she shipped me off, Pet thought? Trapped with no obvious alternatives? But wait a minute, she had me. I was her daughter. Why did I have to leave? Why wasn't there enough money to take care of me? Oh, that's right, nobody cared.

Pet slipped out of bed, threw the pillows on the floor, and stomped out of the room. She and Lily had only been living with the Broussards a few months, and she was ready to go. She felt her mean-thing bubbling up, and it felt good, like self-righteous and fulfilling. The house was quiet, and when she arrived in the kitchen, Broussard sat alone at the breakfast nook.

"Where's everybody?" she said, pulling up a chair beside him.

"Well, for once, my daughter assumed her mother's role, and took all the children to the library," he chuckled. "They were getting antsy since we got some serious Santa Ana winds blowing hard, and they couldn't go outside to play."

Broussard seemed in rare form, still dressed in his white terry cloth robe and slippers, even though it was mid-morning.

"Well, ain't it the wrong time of year for these devil winds?" Pet asked.

"Yep, but they don't always occur in the fall. Winter, too, sometimes, even in the Spring."

He turned his stool to face her, "Look like you got some deep thinking going on. What's on your mind?"

Pet scowled. That damned Broussard could always get her to talk. She marveled at his long, thick black lashes. Them Creoles were some awful pretty people.

Feeling her gaze, he rose, picked up the saltshaker, and sprinkled a few grains into the palm of his hands.

Pet watched his tongue dart in and out as he licked his palm. "You know that Nedra and Ray been trying to talk me into taking all three of Ellen's children, but I can't do it. I done raised my seven children, and I'm too old to start all over again."

"Yes, and I know that we've had this conversation before." He shook some more salt into his palm and resumed licking. "Pet, you need to take one day at a time. I don't know your two younger grandchildren very well. What I do know is that Lily needs you more, and if you don't do anything else, her well-being should be your main focus. The other two were too young; they don't remember anything about what happened, but she does."

Pet became alarmed. She could feel the blood rushing to her face. "And what do you know about what Lily remembers?"

Broussard shook the remaining salt into the sink and turned to face Pet. He knew he had to tread this path very carefully.

"Pet, that girl has confided in me." He stood in front of Pet, looked directly into her eyes, crossed his arms, and wisely chose his words. "Now I don't want you to get your panties in a bunch."

Pet chuckled, and they both visibly relaxed.

"But hear me out. Lily saw everything, but the gun going off. She and Deenie were outside when that happened. I think she knows or suspects who killed her mother."

"What?" Pet loudly interrupted, "That can't be! She would have told me!" Sweat began sliding down her armpits, so she discreetly crossed her arms and firmly pressed her cotton blouse against her underarms to absorb the gathering moisture.

"She can't tell you," Broussard responded calmly. "So, don't be angry with her for telling me. Just be glad that she did. She hasn't told me everything, but she will. It may take her a while, but I think Lily knows everything that happened to her mother. She wants to tell, but I got the impression that except for the police on the day it happened, no one has ever asked her."

Pet winced. She knew Broussard was right. She bowed her head between her legs, allowing her thoughts to run freely through her mind. She didn't want to bring up that terrible day with Lily. The girl might start her screaming fits again. *She thought about Nedra telling her that when Lily howled, it was too heartbreaking for anyone to endure. She said that it went on for weeks, screaming to the top of her lungs, then whimpering for long periods of time. No one could console her. She cried at breakfast, lunch, and dinner, in the bathroom, in the front yard, in the backyard, and by the chicken coop. She even climbed a backyard tree and screamed up there.*

And if anyone asked her to stop, she just cried louder, "I want my Momma!" And who could respond to that demand? Nedra said they just left her alone and let her be. Even the chickens and dogs got used to her cries. After a while, her screams and sobs were as common as the morning and evening backyard rooster's crows.

One day, Nedra said they woke up and were surprised to discover that Lily wasn't screaming. Turns out she had a fever and a very sore throat. So, she couldn't scream anymore. They swathed Vicks Vapor Rub onto her neck and chest and wrapped her in warm blankets. In three days, her fever dissipated, and her voice returned. As far as Nedra knew, she hadn't screamed since.

Pet surmised that Lily had apparently confided in Broussard, like he said. Trying to visualize what she witnessed caused an ache in Pet's chest, a heartache, a cold numbing feeling that wouldn't go away.

Broussard stared down into Pet's glazed eyes. He dropped his arms to his sides and cleared his throat. "Seems like you haven't moved an inch for at least ten minutes. You all right, Pet?"

Pet scowled again. Damn that Broussard. He could get her to talk like no other man. And she wasn't even sweet on him. Who would've thought he had that kind of power over her?

Broussard rearranged his robe, tightening the long white terry-cloth belt around his slender frame. He returned to the kitchen stool, sitting down next to Pet. His loose night slippers dangled awkwardly from the kitchen stool, and he scooted his feet more snugly into them.

Pet's dark, scowling expression and brightly colored muumuu contrasted sharply with his all-white attire. They both stared around the breakfast nook, looking at nothing in particular.

"Look a here, Broussard, none of us want to imagine what that poor child saw. We'd just as soon forget all about it, and we hope Lily does too. Every time she asks about her Momma, I tell her to 'let the dead be dead.'"

This time, it was Broussard's turn to wince. But he said nothing.

"What I do want to say is that me and DH visited the medical examiner and sheriff, and they promised to really investigate Ellen's death. They know they didn't do right by my daughter, and I get the feeling something's going to be done." An involuntary smile brightened Pet's face, and she seemed to relax.

Broussard re-tightened his robe. "What do you think changed their minds? After all, she's been gone over two years now, right?"

"Yeah, and if you ask me, I think the sheriff saw Jesus!" Pet chuckled, and Broussard joined her. "No, seriously, turns out the medical examiner, Albert, is a colored fella, and when me and DH got there—well, I think he helped the sheriff have a change of heart. You should have seen Albert," she boasted proudly, "that little pipsqueak knew his stuff. I didn't even know California had a colored ME!"

Pet rose from her seat and walked out the back door to look at the chickens in the backyard, Broussard followed closely behind her. She spoke with her back to him, "This was the second time I talked to the sheriff, and he has pulled an about-face. First time I spoke with him, he acted like he could care less about what happened, but the other day, well, he was just different. Funny how white folks are. Sometimes out of the blue, they just get a conscience."

CHAPTER 65

I Hope it Wasn't my Stepdad

Sheriff Monroe's conscience was, in fact, clear. He had spoken to the white neighbor who had befriended Ellen. Her exact words were, "You don't invite people to your house for your child's birthday and then kill yourself the same day. No way." And the neighbor had met Ellen's husband. He was extremely jealous. Didn't want anyone, even her, around. She was a pretty colored girl, and he wanted to keep her out there, isolated, without any friends or family around while he was away driving trucks for days at a time.

Monroe had also spoken to the ME, Albert, again. He'd changed the autopsy report's cause of death from suicide to homicide. Albert's exact words were, "You don't have that many defensive wounds on your arms and hands and then kill yourself. Somebody killed that poor girl."

Monroe's next stop would be hauling Orville in for questioning. And talking to his foreman. And his truck driver friend, Lonnie.

It still pained Monroe to think that prior to his newly-found desire to get to the truth, his investigation had centered primarily on an interview with Ellen's eight-year-old daughter and a very brief questioning of her husband, who vehemently denied any knowledge of what happened to her.

He hadn't even bothered to look for gunpowder residue on her hands, and there were police officers and ambulance personnel who had contaminated the crime scene long before his arrival.

And there was the issue of the gun's safety features or lack thereof. He'd recently discovered that the shotgun had a questionable history of prematurely discharging.

Whenever the sheriff encountered what seemed like insurmountable obstacles, he again saw the three children, all in various stages of shock. Even the baby had witnessed what had transpired that day—her crib was in the direct line of sight of her mother's body. The image of three shocked, traumatized, glassy-eyed children was a hard thing to erase from his mind.

As the sheriff approached his office, he heard the shrill sound of his phone ringing. He had forgotten to lower the ringer's volume, and each bell caused the phone to jump around uncontrollably on its wobbly table. Annoyed by the incessant ringing, he snatched the phone's handset and thrust it against his ear.

"Yeah," he growled. He wasn't sure why he was in such a foul mood. Maybe it had to do with the gun manufacturer's representative, a Mr. John Connors, who hadn't returned his numerous long-distance person-to-person telephone calls.

The woman's voice on the other end of the line spoke clearly with a distinct New England nasal accent, "This is the long-distance operator from Springfield, Massachusetts, calling for Sheriff Forrest Monroe. Is he available?"

"Well, I'll be damned!"

"Sir?"

"Sorry, yes, yes, this is Sheriff Forrest Monroe here."

"One moment, please, while I connect Mr. Connors to you."

Forrest heard a hissing static sound, then a few sharp clicks, dead silence, then a deep male voice, with a northern accent. "Sheriff Monroe, this is Connors here, and I'm sorry it's taken so long for me to return your call. My secretary is new, and well, she just found your message under her stenography pad. What can I do for you?"

Sheriff Monroe and Connors were on the phone for over an hour, and Monroe was becoming increasingly frustrated with their conversation. The gun rep said he knew nothing about any issues with the gun's safety and repeatedly steered the all questions and concerns to discussions about the newer models and how he would be visiting the West Coast soon if Monroe was interested in purchasing another rifle.

During Connors' ceaseless sales pitch, the sheriff absentmindedly played with the long black curly handset cord, twirling it around his fingers, and after finally releasing it, watching the curls snap back into place. It was time to end the conversation. He eased the handset away from his ear, listening to Connors' voice becoming more and more faint. He quietly placed the receiver into the phone's cradle.

Sheriff Monroe prayed he'd have more luck on his visit with Lily. As planned, he arrived at the Broussard home in an unmarked, tan Dodge station wagon. When he pulled into the driveway, he noticed curious stares from a half-dozen kids that were playing in the side yard. They were a curious mixture of dark and light-skinned tones. Some even looked Hispanic.

Before he had a chance to knock, Pet met him at the front door. He looked around at the modest home, with furnishings that were too large for its small size; but he appreciated that it was very clean. The front windows were open, and thin blue curtains that matched the dark blue sofa were blowing gently from a slight breeze.

"Can I get you something to drink?"

The sheriff dismissed her offer with a wave of his hand. "No, thank you, ma'am, but I hope you don't mind directing me to your bathroom?" Before she could answer, he continued, "Even though I stayed overnight in the Grapevine, that was a long drive today."

Pet nodded, "Yeah, it's just down the hall; then turn right. I'll fetch her for you."

When Sheriff Monroe returned from relieving himself, one look at Lily brought tears to his eyes. He roughly brushed his face with the back of his hand, and reached out to shake Lily's.

She looked the same as she had two years before, except taller. Her soft brown eyes were those of a wise old sage. Pain had been there. Hurt had been there. And anger, just a tinge of anger.

Lily looked from her grandmother to the sheriff, and back at her grandmother again.

"Come here and sit down. Sheriff Monroe wants to talk to you about your mother."

Lily stiffened, and her squinty eyes abruptly became wide and scared looking.

Sheriff Monroe watched the exchange between Lily and her grandmother and intervened. "Well, Mrs. Jones, I thought maybe Lily and I could go for a walk while we talk, and I could get her some ice cream. I thought I saw the ice cream truck in the neighborhood as I was pulling in."

Pet frowned, pursed her lips, then relented. "Okay, but don't keep her out too long; she got chores to do."

When they stepped outside, Lily instinctively shaded her eyes. The Palm Spring sun had passed its halfway mark and was heading west toward the San Bernardino mountains.

As Lily hurried across the street, Forrest followed, noticing the dark outline of Lily's shadow stretching down the wide paved road in front of the house. She stepped onto the sidewalk, which was broken and uneven, but she intuitively adjusted her footing as they walked along.

They strolled down the street, and Lily watched with curiosity as the sheriff walked beside her. She remembered the last time she had seen him. His glazed, shocked eyes matched everyone's who was present in her mother's bedroom.

But she remembered that the sheriff had picked up baby Lorna who was screaming in her crib that scary day. He had held and quieted her by creating soothing clicking sounds next to her ears, just like her step-dad had done with her and Deenie when they were little. He could be trusted.

"I told Grandpa Broussard that I remember everything," Lily volunteered.

This shocked Sheriff Monroe! He wasn't expecting this announcement! So, instead of watching where he was walking on the uneven pavement, he stared at Lily in bewilderment, and suddenly lost his footing, causing him to stumble, then slip, and fall, butt first onto the sidewalk. He grinned sheepishly as she extended her hand to help him up.

"Well, little girl, I'm glad you didn't try to catch me when I fell. I would've knocked you down!"

They both laughed.

"It sounds like we've got some talking to do. I know it's been a while." He stopped at a crosswalk, and both of them gazed at mothers walking babies in bouncy strollers and children playing catch in the nearby softball field.

Again, Lily shaded her eyes from the afternoon sun. She and Sheriff Monroe resumed walking. She looked up at the sheriff, "I don't think my Momma did that to herself, and I think someone else was in the house with us. But I don't know who it was. Sometimes I dream about somebody being there, but when I wake up, I don't remember who it is. Are you going to help me remember?"

"I'm going to do my best," the sheriff said.

Suddenly, an ice cream truck with speakers blaring "Turkey in the Straw" rounded the corner, and Lily and Sheriff Monroe stopped to watch the throng of children making a mad dash. Several older children had abandoned their game and rushed over just as the truck parked in front of the entrance to the baseball field.

There were a few scraggly-looking children without parents nearby who looked eagerly in the sheriff's direction as he peeled a wad of one's from his pants pocket.

Sheriff Monroe grinned at the enthusiastic faces, "What will you kids be having?" Two rough-looking blond-haired boys and a shy colored girl, all around seven or eight, crowded in front of the tiny window to shout their orders. He paid the driver, and the kids snatched their ice creams and rushed off, lest their good fortunes be taken away.

The sheriff had purchased enough ice cream bars for the entire Broussard family. Lily was torn. Should she tear open the package and gobble the ice cream bar before they walked back home? On the way back, she daydreamed about slowly licking the bar, savoring the rich, chocolate cream as it slid down her throat. She'd eat it slower than the other kids, so she'd be the only one with ice cream left! She liked that idea! So, she decided to wait until she got back to the Broussards.

Neither Lily nor the sheriff talked on the way back. There was no discussion about whether or not to return home or keep walking, but after departing the truck, their feet naturally pointed in the direction of the Broussards.

Just before reaching the house, the sheriff ventured, "Lily, I want you to start writing down everything you remember, no matter how insignificant you think it is, you hear? I mean, you understand 'insignificant,' right?"

"Yes, sir. I hope it wasn't my stepdad, Orville, 'cause I love him so much!" she said, quickly turning her face away from the sheriff as soon as she felt the warm tears streaming down her face, hoping he didn't see them. Lily's hand involuntarily covered her mouth as if she was trying to force herself to shut up, but the words slipped out as soon as she removed her hand. "They were fighting before it happened, and then he left," she said. "I just hope he didn't come back," she whispered.

Lily looked defiantly at the sheriff to see if he heard her. *Oh, no! He did,* she thought as he stared down at her, nodding his head slowly. Lily's eyes bulged, and she broke out in a cold sweat as a soft wail escaped her lips. She really didn't mean to say that out loud. Her shoulders slumped as she stared at the ground. *What have I done? I hope I haven't gotten Orville in trouble.*

The sheriff glanced at the ice-cream sandwich bars which were slowly melting inside the brown paper bag he was carrying. He tapped Lily's shoulder and said, "Come on, we need to pick up the pace, the ice cream's melting."

As they walked quickly back to the house, Sheriff Monroe smirked to himself and thought, *Hmph! This cold case is warming up. That girl did not kill herself.*